ROYAL
Christmas

KATE   SUSAN   HEIDI
HEWITT MALLERY BETTS

MILLS
&
BOON

All the characters in this book have no existence outside the imagination
of the author, and have no relation whatsoever to anyone bearing the
same name or names. They are not even distantly inspired by any
individual known or unknown to the author, and all the incidents are
pure invention.

Mills & Boon, an imprint of Harlequin (UK) Limited, Eton House,
18-24 Paradise Road, Richmond, Surrey TW9 1SR

A ROYAL CHRISTMAS © Harlequin Enterprises II B.V./S.à.r.l. 2011

Royal Love-Child, Forbidden Marriage © Kate Hewitt 2009
The Sheikh and the Christmas Bride © Susan Mallery 2007
Christmas in His Royal Bed © Heidi Betts 2007

ISBN: 978 0 263 89358 8

009-1211

Harlequin (UK) policy is to use papers that are natural, renewable
and recyclable products and made from wood grown in sustainable
forests. The logging and manufacturing processes conform to the
legal environmental regulations of the country of origin.

Printed and bound in Spain
by Blackprint CPI, Barcelona

ROYAL LOVE-CHILD, FORBIDDEN MARRIAGE

KATE HEWITT

Kate Hewitt discovered her first Mills & Boon® romance on a trip to England when she was thirteen and she's continued to read them ever since. She wrote her first story at the age of five, simply because her older brother had written one and she thought she could do it too. That story was one sentence long—fortunately they've become a bit more detailed as she's grown older. She has written plays, short stories, and magazine serials for many years, but writing romance remains her first love. Besides writing, she enjoys reading, travelling and learning to knit.

After marrying the man of her dreams—her older brother's childhood friend—she lived in England for six years and now resides in New York State, with her husband, her four young children and the possibility of one day getting a dog. Kate loves to hear from readers—you can contact her through her website, www.kate-hewitt.com

To Aidan,
Thanks for being such a great friend—and fan!
Love, K

CHAPTER ONE

'How much?'

Phoebe Wells stared blankly at the man slouched in a chair across from her. He gazed back with a sensual smile and heavy-lidded eyes, his sable hair rumpled, the top two buttons of his shirt undone to reveal a smooth expanse of golden skin.

'How *much*?' she repeated. The question made no sense. How much what? Her fingers tightened reflexively around the strap of her bag and she tried not to fidget. She'd been hustled here by two government agents, and it had taken all her self-control not to ask if she was being arrested. Actually, it had taken all her self-control not to *scream*.

They'd given her no answers, not even a look, as they ushered her into one of the palace's empty reception rooms to wait for twenty panic-laden minutes before this man— Leo Christensen, Anders's cousin—had made his lazy entrance. And now he was asking her how much, and she had no idea what any of it meant.

She wished Anders were here; she wished he hadn't left her to suffer the scorn of his damnable cousin, the man who now uncoiled himself from the chair and rose to stand in front of her with an easy, lethal grace. She wished, she realised with a little pulse of panic, that she knew him better.

'How much money, Little Miss Golddigger?' Leo Christensen clarified softly. 'Just how much money will it take to make you leave my cousin alone?'

Shock stabbed her with icy needles, but it was soon replaced by an even icier calm. Of course. She should have expected this; she knew the Christensen family—the royal family of Amarnes—didn't want an American nobody in love with their son. The country's heir. Of course, she hadn't realised that when she'd met Anders in a bar in Oslo; she'd thought he was just an ordinary person, or as ordinary as a man like him could be considered to be. Golden-haired, charming, with an effortless grace and confidence that had drawn her to his side with the irresistible force of a magnet. And even now, under Leo Christensen's sardonic scrutiny, she clung to that memory, to the knowledge that he loved her and she loved him. Except, where was he? Did he know his cousin was trying to bribe her?

Phoebe straightened and forced herself to meet Leo's scornful gaze directly. 'I'm afraid you don't have enough.'

Leo's mouth curled in something close to a smile, the smile of a snake. 'Try me.'

Rage coursed through her, clean and strong, fuelling her and overriding her fear. 'You don't have enough because there *isn't* enough, Mr Christensen—'

'Your Grace, actually,' Leo corrected softly. 'My formal title is the Duke of Larsvik.'

Phoebe swallowed at the reminder of just what kind of people she was dealing with. Powerful, rich. *Royal*. People who didn't want her…but Anders did. That, she resolved, would be enough. Plenty.

She'd had no idea when Anders asked her to meet his family that they actually comprised the king and queen of Amarnes, an island principality off the coast of Norway. And this man too, a man Phoebe recognised from his endless appearances in the tabloids, usually the lead player in some sordid drama involving women, cars, gambling, or all three. Anders had told her about Leo, had warned her, and after just a few minutes' conversation with Leo she believed everything he'd ever said.

'*He's a bad influence, always has been. My family tried to reform him, they thought I could help. But no one can help Leo...*'

And who was going to help *her*? Anders had told his parents about her last night; she hadn't been present. Clearly, Phoebe thought, swallowing a bubble of near-hysterical laughter, that conversation hadn't gone well. So they'd sent Leo, the black sheep, to deal with her...the problem.

She shook her head now, not wanting to speak Leo Christensen's damn title, not wanting him to know just how out of her depth she was. Yet he knew it; of course he did. She saw it in the scornful little smile he gave her, the way his gaze flicked over her in easy dismissal, making her feel like trash.

Still, if he knew it, at least that meant there was nothing to lose. She lifted her chin. 'Fine, Your *Grace*. But there's no amount of money you could give me that would make me leave Anders.' Brave words, she knew, and there was no way she'd take Leo's money, but still...where was Anders?

Leo stared at her for a moment, those sensual, sleepy eyes narrowing, flaring. His mouth twisted and he turned away. 'How quaint, my dear,' he murmured. 'How very admirable. So it's true love?'

Humiliation and annoyance prickled along her skin,

chased up her spine. He made what she had with Anders sound so trite. So cheap. 'Yes, it is.'

Leo shoved his hands in his pockets and strolled to the window, gazing out at the plaza in front of Amarnes's royal palace. It was a brilliant summer morning, the sky blue with faint wisps of cloud, the jagged, violet mountains a stunning backdrop to the capital city of Njardvik's cluster of buildings, the bronze statues of Amarnes's twin eagles—the country's emblem—glinting in the sun. 'How long have you known my cousin?' he finally asked and Phoebe shifted her bag to her other shoulder.

'Ten days.'

He turned around, one eyebrow arched, his hands still in his pockets. His silence was eloquent, and Phoebe felt a blush stain her throat and rise to her cheeks. Ten days. It wasn't much; it sounded ridiculous. And yet she *knew*. She knew when Anders looked at her…and yet now this man was looking at her, his amber gaze sleepy and yet so sardonic, so knowing. Ten days. Ten days was nothing. And judging by the contemptuous curl of Leo's lip, he thought so too. Phoebe straightened. What did she care what Leo Christensen, the Playboy Prince of Amarnes, thought of her? He was a man given over to pleasure, vice. Yet, standing in front of him now, she was conscious of a darker streak in him, something more alarming and dangerous than the antics of a mere playboy. An emotion emanated from him, something dark and unknowable, yet a force to be reckoned with…if only she knew what it was.

'And you think ten days is long enough to know someone?' Leo asked in that honeyed voice that wound around Phoebe like a spell even as alarm prickled along her spine. 'To love him?' he pressed, his voice so soft, so seductively mild, yet still with that thread of darkness that Phoebe didn't understand. Didn't want to.

She shrugged, determined to stay defiant. She wasn't going to defend what she felt for Anders, or what he felt for her. She knew it would sound contrived, as trite and silly as Leo was determined to make it.

'You realise,' Leo continued in that same soft voice that made the hairs on the nape of Phoebe's neck prickle, 'that if he stays with you—marries you, as he has suggested—you will be queen? Something this country is not prepared to allow.'

'They won't have to,' Phoebe returned. The idea of her becoming queen was utterly terrifying. 'Anders told me he will abdicate.'

Leo's eyes narrowed, his body stilling. 'Abdicate?' he said softly. 'He said that?'

Phoebe jutted her chin. 'Yes.'

Leo's eyes met hers and he held her gaze with unrelenting hardness. 'Then he will never become king.'

She would not let this man make her feel guilty. 'He doesn't even want to be king—'

Leo let out a bark of disbelieving laughter. 'Doesn't want to be king? When it's all he's ever known?'

'He told me—'

He shrugged in derisive dismissal. 'Anders,' he said, cutting her off, 'rarely knows what he wants.'

'Well, he does now,' Phoebe returned with more determination than she felt at the moment. Somehow, as the target of Leo's incredulous scorn, she found her determination—her faith—trickling away. 'He wants me,' she said, and it came out sounding childish.

Leo stared at her for a moment, his expression turning thoughtful, then blank, ominously, dangerously neutral.

He could be thinking anything. Planning anything. He cocked his head. 'And you…want…him?'

'Of course I do.' Phoebe fidgeted again; the reception room with its heavy drapes and furniture felt oppressive. A gilded prison. Would she be allowed to walk out of here? She was conscious of her uncertain status as a foreigner in a small and fiercely independent country, and she was even more conscious of the man in front of her, a man with power and authority and clearly no compunction in using both for his own ends.

And where, oh, where was Anders? Did he know she'd been sent for? Why wasn't he looking for her? Since he'd announced their relationship to the royal family he'd been absent, and she now felt a treacherous flicker of doubt.

'You know him?' Leo pressed. 'Enough to live a life of exile?'

'Exile from a family that doesn't accept or love him,' Phoebe returned. 'Anders has never wanted this, Mr— Your Grace.' She swept an arm to encompass the room and the entire palace with its endless expectations.

'Oh, hasn't he?' Leo laughed once, a sharp, unpleasant sound. He moved back to the window, his back to her, seeming lost in thought. Phoebe waited, impatience and worse—fear—starting to fray her hope. Her faith.

'Would ten thousand dollars, American, do it?' Leo asked, his back to her, his voice musing. 'Or more like fifty?'

Phoebe straightened, glad for the renewed wave of outrage that poured through her, replacing the fear and doubt. 'I told you, no amount—'

'Phoebe.' Leo turned around, and the way he said her name sounded strangely gentle, although his eyes were hard, his expression remote. 'Do you honestly think a man like Anders can make you happy?'

'And how could a man like you possibly know?' Phoebe flung back, annoyed and angry that he was making her feel this way. Making her wonder.

Leo stiffened, his face blanking once more. 'A man like me?' he enquired with stiff politeness.

'Anders has told me about you,' Phoebe said, both the fear and the anger spiking her words, making them hurt, making her want to hurt him—although how could you hurt a man like Leo Christensen? A man who had seen it all, done it all and cared about nothing? Or so the newspapers said, Anders said, and the man in front of her with his sardonic smile and cold voice seemed to confirm every awful thing she'd ever heard. 'You know nothing about love or loyalty,' she continued. 'You care only about your own pleasure—and I suppose I'm a little inconvenience to that—'

'That you are,' Leo cut her off. For a second Phoebe wondered if she'd hurt him with her words. No, impossible. He was actually smiling, his mouth curving in a way that was really most unpleasant. Frightening. 'Quite an inconvenience, Miss Wells. You have no idea just how much.' As if drawing a mask over the first one, Leo's expression changed. It became sleepy, speculative, his smile turning seductive. He took a step closer to her. 'What would have happened, do you suppose,' he asked in that soft, bedroom voice, 'if you'd met me first?'

'Nothing,' Phoebe snapped, but even so her heart rate kicked up a notch as Leo kept walking towards her with languorous, knowing ease, stopping only a hairsbreadth away. She could feel his heat, smell the faint woodsy tang of his aftershave. She stared determinedly at his shirt, refusing to be intimidated, to show how afraid—how affected—she was. Yet even so, her gaze helplessly moved upwards from the buttons of his fine silk shirt to where they were undone, to that brown column of his throat where a pulse leaped and jerked, and Phoebe felt an answering response deep inside, a tug in her belly that could only be called yearning. Desire.

She flushed in shame.

Leo gave a low chuckle. He raised one hand to brush a wayward curl from her forehead, and Phoebe jerked instinctively in response, felt the heat of his fingers against her skin.

'Are you so sure about that?' he queried softly.

'Yes...'

Yet at that moment she wasn't, and they both knew it. Heard it in her ragged breathing, saw it in how she almost swayed towards him. Horrible man, Phoebe thought savagely, yet she condemned herself as well. She shouldn't let him affect her like this, not if she loved Anders, which she did.

Didn't she?

'So sure,' Leo whispered, his voice a soft sneer, and his hand dropped from her forehead to her throat, where her pulse beat as frantically as a trapped bird's. With one finger he gently touched that sensitive hollow, causing Phoebe to gasp aloud in what—? Shock? Outrage?

Pleasure?

She could still feel the reverberation of his touch, as if a string had been plucked in her soul, and the single note of seduction played throughout her body.

'Phoebe!'

Gasping again, this time in relief, Phoebe stumbled away from Leo, from his knowing smile and hands. She turned towards the doorway and saw Anders, appearing like the golden god Baldur from the Norse myth, smiling at Phoebe with a radiant certainty that dispelled all her own fears like the dawn mist over the mountains. 'I've been looking for you. No one would tell me where you were—'

'I've been here—' tears of relief stung Phoebe's eyes as she hurried towards him '—with your cousin.'

Anders glanced at Leo, and his expression darkened with a deeper emotion. Phoebe couldn't tell if it was disapproval or fear or perhaps even jealousy. She swallowed and glanced at Leo. She saw with a sharp jolt of shock that he was staring at his cousin with a bland expression that somehow still managed to convey a deep and unwavering coldness. *Hatred.* And Phoebe was reminded of the ending of the Norse myth she'd read about during her travels through Scandinavia: that Baldur had been murdered by his twin brother, Hod, the god of darkness and winter.

'What do you want with Phoebe, Leo?' Anders demanded, and his voice sounded strained, even petulant.

'Nothing.' Leo smiled, shrugged, spreading his hands wide in a universal gesture of innocence. 'She obviously loves you, Anders.' His mouth twisted in a smile that didn't look quite right.

'She does,' Anders agreed, putting an arm around Phoebe's shoulder. She leaned against him, grateful for his strength, yet still conscious of Leo's dark, unwavering gaze. 'I don't know why you were talking to her, Leo, but we're both determined to be together—'

'And such determination is so very admirable,' Leo cut across him softly. 'I will tell the king so.'

Anders's expression hardened, his lower lip jutting out in an expression more appropriate to a six-year-old before he shrugged and nodded. 'You may do so. If he wanted you to convince me otherwise…'

Leo smiled and that simple gesture made Phoebe want

to shiver. There was nothing kind or good or loving about it. 'Obviously, I cannot.' He lifted one shoulder. 'What more is there to say?'

'Nothing,' Anders finished. He turned to Phoebe. 'It's time for us to leave, Phoebe. There's nothing for us here. We can take the ferry to Oslo and then catch the afternoon train to Paris.'

Phoebe nodded, relieved, knowing she should be excited. Ecstatic.

Yet as she walked from the room, Anders's arm still around her shoulders, she was conscious only of Leo's unrelenting gaze, and that dark emotion emanating from him which seemed strangely—impossibly—like sorrow.

CHAPTER TWO

Six years later

IT WAS raining in Paris, a needling grey drizzle that blanketed the royal mourners in grey, and made the images on the television screen blurry and virtually unrecognisable.

Not, Phoebe acknowledged, that she'd met any of Anders's family besides his cousin. Leo. Even now his name made her skin prickle, made her recall that terrible, cold look he'd given Anders as they'd left the Amarnesian palace. That was the last time either she or Anders had seen any of his family, or even stepped foot in his native country.

Six years ago…a lifetime, or two. Certainly more than one life had been affected—formed, changed—in the last half-decade.

'Mommy?' Christian stood behind the sofa where Phoebe had curled up, watching the funeral on one of those obscure cable channels. Now she turned to smile at her five-year-old son, who was gazing at the television with a faint frown. 'What are you watching?'

'Just…' Phoebe shrugged, reaching to turn off the television. How to explain to Christian that his father—the father he hadn't ever even seen—had died? It would be meaningless to Christian, who had long ago accepted the fact that he didn't have a daddy. He didn't need one, had been happy with the life Phoebe had provided, with friends and relatives and school here in New York.

'Just what?' Christian put his hands on his hips, his expression halfway between a pout and a mischievous grin. He was all boy, curious about everything, always asking what, why, who.

'Watching something,' Phoebe murmured. She rose from the sofa, giving her son a quick one-armed hug. 'Isn't it time for dinner?' Smiling, she pulled him along, tousling his hair, into the kitchen of their Greenwich Village apartment. Outside the sunlight slanted across Washington Square, filling the space with golden light.

Yet as she pulled pots and pans from the cupboards, mindlessly listening to Christian talk about his latest craze—some kind of superhero, or were they superrobots? Pheobe could never keep them straight—her mind slipped back to the blurry image of the funeral on television.

Anders, her husband of exactly one month, was dead. She shook her head, unable to summon more than a sense of sorrowful pity for a man who had swept into her life and out again with equal abruptness. It hadn't taken very long for Anders to realise Phoebe had been nothing more than a passing fancy, and Phoebe had understood with equal speed how shallow and spoiled Anders really was. Yet at least that brief period of folly had given her something wonderful…Christian.

'I like the green ones best…' Christian tugged on her sleeve. 'Mom, are you listening?'

'Sorry, honey.' Phoebe smiled down at Christian in

apology even as she noticed that she'd let the water for the pasta boil dry. She had to get her mind out of the past. She hadn't thought about Anders for years, and sometimes it felt as though that short, regrettable episode had never occurred. Yet his death had brought old memories to the surface—namely, that horrible interview at the palace. Even now Pheobe remembered the look in Leo Christensen's eyes, the way he'd touched her…and the way she'd responded.

With a jolt Phoebe realised she was remembering Leo, not Anders. Anders had receded into her memory as nothing more than a faded, blurry image, like an old photograph, yet Leo…Leo she remembered as sharply and clearly as if he were standing right in front of her.

She glanced around the sunny kitchenette of her modest but comfortable apartment, almost as if she would see Leo standing darkly in the shadows. She gave a little laugh at her own ridiculous behaviour. Leo Christensen—all the Christensens, that entire life—was thousands of miles away. She and Anders had quietly separated just months after Leo had offered her fifty thousand dollars to leave him, and she'd never seen any of them again. She'd moved to New York with Christian, started over with the support of friends and family, and relegated the incident to a dark, unswept corner of her mind…that now felt the bright, glaring light of day.

Abruptly Phoebe turned off the stove. 'How about pizza?' she asked Christian brightly, who responded with a delighted smile.

'Angelo's?' he asked hopefully, naming their favourite neighbourhood pizza joint, and Phoebe nodded.

'Absolutely.'

Phoebe went to get their coats, only to stop in uneasy

surprise at the sight of Christian in front of the television once more. He'd turned it back on and was watching the funeral procession, tracking the coffin's progression down one of Paris's main thoroughfares, the flag's twin eagles with their austere, noble profiles visible even in the gloom. 'Is that man dead?'

Phoebe swallowed, a pang of sorrow for Anders's wasted life piercing her. 'Yes, it's a funeral.'

'Why is it on television?' Christian asked with his usual wide-eyed curiosity.

'Because he was a prince.'

'A prince?' Christian sounded moderately impressed. As a New Yorker, he encountered people of all walks of life every day. 'A real one?' he asked with a faint note of scepticism.

Phoebe almost smiled. 'Yes, a real one.' She wasn't about to explain to Christian about Anders's abdication or exile, or the fact that he was his father. She'd always intended for Christian to know the truth of his birth, but not like this, with a grainy image of a funeral on TV. Besides, Christian knew what was important: that Phoebe had wanted him and loved him. Nothing else needed matter.

With decisive determination she turned the TV off, the words of the French commentator fading away into silence.

'*Crown Prince of Amarnes...inebriated...reckless driving...his companion, a French model, died instantly along with him...*'

'Come on, scout,' she said lightly. 'Pizza time.'

They'd almost reached the door, almost missed them completely, Phoebe thought later, when she heard the knock.

Christian's eyes widened and they stared at each other, the only sound the awful, silent reverberation of the knock. Strange, Phoebe thought, how they both knew that knock was different. Three short, hard raps on the door, so unlike the flurry of light taps their neighbour, old Mrs Simpson, would give, along with a cheery hello.

Those short, sharp knocks which felt like a warning, a herald of nothing good, and somehow they both knew it. Phoebe felt that knowledge settle coldly in her bones, even as she wondered who—what—why. Just like Christian, she was filled with questions.

'Who could that be?' she murmured, trying to smile. Christian raced towards the door.

'I'll get it—'

'No.' Phoebe pushed past her son, flinging one arm out to bar Christian's way. 'Never answer to strangers, Christian.'

Taking a deep breath, Phoebe opened the door, and her heart sank at the two dark-suited men standing there. They had the bland good looks and ominously neutral expressions of government agents. In fact, it was men just like these who had summoned her to the palace all those years ago, ushered her into the room with Leo and his abominable offer of a pay-off.

'*How about fifty?*'

Phoebe pushed the memory away and stared at the two men filling up her doorway, trying to frame a thought. A rebuke.

'Madame Christensen?'

It was a name Phoebe hadn't heard in a long while; she'd reverted to her maiden name when she separated from Anders. Yet the presence of these men and the sound of her married name made the years fall away and suddenly she was back in Amarnes, facing Leo...

'Are you so sure about that?'

Even now she could remember—*feel*—how Leo had trailed his finger along her cheek, then lower to the V between her breasts, and she'd let him. Even now, across all the years, she remembered the inescapable fascination she'd had with him in those few brief moments, her body betraying her so quickly and easily.

Phoebe lifted her chin and met the blank face of one of the men. 'Actually my name is Ms Wells.'

The man stuck out his hand, which Phoebe took after a second's hesitation and then dropped almost immediately; her own hand was clammy and cold. 'My name is Erik Jensen. We are representatives of His Majesty, King Nicholas of Amarnes. Would you please come with us?'

'Mommy…' Christian's voice sounded strangled, and when Phoebe glanced back she saw her son's face was bleached white, his eyes huge and shocked. She felt the mirror of that expression on her own face, remembering how men like this had showed up in her grotty hostel, said nearly the exact same words. Six years ago she'd been too young, too bewildered and overwhelmed to do anything but acquiesce. Now she was older, harder, tougher. She knew better.

'I'm not going anywhere.'

Something flickered in the agent's face and Phoebe thought for a second it looked like pity. Fear crawled along her spine and up her throat.

'Madame Christensen—'

'Who is that?' Christian's voice sounded petulant and afraid, his hands clenched into fists at his sides. 'Why are you calling my mom that name?'

'I'm sorry.' Erik Jensen smiled briefly at the boy. 'Ms Wells.' He turned back to Phoebe. 'It would be better,' he said quietly, 'if you came. There is a representative waiting at the Amarnesian Consulate, to discuss—'

'I hardly think there is anything to discuss,' Phoebe replied coolly. 'In fact,' she continued, her voice a little stronger now, 'I think any necessary discussions were concluded six years ago.' When she and Anders had left the palace in a shroud of disapproval. He'd signed the papers of abdication, releasing him from the burden of the throne. Not one family member had said a word or seen them out. They'd slipped like shadows from the palace, unseen, forgotten. Except, perhaps, by Leo, with his cold, unwavering stare that still chilled her all these years later.

'Matters have changed,' Erik replied in that same neutral yet implacable tone. 'A discussion is necessary.'

Coldness seeped through her, swirled through her brain. *Matters have changed.* Such an innocuous yet ominous phrase. She felt Christian inch closer to her, his fingers curling around her leg. She felt his fear like a palpable force, and it angered her that these men could just come in here and in a matter of minutes—seconds—try to change her life. Order it around. 'Just a minute,' she told the agents stiffly, and turned back to the kitchen, Christian at her side.

'Mommy—' Christian tugged at her leg '—who are those men? Why are they so…' he paused, his voice trembling '…so scary?'

'They don't mean to be,' Phoebe said before she thought *I'll be damned if I apologise for them.* 'Anyway, I'm not scared of them.' She tried to smile, although like her son she felt the fear, crawling, insidious.

Why were those men here? What did they want?

She took a deep breath, forcing herself to think calmly. Coolly. Undoubtedly they wanted her to sign some paper, relinquishing her rights to Anders's money. He'd obviously had a lot of it, even though in their few weeks together he'd squandered his stipend with shocking ease. His father, King Nicholas, had insisted on his son's abdication, yet he'd still kept him well provided for with what mattered—champagne and women.

There was no reason to panic, to be afraid. Yet even as Phoebe told herself this, she felt the fear creep in and wind around her heart. She knew how much power the royal family had. Or, rather, she didn't know, couldn't fathom it, and that was what scared her. They were capable of so much. She'd seen it in the way they'd cut Anders out of the royal family as ruthlessly as if wielding scissors. She'd felt it in Leo's cold stare.

'Mommy—'

'I can't explain it all now, Christian.' Phoebe smiled down at her son, 'but I don't want you to be afraid. These men have a little business with me, and I need to deal with it. You can stay with Mrs Simpson for a little while, can't you?'

Christian wrinkled his nose. 'Her place smells like cats. And I want to stay with you.'

'I know, but…' Mindlessly Phoebe stroked Christian's hair, still soft as a baby's. Like the little boy he was, he jerked and squirmed away. 'All right,' she relented. Perhaps it was better if Christian stayed with her. 'You can come.' She tried to smile again, and managed it better. She felt her calm return, her sense of perspective. She didn't need to panic or fear. She'd built a life for herself here, felt it shining and strong all around her, and took courage from that knowledge. The past receded once more, as it was meant to do, as she needed it to.

A few minutes, perhaps an hour at the Amarnesian

Consulate, and this would all be forgotten. Her life would go on as planned.

She linked hands with Christian, and it was a sign of his nervousness that he let her. Resolutely she turned back to the government agents standing in the doorway like overgrown crows.

'I'll just gather a few things, and then we can be on our way.' She took another breath, injected a certain firmness into her voice. 'I'd like to resolve whatever discussion is necessary as soon as possible, and be home for dinner.'

Their silence, Phoebe reflected, was both ominous and eloquent.

It only took a few minutes to pack a bag with a few snacks and toys for Christian, and then she followed the men down the narrow stairs to the street. Mrs Simpson, in a frayed dressing gown and carpet slippers, poked her head out as they descended, her expression curious and a little worried.

'Phoebe, is everything all right?' she called, and Phoebe's voice sounded rusty as she cleared her throat and replied as cheerfully as she could,

'Yes, fine.' She tried a smile, but felt it slide right off her face. She turned away, clutching Christian to her, and willed her racing heart to slow.

A sedan that screamed discretion with its tinted windows and government plates idled at the kerb, and another dark-suited agent exited the car with smooth assurance and ushered Phoebe and Christian into the back.

As she slid into the soft leather interior and heard the door's lock click into place, she wondered if she was making the biggest mistake of her life, or just being melodramatic.

She'd sign a paper, she'd relinquish whatever rights to

money that they wanted, and then she'd go home, she repeated to herself in a desperate litany. And, Phoebe added grimly, forget this had ever happened.

The sun was setting, sending long, golden rays over the mellow brick townhouses and tenements of Greenwich Village as the sedan purred through the neighbourhood's narrow streets, the pavement cafés and funky boutiques possessing only a scattering of patrons on this chilly November day.

Christian sat close to her side, his expression closed yet alert. Phoebe felt a sharp pang of pride at the way he composed himself. He knew she was feeling as afraid as she was…except she was determined not to be afraid.

That time had passed.

She turned towards the window and watched as the narrow streets of the Village gave way to the wider stretch of Broadway, and then, as they headed uptown on First Avenue, to the broad expanse of the United Nations concourse. Finally the sedan pulled onto a narrow side street wreathed with the flags of various consulates, stopping in front of an elegant townhouse with steep stairs and a wrought-iron railing.

Phoebe slipped out of the car, still holding Christian's hand, and followed the agents into the Armanesian Consulate. Inside it felt like a home, an upscale one, with silk curtains at the windows and priceless, polished antiques decorating the foyer. Phoebe's footsteps were silenced by the thick Aubusson carpet.

As they entered, a woman in a dark suit—was it actually a uniform for these people?—her blonde hair cut in a professional bob, started forward.

'Madame Christensen,' she murmured. 'You are expected.' She glanced at Christian, who clenched Phoebe's hand more tightly. 'I can take the child—'

Phoebe stiffened at the words. 'No one is taking my son.'

The woman flushed, embarrassed and confused, and glanced at Erik Jensen, who hovered at Phoebe's shoulder.

'There is a room upstairs, with every comfort,' he said quietly. 'Toys, books, a television.' He paused diplomatically. 'Perhaps it would be better…'

Phoebe bit her lip. She should have insisted on leaving Christian with Mrs. Simpson and spared him this. Yet she hadn't wanted to be parted with him then, and she didn't now. Even more so she didn't want Christian to witness any unpleasant altercations with some palace official determined on making sure she received nothing from Anders's death.

'All right,' she relented, 'but I want him brought back down to me in fifteen minutes.'

Jensen gave a little shrug of assent, and Phoebe turned to Christian. 'Will you be…?'

Her little boy straightened, throwing his shoulders back. 'I'll be fine,' he said, and his bravery made her eyes sting.

She watched as he followed the dark-suited woman up the ornately curving stairs before turning resolutely to follow Jensen into one of the consulate private reception rooms.

'You may wait here,' he told her as Phoebe prowled through the elegantly appointed room, taking in the gloomy portraits, the polished furniture, the Amarnesian insignia on everything from the coasters to the curtains. 'Would you like a coffee? Tea?'

'No, thank you,' she said, resisting the urge to wrap her arms around herself even though the room wasn't cold. Far from it—it was stuffy, hot. Oppressive. 'I'd just like to get on with it, please, and go home.'

Jensen nodded and withdrew, and Phoebe was alone.

She glanced around the room, a gilded prison. This was so much like the last time she'd been summoned to the royal family—had she learned nothing in six years? She'd let herself be bullied then; she wouldn't now. She didn't want Anders's money, she didn't want anything from him that he hadn't been prepared to give her when he was alive, and she acknowledged grimly just how much that had been: nothing.

Nothing then, nothing now. And that was fine, because she was fine. She'd sign their damn paper and go home.

She registered the soft click of the door opening and stiffened, suddenly afraid to turn around and face the person waiting for her there.

For in that moment she knew—just as she had known when she'd heard those three short raps on the door of her apartment—her life was about to change. Impossibly, irrevocably. For ever.

For she knew from the coldness in her bones, the leaden weight of her numbed heart, that a fussy palace official or consulate pencil-pusher was not waiting for her across ten yards of opulence. She knew, even before turning, who was waiting. Who had been sent to deal with her—an inconvenience, an embarrassment—again.

She turned slowly, her heart beginning a slow yet relentless hammering, a distant part of her still hoping that he wouldn't be there—that after all these years it couldn't be him—

But it was. Of course it was. Standing in the doorway, a faint, sardonic smile on his face and glittering in his eyes, was Leo Christensen.

CHAPTER THREE

'WHAT...?' The single word came out involuntarily, a gasp of shock and fear as the sight of Leo standing there so calm and assured brought the memories flooding back. Phoebe threw her shoulders back and lifted her chin. 'What are you doing here?' she asked in a calmer voice.

Leo arched an eyebrow as he strolled into the room, closing the door softly behind him. 'Is this not the Amarnesian Consulate?' he asked, and Phoebe was conscious of how effortlessly he made her feel like an interloper. An ignorant one.

'Then I suppose the question to ask,' she replied coldly, 'is why *I* am here.'

'Indeed, that is an interesting question,' Leo murmured, his voice as soft and dangerous as it had been six years ago. Phoebe felt it wrap around her with its seductive chill and tried not to shiver.

He was the same, she thought numbly, the same as he'd always been. The same sleepy, bedroom eyes, the same aura of confident sensuality even dressed as he was in a dark suit, undoubtedly coming as he did from Anders's funeral, although there was no sign of grief in his saturnine features.

'How did you get here?' Phoebe blurted. 'You were in Paris, at the funeral—'

'I was this morning,' Leo agreed blandly. 'Then I flew here.'

She tried for a laugh. 'Am I that important?'

'No,' Leo replied, and turned from her to move to a small table equipped with a few crystal decanters and glasses. 'May I offer you a drink? Sherry, brandy?'

'I don't want a drink,' Phoebe replied through gritted teeth. 'I want to know why I'm here and then go home.'

'Home,' Leo repeated musingly. He poured a snifter of brandy, the liquid glinting gold in the lamplight. 'And where is that, precisely?'

'My apartment—'

'A one-bedroom in a rather run-down tenement—'

Phoebe stiffened, thinking of the rather astronomical rent she paid for an apartment most people would think more than adequate. 'Obviously your opinion of what constitutes run-down differs from mine.' She met his gaze directly, refusing to flinch. 'I'm not sure what the point of this is,' she continued. 'I assume I was summoned here for a purpose, to sign some paper—'

'A paper?' Leo asked. He sounded politely curious. 'What kind of paper?' He smiled slightly, and that faint little gesture chilled her all the more. Leo's smiles were worse than his scowls or sneers; there was something cold and feral about them, and it made her think—remember— that he was capable of anything. She'd read it in the tabloids' smear stories; she'd felt it the last time she'd stood across from him and listened to him try to bribe her, and she'd seen it in the cold, cold look he'd given Anders.

'Some kind of paper,' she repeated with a defensive shrug. 'Signing away any rights to Anders's money—'

'Anders's money?' Leo sounded almost amused now. 'Had he any money?'

'He certainly seemed to spend it.' Phoebe heard the ring of bitterness in her voice and flinched at what it revealed.

'Ah. Yes. He *spent* money, but it wasn't his. It belonged to his father, King Nicholas.' Leo took a sip of his brandy. 'Actually, Anders hadn't a euro or cent or whatever currency you prefer to his name. He was really quite, quite broke.'

His words seemed to fall into the empty space of the room, reverberate in the oppressive silence. 'I see,' Phoebe finally managed, but sadly, scarily, she didn't. If Anders didn't have any money…then why was she here? 'Then is it about the Press?' she asked. *Hoped.* 'A gagging order or some such? So I don't write some sort of embarrassing memoir?'

Leo's smile widened; he really was genuinely amused now, and it made Phoebe feel ignorant again. Stupid. 'Have you memoirs?' he queried. 'And would they be so…embarrassing?'

Phoebe felt herself flush, and she shrugged, angry now. Angry and afraid. Not a good combination. 'Then just tell me why I am here…*Your Grace*.'

The smile vanished from Leo's face before he corrected with lethal softness, 'Actually, my title is now Your Highness. Since Anders abdicated, I am the country's heir.'

Phoebe stilled, the realisation trickling coldly through her. She hadn't realised Leo was now the crown prince, although of course she should have known. She knew there was no one else. Anders and Leo were both only children, which was why they'd been raised like brothers.

For a second the old myth flashed through Phoebe's

mind as it had the last time she'd seen Leo: Hod and
Baldur. Twins, one dark, one light. One good, one evil.
Except she knew Anders's true colours now, and he was
far from being good or light. Not evil perhaps, but silly,
shallow, selfish and vain. She shook her head, banishing
the memories. 'Your Highness, then. What do you want
with me? Because I'd prefer to get to the point and go
home. My son is waiting upstairs and he's hungry.' Brave
words, she knew. Strong words, but she didn't feel particularly brave or strong. The longer she remained in Leo's
company, bearing the weight of his silence, the more she
felt her strength being tested. Sapped. 'Well?' she snapped,
hating the way he was toying with her, sipping his brandy
and watching her over the rim of his glass as if she was an
object of amusement or worse, pity.

'I don't want anything with you in particular,' Leo
replied coolly. 'However, my uncle, King Nicholas, hasn't
been well, and he has suffered great regret over what
happened with Anders—'

'You mean forcing his son to abdicate? To leave his
country in disgrace?' Phoebe filled in.

Leo smiled over the rim of his glass. 'As I recall, you
told me Anders didn't even want to be king.'

Phoebe coloured, discomfited that he remembered the
particulars of their conversation six years ago...as did she.

'He didn't,' she mumbled, turning away to gaze unsee-
ingly out of the embassy window. Outside, night had
fallen, and a passing taxi washed the room in pale yellow
light before streaming onwards into the darkness. Phoebe
was suddenly conscious of how long she'd been in this
room with Leo, and she turned around. 'I want to see my
son.'

Something flickered across his face—what?—but then

he gave a tiny shrug. 'Of course. He's upstairs, quite happy, but I'll have Nora bring him down as soon as we've concluded our conversation.'

'And what more is there to say?' Phoebe demanded. 'I'm sorry King Nicholas regrets what happened, but the past is the past and can't be changed. And frankly none of it has anything to do with me.'

'Doesn't it?' Leo queried softly, so softly, and yet it felt as if he'd dropped a handful of ice cubes down her back, or even straight into her soul. Those two little words were spoken with such confidence, such arrogance and power and knowledge, and suddenly, desperately, Phoebe wished she'd never agreed to come to the consulate. Wished, almost, that she'd never met Anders—she'd certainly wished that before—except for the saving grace of Christian.

Still, even under the onslaught of Leo's dark, knowing gaze, those sleepy, bedroom eyes with the long lashes and golden irises now flared with awareness, with knowledge, she forced herself to continue. 'No, it doesn't. In fact, you most likely know that I haven't even seen Anders in years. We separated a month after we married, *Your Highness*, and were practically divorced—'

'Practically?' Leo interrupted. 'Had you consulted with a solicitor? Filed papers?'

Phoebe felt yet another telltale blush staining her cheeks with damning colour even as an inexplicable dread settled coldly in her stomach. 'No, I hadn't, but…' She stopped, suddenly, the silence worse than any words she could say, explanations—excuses—she could give.

'But?' Leo filled in, his eyes, nearly the same colour as the brandy in the glass he held, glittering for a moment with—what? Mockery? Contempt? *Anger?* 'Couldn't bear to make that final cut?' he continued in that awful, soft voice. 'Couldn't stand to walk away from a man like Anders?' He took a step closer to her and Phoebe found she couldn't move. She was mesmerised, strangely drawn by his words and yet chilled too by that unfathomable darkness in his eyes and voice, that depth of some unknowable emotion she'd sensed in him at their first meeting. Leo took another step, and then another, so he was standing only a few inches away, and she was reminded forcefully of when he'd stood so close to her before, when his fingers had brushed her in that faint, damning caress and he'd asked her, *What would have happened…if you'd met me first?* Now he asked another mocking question. 'Were you hoping he'd come back to you, Phoebe?'

Phoebe blinked, forced herself to react. His assessment was so far from the truth, and yet the truth was something she could not bring herself to tell. She stepped away and drew a breath. 'No, I most certainly was not. And whether Anders and I divorced or even considered divorcing is of no concern to you—'

'Actually,' Leo corrected, taking a sip of his brandy, 'it is.' He watched, smiling faintly, enjoying her shock and discomfiture. Phoebe felt her hands curl into fists, her nails biting into her palms. She knew Leo was waiting for her to ask why, and she didn't want to. Didn't want to know.

'It wasn't anyone's concern whether we married or not,' she finally said, striving to keep her voice cool, 'so I hardly see why it matters if we divorced or not.' She drew herself up, throwing her shoulders back. 'Now frankly I've had enough of these power games, Your Highness. You may find it amusing to keep me here like a mouse with a cat, but my son is undoubtedly unsettled and afraid and I have nothing more to say to you or anyone from Amarnes. So—'

'Oh, Phoebe.' Leo shook his head, and for a moment Phoebe thought he genuinely felt sorry for her, and that realisation scared her more than anything else.

'Don't call me—'

'Your name? But we are relatives, of a sort.'

'Of a sort,' Phoebe agreed coldly. 'The sort that have nothing to do with each other.'

'That,' Leo informed her, setting his glass down in a careful, deliberate movement, 'is about to change.'

He was trying to scare her, Phoebe decided. Hoped, even. It was about power, about Leo feeling as if he was in control, and she wouldn't let him. He might be a prince, he might have all the money and power and knowledge, but she had her courage and her child. She had her memories, her own knowledge of how the last six years had shaped and strengthened her, and she wouldn't back down now, especially not to Leo. He'd intimidated and bullied her before; she wouldn't let him now.

'Why don't you just spit it out, Leo,' she asked, glad her voice matched his own for strength, 'instead of giving me all these insidious little hints? Are you trying to frighten me? Because it's not working.' Well, it was, a bit, but she wasn't about to tell him that. Leo merely arched an eyebrow, and Phoebe continued, her voice raw, demanding, and a little desperate. 'What do you want? Why did your damn agents bring me here?'

'Because the king wishes it,' Leo replied simply. He gave her a little smile, and Phoebe pressed a fist to her lips before dropping it.

'What do you mean?'

'I told you, King Nicholas regrets his separation from

Anders. I suppose he always did, but he didn't realise it until too late.' Leo's lips twisted in something close to a smile, and Phoebe wondered what kind of man could actually smile at such a moment, at the explanation of such a futile tragedy. Well, she knew the answer…a man like Leo.

'I'm sorry for your uncle's loss,' she finally said, keeping her voice stiff with dignity. 'For everyone's. But as I said before, it has little to do with me.'

'But you see,' Leo countered softly, 'it does. Or perhaps not with you, but at least with your son.' He paused, his words seeming to echo in the oppressive heaviness of the room, of the moment. 'The king's grandchild.'

Phoebe did not reply. She couldn't think of anything to say, to think, so she turned away to the window once more, as if she could find answers there. She blinked, trying to focus on the shapes of passing cars, but she couldn't see. Everything was blurred, and for a second she thought it was because of the rain. Then she realised it was because of the tears clouding her vision.

She took a breath, willed the tears to recede, to feel strong again. The last thing she wanted was for Leo to see her weakness, for surely if he was aware of it, he would use it.

Yet standing there, the lump of emotion still lodged in her throat, she realised she wasn't even very surprised. Of course the royal family of Amarnes wouldn't leave her alone. Leave Christian alone. For while they may have professed no interest in her son while Anders was alive, now that he was dead…?

Her child was all they had of him. And that was what she had to remember, Phoebe told herself, stiffening her shoulders, her spine. He was *her* child…in every way that mattered.

She swallowed again, meaning to turn to face Leo, but suddenly he was there, his presence behind her, like a looming shadow. It was an unwelcome surprise, as was the hand that rested briefly, heavily on her shoulder, the warmth of his fingers burning her even through the layers of her sweater and coat.

'I'm sorry.'

It was the last thing she expected, the words, and, even more so, the raw compassion underneath them. She didn't trust it, didn't allow herself to. How could she? She'd trusted Anders, she wasn't about to trust his cousin, and most of all she wasn't about to trust herself, as much as she wanted to. For in that moment she wanted to believe Leo was sorry, she wanted to believe he could be—what? A *friend*?

The idea was so laughable as to be offensive. Phoebe turned around, shrugging Leo's hand off her shoulder, and he stepped away, his expression bland once more.

'What exactly are you sorry for, Leo?' she asked coolly. 'Bringing me here? Upsetting my son? Thinking you have some kind of control over me just because you're a prince?'

Leo shrugged, his tone matching hers. 'None of the above. I'm sorry because you obviously loved Anders, and now he's dead.'

It was such a flat, matter-of-fact statement; it hardly could be called a condolence. Phoebe inclined her head in acknowledgement.

'Thank you. But anything I felt for Anders ended six years ago. I'm sorry he died in such a tragic way, but...' She drew in a breath. 'What I had with him is far, far in the past. I have a life here now, and so does Christian, re-gardless of what the king of Amarnes thinks or feels. He has not tried to contact us once in the last six years. What is my son to think, to learn he suddenly has a grandfather who cared nothing for him before?'

'I imagine he'd be grateful to learn he has some family,' Leo replied, his tone still cool.

'He has my mother—'

'On his father's side. But you've never even told Christian about Anders, have you? He doesn't even know that his father is—was—a prince.'

'And why should he?' Phoebe flashed. 'Anders abdicated the throne and had no interest in being a father to Christian. We're far better here in New York with our friends and family. My mother has been a doting grandmother to Christian, and he's wanted for nothing.'

Leo merely arched one eyebrow in silent scepticism, making Phoebe fume. 'You don't need to live in a palace or ride in a Rolls-Royce to be considered cared for, you know,' she snapped. 'Christian has had a perfectly acceptable and happy childhood—'

'He is the son of a prince, descended from royalty,' Leo said quietly. 'And you don't think he should know?'

'None of you wanted to know,' Phoebe returned. 'Not once—'

'Ah, but you see, we didn't know about Christian,' Leo told her softly. 'By the time he'd made an appearance, you'd already separated from Anders—or should I say he separated from you? Either way, you disappeared from his life. And the royal family had no interest in you…until we learned you had a child. How old is he, Phoebe? Five, six?'

'Five.' Almost six, but she wasn't about to tell that to Leo. Let him draw whatever conclusions he wanted.

Leo paused, took a step closer. 'You must have fallen

pregnant right away. Or did it happen after he left you? You were together for how long? A few weeks?'

'A little over a month,' she answered tightly.

'What happened, Phoebe?' Leo asked, his voice as soft as a caress. 'Did Anders smile and say sorry as he always did? Did he make it up to you?' Another step and she could feel his breath on her cheek, felt his hand touch her shoulder, trailing his fingers, and even now she felt a sharp, unwanted pang of need—desire—at the simple touch. She shrugged away. 'Is that how Christian came about?'

'It's absolutely no concern of yours,' she said coldly. The last thing she wanted Leo to know was the truth of Christian's birth. Let him believe she'd, however briefly, made up with Anders. The idea was repellent, but so was the alternative…Leo knowing the truth.

'Perhaps not,' Leo agreed, 'but the fact remains that Christian is my concern, or at least my uncle, the king's.'

'No.' The word was torn from her, and Phoebe turned to see Leo looking at her again with a strange compassion that rested oddly on the harshly beautiful features of his face. She wasn't used to seeing a gentler emotion softening his mouth, lighting his eyes. She didn't like it and she didn't trust it.

'Yes,' he corrected her softly, spreading his hands for a moment before dropping them again, 'and I'm afraid there's nothing you can do about it.'

The words buzzed like flies in Phoebe's brain and she tasted bile. She wasn't ready for this, she realised. She didn't have the strength for a second round with Leo. She drew in a shaky breath. 'I'd like to check on Christian,' she said, and was glad her voice was steady. 'Alone. And then we can continue this conversation.'

Something sparked in Leo's eyes, something almost

like admiration or at least a certain grudging respect, and he inclined his head. 'Very well.' He moved to the door and pressed an unseen button. Within seconds a dark-suited official entered almost soundlessly. Leo spoke to the official in Danish, and Phoebe could only make out a few words.

'Sven will take you upstairs,' Leo told her. 'When you are satisfied Christian is comfortable, we will continue.'

Phoebe nodded, turning to follow Sven. Leo had turned his back on her and was pouring himself another drink, staring out at the black night as if he too was seeking answers in the darkness.

The door clicked softly shut behind him and Leo took a strong swallow of his drink, the alcohol burning all the way to his gut. He needed the sensation, the sedation from feeling. Remembering.

Regretting.

Anders was dead. That was enough to damn him. Dead. A wasted, reckless life, and not once had Leo tried to rein him in, teach him control. No, that hadn't been his job. His job, Leo acknowledged sourly, had been to stay out of the way, to be the unneeded spare, and of course to keep Anders happy. Entertained.

It hadn't been very much of a job.

Even now Leo remembered the slow burn of constant dismissals and rejection. Stay out of the way, Leo. Be quiet and do what you're told. Do not anger the king… His mother's pleas, the desperate attempts of a woman who had been cast off by the royal family as soon as she'd been made a widow. She hadn't wanted the same fate for Leo.

So his fate—his duty—had been to exist as Anders's

older shadow. He'd accompanied his cousin on his escapades and he'd enjoyed them himself and now...

Now those days were over, and his duty lay elsewhere.

Leo turned away from the window, impatient with his own maudlin reflections. He thought of Phoebe, felt a flicker of reluctant admiration for her strength and courage, even though she was clearly shocked by Anders's death...and its repercussions. Sometimes, Leo thought, he wondered if they'd ever be free of Anders's repercussions, the messes he made, the people he disappointed.

And Phoebe and her son were just another problem Leo had to solve. Leo took another long swallow of brandy and closed his eyes. He knew what was required of him; the king had made it clear. *Bring the son, pay off the girl.* So simple. So cold-hearted. So treacherous.

Already he doubted the success of such a plan. Phoebe showed a fierce and unwavering loyalty to her child, and no doubt an offer of cold cash would enrage her, as it had before, and entrench her even more deeply in her disgust of Amarnes and its royal family. A subtler tactic was needed, a more sophisticated deceit.

He needed to keep her pliable, sweet, until he could decide just what he would do with her. What he *wanted* to do with her... Leo felt a tightening in his gut as he thought of how she responded to his lightest touch... She was so transparent in her desire. And yet he felt it as well, deep inside, a need...

He pushed the thought—as well as the feeling—away. He couldn't afford to desire Phoebe. She was a problem to be solved, an inconvenience to be dealt with, just as she'd surmised all those years ago. Even now he remembered every word of the conversation, could feel the smooth silk of her skin against his questing hand...

No. He clamped down on the thought, straightening his shoulders, and tossed back the last of his brandy. As the first stars began to glimmer in the sky, he considered his next move.

CHAPTER FOUR

PHOEBE followed Sven up the thickly carpeted stairs, the long velvet curtains drawn against the night. Everything was silent and still, hushed and muted, so she could hear the relentless drumming of her own heart, loud in her ears.

Sven came to the end of an upstairs corridor and opened the door.

'Mommy!' Christian sprang up from where he'd been sitting with a scattered pile of Lego.

'Having fun?' Phoebe asked lightly, even as her arms ached to clasp her son to her in a tight hug and never let him go. Dash out of the consulate and run from the ever-grasping claws of the royal family, with their power and their ruthless arrogance.

'Yes…' Christian admitted a bit grudgingly. Looking around the room, Phoebe could see that was indeed the case. The sumptuous carpet was scattered with Lego and action heroes, and a pile of Christian's favorite DVDs rested by the large-screen plasma TV.

'Can we go?' Christian asked, and Phoebe saw him chew nervously on his lip. 'I'm hungry.'

'You can have dinner here,' Phoebe suggested. 'I'm sure they'll let you order whatever you like. You can have that pizza you wanted.'

'Of course,' Nora murmured.

'But I want to go now…'

So do I, Phoebe thought grimly, but she simply rested a hand lightly on Christian's head, resisting yet again the urge to grab him and run. 'Soon, I promise. Why don't you watch a DVD?' She gestured towards the huge television. 'You've been asking for one of those for ages.'

'I don't want to watch a DVD,' Christian said at his most obstinate, and Phoebe sighed, crouching down so she was at eye-level. 'Christian, I'm sorry, but we have to stay a bit longer. I told you I had some business to take care of, and it will be finished—soon. I need to talk to—to Prince Leopold for a few more minutes—'

'Prince?' Christian repeated, his voice sharpening with curiosity and then, worse, realisation. 'Like the prince on TV? The one who died?'

Phoebe silently cursed her son's mental agility. 'Ye-es,' she agreed reluctantly, adding a caveat, 'sort of.'

'You know a prince,' Christian said, sounding impressed, and then he actually puffed out his chest. 'And so do I.'

'A prince with a big-screen TV,' Phoebe reminded him, desperate for a diversion. 'I'll just be a few more minutes, OK?'

'OK.' Christian nodded slowly, won over by the promise of pizza and a DVD.

Phoebe straightened, smiling in relief, even as she steeled herself for another round with Leo. Yet at that moment all she could remember was that dark look of compassion in his eyes, and the way his fingers had burned through her coat.

Sven took her back downstairs, but instead of returning to the large reception room at the front of the consulate he led her to a smaller, more private room at the back.

He opened a door and ushered her inside, retreating and closing the door softly behind him before Phoebe even had a chance to register where she was.

'What is this?' she demanded, and Leo turned to her and smiled.

'Dinner, of course.'

But it wasn't just dinner, Phoebe acknowledged with a fluttering of panic she knew she shouldn't feel. It looked—and felt—like some kind of seduction.

The room was dimly lit by a few small table lamps, and a table for two had been laid by the marble fireplace, set with a creamy damask cloth, delicate porcelain and the finest crystal, glinting in the light. The flames of the fire cast leaping shadows over the room, and half of Leo's face was in shadow, so she could only see the faint curling of his mouth in what she supposed was a smile.

He looked far too confident, Phoebe thought as the panic rose, far too powerful, too predatory. Too sensual. For there could be no denying that Leo Christensen was a completely sensual being.

He'd taken off his tie and undone the top two buttons of his shirt so that Phoebe's gaze was instinctively drawn—as it had been six years ago—to the strong column of his throat. She jerked her gaze upwards, felt herself flush as she saw how Leo had been watching her. Knowing.

'I'm not hungry,' Phoebe said, taking a step towards the door.

'Aren't you?' Leo murmured, and Phoebe's flush intensified as though her whole body was burning. Burning not just with awareness, but with shame, for something about Leo invoked a helpless response in her that she hated.

Desire.

She felt it stretch and spiral between them, sleepy, seductive and far too powerful. No, Phoebe corrected fiercely, not desire. Fascination. It was like a child's fascination with fire, fingers aching to touch the flickering flame, so forbidden and dangerous. It didn't *mean* anything. It wouldn't, of course it wouldn't. She didn't even *like* Leo. As long as she remembered that and kept herself well away from the flames, she'd be all right. Safe.

Except now the source of heat and danger was walking right towards her with that long, easy stride, smiling with sleepy sensuality as he held out a glass of wine he'd just poured while she'd been standing here, her mouth hanging open and her eyes as wide as a child's, or worse, a lovesick girl's.

'Here.' He handed her the glass of wine, which Phoebe accepted before she could think better of it, her nerveless fingers curling around the fragile stem.

'You've gone to rather a lot of effort,' she finally said. Leo merely raised his eyebrows.

'I must admit I did little more than bark a few orders, but I thought we'd both be more comfortable having eaten something.'

'Did you?' Phoebe mumbled, taking a sip of wine, wishing she didn't feel this helpless fascination. Already she couldn't keep her eyes from wandering up and down the length of him, the long legs, trim hips and broad shoulders, finally resting on those full, sculpted lips, wondering how—

Stop. This was ridiculous. *Dangerous.*

'Yes, I did,' Leo replied, amusement gleaming in those golden, hooded eyes, eyes like an eagle's, the eagles that were stamped on every piece of priceless porcelain on the table, reminding her just who she was dealing with, *what*—

Phoebe put her glass down with an unsteady clatter. 'I appreciate your effort,' she said, forcing herself to meet Leo's gaze directly, 'but I'd really like to finish things here and go—'

'Home. Yes, I know. However, I'm afraid it's not going to be that simple or quick. And I, for one, am starving, having travelled across the Atlantic this afternoon with very little to eat.' He went to the table and began to remove the covers from several silver chafing dishes.

Leo began serving them both food, fragrant offerings that made Phoebe's stomach clench and rumble despite her protestations that she wasn't hungry. 'Come, sit down,' he said mildly. 'There's no reason to refuse to eat, is there?'

'I'm not—'

'Hungry? Yes, you are. I can hear your stomach rumbling from here. And if you're worried about Christian, I had Nora order pizza. He doesn't have any food allergies, I trust.' He spoke with such confidence Phoebe knew he'd already checked. Yet despite his knowing arrogance, she was touched that he had thought to consider Christian's needs. It was a small detail, irrelevant really, yet it still, strangely, meant something.

'Thank you,' she murmured, still somewhat grudgingly. 'Christian loves pizza.'

'Come.' He beckoned her, holding aloft a dish that was steaming and fragrant. 'You know you want to.'

Phoebe almost resisted simply for the principle of it. She didn't want to be seduced by Leo, not even by the food he offered. He was toying with her, she knew, teasing her because he knew he affected her, knew that there was something basic and primal that she responded to, helplessly, hopelessly.

She'd felt it back then, a little spark leaping to life deep inside her, and now she felt that spark flame to life once more, licking at her insides, threatening to burgeon into a full-grown inferno of need.

'Fine.' Phoebe moved over to the table and sat down, accepting the plate of boeuf Bourguignonne in its rich red wine sauce that Leo handed her. It smelled and looked delicious. 'And now you can tell me what this is all about.'

'Of course.' Leo took a sip of wine, watching her over the rim of his glass. 'Tell me, when was the last time you saw Anders?'

'That's hardly relevant,' Phoebe snapped. She shifted in her seat, uneasy at this line of questioning and where it might lead.

'I'm curious.'

'Too bad.' She took a bite of beef, barely registering the rich gravy or succulent meat. Her heart was thudding with heavy, hectic beats and her hands felt clammy. And all because of Leo. Why did she let him affect her this much?

'Did Anders ever meet his son?'

Phoebe pressed her lips together. 'Let's just say,' she said tightly, 'that he wasn't interested.'

'I see.' Leo gazed at her with a shrewd compassion Phoebe didn't like. She didn't want to be pitied or even understood. She just wanted to be left alone. 'All right, Phoebe,' Leo said. 'It's really rather simple. King Nicholas regrets his separation from Anders. He was furious six years ago, as you probably know—he'd already arranged Anders's marriage with a minor European royal when he announced his relationship with you. It would have been a good match.'

Phoebe's fingers clenched around the heavy sterling-silver fork. 'Maybe so, but Anders obviously thought differently.'

'Perhaps,' Leo replied, and Phoebe felt it as an insult, even though in essence it was true. Anders *had* felt differently...for about a month.

'I already know the king regrets his separation,' Phoebe said, and heard the impatience fraying her tone. 'You've made that abundantly clear. I just don't see what it has to do with me—'

'Nothing to do with *you*,' Leo replied blandly, 'but everything to do with Christian.' He smiled, that sensual mouth curving, curling, making Phoebe want to shiver. 'The king,' he told her, 'wishes to see his grandchild.'

Phoebe said nothing. Again, she found she wasn't surprised. Horrified, but not surprised. Wasn't this what she'd been waiting for, secretly, silently dreading? A claim on her child, no matter how small. A claim that could become stronger than her own. She opened her mouth, groping for words, for a cutting rebuttal, yet nothing came. Her mind was spinning in horrible circles, looking for an escape, some way out of this mess—

'In Amarnes,' Leo clarified in a terribly implacable tone. He paused. 'You're welcome to accompany him, of course.'

Outrage finally gave her voice. 'Of course I'll accompany him! That is, *if* he was going anywhere—which he's not.'

Leo gazed at her, rotating the stem of his wine glass between long, lean fingers. 'Phoebe,' he said finally, his voice surprisingly, strangely gentle, 'do you really think you can make such a statement?'

'I just did—'

'And back it up?' Leo cut her off, his voice still soft yet with a chilling knowledge that made Phoebe blink. And blink again.

'He's my child. I don't need to back anything up,' she finally said, but even to her own ears her voice sounded uncertain. Afraid.

'And my uncle is the king of a small but wealthy and well-connected country,' Leo told her. 'What he wishes, he gets. And frankly there isn't a court in the world that would rule in your favour. My uncle would make sure of it.'

'A court?' Phoebe repeated blankly, and a second later the single word caused a host of unpleasant connotations and images to tumble through her mind: trials and lawsuits, custody battles—all things she couldn't afford, not emotionally or financially. 'Your uncle would take me to court?'

Leo shrugged. 'If you refuse him this small request—'

'And how is this request small?' Phoebe demanded. She rose from the table, spinning away, her fists pressed to her eyes as if she could shut out Leo's voice, the reality he was forcing upon her.

From behind her she heard Leo rise from the table and come to stand behind her; she could feel the heat emanating from him, and for one crazy moment she wanted to lean back against him, feel the strength and hardness of his chest, find some kind of comfort there.

With *Leo*? her mind mocked. She really was falling apart if she thought there was any comfort to be had from him.

'I'm sorry,' he said in a tone that managed to be both compassionate and final, 'but this is how it is, and you cannot change it.' He paused. 'Prepare for a holiday in Amarnes. You might even enjoy it.'

Phoebe whirled around. 'For six years your family has completely ignored me. And now suddenly they want something from me? And think they can have it?'

Leo didn't even blink. 'Essentially, yes.' His voice was flat, but she thought she saw a flicker of compassion in his eyes, and in desperation she appealed to that faint, frail hope.

'Leo, please. It doesn't make sense to drag Christian from the home he loves, the life he knows, and for what? To appease an old man's sense of regret? It's not fair to me or to Christian.'

Leo hesitated, and for a moment—a second—Phoebe thought she had a chance. Prayed that he understood, that he'd relent—then his face closed, like a fan snapping shut, and despair fell over Phoebe like a dank fog.

'I'm sorry,' he said, his voice flat, expressionless. 'There is nothing I can do.' He gave a little shrug, dismissing her pain and distress in so tiny, so indifferent a gesture. 'It is only for a fortnight.'

Two weeks. Two weeks in Amarnes, facing the royal family, reliving that unwanted episode of her life. And would it end then? Phoebe wondered dully. Would King Nicholas be satisfied? Or would he just go on asking for—demanding—more, and more, and even more, until Phoebe and Christian's lives were siphoned away in sacrifice to an old man's selfish whims, drop by tiny drop, week by painful week.

She turned to Leo. 'And it will end there? We'll go home, and the king will never want to see us again?' She let out a sharp, incredulous laugh. 'You honestly expect me to believe that? That he won't want—demand—more?'

Leo's face was utterly impassive. 'Perhaps he will be satisfied,' he said. 'This might be no more than a passing fancy.'

'And that should make me feel better, I suppose,' Phoebe tossed back. 'I'm sure Christian will be happy to have served his purpose and then be thrown away like rubbish!'

Annoyance flashed across Leo's face like a streak of lightning. 'You are being melodramatic. There is no reason why a two-week trip to a beautiful country should be nothing but a lovely holiday for both you and your son. You look exhausted,' he continued bluntly, 'and I'm sure you could use some relaxation.'

'I'm hardly going to relax—'

'You might try,' Leo cut her off. 'It would certainly make the trip more pleasant for you.' His voice was sharp with impatience, and Phoebe knew he was done with her objections. Her fate, and her child's, had been decided. And there wasn't a single thing she could do about it.

She saw that now, starkly, understanding once again the kind of people—the kind of power—she was dealing with. She couldn't face a royal family in the courts. She couldn't face the tabloids and the paparazzi that would swarm over her little family like greedy vultures when they caught wind of this story.

'Come, why don't you eat?' Leo said mildly, sitting down again. Phoebe shook her head.

'Now I've really lost my appetite.'

'Suit yourself. But just because you don't like the state of affairs doesn't mean you can't enjoy yourself in the meantime.'

Phoebe glanced around the sumptuous room flickering with firelight, their decadent meal spread on the table. She thought of what she'd seen of Leo in the papers, years before, and wondered how many meals like this he'd enjoyed with the models and starlets he liked to have on his arm…and no doubt in his bed. A resentment she didn't quite understand spiked her voice as she said, 'Like you do, I suppose.'

There was a second's hesitation before Leo shrugged

and poured them both more wine, even though Phoebe's glass was still mostly full. 'Of course.'

Phoebe took a breath, opened her mouth and prepared for a fight. Yet suddenly, looking at the magnificently laid table and the remains of her delicious meal, she felt all the fight—all the anger and outrage and self-righteous fury—trickle out of her. Leo was right, even if she didn't want him to be. She had to accept this. The problems her refusal could cause were too dire to consider.

Two weeks in Amarnes, and then they could return home, to the life she'd built for them both here in New York. Two weeks in Amarnes, and Christian could get to know his father's side of the family. Perhaps she could even see the positive side of things, make it an adventure…

And in the meantime, she would eat and enjoy this meal. Resolutely she returned to the table and raised her wine glass to Leo in an ironic toast, earning her a faint smile. 'Very well,' she said stiffly. 'Cheers.'

'Cheers,' Leo murmured, and they both drank in silence. Phoebe fought the temptation to drain her glass.

'So,' she said when they'd both finished drinking and she'd picked up her fork, toying with a bit of beef. 'What's happened in Amarnes these last six years?'

'More of the same, really,' Leo replied in a deliberate drawl. 'Nothing much happens in these tiny little countries, you know, although we like to think it does.'

Phoebe choked back a surprised laugh. 'I suppose Anders's abdication was the news of the century, then.'

'Just about.'

'And it made you king.'

'Heir,' Leo corrected, his tone light although his expression had hardened. 'King Nicholas is still alive, as far as I know.'

Phoebe took another sip of wine. 'The Playboy Prince will become the Playboy King one day,' she quipped a bit sardonically, and Leo's mouth tightened, his eyes darkening to a deep umber. She wondered if she'd actually offended him. 'Your reputation is well-known, you know. At least it was when I—'

'Yes, I'm aware,' he said in a bored voice. 'Although in that regard, I suppose some things have changed in Amarnes.'

Phoebe regarded him curiously. Was he actually trying to say *he'd* changed? Yet he seemed so much the same— even as that thought took hold of her, another realisation swept through her. He *had* changed. Gone were the rumpled curls, as if he'd just risen from bed—from being with a lover. His hair was cut short, and more grey streaked his temples. And even though he'd treated her with the same lazy arrogance as he had six years ago, Phoebe sensed something new—something harder—in him now, a resolute sense of purpose that had been lacking before— or was she simply being fanciful? Imagining things, rewriting history, the man she'd known?

Except, Phoebe thought, she'd never really known Leo. She'd met him for ten minutes and read about him in the tabloids. That was all, and it occurred to her how very little it was. Now, suddenly—stupidly, perhaps—she found herself wondering just what kind of man he was. What kind of man he'd been, and then, more intriguingly, how he might have changed.

'So what have you been doing, then?' she finally asked. She took a bit of beef and chewed slowly, watching him. Swallowing, she continued. 'How have you been keeping yourself?'

Leo shrugged. 'A bit of this, a bit of that.'

'That's hardly an answer.'

'I'm sure a more specific answer would bore you. Do you really want to know the monotonous details of royal duty?'

'You're not a playboy any more?' Phoebe pressed.

Leo smiled, the sleepy, sensual smile Phoebe remembered, and as awareness coiled in her belly and raced through her veins she knew one thing that hadn't changed: her response to him.

'You know what they say. You can take the man out of the country, but you can't—'

'You mean,' Phoebe cut him off, 'you haven't changed?'

Leo shrugged. 'Judge for yourself. But...' he leaned forward, his eyes glinting into hers '...enough about the boring, sordid details of my own life. I want to know about you.'

Phoebe raised her brows, a strange, surprising smile lurking inside her, quirking her mouth. 'Can something be sordid *and* boring?'

'Most definitely.' He dismissed the topic with a shrug of one powerful shoulder. 'Now, I know a bit about how you've been keeping yourself—'

'How?'

Leo smiled. 'Phoebe, I always do my research.'

'You had me investigated?' she demanded sharply.

'Of course. That's how Christian's existence was discovered.'

'Why—why would you do that?' Phoebe asked in a whisper, thinking, *if only he hadn't...*

'I'm afraid when Anders died, he left a few skeletons in the cupboard that had to be dealt with. You were one of them.'

'And now you're dealing with me,' Phoebe filled in. 'Once again I'm an inconvenience.'

'But an interesting one,' Leo told her with a faint smile. 'I learned, for instance, that you have your own business, designing jewellery.'

Phoebe nodded, a sense of pride burgeoning within her when she thought of what she'd accomplished. 'Yes, I do. I have a small boutique on St Mark's Place and a mail-order service as well.'

'You've made a life for yourself,' Leo observed, and Phoebe's eyes flashed.

'Despite my supposedly squalid apartment?'

His answering smile took the sting out of her remark. 'I suppose your apartment could be seen as…adequate,' he said with a heavy sigh that made a reluctant smile tug at Phoebe's mouth. She could hardly believe she was sitting here, talking and laughing with Leo Christensen… almost as if they were friends.

Had he simply lulled her into a false sense of security, comfort? Or was this real?

She realised with a surprising pang of longing that she wanted it to be. Despite the fullness of her life, her business, her friends and family, she'd been without a man. A companion. With a son to raise and a growing business to manage there hadn't been time, or, Phoebe acknowledged, much inclination. The wreck of her one-month marriage kept her wary and distant, although she'd had a few relationships—well, dates at least—over the years.

Leo leaned forward, his fingers reaching out to touch Phoebe's throat, his fingers lightly caressing its hollow. 'Is this one of your pieces?'

Phoebe swallowed, far too affected by Leo's casual caress. His fingers were still brushing her skin as he touched the necklace, an uncut sliver of fiery agate encased in twisted gold wire.

'Yes…' Her voice came out in a shuddery hiss of breath. Leo looked up, and Phoebe was transfixed by his gaze, his eyes the same colour as the stone he caressed.

'It's beautiful. Unusual. I can see why you've been successful.'

'Thank you.' He was still touching her, and Phoebe knew she should withdraw, should demand he drop his hand. Yet she couldn't. She was enjoying it too much, savouring the feel of his fingers against his skin, revelling in the desire that uncoiled and wound its way through her.

Why was she so helpless when it came to this man? And did it even matter why? It simply *was*.

Leo's eyes met and clashed with hers, and after another heightened second he slowly—almost reluctantly—withdrew his hand. 'How did you get started in jewellery?' he asked. He leaned back in his chair, leaving Phoebe feeling stupidly, ridiculously, *overwhelmingly* bereft. She looked away, afraid Leo would see the disappointment in her eyes.

'My mother is a potter, and so art was always part of my upbringing. We'd go to Long Island for summer every year, and I loved collecting stones on the beach. Pretty ones, different ones. I'd twist string around them to make necklaces and bracelets and things.' She shrugged, suddenly self-conscious. 'And that's where my jewellery comes from, really. Childish crafts, but grown-up.'

'Very grown-up,' Leo murmured. 'I can't imagine it's cheap to rent retail space in Manhattan.'

'No, indeed,' Phoebe agreed. 'And apartments aren't cheap, either.'

'Touché.' Leo grinned, his eyes lightening to amber, his teeth strong and white. He raised his glass in a mock-toast. 'You're not going to forgive that one remark, are you?'

'Not any time soon,' Phoebe retorted, trying to be flippant although she felt far from it. Leo's full-fledged grin had had a devastating effect on her; she'd never seen him smile properly before, without irony or contempt or derision. She looked away, taking a slug of wine, willing her heart rate to slow. She couldn't keep on like this, every sense on high alert, responsive to his every gesture. Craving more.

One of the consulate's staff slipped in quietly to clear the remains of their meal. The fire snapped and crackled, and Phoebe knew she should go. Even more importantly, she should *want* to go. Yet somehow she didn't. Somehow she wanted to stay in this warm, comfortable room, with the fire casting leaping shadows along the panelled walls, and the glow of Leo's smile starting a fire in her soul. In her body, too, for her throat still burned where he'd touched her all too briefly.

Stop it. Phoebe closed her eyes in private supplication. *Please.* Wanting Leo was such a bad idea. It would cloud her judgement, make her weak…

She had to think of what was best for Christian, not her own unsatisfied body. She had to keep them both safe.

Somewhere in the consulate a clock struck eight, low, sonorous chimes that reverberated through Phoebe and made her reluctantly stir. 'I should go.' Yet she didn't move. 'It's late, and we can continue this discussion another day—'

'I'm afraid not,' Leo said, and he sounded genuinely regretful. 'You see, the king is not very well at the moment and he wants to see Christian as soon as possible. We need to leave for Amarnes tomorrow.' Phoebe's mouth dropped open in soundless shock. *Tomorrow…?* 'The arrangements have been made,' Leo continued, 'and I will fetch you and Christian at eight o'clock tomorrow morning.'

Her earlier stirrings of desire gave way to sheer outrage. 'That's impossible! I can't arrange travel details so quickly. Christian is in school and I'm not even sure his passport is current—'

Leo shrugged. 'Ring the school, and the passport is irrelevant. We will be travelling on a private jet, and—' his smile glimmered briefly '—I think Customs will let him through, as a royal.'

As a royal. Phoebe wasn't ready to process that statement or its frightening implications. She shook her head. 'And what about my work?'

Leo's expression didn't even flicker. 'Since you manage your own business, I'm quite certain you can arrange a leave of absence.'

'I have orders to fill—'

'And they can't wait for two weeks?' Leo raised his eyebrows. 'Surely you have an assistant of some kind who can do what is necessary. If not, hire one and the Amarnesian government shall pay for it.'

'Hire one by tomorrow morning?' Phoebe demanded, and Leo simply shrugged again.

'I do have an assistant,' she admitted grudgingly, 'but she's part-time and I can hardly ask—'

'Yes,' Leo replied, his tone managing to be both friendly and implacable, 'you can.'

Phoebe bit back yet another angry retort. She knew there was no point in arguing. Leo would meet each objection with that irritating indifference before reminding her once again of the royal family's power and reach. She was beaten…for the moment.

'Fine,' she finally said, her teeth gritted, 'but at the end of two weeks I'm returning home with Christian and I plan to never see any of you ever again.' The words sounded petulant, she knew, and also a bit desperate. Could she guarantee such a thing?

Leo regarded her for a moment, his head tilted to one side, those amber eyes softened in what, once more, unsettlingly, looked like compassion. 'Yes,' he said, his voice carefully expressionless, 'of course you are.'

The fire had died to a few embers in the grate, the moon a lonely silver sickle high above in the sky as Leo poured himself another brandy. Phoebe had left with Christian hours ago, and now he pictured her putting her little boy to bed in her apartment, sitting alone on the sofa, her knees drawn up to her chest as she contemplated her changed and uncertain future.

And she had no idea just how changed and uncertain it was. Leo smiled grimly. King Nicholas had not wanted Phoebe to come to Amarnes at all; he simply wanted the boy. Yet Leo knew that was an impossible task, and one he had no wish to perform. He wouldn't—couldn't—separate the boy from his mother, not when she was so obviously attached to him. He knew what that felt like, remembered his mother's pale, stricken face as she left on the royal jet for her home country of Italy, while Leo, six years old and stoic, stood silently at the nursery window, trying not to cry.

From that moment his life had been consecrated to the crown, to serve it and yet never wear it. For the last six years he'd been considered the heir apparent, much to Nicholas's fury. Leo knew Nicholas would rather have the monarchy crumble to nothing than have him as his successor, yet he had had no choice. And for the last six years Leo had been doing his damnedest to prove to Nicholas and to the people of Amarnes—to the whole world—that he was worthy of the crown.

'*Have you changed?*'

Phoebe didn't believe he had; she still saw him as a reckless playboy, cut from the same cloth as Anders. And perhaps he was. The old, familiar guilt, as corrosive as acid, roiled in his gut.

'You don't deserve it...you don't deserve to be king.'

Yet he would be, deserving or not. He was his uncle's only heir now, and nothing could change that. Anders's abdication was absolute. So Leo would continue to serve his country and his sovereign, and do what was required of him...no matter what it meant for Phoebe.

He drained the last of his brandy and stood up, preparing for bed. He couldn't afford to think about Phoebe, her feelings...or the way she'd felt when he touched her. For a moment he savoured the memory of the silkiness of her skin, how her grey eyes had darkened to slate, her lush body almost quivering with desire...

And he'd felt it too, a current running through him, hot and electric, needing an outlet. He still felt it now; his body was restless and unsated, yet Leo knew he would have to ignore it. Seducing Phoebe was not part of his plan. Couldn't be.

Yet what was his plan? Leo mused. He would bring them both to Amarnes, even though Nicholas would be furious. Perhaps the old man would grow bored and let them go, as Phoebe so obviously hoped, yet Leo doubted it. And what would Phoebe do then? Leo rubbed his face tiredly. He had no answers, not yet, but at least he'd done his duty. He always did his duty. He was bringing the boy back, and Phoebe—for the moment at least—was proving to be biddable. The rest, he decided, would have to wait.

CHAPTER FIVE

PALE sunshine slanted through the gauzy curtains of Phoebe's bedroom as she slowly swung her legs over the side of her bed and rested her head in her hands. It had only taken a second of consciousness for the comforting veil of sleep to be ripped away, replaced by the clamorous memories of last night.

Leo. Leo was here in New York, and would be coming to fetch them to take them to Amarnes in—she looked at the clock and felt a lurch of panic. In less than two hours. Quickly Phoebe rose from the bed, showered and dressed before Christian woke up and demanded his breakfast. She peeked in on Christian, and saw him sprawled across his sheets.

When she'd taken him home from the consulate he'd been bubbling over, fear so easily replaced by excitement. Phoebe had told him they were going to Amarnes for two weeks, preparing herself for questions, demands, even tears. But Christian's eyes had simply widened and he'd breathed one word: '*Cool*.' Five-year-olds, even ones as precocious as her son, were easily appeased.

She'd also had to break the news to her mother, Amelia, in Brooklyn. She'd called her mother after Christian was asleep, her heart aching slightly at the sound of her cheerful hello.

'What's up?'

'A lot, actually,' Phoebe had said, trying for a laugh, but her mother, as always, heard the concern and worry underneath.

'Phoebe, what's wrong?'

Phoebe knuckled her forehead and closed her eyes, fighting a sudden, overwhelming wave of weariness. 'Two government agents from Amarnes showed up at my door a few hours ago.'

'What?' Her mother's breath came out in a hiss of surprise. She knew everything about Phoebe's hasty marriage to Anders; she'd been waiting at the airport with a hug and a smile when Phoebe arrived, weary and heart-sore, with a three-month-old Christian in her arms. 'Why?'

Phoebe pressed her lips together before she said shortly, 'Christian.'

Her mother was silent. 'They don't…'

'No,' Phoebe said quickly. 'They don't. And they won't know if I can help it.'

'Oh, Phoebe.' Phoebe nearly buckled under her mother's compassion. She was just about holding it together, making herself see this as the little adventure she'd promised Christian it was, but hearing the sorrow and worry in her mother's tone made Phoebe want to cry and confess all her fears.

What if they want him? What if they keep him? What if there are custody battles and lawsuits and horrible things I can't control? I'm so afraid.

She didn't give voice to any of these questions, merely continued in a rather flat voice, 'We're leaving tomorrow for Amarnes.'

'No—'

'For two weeks,' Phoebe clarified. 'Apparently the king wants to see his grandson. And then we'll come home.'

'Phoebe, don't give in to them. Once you're in Amarnes you'll have very few resources, very little power—'

'I have no choice, Mom,' Phoebe said. 'They're royal. They have millions. Billions, probably, and if it came to a court case—'

'Will it?' her mother asked quickly and Phoebe closed her eyes once more.

'I hope not. I pray not. But…I don't know.' Her hand felt slippery around the receiver. 'If I go willingly now, it might…help me later.'

'Or not,' Amelia said darkly and Phoebe blew out an exasperated sigh.

'Then what should I do?'

'I have a friend, a human-rights lawyer…' Phoebe could hear her mother scrabbling for one of the many business cards she kept stuck on her fridge with colourful magnets.

'Oh, Mom, I can't afford a lawyer. Not for the kind of court case we're talking about, and I don't want to drag Christian through that anyway.' Besides, she added silently, she doubted one of her mother's hippie friends, leftovers from the flower-power days of the sixties, would give her much credibility in court. 'Anyway,' she continued, keeping her voice firm, 'I've been thinking that Nicholas should see Christian anyway. I always felt the way they cut Anders out of their lives was so unfair, and I'd be a hypocrite to do the same thing with Christian.'

'Phoebe, these people don't deserve your sympathy—'

'Perhaps not,' Phoebe agreed, 'but that doesn't mean I'm going to be like them.' Strong words, she knew. She only wished she felt as strong and certain inside.

After speaking to her mother, she'd called her assistant, Josie, who had been more than happy to take over the boutique for two weeks.

It was, Phoebe thought, all too easy to arrange, almost as if it were meant to be. And perhaps it was. If she simply clung to the belief that this was for merely two weeks, she could be generous. She could allow the king access to her son, she could forgive them all for being so cold-hearted and bloody-minded, she could accept that Leo was simply doing what he had to do…

Leo. And, Phoebe asked herself with uncomfortable shrewdness, did any of this have to do with Leo, with the wellspring of desire he'd plumbed in her, with the memory of his brief touch still burning up her senses? Was all this magnanimity simply because she wanted a chance to see Leo again?

He's a playboy, a rake, a reprobate, Phoebe lectured herself, but the words bounced off her heart meaning-lessly. She didn't know *what* Leo was any more. And this trip to Amarnes gave her a chance to find out.

Now, as morning broke, the Washington Square Arch bathed in the pink light of dawn, Phoebe steeled herself for the day ahead. She'd packed quickly last night, throwing in most of their clothes as well as a few of Christian's books and toys. She dressed simply in grey wool trousers and a pale pink sweater and tried to ignore the flutter of nerves—or was it actually excitement?—in her stomach.

The next hour passed in a flurry as Christian awoke and Phoebe rushed to get breakfast and pack last-minute things. Harassed and her hair half-brushed, Phoebe watched in dismay as a limousine with tinted windows pulled up to the apartment building, idling at the kerb. Her heart leapt into her throat as she watched Leo, dressed superbly in a dark suit, a wool trenchcoat over one arm, exit the car and press the bell.

Leo's dark gaze swept over the apartment building with its crumbling steps and soot-stained walls. It was charming, he supposed, in a slightly run-down way. His lips twitched as he imagined teasing Phoebe about it, before he clamped down on that thought. He couldn't afford it, couldn't allow Phoebe to matter at all. It would only hurt them both in the end.

Leo pressed the bell again, impatience biting at him. He knew this had to be difficult for Phoebe, knew it was the last thing she wanted, and who could blame her? The royal family had spat her out six years ago and now they wanted to chew her back up. Hardly an enticing proposition, yet one she would have to accept, just as he had.

He pictured her then, not as he remembered her six years ago with her still childishly rounded face and college student's clothes of torn jeans and a T-shirt, but the woman she'd become. The woman he'd seen yesterday, whose hair was still curly and dark, whose slight figure still possessed improbably lush curves. He thought of how her wide grey eyes sparked defiance—and an irrepressible desire—when she looked at him.

It infuriated her perhaps, that desire, but it was there. It had been there last night; he'd seen it, *felt* it humming in the air between them when she'd entered the room and had seen the candlelit room with a meal laid out like a planned seduction.

Of course, he couldn't seduce her, as much as his body begged for that release. Sex was a complication he couldn't afford. Last night had simply been a way to gain her confidence, her trust, even her friendship.

He needed Phoebe pliant and willing, ready to do the royal family's bidding...whatever it might be.

Phoebe called for Christian, who had been racing around the apartment like a wild thing, and reached for her suitcase. She didn't want Leo in her apartment, filling up the small space with his formidable presence, yet she realised it was unavoidable as she heard his tread on the stairs, light yet purposeful. Mrs Simpson must have let him in, Phoebe thought. She never could resist a handsome face or a charming smile, and Leo had both.

And then he was there, knocking on the door, which Christian wrenched open before Phoebe could stop him—not that there would be any point, delaying the utterly inevitable.

'Hello.' Leo stood in the doorway, dressed in a dark suit, looking calm and unruffled and unusually solemn. He surveyed Christian, who stared at him in open curiosity. 'My name is Leo, and I suppose I'm your cousin.'

Christian's eyes widened. 'I have a cousin?'

Leo's gaze moved questioningly to Phoebe, who bit her lip. 'We hadn't quite got round to discussing that yet,' she said quietly and Leo inclined his head.

'Well, it's quite a nice surprise for you, isn't it, Christian?' He smiled easily. 'I like surprises. Do you?'

'Ye-es,' Christian agreed after a moment, and Leo reached for the rather large, green plastic dinosaur poking out of Christian's backpack.

'My goodness, I wouldn't want this fellow to catch me in a dark alley,' he said, inspecting the toy with considerable interest. 'He's got a lot of teeth, hasn't he?'

'And he makes a noise, too,' Christian said eagerly, pushing a button so the dinosaur let out a fearsome mechanical roar and clawed the air for a few seconds. Leo let out a little yelp, pretending to jump back in fright, thus earning a great belly laugh from Christian. 'It's just pretend,' he said with a child's scorn, and Leo returned it to his backpack.

'Thank goodness for that,' he said, his eyes meeting Phoebe's over Christian's head. Phoebe smiled in gratitude, amazed and thankful at how effortlessly Leo had diverted Christian from the thorny question of his relations. Yet Leo was charming, always had been; why not with children as well as women? That was why he was so dangerous.

'We should go,' she said a bit stiltedly, conscious of Leo's warm gaze on her, as well as the fact that she hadn't had time to blow-dry her hair. It framed her face in wild, dark curls, and she could see Leo eyeing them. Did she not look smart enough? He turned back to Christian.

'Yes, we should. The car, not to mention the royal jet, is waiting.'

'Royal jet?' Christian repeated, and his eyes bugged out. 'Really?'

'Yes, Amarnes is an island. We'll take my limousine to the airport, and fly from there.'

'Wow.' Christian looked completely thrilled now, and Phoebe managed a smile.

'Pretty cool, eh?' she said, keeping her voice light even as her heart hammered within her in a staccato beat that seemed to say *two weeks, two weeks, two weeks*. Only two weeks.

Leo stepped in front of her, taking the suitcase from her with an easy smile. 'Please. Allow me.'

'Thank you,' she murmured and with Christian by her side she followed Leo down the stairs.

They didn't speak as he loaded the cases in the back of the limo himself, or even when they arranged themselves on the plush leather seats, Christian's eyes wide as he took in the mini-bar and fresh flowers.

Leo slipped into the limo across from her, and she was achingly aware of his presence, his heat, his scent. Her fingers felt thick and clumsy as she fumbled with Christian's seat belt, wishing her senses were not so heightened when it came to Leo and yet craving it—him—anyway.

'Here.' Quietly, competently, Leo clicked Christian's buckle closed, his long brown fingers over hers. Touching hers. And in her emotionally heightened state, Phoebe felt a rush of something—what? Gratitude, or something more? No, something less, something so basic, this fascination with Leo, with his aura of excitement and danger.

Except right now he wasn't being dangerous. He was just being kind.

'Thank you,' she mumbled before sitting back and buckling her own seat belt.

'Not a problem.' Leo leaned back against his seat, stretching his legs in front of him. 'Now, Christian, would you like something to drink? I think there's orange juice in the fridge, as well as some cola if your mother allows it.'

'Christian doesn't…' Phoebe began, but her son was already leaning forward to inspect the contents of the mini-bar.

'All right, fine,' she finally said, striving for that light tone once more. 'This is a holiday after all.'

'Exactly.' Leo smiled, and Phoebe tried to ignore the

effect of that gesture on her insides, tried to think of something else—anything else—as the limo pulled away from the kerb and headed into town, towards the Holland Tunnel.

They rode in silence to a private airstrip on the outskirts of the city. A sleek silver jet waited there, with the recognisable emblem of the twin eagles emblazoned on its tail.

'Wow,' Christian breathed as they boarded the plane. Leather sofas and a mahogany coffee table adorned with yet more freshly cut flowers made Phoebe feel as if she were entering a living room rather than an airplane. Christian was looking at all the luxury with wide eyes, and Phoebe tried to suppress a spurt of anxiety. She'd been afraid the royal family would want more of Christian…but what if he wanted more of them? How could she compete with all of this?

'Just enjoy it,' Leo murmured, his lips nearly brushing her ear, his breath fanning her cheek. Uneasily Phoebe wondered if she'd spoken aloud. Or had Leo just read her mind?

She chose not to answer, busying herself with settling Christian. Soon enough they were all seated and the plane was gliding down the runway and then up into a grey November sky.

'I've never been on a plane before,' Christian said after a few minutes of rather tense silence. His cheeks were flushed and he was clutching his dinosaur to him. 'That I remember, anyway.'

Leo glanced at him, his features seeming to soften. 'Then this should be quite an adventure for you.'

'I guess so,' Christian mumbled, shooting Phoebe an uncertain look. Phoebe knew that underneath the excitement her son was confused, and she would have to talk to him soon. Explain…except how could she explain? She wasn't even sure what was going to happen, and the last thing she wanted to do was tell him about relatives who might ultimately reject him.

Two weeks, her mind reminded her, her heart still beating fast. *Two weeks, two weeks, two weeks.*

The next few hours passed in silence punctuated only by Christian's occasional question—did they have pizza in Amarnes, and what about milkshakes?—as well as the tinny roar of his dinosaur as he played.

Phoebe sat tensely across from him, watching as Leo took out a sheaf of papers and a gold-plated pen and set to work. What was he working on? she wondered. What kind of work did a playboy prince have to do? Except he wasn't a playboy prince any more, she reminded herself. He was the heir apparent.

'What are you doing?' she asked when Christian had fallen into a doze and the silence seemed to stretch on for ever, taut and unyielding. Leo glanced up.

'A pet project of mine,' he said with a little shrug. 'Facts and figures, very boring.'

'You're quick to dismiss many things as boring,' Phoebe replied, and with surprise she heard the teasing lilt in her voice. Was she actually flirting? Or just being friendly?

Leo shrugged again. 'It's a charity,' he said after a moment. 'I'm one of the trustees and I'm simply going over the endowment figures.'

'What kind of charity?' Phoebe asked, now genuinely curious.

'A relocation programme for political refugees. Amarnes was a neutral country during World War Two, and we took in many of those fleeing persecution. I like to see the tradition continue today.'

'Very admirable,' Phoebe said, yet her mind was spinning. This new version of Leo—a man who concerned himself with refugees—bore little resemblance to the pleasure-seeking playboy she'd encountered six years ago.

Had he really changed so much? Yet his smile was as sardonic as ever as he remarked in a drawl, 'It's easy to be admirable when you have the money and time.' He capped his pen and put his papers away. 'You should get some sleep. The jet lag can be brutal.' And, seeming to dismiss her, he settled back in his own seat and closed his eyes.

Although he kept his eyes closed, sleep remained elusive. Leo was aware of the uncomfortable prickling of his conscience as he'd spoken with Phoebe. He wanted to gain her trust, he needed her pliant, and the best way to do that was to show her how he'd changed. How he was on her side. It would be all too easy, and yet when the opportunities came Leo found he didn't want to take them. He didn't want to use Phoebe. He wanted to…*protect* her. What a ridiculous and inappropriate notion. The only reason he was bringing her to Amarnes at all was because he knew he couldn't pay her off in New York. Sooner or later he would find a way to keep her out of the picture—or at least removed from it.

Just like your own mother was.

His jaw clenched and he forced his conscience back into the shadowy corner of his mind, where it had remained for most of his playboy years. Back then he hadn't had a conscience because he hadn't cared; he was the unneeded spare, and so he'd do what he damn well liked.

Yet Anders's abdication had changed everything. Leo felt the familiar guilt eat at him and he pushed it resolutely away. For the last six years he'd lived the life of a monk, a *saint*, chaste and diligent, and had won the respect of his people. He'd put his country and crown first, always, and he would continue to do so. No matter what it cost him…or Phoebe.

They were more important than the tender feelings of a woman he couldn't afford to care about. He shouldn't even want to care, he told himself irritably. Phoebe was an inconvenience, that was all. All she could be.

Forcing himself to relax, to forget that woman sitting across from him with every anxiety and fear reflected in her wide grey eyes even as she kept her tone light and upbeat for the sake of her son, Leo finally—by sheer force of will—drifted into a doze.

Phoebe couldn't sleep. Christian was snoring, his cheek pillowed against the plastic back of his dinosaur, and even Leo seemed to have dozed off, yet Phoebe sat there, tense, anxious, too many emotions and questions and desires coursing through her. What would happen when they arrived in Amarnes? How would the king receive Christian…and her? What was she going to *do*?

Too many questions, and none of them had answers. Yet. Phoebe pushed them away, and her gaze fell on Leo's sleeping form. He'd shed his jacket and rolled up the sleeves of his crisp white shirt, exposing strong, tanned forearms now loosely crossed. Phoebe's gaze fell on those arms and stayed there, noticing the fine dark hairs, the sinewy muscles, the long, elegantly tapered fingers. She knew she should look away—she should want to look away—but she couldn't.

That dark tug of fascination was pulling at her insides, and while Leo slept she found her gaze roving over him almost hungrily, noting the cropped, dark hair, the chiselled cheekbones and sculpted lips, the ridiculously long eye-lashes. She let her gaze drop from his face to his shoulders—how did a plain white shirt emphasise the powerful muscles of his chest so wonderfully?—and lower still to his trim waist and hips and long legs, stretched out in front of him, his butter-soft leather loafers just inches from her own feet.

He was a beautiful man. A dark angel with the heart of a devil...or so he'd seemed all those years ago. But now...?

'What would have happened, do you suppose, if you'd met me first?'

The question he'd asked her six years ago slipped slyly into her mind, and the answer Phoebe had given back then—nothing—seemed to echo uselessly through her.

All right, so she was attracted to him. Phoebe straightened in her seat and forced herself to look away, out of the window. The plane had risen above the city fog and now there were only a few wisps of cottony cloud in an otherwise perfect blue sky.

Of course she was attracted to him; he positively oozed sexuality and charm. And, to be perfectly blunt, she'd been without male companionship of any kind for too long.

Yet it still shamed her to admit to something so basic, so impossible to ignore or deny. How could she be attracted to Leo, the man who had insulted her, belittled her, tried to buy her? Was she so enslaved to her own senses?

Again Phoebe felt that dark tug of longing, of need.

Apparently she was.

'You mean you haven't changed?'

'Judge for yourself.'

Was it possible that Leo had really changed, put his playboy days behind him? She thought of him bantering with Christian, the glimmer of humour in his amber eyes, and forced back another treacherous wave of desire and, worse, hope.

She couldn't afford to believe Leo had changed. As much as she wanted to, she couldn't afford to trust him. She was on her own here, and she'd better remember that.

'Look.' Leo reached over and touched her shoulder, causing Phoebe to jump as if he'd branded her with a hot poker. She must have fallen into a doze without realising it. 'Amarnes,' he told her, and, swallowing audibly, Phoebe refocused her gaze on the vista outside.

Amarnes. It nestled in a slate-blue North Sea, a tiny, perfect jewel. The eastern side of the island was carved into deep fjords; from the sky Phoebe could see the steep sides of the valleys they created, lush and green, their rocky peaks capped with snow. As the plane moved over the fjords, Phoebe saw a cluster of brightly painted fishermen's cottages near the shore, and then, on a plain on the northern end of the island, Amarnes's capital city, Njardvik.

For a moment Phoebe let herself remember the last time she'd come to Amarnes, standing on the deck of a ferry, the salt spray stinging her face, Anders at her side. Back then she hadn't known Anders was a prince, hadn't known anything. She'd met him ten days earlier, while backpacking through Norway, and she'd fallen for him right away. Anders had had a gift of making her feel as if she were permanently fixed at the centre of his universe. It was only later—when a single piece of paper declared them married—that she realized he made *everyone* feel that way.

On the ferry he'd pointed to Amarnes, just a smudge of dark green on the horizon, and said, 'That's my home.' He had leaned against the railing and with a self-conscious smile added, 'I should probably tell you, I'm a prince.'

Phoebe had laughed disbelievingly, until Anders explained that he wasn't joking; he was actually heir to a throne. Phoebe had stared.

'I don't want any of it,' he'd told her. 'You can't imagine the pressure, the expectations.' His brilliant blue eyes had met and held hers. 'I just want you, Phoebe.'

What a joke. An outright lie. Anders might have believed it at that moment, Phoebe thought fairly, but it was simply that. A moment. Yet six years on Phoebe couldn't summon the energy to feel bitter or angry. She'd been as reckless as Anders, plunging into a marriage with a man she barely knew, and now that he was dead she only felt a distant kind of sorrow and even pity for the man he'd been and the life he'd wasted.

The plane began its descent, and Christian stirred. Phoebe's gaze slid involuntarily to Leo, and she was unsettled to realise he'd been watching her, his lips curved in a knowing smile that she didn't like.

'Welcome home,' he said softly, just for her ears, and Phoebe bristled.

'Hardly.'

Leo just smiled.

The next few minutes were a blur as they exited the plane, the cold, clean air hitting Phoebe like a slap—she'd forgotten how fresh everything was here, so new and bright and clean. Even the colours seemed sharper, the deep green of the fir trees that flanked the winking blue sea, the grey, craggy mountains with their majestic white peaks. And the sleek black limousine that purred to a halt as Leo directed their luggage to be loaded in a van and ushered them into the car.

'The palace is only a few minutes away,' Leo said as the limousine pulled away from the airstrip, heading down a narrow road that snaked along the valley floor. Phoebe glanced at Christian; he was taking in everything with wide, amazed eyes. He must, Phoebe thought, feel as if he'd stepped into a TV show, or a fairy tale.

Within minutes the limousine emerged from the closed valley to the outskirts of Njardvik, the boulevard into the city lined with pastel-coloured townhouses, a leftover relic of the island's Dutch possession four hundred years earlier. Unwillingly Phoebe gazed around at the quaint plazas with their flowerpots and pavement cafés, now shuttered for the oncoming winter. There could be no denying that Njardvik was an unspoiled jewel of a city, and just the sight of its pretty streets and elegant homes made her remember the optimism and excitement that had buoyed her along this very route with Anders.

Was her hope that this would end after two weeks just as misplaced?

'Wow,' Christian breathed, and Phoebe turned to see the limousine enter the eagle-crested gates of the palace court-yard. The palace itself was several hundred years old, a rambling and impressive edifice of mellow gold stone. A rather grim-faced official in royal livery waited by the main entrance, guarded by two soldiers resplendent in their royal blue uniforms and polished helmets.

'Here we are,' Leo said lightly, and opened the door.

Numbly Phoebe followed him, Christian clutched in her arms. She heard Leo speak a few words of Danish to the official, who opened the doors to the palace and, with a sweep of his arm, bade them enter.

She'd only been to the palace once before, hustled like some criminal by royal agents, afraid, alone, to be con-fronted by Leo. It almost made Phoebe feel dizzy and sick to be back here. Once again she was afraid, alone, and she had no idea what was going to happen.

She pushed the feelings away, tried to summon back her courage. Her confidence. She was changed, no matter if Leo was or wasn't. She was stronger now, and she had to remind herself of that strength as she stood in the palace's huge foyer, feeling tiny and insignificant on about an acre of black and white checked marble.

'The king would like to see you,' Leo said. 'But first you will want to rest, freshen up. Johann will lead you to your rooms.' Another servant, also in royal livery, seemed to appear almost magically, and wordlessly Phoebe followed him from the cool marble foyer up the ornate curving staircase, Christian at her side.

Johann led them to a suite of rooms in the back of the palace. Phoebe took in the two king-sized bedrooms, joined by an elegant little parlour, and the wide terrace overlooking the palace gardens, now rimed in frost.

She dropped her handbag next to her suitcase on the floor, the carpet thick and sumptuous, and took a deep, steadying breath. Christian was already investigating the huge walk-in wardrobes, the big-screen plasma TV hidden behind mahogany doors, the king-sized bed with its fluffy feather mattress.

'This place is so cool,' he said, reaching for the TV's remote control and stabbing curiously at the buttons. 'How long are we staying?'

'Two weeks,' Phoebe replied tightly. She felt wound up, ready to snap, and they hadn't even seen the king yet. They hadn't seen anything, done anything, and already the tension was biting at her, fraying her calm, her strength. She went to the bathroom to splash water on her face, and grimaced at her pale, strained reflection.

Christian wandered in, the remote control still clutched

in one hand. 'If the prince is my cousin, what should I call him?' he asked, wrinkling his nose. 'And if he is a prince, does that make me one too?'

A light knock on the door kept Phoebe from answering those alarming questions. She opened the door to another blank-faced servant, who informed her in flawless English that King Nicholas awaited in the throne room.

'Already?' Phoebe asked, to which the servant simply gave a helpless little shrug. She hadn't changed or even brushed her hair, but if the king was going to be so rude as to demand her attendance before she'd even caught her breath, he could take her as she was.

She gestured to Christian and, ever ready for an adventure, he quickly trotted to her side. They followed the servant through a maze of corridors and down another, more private staircase until finally they were standing in front of a pair of ornate doors decorated in gold leaf.

Phoebe swallowed. This part of the palace she'd never seen.

'His Majesty, King Nicholas the First of Amarnes,' a servant intoned, and the doors were thrown open. Phoebe started forward, Christian at her side, only to have a burly, solemn-faced servant step straight in front of her, so she smacked into his chest.

'What—?' she cried in dazed confusion. A hand came down hard on her shoulder.

'Only the boy,' a voice, low and final, spoke in clipped English, and before Phoebe could frame a protest she was hustled away as Christian disappeared behind the heavy, ornate doors.

CHAPTER SIX

'*WHAT?*' Leo looked up from the mail he'd been rifling through, his brows drawn sharply together in a frown. His top aide, Piers Handsel, gave a nod of confirmation.

'I thought you'd like to know. The king summoned the boy ten minutes ago.'

'But they've just arrived,' Leo said, his voice no more than a growl. Had the king no tact, no sensibility? Running roughshod over Phoebe was not the way to gain her trust.

'Just the boy,' Piers clarified. 'Not…' he paused delicately '…the mother.'

Leo dropped the letter he'd been holding and glared at his aide. 'What do you mean?' he asked, his voice menacingly soft.

Piers shrugged in apology. 'The king has no wish to see her, apparently. He refused her entrance into the throne room.'

'She would have resisted—'

Piers coughed. 'I believe Lars escorted her to the blue salon.'

'Lars!' Leo repeated in disgust. Lars was little more than a thug, paid to do Nicholas's dirty work. And when Piers said *escorted*, Leo had no doubt he really meant *forced*. So, only minutes after arriving at the palace, Phoebe was being treated like an unwanted prisoner, and her son was alone with the king. A stranger.

Rage, white-hot and electric, coursed through Leo. For a moment a memory of his own mother's treatment blazed through him. Just like Phoebe, she'd been shunted from the palace and her son's life because she'd been surplus to requirements. He felt sick at what Phoebe had to endure. What he had allowed her to endure.

'I will speak to the king,' he said shortly and, tossing the rest of his mail aside, he strode from the room. Rage fuelled him as he navigated the palace's many corridors before arriving at the throne room. He paused at the doors, for if Christian was still with the king he had no desire to frighten the boy. All was silent from within. Leo threw open the doors and strode in.

Nicholas sat on the throne, a small, grey-haired man, diminished by age, wearing his usual three-piece suit, his thin, liver-spotted hands folded over his middle.

Leo didn't bother with the preliminaries; he was too angry. 'What were you thinking,' he demanded tersely, 'to separate Phoebe from her child practically the moment they arrived?'

Nicholas regarded his nephew shrewdly. 'Phoebe, is it? I told you not to bring her.'

'I had no choice,' Leo replied, his voice curt despite the anger that still coursed through him. He curled his hand into a fist at his side, resisting the urge to plough it straight into the king's sagging belly. 'She wouldn't be bought.'

'Everyone can be bought.'

Leo pressed his lips together. 'Phoebe is utterly dedicated to her son. I've seen it myself.' He paused. 'Before I went to New York, I didn't realise quite how much.' He'd gone to New York anticipating a flighty, careless woman... the kind of woman who had married a man she'd known for little more than a week, and separated from a month later. Yet Phoebe hadn't been that woman. She'd changed, he realised, changed and grown, and he felt a surprising flash of both pride and admiration at the thought.

Nicholas shrugged. 'No matter. I'm sure we can find a way to dispose of her.'

Dispose of her. Like rubbish, Leo thought, just as Phoebe had feared. Twenty-four hours ago such a statement would have caused barely a ripple of unease; Phoebe had just been an inconvenience to deal with. Yet now his uncle's callousness infuriated him. Enraged him, touching and hurting him in a deep place inside he couldn't bear to think about. 'Your sensitivity astonishes me,' he said in a clipped voice that belied the emotion coursing through him in an unrelenting river, 'but she has a legal right to her son—'

'As did your mother,' Nicholas replied with a glimmer of a smile. 'Yet she saw fit to step aside.'

Leo struggled to speak calmly; the mention of his mother caused that river of emotion flowing through him to become a torrent, an unstoppable tide. For a moment he was that boy again, standing at the window, struggling not to cry, yet wanting desperately to shout out, to beg her to come back or at least turn around. She never had.

Mio Dio, did he see himself in Christian? His mother in Phoebe? How could he have ever considered separating them for a moment?

Yet he hadn't, Leo realised. From the moment he'd entered the salon at the consulate and seen Phoebe standing there, so proud and afraid, so much the same as he remembered with her wide grey eyes, as clear as mirrors, and her dark, curly hair, irrepressible and wild…his plans to buy her off had disappeared. Evaporated, like so much meaningless mist. He would never separate a mother from her child…yet what could he do with her now? What life could she have in Amarnes? Or would the king tire of the boy as Phoebe hoped?

'What do you intend,' he asked now, trying to sound unconcerned, 'with the boy?'

Nicholas shrugged. 'I like him,' he said, his tone that of a child with a new toy. 'He has courage. He was obviously afraid when he entered the throne room, but he didn't succumb to tears. He threw back his shoulders and greeted me like a man.' Nicholas paused, and Leo turned around to see the king give him a sly, sideways smile. 'He will make a good king.'

For a moment all Leo could do was stare blankly at the king as his words echoed through him. '*He will make a good king…a good king…a good king…*' 'What,' he finally asked with soft menace, 'do you mean?'

Nicholas chuckled. 'You didn't realise, did you? Why do you think I sent for the boy?' Nicholas's mouth twisted cynically. 'To play happy families?'

Leo didn't trust himself to answer. Suddenly he realised how ridiculously sentimental, how glaringly *false* Nicholas's desire to see his grandson was. Of course he had an ulterior motive…but *king*?

'Anders abdicated,' Leo finally said in a low voice. 'You can't undo—'

'Can't I?' Nicholas looked positively gleeful, causing rage to course through Leo once more. Rage and regret and guilt, all wrapped together, consuming him, choking him— He'd been so blind. So blind to follow the king's bidding, to ignore his own memories, to bring Phoebe and

Christian here—to think he could be king. That he deserved to be.

'I've called a session of Parliament,' Nicholas said. He sat back on the throne, an ageing tyrant still determined to wield his power. To hurt.

'And just like that,' Leo demanded in a hiss, 'you're going to change the line of succession, make a child you don't even know your heir—?'

'The line of succession is intact,' Nicholas informed him coldly. 'You were the aberration.'

Of course he was. He always had been. The older son of the younger brother. What a useless position that was. Leo laughed, a harsh, ugly sound. 'I know how much it infuriated you that I was made heir—tell me, was it pride that kept you from begging Anders not to abdicate? Perhaps in time you would have accepted his bride, as long as it meant your son could be king.'

Nicholas's eyes narrowed to two slits blazing hatred and contempt, the only weapons he had. 'And now my grandson will be king instead,' he said coldly.

'If Parliament agrees to reinstate Anders posthumously.'

'They will.' Nicholas spoke with such certainty, and Leo knew he had reason to. Parliament did what the king wanted it to. He shook his head, the implications of Nicholas's pronouncement filtering through him.

He wouldn't be king. For six years he'd been the heir, serving the crown, serving Nicholas in attempt after attempt to show how worthy he was. Even if he didn't believe he was himself.

It had taken several years of honest living before the Press—and the people—started to believe in him, in the idea of him as king, but he'd won their trust. Their respect.

He'd never won the king's.

He was the son of a second son; he'd been a playboy, a reprobate, a rake. And deeming him even more unworthy were the feelings he'd locked inside himself, feelings he refused to consider or acknowledge because to do so would be to open a Pandora's box of emotions that might never be shut again.

And now it was going to be taken away, his life—and Christian's—irrevocably changed by the whim of an ill, old man. The twin demons of regret and guilt lashed him. He'd brought Phoebe straight into the lion's den— a pit of vipers! For if Christian was heir, there was no question of him returning to his life in New York…ever. And Nicholas would want Phoebe completely and utterly out of the way…out of the country, out of Christian's life, and he'd do whatever he could to achieve his goal.

And Leo…Leo had practically been his stooge. He'd thought he was serving the crown, but now he saw he'd only been serving the greedy whims of a vicious old man. He shook his head slowly, steeled his spine.

'If you're so determined to see the boy king, so be it,' he said coolly. 'I suppose you'd rather see the monarchy crumble to nothing than have me on the throne.' Nicholas's mouth tightened, but he didn't reply. 'But you won't get what you want by bulldozing over Christian's mother. As much as you might loathe her presence, she can't be bought or intimidated.'

'We'll see about—'

'She's American,' Leo cut across him coldly, 'and that boy is her whole world. She has no notion of royal duty as my mother did, and she won't be frightened or bullied the way my mother was.' Again he felt the old rage, the guilt and sorrow and regret. How could he have acted in such a way, putting Phoebe in the same utterly untenable position as his mother? How could he not have seen what was happening, what Nicholas was planning? Or had he just closed his mind to it, an act of bloody-minded will, because he was determined to do what he could to protect his crown?

Except the crown wasn't his any more.

Nicholas shrugged impatiently. 'I'll find a way—'

'No,' Leo cut him off, 'you won't.' Determination filled him, a cold sense of purpose that made him gaze directly, unflinchingly, at the king, allowing the old man to see his scorn. 'And if you want Christian to remain in this country, in the crown's protection, then you need a subtler method.' The smile he gave his uncle was cold and feral. 'From now on we'll do it my way.'

Phoebe rubbed her arms, fighting a rising sense of panic— near hysteria—as she paced the room, one of the palace's many salons. The doors, she knew, were locked. She'd tried them, rattled the handles helplessly, unable to believe they'd actually locked her away without a word of explanation…without her *son*.

She was a prisoner, and the realisation that she'd walked straight into this gilded jail made her choke. She'd trusted Leo—she hadn't even known she'd been doing so, he'd insinuated himself into her thoughts, her *heart* so insidiously—and now look where she was. Locked up like a criminal, and Christian—

She pressed a fist to her trembling lips and willed the panic to recede. She needed to be calm, to think clearly, rationally—

They couldn't just take him from her. Surely, *surely* in

this day and age, in the Western world, a mother couldn't be forcibly separated from her son—

Except she really had no idea what could happen, what the royal family could do. Lord, where *was* he? It had been half an hour, an endless thirty minutes. She resisted the urge to go to the door and rattle the knob once more, to pound and kick and scream until she was heard. Such antics would surely only weaken her position, and she needed to be *calm*—

A sound at the door had all sense of calm leaving her as she flew to it, her breath heaving in her chest. The door opened and Leo stood there, looking all too calm, all too unruffled—

'You lied!' Her voice came out close to a scream. 'They took him from me, and locked me in here—' She choked back a helpless sob.

Leo moved into the room, closing the door quietly behind him. 'I'm very sorry for what happened,' he said in a careful voice. 'That was never my intention.'

'Wasn't it?' Phoebe threw back at him. 'Somehow I have trouble believing you didn't know exactly—'

'I promise you, Phoebe, I didn't.' The intensity in his voice, the throbbing sincerity, made her still. She believed him, she hadn't been wrong to trust him, and the realisation—the *hope*—gave her comfort.

'Then what?' she asked, drawing in a steadying breath. 'The king acted on his own?'

'Basically, yes.' Leo thrust a hand into his pocket and strode to the window, gazing out at the cloudless blue sky, the palace courtyard glittering under a winter sun. Phoebe watched him, saw the tension in every taut line in his body, felt the anger simmering under his calm exterior. Perhaps he wasn't so unruffled after all.

'I thought the king wanted to see his grandson,' he said abruptly, his eyes on the sun-filled view outside. 'That's why I brought you here.'

Phoebe frowned, an uneasy confusion filling her. Even though Leo was still, his gaze on the palace courtyard, she sensed an anger in him…a restless darkness that she remembered from six years ago. 'Has something changed?' When Leo remained silent, gazing outside, she continued more forcefully, 'What does he want, Leo? Why did he separate us?'

'Because he's more interested in Christian than you,' Leo replied flatly.

Phoebe paced the floor again, rubbing her arms. 'I know that,' she said. 'I'd be an idiot not to. But…' All the unspoken fears—fears she couldn't afford to confess—clamoured up her throat, clawing their way out. Was the king going to seek custody, remove her from Christian's life completely? Her mother was right, she never should have come, she should have hired that dippy lawyer friend, something, *anything*—

'Phoebe.' Phoebe skidded to a halt, for suddenly Leo was there, his hands warm and steady on her shoulders, his eyes meeting, melting into hers. 'I'm not going to let anything happen, I promise.'

'How can you stop it? What's he planning, Leo?' She felt a hiccupy sob rise from her throat and she swallowed it back.

'I didn't realise…' Leo stopped, his lips pressed together, his face turning hard again.

'Realise what? Leo, what are you not telling me? What is the king planning?' Her voice rose with each question until it neared a shriek. 'Please,' she said in a whisper. 'Please be honest with me.'

Leo glanced down at her, and a surprising tenderness

softened his features. 'I will,' he told her. He raised one
hand to brush her cheek with his knuckles, and it took all
of Phoebe's strength to resist leaning into that caress. She
wanted to lean into it, into him, to let someone share the
burden of her fear and anxiety. She longed to trust Leo—
he was the only one she could—and yet she was afraid that
trusting him might be the biggest mistake of all. 'I will tell
you,' he continued, 'but not now. You've only been in the
country for little more than an hour, and I'm sure you
want to see Christian.'

'Where is he?'

'Upstairs in the nursery, with my old governess. He's
fine.'

Phoebe nodded. She still felt shaky and far too afraid,
but Leo's words, his presence, his hand still cupping her
cheek made her less so. Perhaps they shouldn't, but they
did and she was even glad.

Leo smiled, his fingers drifting down her cheek to cup
her chin. 'Tomorrow,' he told her, and bent his head so his
lips brushed hers in the softest whisper of a kiss. He
stepped back, his eyes widening slightly, and Phoebe wondered if he felt as dazed as she did. It had been the slight-
est kiss, their lips barely touching, and yet…! It had lit a
fire of yearning in her body, that latent little spark igniting
suddenly into a raging blaze.

'Leo…' she said, and heard the longing in her voice.

Leo touched her lips with his finger as if he was sealing
the memory of his touch. 'We'll talk tomorrow.'

'Tomorrow?' She couldn't wait that long.

'You need rest.' Leo smiled, and Phoebe found herself
fixated on his mouth, his lips so full, sculpted, *perfect*. Her
own lips parted in memory and desire. 'I'll have someone
see you to the nursery.'

'All right…' She knew she needed to process everything that had happened—including Leo's kiss—even though already she longed to see him again. Touch him again. Yet exhaustion was crashing over her in a numbing wave, and she knew Leo was right. She needed to see Christian, to restore some balance, some *sanity* to their lives. Still, as Leo turned away, clearly distracted, a prickle of unease rippled along her skin. What was he thinking, feeling and, more importantly—more frighteningly—what was he not saying?

The door clicked shut behind him and, alone in the salon, Leo swore aloud. His plan was working all too well. Phoebe trusted him, had responded to him—*mio Dio*, that kiss! He'd barely touched her, yet it hadn't mattered. That simple touch had set off an unstoppable response in both of them. He'd felt it before, all those years ago, and he certainly felt it now. His whole body ached with memory and desire, a longing to deepen that almost-kiss and join his body to hers…

No. Not yet. There was still more work to be done.

Guilt roiled within him, as bitter as bile. He was using Phoebe, using her with cold-hearted calculation. And if she discovered it…

He couldn't think that way. Couldn't afford to. The king's nefarious plans justified his own. This was the way it had to be; the only way it could be.

Numbly, Phoebe followed one of the royal servants to the top floor of the palace, where the nursery suite was located. She was met at the door by a pink-cheeked matron in a staid blue uniform.

'We've been waiting for you,' the nurse said, smiling with easy good humour.

'Where's my son?' Phoebe asked tersely, and Frances stepped aside to let her enter.

'He's right here, never you worry.'

'Mommy!' Christian stood up from his place on a colourful rug on the floor, bits of Lego scattered around him. 'Where have you been?'

Phoebe let out a shaky laugh of relief as she bent to scoop him into her arms. Christian squirmed, but she couldn't resist pressing a kiss to his head. 'I was talking to Leo,' she murmured, kissing him again. 'Are you all right?'

'Of course I am.' Christian wriggled away, returning to his Lego. 'I met the king.'

Phoebe sat back on her heels, her heart beating fast once more. 'Did you?' she asked lightly. 'Was he nice?'

'He was OK,' Christian said with a shrug, then glanced up. 'Why didn't you come with me?' His eyes widened, and Phoebe saw the fear lurking behind his boyish bravado.

'I wanted to,' she said carefully, 'but the king wanted some special time with you.'

Christian considered this as he placed another piece of Lego on the tower he was building. 'Oh,' he said, and just when Phoebe was about to let her breath out in relief of a confrontation avoided, he looked up with his clear, candid gaze. 'Why?'

'Time for elevenses!' Frances swept in with a tray of jam and bread as well as glasses of milk. 'You must be hungry, young man. Come and have a bite to eat.' Dutifully Christian sat at the table for his snack, and Phoebe rose, turning to Frances, who busied herself tidying up the toys.

'Thank you for taking care of him.'

'He's a lovely young man,' Frances replied. 'It was no trouble.'

'You've worked for the royal family for a long time,' Phoebe said slowly.

Frances nodded. 'Thirty-five years, since Leo was born. I took care of him as well as Anders.' Her expression sobered. 'Such a waste, that one. A loss.'

It was, sadly, a succinct and accurate summary of Anders's life. 'Yes,' Phoebe agreed quietly.

'You know, of course,' Frances continued with a nod and Phoebe started at her plain speaking. 'He couldn't keep his hand to anything.'

'No, I don't suppose he could.' Phoebe reached down to place a dog-eared book in the toy basket. 'You must have known them quite well, then? Anders…and Leo?'

Frances glanced up quickly, her expression shrewd before she shrugged and nodded. 'Yes, of course.'

Curiosity bit at Phoebe, made her want to ask questions. To know more, and even to understand. 'What were they like…together? Were they friends?'

Frances gave a short, derisive laugh. 'Friends? Those two? Not even for a moment.'

The abruptness and certainty of her answer made Phoebe ask, 'Why do you say that?'

'Because Anders was frightfully spoiled from the moment he was born. I did the best I could, but his parents doted on him dreadfully. He could do no wrong, and if he did…' she shrugged '…Leo was blamed.'

'Leo…?' Phoebe glanced quickly at Christian, but he was absorbed in a game he was playing quietly with himself at the table, his face smeared with jam. 'What do you mean?'

Frances sighed. 'It's not my place to say, but I can only imagine how difficult your position here must be, and the more information you have…' She stopped and shrugged again. 'Nicholas and Havard were brothers. It starts with them, you see. Nicholas hated Havard…he was jealous of him, of course. Everyone loved Havard. He was the younger brother, but I'm sure everyone wished he were the heir instead of Nicholas. He was handsome, charming, kind to everyone, while Nicholas was sour and spiteful. He couldn't help it, really. He was sickly as a child, pale and thin, while Havard was bursting with health. Or so I've been told…he was a husband and father by the time I met him. But it seemed that Nicholas had reason to be jealous, and that jealousy poisoned him.' Frances put the basket back on the shelf and brushed off her hands. 'Nicholas married first, a Danish woman, Johanna. She retired to Monaco when Anders abdicated, and died two years ago. But back then it seemed as if they might make a good match, until no children came. For ten years.' She shook her head. 'Ten long years. Meanwhile Havard married Ana, an Italian heiress, and had Leo practically nine months later. Nicholas was even more eaten up with jealousy. Everyone could see it, even me. I had been hired by then, to take care of Leo.'

'But Leo had no chance to be king,' Phoebe said. 'As the son of the younger son.'

'Well, that would be the case, if Nicholas didn't have any heirs. And Havard probably began to think his son might be king—he actually might be king—if Nicholas remained childless. There were rumours and whispers, as there always are, and no doubt they enraged Nicholas.'

Phoebe couldn't even imagine the tensions and rivalries that must have poisoned the royal household, the home Leo had grown up in. How had it affected him? *Changed* him? 'What happened then?' she asked in a whisper.

'Anders was born and Havard died,' Frances said simply, 'and everything changed.'

'How…?'

'Nicholas had an heir and Leo had nothing. His mother was sent back to Italy post-haste and Leo was treated like the poor relation. It's no wonder—' Frances stopped, shaking her head. 'But I shouldn't gossip like this, even if you deserve to know.'

Phoebe laid her hand on Frances's arm. 'Please,' she said, 'tell me.' She needed to know this history, needed to understand Leo.

Why…?

She couldn't even say, couldn't untangle the kaleidoscope of feelings tumbling through her. Fear, of course, was prevalent, but there was also compassion, wonder, hope.

Hope…?

That made no sense.

Phoebe turned back to Frances, who pursed her lips then gave a little shrug. 'It's no wonder he went off the rails a bit, that's all,' she finally said.

'The Playboy Prince,' Phoebe murmured, and Frances nodded.

'Exactly.' Christian rose from the table, gleefully holding out his jam-covered hands. 'Come here, love,' Frances said, bustling over to him, clearly glad to have a reason to end the conversation with Phoebe. 'Let's get you washed off.'

Christian went for a wash off with Frances, and Phoebe was left alone in the nursery with its high sashed windows and pale oak floor. She sank onto a sofa, her mind spinning. She felt she understood Leo so much more now…why he'd been such a playboy, so cynical, and why he'd changed. For he *had* changed, she thought. The unneeded spare had become the heir, the prince who would be king, and duty rather than desire—a lust for pleasure—drove him now.

Yet could she really think she knew—understood—Leo? She *wanted* to know him, to trust him, even to like him. She touched her finger to her lips, and knew she wanted more than to like him. Desire, consuming, endless, flooded her.

Yet was it wise—safe—to trust such a man? To desire him? Was Leo truly being kind, or just softening her for the kill? Did he intend to take away her son? Phoebe swallowed back the acid taste of fear. She didn't, Phoebe realised, really know Leo at all.

'Mommy!' Christian came back into the nursery, his face brightening as he turned to the door. 'Leo!'

Phoebe froze. The room, the whole world seemed to stand still as she turned slowly. Leo stood in the doorway, smiling, natural, and entirely at ease, his relaxed stance starting to dispel her fears of moments before even as her heart rate kicked up at the sight of him. She could almost taste the memory of his lips on hers, inhale his scent…

'Hello, Christian,' he said. 'I thought I'd come and see how you are.'

'There are lots of toys here,' Christian told him matter-of-factly, 'but some of them are old.'

'Ah.' Leo's laughing eyes met Phoebe's over Christian. 'Those would be mine.'

Phoebe let out a little bubble of surprised laughter, and Leo smiled back, his eyes so very warm on hers, melting her fears clear away. *If only I could stay in the same room with this man*, she thought suddenly, *and have him smile at me forever*.

Strange, when his smile had used to scare her. Years ago it had been so cold, so cruel and callous and calculating. Yet now she basked in the sunlight and warmth of Leo's smile and wondered how she could have ever doubted that he'd changed. At that moment, it seemed so wonderfully obvious.

'I thought,' Leo said, coming farther into the nursery, 'that you could have dinner in your rooms tonight. Since you're most likely tired.'

'I'm not—' Christian began and Leo's eyes met Phoebe's once more.

'I think,' he said softly, 'it would be best.'

Phoebe nodded slowly. 'Thank you,' she said slowly. The farther away she stayed from King Nicholas, the better.

'And tomorrow,' Leo continued, 'I thought we'd go ice-skating. Every year a rink is created in Njardvik's main square, by the biggest Christmas tree you've ever seen. It is quite a sight.'

Christian cocked his head, clearly sceptical. 'Bigger than the tree at the Rockefeller Center?'

'Hmm.' Leo pursed his lips. 'I'm not sure about that, actually. But the rink is most certainly bigger.'

Christian nodded in acceptance, excitement lighting his eyes, and Phoebe touched Leo's sleeve. 'Leo—' she said quietly, and he turned to her, his gaze warming her once more.

'There will be time for us to talk later, Phoebe,' Leo said softly, so only she could hear. 'When we are rested…and alone. I promise.'

Alone. And what would happen when they were alone? Nerves and something else—something wonderful and intoxicating—fluttered deep in Phoebe's belly. 'And when will that be?' she asked, knowing Leo could hear the longing in her voice. Desire had made her transparent.

'Soon.' His voice was a caress. 'I promise.'

Phoebe nodded, knowing she would have to leave it at that, even though her mind seethed with questions and her body ached with unfulfilled yearning. 'All right,' she murmured, and a few minutes later he excused himself to return to work. Phoebe took Christian back to their suite and, despite many mighty protests, he quite promptly fell asleep.

Phoebe remained awake, restless, anxious, both her body and mind unsated, unfulfilled. And yet, even so, amidst all the turbulent uncertainty coursing through her, she felt hopeful as well. She gazed out at the palace gardens, the bare branches of the trees stark against the darkening sky, the grounds shrouded in winter, and wondered what on earth she had to hope for.

Yet it was there, deep inside her, a tightly furled bud ready to burst open and bloom in the light of day, in the warmth of a man's smile, in the memory of his kiss, in the belief—naïve and misplaced as it might be—that she could trust him, that perhaps he could be a friend…or perhaps—*perhaps*—even something more.

'The king is expecting me,' Leo coolly informed the aide standing guard outside Nicholas's bedchamber. The aide moved aside and Leo let himself into the darkened room.

King Nicholas sat up in bed, an ornately carved four-poster, several pillows piled behind him and the coverlet folded over his knees.

'Well?' he demanded in a rasp. 'Did it work?'

'Did what work?' Leo asked laconically, and Nicholas gave a growl of impatience.

'Whatever this plan of yours is, to get the girl out of the way.'

'Oh, yes,' Leo replied. He propped one shoulder against one of the bedposts as he surveyed Nicholas's frail form. 'It's working.'

'I don't see why we couldn't just buy her off,' Nicholas grumbled. 'Or run a smear campaign—'

'Trashing her in the tabloids would hardly benefit your heir,' Leo pointed out sardonically, 'and I told you, she can't be bought.'

'And as I told you, everyone can be bought, Leo,' the old man said. He paused, his eyes glinting with malice. 'Your own mother's price was fifty thousand.' He paused, clearly savouring Leo's surprise. 'American.'

Leo froze, his gaze sweeping over his uncle in icy assessment. He didn't want to believe what he'd just heard; he wanted to call the king a liar. Desperately. Surely his mother wouldn't have accepted money in the place of her son. Yet, looking at Nicholas's sleek smile of satisfaction, he knew he wasn't lying. His mother had accepted cash to abandon her child to the royal family and their machinations, and clearly Nicholas had been waiting for such a moment as this to tell him so.

He felt a wave of icy shock at the realisation, and underneath a deeper hurt he couldn't bear to probe. He snapped his unfocused gaze back to his uncle and smiled lazily.

'At least she got something out of it, then,' he said in a drawl, and Nicholas let out a raspy laugh.

'So what is your plan with this American?'

Leo smiled coldly. It was a sign of the old man's unbelievable arrogance that he trusted Leo to carry out his bidding even now, when he'd told him he would no longer be his heir. He'd cut him out of the succession as ruthlessly as if he'd wielded scissors, yet Nicholas didn't doubt or question Leo for a moment. He simply wasn't accustomed to disobedience. The only one who'd dared to go against him in a moment of childish folly had been Anders, and look where it had got him...abdicated, exiled, dead. A waste of a life. Leo swallowed back the rush of guilt such thoughts always caused him and turned to address his uncle.

'There's no need for you to know the details,' he said coolly. 'I'm carrying it out and it will deal with...the inconvenience...in due course.'

'Inconvenience.' Nicholas snickered. 'Yes, she is that.' He shifted in his bed, adjusting the pile of pillows behind him. 'Well, as long as you take care of it, and soon.'

'Oh, yes,' Leo assured him, his voice terribly bland. 'I'll have it dealt with by tomorrow night.'

'Good.' Nicholas pulled the coverlet up over his chest, a cough rattling in his bony chest. For a moment Leo felt a flicker of sympathy for the old bastard; even he couldn't defeat Father Time. 'Now I'm tired,' Nicholas said. 'I'll speak to you in the morning.'

'Of course.' Leo sketched a short, mocking bow before leaving his uncle's bedroom.

Back in his own suite of rooms, Leo automatically went to the drinks tray before, with a muttered curse, he turned away. He unlocked the French doors leading to a terrace and stepped outside.

The wrought-iron railing was cold under his bare hands, the night air freezing and sharp, like a knife to the lungs. Stars glittered in a mercilessly black sky, the moon no more than a pale sliver of silver. In the distance the harbour gleamed blackly in the moonlight, and Leo smelled the promise of snow in the frigid, damp air.

He cursed aloud.

He'd never felt so trapped, so backed into a corner, as

he did right then, and the king didn't even realise. No one did. He had to protect Phoebe. He had to protect the crown. And he could see only one solution. A solution that required him to manipulate and use Phoebe with cold precision.

He had to make Phoebe his wife.

It would save her, but it would also condemn her. Condemn her to the politics of the royal family, a life she didn't choose in a foreign country, a loveless marriage to him.

There was passion between them, Leo knew—oh, how he knew; he still felt it in every restless, unsatisfied sinew and limb. He felt it every time he saw her, uncoiling deep within him, radiating out to his fingertips that ached to touch her, brush the creaminess of her skin, the softness of her lips, her hair…

It was that latent sense of need that had given him the idea in the first place, and yet was it enough? Would Phoebe agree? Accept…?

And would she hate him when she knew…discovered what he'd done, what kind of man he was?

Would it even—ever—come to that?

Leo closed his eyes. Phoebe was a good woman, a better woman, perhaps, than even his own mother, who, he now knew, had given in to if not greed, then desperation. Thirty years after the fact he could feel pity—despite the pain—for a woman who had been so bullied by the royal family she'd allowed herself to be bought off.

Yet Phoebe didn't let herself be bullied or bought; despite her fear, she'd stayed strong. She was a good woman, Leo thought with a pang of guilty regret. Far too good for him.

A cold wind blew over him, rustling the tree branches, making him shiver. Suppressing another curse, Leo resolutely turned and went back inside.

CHAPTER SEVEN

PHOEBE awoke to a pearly pink sky and dawn streaking its pale fingers along the floor. Next to her Christian lay sprawled across the bed. He'd had a restless night and sometime between midnight and dawn Phoebe had brought him into bed with her.

Now she lay still, enjoying a moment of peaceful solitude even as the memories and implications of yesterday trickled slowly through her.

They were in Amarnes. Nicholas might very well want custody of her son. Leo had kissed her.

She rolled off the bed, carefully extracting herself from the rumpled covers so as not to wake Christian. The sun was rising now, a pale sliver of yellow above the mountains, turning their snow-capped peaks to the colour of cream. A glance at the clock told her it was already after eight o'clock; in November the sun didn't rise until quite late in this part of the world.

Hurriedly, Phoebe washed and dressed. Today they were going ice-skating with Leo. And despite all her fears and anxieties, the terror that Nicholas would find a way to take Christian from her and, even worse, that Leo might aid him, she found herself looking forward to the outing with absurd excitement.

An hour later they were leaving the palace, just the three of them, bundled against the chilly wind blowing in from the sea.

'What, no entourage?' Phoebe asked as they simply strolled through the palace gates. 'No guards?'

'Amarnes is a small country,' Leo replied with a shrug. 'Very safe. And I think I can take on any comers.' His wry smile as he flexed one arm made Phoebe laugh aloud. She needed this, she realised. She needed to laugh, to let go, to enjoy a day apart, a day just for pleasure…with Leo.

Next to her, Christian was practically dancing in excitement. So much for the Rockefeller Center, Phoebe thought wryly. He obviously thought this was much more fun.

She'd certainly agree with that.

The sun was just emerging behind some ribbony white clouds as they entered the city's main square. Phoebe's last visit to Njardvik had been such a blur that she now found herself looking around in genuine interest. The square was surrounded by tall, narrow townhouses painted in varying pastel shades, elegant and colourful.

In the middle of the square, now strung with fairy lights, an ice rink had been formed, sparkling with sunlight. A Christmas tree decorated in red and gold, at least forty feet high, towered over the rink. Even Christian was impressed by its size, and declared it better than the tree at the Rockefeller Center.

'I'm so relieved,' Leo told him with a little smile.

They fetched skates from a hut erected near the rink, and then sat on a rough wooden bench to put them on. Phoebe saw the way the people—the man who rented them the skates, the red-cheeked woman who sold *pebber nodder*, the little shortbread cookies flavoured with cinnamon—looked at him. Spoke to him. She saw and heard respect, admiration, even affection. Leo, Phoebe realised, had won his people over.

The thought made her glad.

'Have you skated much?' Leo asked with an arched brow, and Phoebe smiled, suddenly mischievous.

'A bit.' She tightened the laces on her skates. 'What about you?'

'A bit as well,' Leo replied.

'I fall a lot,' Christian confided. He stretched out his legs for Leo to lace up his skates. Phoebe watched the simple sight of Leo doing up her son's skates and felt her heart both constrict and expand all at once. There was something so *right* about this, and it scared her. It was all too easy to imagine them as a family, to imagine this was more than just a day's outing. To imagine—and want—this to be real.

'There.' Leo stood up, reaching a hand down to Christian, which the little boy took with easy trust. He held out his other hand to Phoebe, and after the briefest of hesitations she took it. They both wore gloves, yet even so it felt all too good— too right and too wonderful—for his hand to clasp hers.

They walked awkwardly on their skates to the rink and Christian's bravado faltered at the sight of the sheer ice. Skating backwards with long, gliding movements, Leo took the boy's hands and helped him move along. Phoebe watched from the side as they skated around the rink. Leo had skated more than a bit, she thought wryly. He skated backwards with effortless ease, helping Christian along, encouraging him with ready smiles and praise. Christian beamed back, delighted when he was finally able to let go of Leo's hands and skate for a few wobbly feet by himself.

Leo skated towards Phoebe, who remained leaning against the rink wall.

'You're good,' she said and he gave a modest shrug.

'Growing up in Amarnes…all children learn to skate.' He gave her a little smile. 'Are you going to get out on the ice?' His eyes glinted with humour. 'You're not afraid, are you?'

'Me? Afraid?'

'You said you'd only skated a bit…'

'So I did,' Phoebe agreed, and then pushed off the wall. She wasn't able to see the expression on Leo's face as she glided to the centre of the rink, did a graceful figure-of-eight before spinning in a dizzying circle, one leg stretched out in a perfect right angle.

'Way to go, Mom!' Christian crowed, then turned to Leo. 'She used to skate a lot.'

'So it would appear,' Leo murmured, and Phoebe, skating back, couldn't help but grin.

'I took figure-skating lessons for five years. I had dreams of being the next big star, actually.'

'And what happened?'

Phoebe smiled wryly. 'I wasn't *that* good.'

'Better than me,' Leo told her. 'And you don't need to look so smug,' he added as she leaned against the wall once more. 'I was looking forward to giving you lessons.'

'Perhaps it should be the other way round,' Phoebe replied, and he laughed aloud.

'Or perhaps,' he murmured for only her ears, 'we should have lessons in some other…field of interest.'

Suddenly Phoebe was breathless, the camaraderie of the moment replaced by something deeper, needier and more elemental.

She wanted him. She wanted to touch him, kiss him, to feel every bit of his skin, his hair, his mouth and eyes—his body. She wanted his body inside her, wanted to feel him move against her—

She turned away, afraid her thoughts—her need—would be reflected in her eyes. Leo was so adept at reading her emotions, and she wasn't ready for him to know this.

Although perhaps he already did. Perhaps he'd always known it, from the moment he'd first touched her all those years ago, and she'd felt as if he'd reached right inside to her soul. Perhaps he had…perhaps her ill-fated marriage had never had a chance from that moment.

Perhaps, Phoebe thought hazily, it had always been Leo.

'Aren't we going to skate some more?' Christian demanded, and Leo reached for his hands.

'Yes, we are,' he said as he started skating backwards again, Christian following him. 'And then we're going to get some hot chocolate.'

They skated for another half-hour before the cold defeated them, and they returned their skates.

'There's a café near here,' Leo said, 'with the most delicious hot chocolate.' He smiled at Christian. 'With whipped cream.'

The air was sharp with brine and damp with cold as they left the rink, even though the sun was shining.

They walked in easy silence down the narrow streets to the promised café, a small, wood-panelled room in the front of a townhouse, its scarred oak tables and chairs relics from another century.

The owner hurried towards them, all welcoming smiles and excited chatter, which Leo, looking almost discomfited, waved away. Within seconds they were seated at a more private table in the back, scarves and mittens shed, and coats hung over their chairs.

One of the waiters brought Christian a colouring book and some crayons, and he was soon hard at work. Phoebe took the opportunity to study Leo, her heart—and something else—lurching at the sight of him. A few stray snow-flakes glittered in his hair, and his cheeks were bright with cold. She could see the glint of stubble on his jaw, and it made her ache to reach out and touch the bristles, compare the feel of it to the softness of his lips…

On the table she curled her hand into a fist, deter-mined—for the moment—to resist the impulse. Leo glanced at her, amusement quirking his mouth.

'You look as if you're deep in thought,' he said. 'Or per-haps working out a difficult maths problem. What are you thinking about?'

Phoebe had no intention of telling him the nature of her thoughts. She smiled and began to shrug, surprising them both when she suddenly said, 'You *have* changed.'

Leo stilled, his long, brown fingers flat on the table. He didn't quite look at her as he asked lightly, 'Have I?'

'Yes,' Phoebe said more forcefully. 'You're not… you're not…'

'A reckless, womanising playboy any more?' he asked, his voice still light, but she heard—felt—the darkness underneath. The same emotion she'd felt from him all those years ago, a kind of pain or sorrow.

'No,' she said quietly. 'But it's more than that.'

Leo opened his menu and scanned the pages. 'How in-triguing,' he murmured, but Phoebe could tell he wanted to deflect the conversation from himself, and she won-dered why.

A waiter returned with mugs of creamy cocoa, and Phoebe dipped her spoon in the frothy confection. 'So did you put your partying days behind you when you realised you'd become king?'

Something flashed in Leo's eyes—something bleak and angry—and then he shrugged. 'Something like that. I told you before, didn't I, some things can be sordid and boring?'

She felt a flicker of disappointment. 'So the party scene just got old?'

'It always does.'

Christian looked up from his mug of hot chocolate, his entire face flecked with whipped cream. 'What does sordid mean?'

And that, Phoebe thought, was a signal to change the conversation if there ever was one. Yet she was curious, far too curious, about Leo. About his childhood, about his change of heart, about the man he was now. A man, she realised with both alarm and excitement, that she could more than like. A man she could love.

They finished their hot chocolate in comfortable silence, before Leo said they should return to the palace. 'You, young man, look tired.'

'I am not!' Christian protested with five-year-old indignation.

'Well,' Leo relented, 'perhaps your mother is. Maybe I could show you the palace games room while she has a nap? I play a mean game of air hockey.' He glanced at Phoebe in silent query, and she gave a little nod. A nap sounded heavenly.

Outside the café they came across one of Njardvik's little Christmas markets, a narrow street lined on both sides with stalls, each one strung with lights and offering various handicrafts, baked goods and Christmas ornaments.

'Are these all Santa Clauses?' Phoebe asked as she examined a row of carved wooden figures, each with a long white beard and red cap.

'Santas, no. They're *nissen*,' Leo replied. 'Sort of like Santa—but a *nisse* is a bit of a trickier fellow.'

'Trickier?'

'Yes, he was originally a protector of family farms. But he might steal the cows' hay to give to the horses—that sort of thing. Now he's become a bit more like Santa. On Christmas Eve someone dresses up as a *nisse* and brings presents, asking if there are any good children.'

'Did someone do that for you as a child? In the palace?' Phoebe asked suddenly. She pictured Anders and Leo at Christmas, waiting for the *nisse*. Knowing what she did, she could imagine Anders vying for all the attention while Leo stood in the shadows, watching.

'Oh, yes.' Leo's expression was strangely shuttered. 'Always.'

'And what did you answer?' Phoebe asked, keeping her voice light. 'Were you a good child?' She meant to sound light, teasing, but instead the question sounded serious. Leo's mouth stretched in a smile and he put the *nisse* back on the shelf. 'Oh, yes,' he said, 'of course I was.'

Yet Phoebe could only imagine what he wasn't saying, what memories he was keeping to himself. Ignored, neglected, a virtual orphan. He might have been a good child, she thought, but she doubted he had been a happy one. She glanced back at the *nisse*; the look on the little statue's face suddenly seemed closer to a sneer.

They left the Christmas market and began to walk back to the palace, Leo leading them down the city's narrow cobbled streets, his hand easily linked with Christian's. Phoebe trailed a few steps behind, watching them, thinking how much like a family—a father and son—they looked.

What if Leo had been Christian's father, instead of Anders? What if all those years ago, she had met him first? What if they'd fallen in love?

Useless questions, Phoebe knew, and ones she couldn't

possibly answer. The past was the past; it had been written, finished. The present was intriguing enough.

And as for the future…

What could there possibly be between her and Leo, the heir to the country's throne? She'd been considered an unsuitable candidate for queen six years ago, and she doubted anything had changed on that score.

Besides, wasn't she getting a little ahead of herself? All Leo had done was kiss her, and such a little brush of a kiss it barely counted.

Except it hadn't *felt* little.

And yet in two weeks she would be returning home with Christian—at least, that was what she wanted, what she'd hoped for. Her fears about the king's plans and intentions still gnawed nervously at her insides. Even so, amidst the fear and the uncertainty, she now felt a longing for these two weeks to never end.

It was working, Leo thought grimly, his hand still loosely clasped with Christian's. With half an ear he listened to the boy chatter on about some kind of toy—a robot or a dinosaur?—as his own mind spun in circles. He'd had a plan, he'd carried it out, and it was clearly a success.

Phoebe was falling in love with him.

So why did that make him feel so miserable?

Because I don't deserve it…I don't deserve any of it, I never did or will…

He pushed the thoughts away, the tormented voices of his conscience, his memory. He couldn't afford to have either. He needed to focus, to keep working towards his goal. And even if Phoebe hated him, even if she discovered the truth, he knew he was doing only what he had to.

For Phoebe's sake.

* * *

Phoebe gazed at herself in the mirror, amazed at the transformation. That afternoon several gowns had been sent to her room with instructions she choose one to wear that evening. A single card had been inserted among the folds of tissue paper, with a single sentence upon it, written in a bold scrawl: *Have dinner with me.*

Her heart hammered in anticipation and her nerves jangled as she undid the dresses from their folds of paper and hung them on the door, gazing at each one in turn. What to wear to dinner tonight? Dinner alone with Leo. Now finally he would explain what he knew of the king's plans, yet Phoebe found she could barely think of that.

All she could think of, her body's insistent needs drowning out her mind's, was being alone with Leo. What would happen? What would he do? What would *she* do?

'Which one should I wear?' she asked Christian, who was sprawled on the bed, watching a children's show in Danish with an expression of endearing perplexity.

He glanced up at her, frowning at the sight of the clothes. 'Are those dresses?' he asked and Phoebe laughed, reaching over to ruffle his hair. Christian promptly ducked out of the way and returned to watching the television.

'Yes, silly. And can you actually understand that show at all?'

'I saw it back at home,' Christian replied with a shrug and Phoebe rolled her eyes.

'Come on, sport. Help me out here.'

With a long-suffering sigh, Christian turned away from the TV once more. He glanced at the three gowns, his brow furrowed. 'The silver one.'

'You think?' Phoebe reached out to stroke the slippery, silky material. It was a bit pathetic, getting fashion advice from a five-year-old, but she needed to talk to someone.

To let out some of this energy, this excitement bubbling away inside of her.

'Yeah.' Christian had clearly had enough of fashion talk, for he turned back to the show, which featured a talking lion that happened to be friends with a zebra. 'It's the same colour as my robot.'

'And that's as good a reason as any,' Phoebe murmured, slipping the dress off its hanger. She went into the bathroom to change, and the dress's material flowed over her like liquid silver. It was deceptive in its simplicity, two skinny straps and a bodice decorated with tiny jet beads that ended in a swirl of shimmery silk around her ankles.

'It matches your eyes,' Christian said when she came out to show him. She laughed, twirling around, feeling beautiful.

'How kind of you to notice.'

'Did you bring your hair stuff?'

Christian knew how she disliked her curly hair that always tended to frizz. When she had time, she used a special hair serum and blow-dried it straight. 'No, I didn't,' she said with some reluctance. 'Leo will just have to take me as I am.'

'You're eating with Leo?' Christian asked, astute as ever, and Phoebe flushed.

'Yes, we're having dinner together while you get to be with Frances.'

Christian narrowed his eyes. 'Are you going to marry him?'

'Christian!' Phoebe stared at her son in shock. 'What makes you think such a thing?'

He shrugged. 'He's nice and I don't have a dad,' he said simply. Phoebe's heart ached.

'I didn't realise you wanted one,' she said quietly, and

Christian gave her a look that clearly said such a thought was incredibly stupid. And wasn't it? Phoebe asked herself. No matter how many friends she surrounded Christian with, no matter how much love she showered him with, didn't he still want a father?

Didn't he still need one?

And could Leo be it—him?

Whoa, Phoebe told herself. You're getting way, way ahead of the game. Leo had merely asked her to dinner. He'd only kissed her once. And yet…and yet…

She wanted so much more. She was ready for so much more. For the last five years she'd put her own romantic life on hold, for Christian's sake. Building her business and caring for her son had been enough.

Now it wasn't.

Now she wanted more. She wanted Leo.

At seven o'clock Phoebe took Christian up to the nursery and was met at the door by a smiling Frances.

'My, don't we look nice tonight!' she exclaimed, taking Christian by the hand. She winked at Phoebe. 'You're not going on a date, are you?'

'Just dinner,' Phoebe murmured, blushing. What was with everybody? she wondered. Were her hopes so transparent?

'Well, enjoy yourself,' Frances replied comfortably. 'I'm sure we will.'

Leaving Christian in the nurse's capable hands, Phoebe made her way downstairs. A servant directed her not to the main dining room, but to a private salon in the back of the palace.

The servant opened the door, disappearing quickly and quietly before Phoebe had even properly entered. And then she stopped, for the room, with its fireplace and dancing shadows, the rich wood panelling and the heavy velvet curtains the colour of wine, was sumptuous and beautiful and reminded her of the room at the consulate.

For just as before there was Leo standing by the fireplace, dressed in an immaculate suit, his hair brushed back from his forehead and curling on his collar. He looked amazing, seductive and beautiful and she wanted him more than anything she'd ever wanted in her life.

For, while the room seemed so similar to that room at the consulate, the mood was different. She was different…and so was Leo. Gone was the fear, the outrage, the anger. She came into the room smiling.

'Did I really need to wear a formal gown?'

'I was hoping you'd choose the grey one.'

His words caused a prickly heat of awareness to creep along her arms and flush her face and bare shoulders. 'You selected those gowns?'

Leo arched one eyebrow. 'Are you questioning my taste?'

Laughing a little, Phoebe shook her head. 'No. They were all beautiful.'

Leo started forward, towards her. 'But the grey one matches your eyes.'

'That's what Christian said.'

'Smart boy.' He stopped in front of her, close enough for her to touch him if she reached her hand out and yet still too far away.

Phoebe's heart bumped in her chest; she felt as if Leo could see it through the tissue-thin fabric of her dress. She stared at him, unspeaking, helpless, because she had so many things to say and she didn't know how to begin. 'I'm hungry.'

Leo's lips curved in a smile and Phoebe flushed. She

hadn't meant to say that, but the words had come out anyway. 'So am I,' he said, and Phoebe knew he wasn't just talking about food.

He reached out one hand to touch hers, lacing their fingers together, and drew her deeper into the room. His touch created an instant and overwhelming response, so her legs felt like butter, soft and melting as she practically swayed towards him.

'Leo...'

'Let me pour you a glass of wine.'

But she didn't need wine; she felt drunk already, dizzy and light and free. 'All right,' she whispered. She watched as he poured from the bottle already opened on the sideboard and then handed her a crystal glass, raising his own in a toast. 'To tonight,' he said, and the words were surely a promise of what was to come.

Phoebe drank, letting the rich liquid slide down her throat and fire her belly. She felt floaty and weightless, suspended in the moment, unable to think or care about anything else. She knew, absolutely knew, she shouldn't feel this way. Wasn't this evening meant to be about the future? About the king and his plans? About what Leo knew? Yet all the questions she'd meant to ask, all the answers she'd meant to demand, seemed to float away to nothing, meaningless in the face of the consuming desire she felt for this man.

'Shall we eat?' Leo asked, and Phoebe nodded, for, though she'd claimed to be hungry, surely the meal was simply something to be got through, to be endured before the rest of the evening began.

She moved to the table, her gown swishing sensuously against her bare legs, and sat down.

'Please. Allow me.' Leo set down his wine glass and

took the heavy linen napkin from the table, unfolding it with a flourish and then spreading it on her lap, his fingers brushing and even lingering on her thighs. Phoebe closed her eyes, savouring the caress.

Leo moved to the other side of the table and sat down, and Phoebe forced herself to open her eyes, to act normal. To feel normal. His knee nudged hers under the table, a subtle, steady pressure that had fiery sensation flooding through her once more.

This had to stop. It had to *begin*.

'Something smells delicious,' Phoebe said.

'Indeed.' Leo lifted the lids on several silver chafing-dishes; a tantalising aroma of rosemary and lemon wafted from a dish of roasted chicken. Leo placed some on her plate, along with fresh asparagus and new potatoes. He handed her a basket of bread; the rolls were soft and flaky.

Yet Phoebe couldn't taste it, or at least the taste was overwhelmed by her other senses. The feel of Leo's knee against hers, the sight of him, the *scent* of him.

She couldn't take any more, she thought almost frantically. She was burning up, her body aching and restless—

'Phoebe,' Leo said quietly, putting down his fork, 'the king wishes to make Christian his heir.'

The words didn't make sense. They penetrated Phoebe's haze of desire like buzzing flies, circling in her fevered brain. *The king wants to make Christian his heir...his heir...his heir...*

'But...that's impossible.' The words felt thick and clumsy on her tongue, and she blinked, struggling to find clarity amidst her body's clamouring needs. 'Anders abdicated. Christian has no right—'

'The king has decided otherwise.' Leo gazed at her

directly, watched her carefully. Did he think she was going to throw a fit? To scream and shriek and cry?

For now the lovely fog of desire was burning off under the cruel light of dawning realisation. If Christian was the king's heir, then he would be king one day. Of Amarnes. He would live his life here, his life would be forfeit to the crown, and Phoebe—what role would she have?

The answer was obvious. None. She rose from the table on legs made shaky now by fear. '*This* has been his plan?' she asked sickly, though she knew, of course, it was. 'All along?'

'Yes…although I did not know it.'

She shot Leo a dark glance. 'No, you wouldn't, would you? If Christian is named heir, then you won't be—'

'King. No.' Leo spoke with no intonation, no inflection, no emotion at all. Phoebe turned around to stare at him helplessly. What was he thinking right now? Feeling? She had no idea, no clue, and it scared her. The heady hope of the last twenty-four hours, brimming as they had been with possibility, suddenly seemed ludicrous. False. Who *was* this man?

'Are you disappointed?' she asked and Leo shrugged one shoulder.

'I could hardly say I did not feel some disappointment at the news. But if the king wishes it, there is little I can say or do about the matter.'

'And what can I do?' Phoebe demanded. 'I don't want Christian to be king!' She thought of her mother's lawyer friend. How did you contest a line of succession? Was it even possible?

'I wouldn't go down that route, Phoebe,' Leo said quietly, and she heard a raw note of compassion in his voice. 'It won't get you anywhere.'

'But how can he…? This isn't a dictatorship—don't you have a parliament or something—?'

'Yes, and I'm afraid they'll do what Nicholas says. He is—and has been—a strong ruler.'

Just like that, Phoebe thought, too shocked and sick at heart even to feel angry. Just like that, Nicholas could change everything, everyone's lives.

'So what am I supposed to do?' She finally asked brokenly. 'Just…roll over? Accept this?' Her voice rose and her hands fisted at her sides. 'Leo, he can't become king! Frances told me how awful the royal family—your family—is!' she continued wildly, driven by desperation. 'All the jealousies and rivalries—your own mother was sent away!'

Leo stilled, his face now utterly blank. 'Yes, she was.'

'And is that what's going to happen to me?' Phoebe demanded. 'Is the king going to send me away, or will he just try to buy me off again?'

'No,' Leo replied calmly. 'He wanted to buy you off in New York, but I never made the offer.'

'What…?' The single word came out in a hiss.

'A million euros,' Leo clarified dispassionately. 'But I knew as soon as I saw you, Phoebe, that you would never take such an offer, and I would never make one.' He paused, turning his head so his face was averted from her, cast in shadow. 'You were right, my mother was sent away when I was six. When Anders was born. My father died the same year, and Nicholas couldn't wait to get rid of me. Or at least put me in my proper place.' He laughed shortly. 'Of course, he couldn't do so without first getting rid of my mother. She wasn't needed any more, and Nicholas wanted a clear playing field.' Leo let out a long, ragged breath. 'He bought her off.'

Phoebe's eyes widened in shock; she still couldn't see Leo's face, but she could feel the pain emanating from him in sorrowful waves. 'Leo, I'm sorry.'

'I saw her only a handful of times after that, and she died when I was sixteen. She had a weak chest.' He turned his head, met her gaze. 'So I could hardly let the same happen to you,' he continued, and Phoebe saw the bleak honesty in his eyes. 'Even though I was tempted.'

'Tempted...?'

'You were an inconvenience, remember?' Leo gave her the ghost of a smile. 'At least, I thought of you as one until I saw you again.'

Her heart bumped painfully against her ribs. She wanted to ask Leo what he meant, wanted to hope, *needed* to, but the future—Christian's future—was too over-whelming. 'So what can we do?' she whispered. 'We can't— I can't—' She stopped, took a breath, and started again in a stronger voice. 'I won't be bought, and I won't leave Christian.'

'I know.' Leo smiled, his mouth curling upwards in a way that made Phoebe's insides tingle with awareness, with anticipation. 'I have another solution.' He paused, and in that second's silénce Phoebe felt as if the room—the whole world—became hushed in expectation, as if every-thing had led to this moment, this question, this possibility. As if she already *knew*. Leo took a step towards her, his hand outstretched. 'Phoebe,' he said, 'you can become my wife.'

CHAPTER EIGHT

PHOEBE stared at him in wordless disbelief. She'd been expecting…something—and yet this? Marriage? 'Your *what*?'

'My wife.' Leo's smile widened. 'It's really very simple.'

'Is it?' she asked incredulously, and Leo took another step towards her.

'Of course. If you marry me, you can stay in Amarnes. More importantly, you can stay in Christian's life. You'll have a place, guaranteed.'

'As Queen of Amarnes.'

'I'm afraid not,' Leo corrected softly. 'It'll be back to the Duchy of Larsvik, I'm afraid.'

'Oh, well.' Phoebe tried to laugh; the sound that emerged was something between a hiccup and a ragged sob. 'I suppose I'd have to settle for being a duchess.'

'Sorry to disappoint,' Leo said, his mouth quirking, but she saw the darkness in his eyes. This was no joking matter.

'Leo…'

'Is there any reason why you should refuse?'

She shook her head. There were too many reasons to

name, and yet there was also a terrible desire to simply say *yes*. How could she do something so impractical, so *insane*? 'What is this?' she finally managed. 'Some kind of pity proposal?'

'Do I seem the kind of man to marry someone out of pity?' Leo asked, arching one eyebrow.

'You don't seem the kind of man to marry at all.'

Leo gave a small nod of acknowledgement. 'Perhaps, but I have always accepted that I will have to settle down one day. It is expected.'

'Is that supposed to make me feel better?'

'It is simply the truth. Besides, our marriage will help stabilise the monarchy. A child king…'

'Nicholas isn't dead yet,' Phoebe reminded him, and Leo gave a little shrug.

'And Christian is only five. I would not want to see him at the mercy of a regent who did not have his best interests in mind.'

'And you would?' Phoebe asked. Leo regarded her levelly.

'Of course.'

It was too much to take in. Ruler, regent, kings and queens and even a duchy—she felt as if she'd stumbled into a fairy tale.

Was this the happy ending?

'So.' Leo waited, hands spread wide, for Phoebe's answer.

She didn't want to state the obvious, but she knew she had to. 'We don't love each other.'

Leo hesitated, and when he spoke his voice was careful. 'No, but we've certainly enjoyed each other's company these last few days. Who knows what could happen in time?'

Was he actually saying he might come to love her? Phoebe wondered, her heart swelling with awful hope. This was such an insane idea. She couldn't marry Leo. A few days ago she hadn't even liked him. She'd hated him, despised and mistrusted him, the sardonic, cynical Playboy Prince—

Except that wasn't who he was any more. The last few days he'd seemed like someone else entirely. She spun away, staring out at the unrelieved darkness of the palace gardens, the snow-covered lawns glittering in the moonlight. 'And how would your uncle take this news?'

Another hesitation. 'He'd have no choice but to accept it.'

'Really? He doesn't seem the kind of man to just…accept things.'

'No, indeed not,' Leo agreed, 'but there is little he can do with the hard fact of a marriage certificate.'

'He could make our lives miserable,' Phoebe pointed out.

'I would not allow it.' Leo took a step forward. 'And I would not allow him to bully or control Christian either—'

'No—' The thought of Christian being manipulated by these people made her ill. Phoebe pressed a fist to her lips. Christian was the country's *heir*. It couldn't be, couldn't be so, it was impossible, unbelievable… Something was skimming on the edge of her conscience, a realisation that she couldn't quite grasp or understand—too much had happened, too much to absorb, to accept, and yet—

And yet…

Leo was walking towards her, his stride long and sure, a look of decision in the hard planes of his face even as his eyes fastened on hers, sleepy and sensual. Phoebe took a step back, suddenly afraid. Afraid how easily she would give in if Leo touched her. She wouldn't resist at all and, while moments ago the thought had been welcome, now— now everything had changed.

'As my wife and Duchess of Larsvik you would have position, security,' Leo told her. He stood in front of her, his hands sliding along her bare shoulders, his thumbs brushing the sides of her breasts. Phoebe shuddered. She wasn't even moving or batting his hands away. 'If you don't marry me,' Leo continued, his tone so reasonable even as his hands continued to slide up and down her shoulders, skimming the curve of her breasts, making her want more, and even more still, 'where will you live? What will you do? No matter how much you try to stay in Christian's life—if you're allowed at all—you'll feel like a hanger-on. Nicholas will take every opportunity to weaken your position, your relationship with your son.'

'This can't be happening…' Yet the words came out in a moan, and she arched her body, desperate to give Leo more access. Yet he didn't deepen his caress, merely continued as he had before, his fingers skimming her body, his words no more than a breath of sound.

'But it is.'

'Your mother was married and it didn't protect her,' Phoebe gasped, and Leo's hands stilled for a moment before he resumed his caresses.

'She was a widow, young, alone, easily bullied. Your situation—our situation—is very different.'

'Is it?' She couldn't think, felt as if she could barely string two words together. Leo moved his hands to her front, his palms cupping her breasts through the thin fabric of her dress. His eyes met hers, glinting with challenge, with knowledge.

'You know it is.'

Phoebe closed her eyes, her mind spinning, her body swaying. 'I don't,' she managed, 'feel like I know anything…'

Leo reached up to lay one finger against her lips. His finger was cool and tasted slightly of salt. Phoebe realised her mouth had parted instinctively; she was practically *licking* him. 'Just say yes.'

'I…' Even in her haze of desire she hesitated, afraid, uncertain…and desperate for Leo to kiss her.

Yet Leo didn't kiss her; he simply smiled and traced the delicate line of her jaw with his thumb, the touch featherlight and yet incendiary. 'Can't you see how good it would be between us?' he murmured.

And from somewhere Phoebe found the strength to say, her voice still no more than a husky whisper, 'Sex. Just sex.'

'*Just* sex?' Leo repeated, and there was laughter in his voice, deep and rich as chocolate, and certainly just as sinful. 'You haven't had very good sex if you can say that.'

No, she hadn't. For she'd never felt like this before, as if her whole body was burning, focused on a single point, one desperate need.

Kiss me.

'You know what I mean,' Phoebe whispered. She still hadn't moved; she still stood in the circle of Leo's arms, his fingers still tracing her jaw, dropping to her collarbone, and she remembered how he'd let his finger drop lower, deeper, and she'd wanted him to…

She wanted him to now. A tiny moan escaped from her, breathless and revealing, and with a low chuckle Leo bent his head and claimed her mouth with his.

His lips were both hard and soft, Phoebe thought, cool

and warm at the same time. An exciting blend of contradictions, just like the man himself…and then she lost all track of rational thought as she was swept up into sensation, sensual pleasure, the feel of Leo's mouth moving on hers as sweet and tempting and wonderful as anything she'd ever felt or done. Even more so.

And still she wanted more. Her hands crept up to tug on the lapels of his suit, the finely cut wool sliding and catching under her grasping fingers, and with an impatient jerk she pushed the expensive fabric aside and slid her hands along his muscled shoulders, the thin cotton of his shirt the only barrier between the skin-on-skin contact she craved.

And Leo must have craved it too, for with an almost animalistic growl he lowered his head to her bare shoulder, his lips tracking kisses along her throat, and then following where his finger had gone, to the deep V between her breasts, pushing the silk of her dress aside to give himself more access to her flesh.

It was access that Phoebe eagerly, impatiently granted, and in a distant part of her pleasure-dazed mind she heard the clatter of porcelain and silver as Leo swept aside the dishes and, cradling her hips in his hands, sat her on the table.

There was something naughty and decadent about sitting on the table, her dress rucked up to her thighs, her legs wrapped around Leo's waist—when had that happened?—as if she were yet another delicious offering.

And she was an offering, Phoebe thought hazily, an offering to Leo, her body pliant beneath him, open and ready.

Her hands fisted in his hair as he moved above her, and she longed for their bodies to be joined, to feel him inside her. She *ached* with it.

And then it happened, and she gasped with surprise and

pleasure as he moved inside her, his body finally joined with hers, sliding in and fitting so perfectly, so rightly, Phoebe felt as if she'd been missing a crucial piece of herself and was finally whole.

Leo's eyes met hers as he moved; he held her gaze and neither of them looked away, needing no words. This was more than words, more necessary, more elemental.

For she'd never felt this way, this endless aching, desperate craving finally satisfied so utterly, and in the aftermath of their spent desire there emerged a new hope, a tremulous joy. This wasn't *just sex* at all. It was what she wanted, needed, and craved; it was, indeed, the purest form of communication between a man and a woman.

Leo stared at Phoebe's face, her flushed cheeks and swollen lips, framed by a wild mane of tangled curls. She looked dishevelled, beautiful and so very much his. He'd made her his.

He felt a deep, primal sense of possession as he looked at her, lying still dazed amidst the detritus of their meal. He hadn't meant it to happen like this; a bed, candles, every romantic thing he could think of waited upstairs, but he hadn't been able to get that far. From the moment he'd touched her, his mind, his sense of reason had been lost to his body's needs. And not just his body, Leo thought, for despite the urgency of their coupling he'd felt some deeper need satisfied when he'd made love to Phoebe, a final piece of himself—the most necessary piece—sliding into place.

He stood up, turning away, disturbed by the nature of his thoughts.

Slowly Phoebe slid off the table, pulling down her gown with shaky movements. Leo knew he should say something, do something besides adjust his clothes and run his hands through his hair, his movements just as shaky as Phoebe's. This was when he was meant to hold her in his arms, gain her acceptance and savour the fact that his plan had worked.

Yet he couldn't do anything.

'Leo…' Phoebe said, her voice husky.

He turned slowly to face her. 'Yes?'

She stared at him with dazed eyes, pushing her hair away from her face. 'Christian…Christian can only be named heir because he's Anders's child.'

'Of course.'

'His legitimate offspring,' Phoebe clarified, and Leo felt a well of foreboding open up inside him.

'Of course. There is no question of that. I saw your marriage certificate myself.'

'I know, but…' Phoebe licked her lips, her expression turning guarded, even fearful. Leo tensed, waiting.

'What is it, Phoebe?'

She stared at him, clearly torn between confession and self-protection. What, Leo wondered grimly, was she hiding?

'Christian…' she began, then stopped. She let out a breath and started again. 'Christian is not my son.'

CHAPTER NINE

PHOEBE couldn't read Leo's expression. She wasn't sure she wanted to. He stood there, staring at her with such ominous blankness even as her body quivered with the aftershocks of their lovemaking, the memory of his touch.

Even now she wasn't sure she should have said anything, confessed the secret she'd held so closely to her heart ever since those two government agents had shown up at her door. Yet this was the realisation that had been skimming the surface of her consciousness as Leo had begun his seductive onslaught—that, since Christian was illegitimate, he couldn't be heir.

The realisation had only fully dawned as she'd lain there, sated and dazed, after they'd made love.

Should she have told Leo? Phoebe wondered, panic starting its inevitable flutter inside her. Would he use the information against her? Yet surely not—surely not, when he'd just made love to her, asked her to marry him…

And yet, Phoebe realised dully, now there would be no reason for him to marry her. He could rescind his offer and she had absolutely no right—no reason—to feel so disappointed by the thought.

'Phoebe,' Leo finally asked, his voice so soft and yet so dangerous, 'what are you saying?'

She swallowed, knowing she would have to tell the full truth. 'He's not my son,' she repeated. 'I legally adopted him when he was three weeks old.'

Leo shook his head slowly, clearly incredulous. 'Is he *Anders's* son?'

'Yes,' Phoebe said quickly. 'Of course he is. Just look at him. You can have a paternity test done if you wish.'

Leo let out a harsh bark of laughter. 'But there's no need, if he's not legitimate.' He shook his head again. 'You'd better tell me all of it.'

'There's not much more to tell,' Phoebe said. 'Anders had an affair with a waitress in Paris before we even met. He didn't find out about the pregnancy—about Christian—until after we'd married. The girl came to him—to us—wanting to give him away.' Phoebe saw Leo's features twist with contempt. 'It wasn't like that,' she said quickly. 'If you can feel some pity for your mother, who was shamed and bullied into leaving you, then save some for this girl. She was young, only nineteen or so, and a stranger to Paris. She couldn't return home with a baby, her family would have disowned her. And she didn't have the resources to support him herself—'

'Why not ask Anders for money? Child support?'

'Perhaps she didn't know of such things. Or perhaps she knew Anders well enough not to trust him to give reliable financial support.' She sighed, remembering the fear etched in the gaunt lines of the girl's face. 'In any case, she wanted to give Christian to us, and return to her family. I was happy to take him.'

'Were you? A few weeks into your marriage?' Leo gave an incredulous laugh. 'Not much of a honeymoon.'

'No, indeed not. And I suppose that's when things

started to go sour for Anders. Married, with a child…well, it wasn't what he'd thought he was getting into.'

'So he left.'

'Yes.'

'And you kept his bastard.'

Phoebe flinched. 'You don't have to be crude,' she said. 'I'd only had Christian for a few weeks by that point, but I loved him.' She paused. 'You might as well know I was adopted myself. My biological mother was similar to Christian's—a teenaged girl without resources or support. My adoptive mother volunteered in a crisis pregnancy centre, and she encouraged my biological mother—Vanessa—to keep the pregnancy. Vanessa agreed, and my mother adopted me.' Phoebe straightened, meeting Leo's gaze. 'She was a single woman and she raised me successfully. I had a very happy, a very full childhood. So I thought I could provide the same for Christian…and I have.' Yet Christian's words from earlier that afternoon echoed through her. '*He's nice and I don't have a dad.*' She might have saved Christian from becoming king, but she'd also kept him from gaining a father.

Would Leo have made a good father, a good husband? Phoebe's heart ached. Now she would never know.

Leo raked a hand through his hair before dropping it wearily. 'Well,' he said, 'this is all very admirable.' There was a cynical edge to his voice that Phoebe hadn't heard in a while, and she didn't like it.

'I didn't tell you before because I was afraid,' she confessed quietly. 'That the king would use it as a way of taking Christian from me. But if he really is only interested in Christian as his heir…'

'Yes,' Leo agreed shortly. 'Well. I wish you'd told me this before.'

'Before,' Phoebe repeated slowly, and flushed in comprehension, and then shame. Before they'd made love. 'Why…?' She stopped, for an awful, awful realisation was starting to dawn, to creep over the horizon of her consciousness and flood her mind with damning light. 'You just made love—had sex with me to convince me to marry you,' she said. 'That's all it was.' More realisations came one on top of the other, swift and condemning. 'That's all any of it was.' She swept an arm to encompass the strewn remnants of their meal. 'This—this dinner was no more than a deliberate seduction.'

Leo's face was blank, terribly, terribly blank. He said nothing. 'And the ice-skating—the way you've been so *kind*—' She choked on the words, the thought, and spun away. Everything had been contrived, deliberately planned. None of it was real. She stared out of the window at the palace gardens, cloaked in darkness. Moonlight glinted off a bronze statue of an angel, her arms arced above her head, her face as pitilessly blank as Leo's. 'Why?' Phoebe whispered. 'Why did you do all this?'

Leo hesitated, and Phoebe spun back to face him. 'Was it just to make a fool of me? Or was it…was it some kind of revenge?'

'Of course not.' He spoke calmly, dispassionately, his face as hard as it had been that night six years ago, when he'd asked her how much money it would take to make her leave Anders.

He *was* the same man. Or he seemed like it at that moment. Phoebe closed her eyes.

'Just because something is planned,' Leo finally said, 'doesn't make it less genuine.'

Phoebe opened her eyes, stared at him in disbelief. 'You don't think so?'

'Phoebe—'

'Everything you ever did was calculated. And you told me, didn't you? "I always do my research." You probably knew pizza was Christian's favourite food, you knew—'

'Don't overreact—'

'Overreact?' Phoebe laughed shrilly. 'My entire life has been upended in the space of twenty-four hours, and the one person I was beginning to trust, to…' She stopped, not wanting to confess how deep her feelings for Leo had almost run. 'He turns out to be jerking me around.'

Leo ran a hand through his hair, exhaling in impatience. 'If it seemed like I was manipulating you, Phoebe, it was for your own sake.'

'Thanks, but I actually prefer people to be honest with me.'

'And you're one to talk of honesty!' Leo snapped. 'Keeping the truth of your son's birth to yourself! A rather important detail.'

'I was afraid—'

'Obviously you didn't trust quite so much.' Leo shook his head, his eyes now glinting with scorn. It seemed incredible to Phoebe that mere minutes before they'd been lovers. They'd looked into each other's eyes as their bodies joined and she'd felt as if she'd never known another person so perfectly, so purely. And now—

'Why do you think I tried to befriend you?' Leo demanded. He gave the answer himself, his voice hard and angry. 'So a wedding proposal from me didn't seem so *insane*.'

'You were trying to make me fall in love with you,' Phoebe whispered.

Leo laughed harshly. 'Well, it didn't work, did it?' He turned away, his hands shoved in his pockets, his body radiating anger and frustration.

Yet it had, Phoebe thought disconsolately. Or almost. She'd been on the brink of falling in love with Leo—she'd so desperately wanted to say yes to his proposal. She'd wanted to marry him—but not as a matter of convenience, but of love. The realisation levelled her, made despair flood through her in empty yet consuming waves. She shook her head now. 'It's just as well that there's no reason for us to marry, then.' As she said the words, she felt her heart twist. Amazing how quickly hope could lodge in your heart, how mere possibility could become so real—

'Actually, there is.' Leo spoke almost lazily, and Phoebe froze.

'What are you talking about?'

'We just had unprotected sex,' Leo informed her bluntly. 'I didn't wear a condom, and I'm assuming you're not using birth control.' He paused, his gaze sweeping over her, making her flush. 'Or are you?'

'No,' she admitted quietly. She hadn't any reason to use birth control, and Leo obviously had known it. He'd done his research, after all. She glanced at him, eyes flashing. 'Was that part of your plan too?'

'No,' Leo said after a moment, colour high on his cheekbones. 'It was not. But the fact remains that it happened, and so there is a possibility you could be carrying my child.'

'A very small possibility,' Phoebe snapped.

'A real one, none the less,' Leo replied.

Her flush deepened as she realised the truth of what Leo was saying. She was in the middle of her cycle, and pregnancy *was* a possibility. She swallowed. 'Still, even if I am pregnant—'

'Your child will be my heir—'

'Not this again!' Phoebe snapped. 'The child won't be legitimate—'

'Yes,' Leo cut her off, his voice final, 'he will.' He gave her the glimmer of a smile, making Phoebe's heart lurch far more than it should. 'Or she. Queen Helena reigned for over thirty years.'

Her hand stole inadvertently, instinctively to her middle, imagining the little life nestled there. Which was ridiculous, since they'd had sex less than an hour ago. The life—the baby—they were talking about had not even been formed yet.

She looked at him curiously. 'You want this baby? That is, if this baby exists—'

'This baby,' Leo told her, 'is my heir.'

Of course. With Christian's illegitimacy, Leo was king again…which was just what he wanted.

'My news should delight you,' Phoebe said. 'With Christian out of the way, you can be king.' She smiled, as cynical as Leo had ever been. 'You should be thrilled.'

Leo paused, his face turned from hers. 'Yes,' he said tonelessly, 'of course I am.'

'But you'll have to tell the king,' Phoebe continued, a new realisation creeping over her, chilling her. 'He'll know—'

'Of course he will.'

'But who knows what he'll do? He could try to take Christian away—'

Leo gave a little snort of disbelief. 'You didn't think this through very carefully, did you?'

'Of course I didn't!' Phoebe snapped. 'I've had a dozen different things thrown at me in the last two days—I don't know what to think.' Her voice wavered and broke, and she turned away, not wanting Leo to see how overwrought she was.

'I don't think Nicholas will have much interest in

Christian once he's learned the truth of his birth,' Leo said quietly. 'He'll be of no use to him.'

'And I suppose I should be glad of that.'

'Absolutely.'

'So even though he's family, none of you want him any more,' Phoebe said dully. It should relieve her, but it still was a rejection.

'I rather thought,' Leo said after a moment, 'that it was more a case of you not wanting us.'

They were silent for a moment, the only sound the wind rattling the panes of the salon's windows and the crackle of the dying fire.

'Still,' Leo finally said, 'until we find out if you're pregnant you need to stay in Amarnes. And if it turns out you are carrying my child…' Phoebe sucked in a breath, her heart starting to hammer '…we will marry.' Leo's tone was flat, implacable. No more seduction, Phoebe thought grimly. No more pretending. Just cold, hard truth.

'I'm hardly suitable to be queen,' Phoebe pointed out. 'I wasn't before, and I haven't changed.'

Leo regarded her with assessing eyes, his head tilted to one side. 'That,' he said, 'is my decision.'

'And not mine?'

'If you are carrying my child, then no.'

It was all about the child, Phoebe thought. The heir. It wasn't about her at all. A fresh wave of realisation swept over her. It had *never* been about her. Had Leo only wished to marry her to have some control over Christian, the future king, himself? To safeguard his own interests, never mind hers?

'I'd like to go to bed,' she said in a shaky voice, and inwardly flinched as Leo's gaze flicked to the table where they'd just lain.

'Very well. We will speak tomorrow.'

Phoebe nodded, too exhausted both emotionally and physically to argue. She needed to escape the prison of this room and of her own mind—for a few hours to be blissfully blank, to think of nothing, feel nothing.

'Goodnight,' she whispered. Leo looked at her for a long moment, and she remained there, transfixed, as if he were forcibly holding her still. A darkness lingered in his eyes, a sorrow. Finally he looked away, let her go.

'Goodnight, Phoebe.'

Back in her suite of rooms, Christian settled in his own bed, she found that sleep eluded her. Phoebe lay in the middle of the king-sized bed and watched the moon cast silver shadows on the floor, her mind spinning in circles. Had she judged Leo too harshly, accusing him of being manipulative and deceitful? Perhaps he did have her best interests at heart…even if it no longer mattered. There was no reason for him to marry her, or even to be kind to her. No reason for them to have a relationship of any kind at all.

Unless she was pregnant.

Once again Phoebe's hand crept to her middle and rested there, imagining a tiny bean of a baby nestled inside her womb, starting to grow. Of course, she reminded herself, everything she and Leo had discussed was still hypothetical. *Impossible.*

Did she actually want to be pregnant? Did she want this life to grow inside her, part her, part Leo, making them a family? It would be a reason to marry Leo, even if he'd manipulated her, even if all he cared about was the crown.

I want him to be the man he's been these last few days. I want him to be real. And then, another thought that sprang unbidden from the deepest corner of her heart: *I want him to love me…as I love him.*

How could she love Leo? *Leo*…a man she'd once hated—or had that been her mind's way of protecting her heart? For even six years she'd felt that irresistible fascination with him, that dark tug of longing.

And now she loved him. She loved the man he'd shown himself to be—kind, compassionate, *passionate*… She still ached from the memory of his lips on hers, his body joined to hers…She'd never felt such pleasure, such intimacy as she had with Leo, such exquisite understanding and even joy.

Phoebe closed her eyes, desperate for sleep to come and rescue her from the endless circling of her own thoughts. She loved Leo, the Leo she'd known these last few days, and the thought that all his actions, his kind words, the way he'd *touched* her, had all been simply part of some cold-hearted plan was too awful to bear, no matter what his motive had been. She wanted him to love her, she thought despondently, and love wasn't manipulative or planned…it simply *was*.

'The king is sleeping.'

Leo gazed at the impassive face of one of Nicholas's aides and shrugged. 'Very well. I'll talk to him in the morning.'

His news about Christian could wait. Part of him wanted to gloat, to crow, to shove his victory in the old man's face. It was a childish impulse, and Leo repressed it. The information Phoebe had given him was precious, dangerous. He wasn't going to part with it so quickly.

He turned to walk down the long, dark corridor to his own room. His footsteps fell silently on the soft carpet, and all around him the palace was silent and dark.

He knew he should be feeling the thrill of victory; he'd bested Nicholas, and the old man didn't even know it yet.

He'd won the long, drawn-out battle of the last few years; he could forget all the taunts and slights, the years of being ignored, passed over, discarded. He would be king.

He wouldn't marry Phoebe.

Why did he feel so empty, so flat, so *disappointed*?

He'd enjoyed these last few days, he realised, had even come to care for Phoebe and Christian, for the family the three of them were together.

And when he and Phoebe were alone…Leo closed his eyes, sweat prickling along his shoulder blades as he remembered the touch and feel of her, all creamy skin and tangled curls…the look in her eyes, like two endless wells of longing, as he'd held her gaze and moved inside her.

He wanted that again. He wanted it forever.

Leo swore under his breath as he let himself into his private suite. The room was cast in shadow, and in the darkness he felt the old demon of guilt rise to ride him once more.

I've worked hard. I've worked so hard for it all…

He could almost hear Nicholas taunting him. *You are the aberration.*

And he was. He'd never been meant for the throne, or for Phoebe, and even now he fought the feeling—unreasonable as it might seem—that to ascend it, to marry Phoebe, would be almost a crime. The actions of a thief, who crept in quietly and took what wasn't his.

Yet if Phoebe had his child? His heir…? And he became king? Then, Leo thought grimly, he'd have everything he'd ever wanted…and he wouldn't deserve any of it.

CHAPTER TEN

THE next morning Phoebe took Christian to the nursery for breakfast. She felt an instinctive need to avoid both Leo and the king, to protect herself.

The nursery was warm and welcoming, filled with sunlight. When Frances saw them she sent for breakfast, her gaze resting on Phoebe's pale face and shadowed eyes with a little too much shrewdness.

'And how was your dinner last night?' she asked when Christian was occupied with some toy cars in the corner of the room.

'Fine,' Phoebe replied. She tried to keep her voice light but she still blushed, and Frances obviously noticed.

Desperate to change the conversation, she glanced around the room with its wide oak floorboards and comfortable furniture, the baskets of toys lining the walls. 'I'm surprised the nursery has been kept all these years. It must have been thirty years since any children were here.'

'Yes, Leo and Anders were the last ones.' Frances glanced around the room as well, and Phoebe imagined Anders and Leo there as boys, one blond, one dark. One indulged, one ignored. Baldur and Hod. Yet she suddenly found herself wondering, which was which?

She turned back to Frances. 'And have you been kept on as a governess all these years?'

Frances chuckled. 'What, twiddling my thumbs? No, indeed. I've been a nursery teacher in Njardvik. My husband was Amarnesian, and after he died I stayed on here.' She paused. 'No, I was just brought back in the last week, for this little lad.' She gestured to Christian. 'At least now the nursery will be full of laughter again. I fear it's been waiting—the whole kingdom has been waiting—for it to be used again.'

'The king hired you?' Phoebe asked, a bit too sharply, for Frances gave her a wary look.

'Not directly, of course, but yes.'

'For how long?'

Frances shrugged. 'Indefinitely. Until this little man grows up, I should think.'

Phoebe nodded slowly. It shouldn't surprise her, this news. It was no more than what Leo had told her; the king had intended to keep Christian in Amarnes. Yet still it reminded her of what Leo had known, had always known. He'd lied to her in New York, promising a two-week holiday, simply to get her to come to Amarnes. He'd kept the king's intentions from her, and then used his oh so persuasive body to convince her to marry him for his own purposes, the kingdom's purposes. To protect—and control—the heir to the throne. His throne.

It was all so obvious, so terrible, and yet Phoebe didn't want to believe it. She wanted to believe in the Leo she'd fallen in love with, yet hadn't Leo practically admitted that man was false, a charade he'd performed to win her trust?

A maid bustled in with breakfast, steaming, fragrant coffee and Danish *kringle*. Frances called to Christian, and he came over eagerly.

'Where's Leo?' he asked as he blew on his hot chocolate, a slice of *kringle* in front of him. Phoebe started in surprise.

'I don't know, scout. Does it matter?'

Christian gave her one of his looks; Phoebe had used to joke that it was the look that said he clearly knew much more than she did. 'I want to see him. He said we'd go sledging.'

'Did he?' More promises, more ways to win them over, and with a lurch of alarm Phoebe realised she needed to protect Christian's heart as well as her own. What if he became too attached to Leo? Even though their future still hung in the balance, the very real possibility remained that they would return home in less than two weeks and never see Leo again. 'I think,' she said carefully, 'that he might be busy today. Princes do work, you know.'

Christian wrinkled his nose, considering. 'Doing what?'

'Oh, lots of things…' Phoebe thought of Leo's charity for political refugees. Such generous, important work, and yet he'd been dismissive of it. *'It's easy to be admirable when you have the money and time.'*

No, she thought, it's not. Look at Anders, look at King Nicholas. Spoiled and selfish, vain and petulant. Leo was different. He *was*.

She wanted to believe it so much.

'Mom…' Christian interrupted her thoughts, his tone telling her that he'd been trying to get her attention for some minutes.

'Sorry, honey.' She smiled in apology. 'I was a million miles away.'

'Do you think we can still go sledging today?'

She glanced helplessly at Christian, who had far too

much hope in his eyes. She'd worked so hard to give him everything he needed from the moment he'd been handed into her arms, and yet now fear clutched at her heart and made her eyes sting. *I don't want you to be hurt.* 'I don't think so, Christian,' she said quietly. 'I think Prince Leopold is most likely busy today,' she told him again. With no time for them, no need to have time for them.

Christian's lip jutted out. 'I want to see him.'

'Perhaps later—'

Christian's mouth remained in a half-pout for a moment before he squared his shoulders and, nodding in acceptance, turned back to his hot chocolate. Crisis averted, Phoebe thought, but still felt a well of sadness inside her at the thought of what Christian wanted…what she hadn't even realised he'd been missing.

She reached for her coffee. 'Thank you for this,' she told Frances, who waved her hand in dismissal.

'No trouble at all.' She glanced thoughtfully at Phoebe. 'And for the lad's sake, I hope the prince is able to take you both sledging. There's meant to be snow.'

Phoebe took a sip of coffee, averting her eyes. 'I'm sure he's very busy.'

'He is, that,' Frances agreed. 'You've probably realised that Nicholas is king in name only. He's growing old, of course, and he had a stroke last year. Leo has taken on much of the day-to-day administration of the monarchy.'

Phoebe stared at the governess, her coffee cup cradled in her hands, forgotten. 'He has?' she said, and heard the blatant disbelief in her voice.

'Yes, he has. And the people love him. He has a way with them, you know, an affection and a kindness that Nicholas never had. He's like Havard, his father, that way.' She made a face before laughing a little bit. 'Nicholas hates that he can't do it all any more, of course. He's always resented Leo…but I told you that before, and you've probably seen it yourself.'

'Actually,' Phoebe said, 'I've never even met the king.' She gave a little laugh, thinking how ridiculous it was for a man she'd never met to have so much control over her life. 'I knew he resented Leo, but I didn't realise how much Leo had already taken over.'

'Nicholas still signs everything, of course,' Frances said. 'Prince Leopold is given a rather short leash, but that's just the king's way. Still, he's done so much. A new hospital in Njardvik, with a special research centre for pulmonary diseases.' Phoebe jerked in surprise, remembering Leo talking about his mother: '*She died when I was sixteen. She had a weak chest*.' 'He works for several charities,' Frances continued, 'and just recently he's authored a bill for harsher penalties for drunk-driving.' Because of Anders's death, Phoebe thought. Frances sat back complacently, her cup of coffee resting on her middle. 'Yes,' she said, 'he'll make a good king.'

Obviously Frances didn't know the king's plans regarding Christian, Phoebe thought, and was glad. She only hoped that such ignorance would continue.

They ate the rest of their breakfast in companionable silence, Phoebe lost in thought as she mulled over Frances's revelations. No wonder Leo wanted to be king, she thought. He certainly deserved it.

'Leo!' Christian's happy cry had Phoebe stiffening in her seat, afraid to turn her head, to see him and the expression in his eyes. She wondered how long he'd been standing in the doorway. How could she have not known he was there? Her body hummed and sang with awareness, and as she turned she braced herself to see him, feel his gaze on hers, cold and distant as it had been last night, when they parted.

Yet when she finally faced him, he wasn't looking cold. He was smiling, his eyes warm on hers, and Phoebe felt a ridiculous surge of relief.

'Hello, Christian,' Leo said as the boy tackled him around the knees. 'It's good to see you, too.'

Frances made herself busy cleaning up the breakfast things, and Phoebe rose from the table. 'Hello,' she said, her voice coming out a bit rusty.

'Hello.'

And then they didn't say anything, just stood there, while the memories poured through her, as warm and golden as honey, of Leo kissing her, his hands cupping her breasts, sliding down her midriff, cradling her hips.

Christian tugged on Leo's hand, and he glanced down. 'Are we going sledging?'

'Christian—'

'As a matter of fact, we are,' Leo replied easily. 'Or to-bogganing, at least.'

'What's a toboggan?'

'A very large sledge.' He glanced back at Phoebe. 'I thought we could spend a few days at the royal chalet up in the mountains.'

'Chalet?' Phoebe repeated, surprise streaking through her, even as Christian squealed in delight at the prospect.

'Yes. It's very secluded there, very private and peaceful.' He lowered his voice. 'I think it's a good idea to stay away from the palace for a little while, not to mention the Press.' He slipped a folded newspaper from his pocket and silently handed it to Phoebe.

'Oh, no.' She read the lurid headline: 'PALACE'S

MYSTERY CHILD?' There was even a blurred, grainy photo of the three of them ice-skating.

'It was bound to happen,' Leo said with a shrug. He took back the paper and put it in his pocket. 'But the less speculation, the better and, frankly, I'd rather be somewhere else.'

'Would you?' Phoebe asked in surprise. Somehow she imagined that Leo would want to be right in the centre, managing things. Yet what was there left to manage? The threat to his throne had been taken away. He could relax.

So could she, for that matter, if she didn't feel so utterly wretched.

'The chalet is only an hour from here,' he continued. 'We can drive, just the three of us. Have some proper time together.' Then, as if he'd said—revealed—too much, he added coolly, 'Unless you object?'

'No,' Phoebe said quickly. 'It sounds great.'

'Yeah,' Christian chimed in. 'Let's go!'

Leo glanced down and tousled his hair. 'My sentiments exactly.'

He was playing a dangerous game, Leo thought as he exited the nursery. He should be using the next two weeks to distance himself from Phoebe. Slowly but surely separating himself from her, from the hope she gave him, the belief that he could have it all, he could have *her*.

Yet he'd failed at the first opportunity. He'd spent several hours that morning trying to work, to keep his mind from Phoebe and the intense desire he had, in both his body and soul, to find her and drag her to the nearest bed—or table—and make love to her again. And again.

He thought he'd succeeded, had managed to get through the morning without looking for her, until he'd seen the papers. The damn newspapers, with their stories and photos and rumours and lies. And, he acknowledged starkly, too much truth. Far too much truth. The palace's mystery child, indeed.

He didn't even have a plan or thought when he'd left his study in search of Phoebe. He'd gone instinctively to the nursery, told her about the chalet, surprising himself as much as he had her. He had never intended to take her there, to have some kind of holiday, practically a *honeymoon*, even though they weren't married. Yet, if ever.

The words had been out of his mouth before he could stop them or even process his suggestion, and as Christian looked at him in delight and Phoebe in stunned silence he realised how much he wanted this. Them. A family.

A few days, he told himself now. That was all it was, all it could be. A respite for both of them, and then…

Then it would be over. Phoebe and Christian would return to New York, never to see him again. Perhaps there would be a few visits, for form's sake, as Christian was still a relation. But those would taper off eventually, and Leo would be left with nothing. He would be a stranger.

Unless she was pregnant. Leo couldn't bear to think of the possibility; it was too precarious, too precious. A child. His child. His and Phoebe's, yet if she didn't want to be married to him—if the child was a leaden chain rather than a golden cord roping them together—he shouldn't want it, surely?

Yet he did. So very much. He wanted all of it, the child, the throne, the queen.

You don't deserve it…

It didn't matter.

* * *

An hour later Phoebe and Christian waited in the quiet foyer of the palace for Leo. Christian shifted impatiently by her side.

'Where is everybody?' he asked, his voice a hushed whisper.

Phoebe shrugged. 'The king is still sleeping,' she said, 'or so I heard. I suppose you tired him out.'

'He's just tired because he's old,' Christian said with childish bluntness. 'Where's Leo?'

'I'm sure he's coming…'

'Here I am.'

'Leo!' Christian turned eagerly towards his uncle. He was coming down the stairs, dressed in jeans and a heavy parka, smiling easily.

'The Land Rover is packed and out the front, so we'd better make haste if we want to beat the snow.'

Phoebe didn't see any sign of snow as she followed Leo outside. The sky was brilliant blue, the air clear and cold. Leo took Christian from her and settled him into the car seat while Phoebe seated herself in the front. Within a few minutes they were driving out of the palace gates, through Njardvik, and then along a narrow road that snaked along the valley floor.

Phoebe didn't try to make conversation, for, despite the easy affability with which Leo addressed Christian, she saw a steeliness in his eyes, in the set of his jaw, in the way he gripped the steering wheel, that had any conversation openers dying in her throat. She had no idea what he was thinking, feeling, she realised as she turned to face the window and gaze out at Amarnes's stunning countryside.

After half an hour Leo turned onto an even narrower road that wound up the mountainside. Phoebe glimpsed a few wooden cottages and chalets among the dense evergreen trees, but other than those few buildings there was no sign of life.

They drove higher into the mountains, the rocky ground now dusted with snow, and the dazzling blue sky of that morning was now replaced with a pearly grey-white. As Leo turned the Land Rover onto a steep lane flanked by ornate iron gates, the first snowflakes began to fall.

It was perfect, Phoebe thought as they all clambered out of the car. The chalet was a rambling wooden structure with painted balconies and shutters. Perched on an out-cropping of jagged rock, it looked like something out of a fairy tale.

Their boots crunched on the snow as they walked towards the chalet, Christian racing ahead, his shouts of glee echoing around them.

Inside, the living room boasted a cathedral-like ceiling, a huge stone fireplace and a two-storey picture-window that showcased the stunning vista of both mountain and sea.

'This is amazing,' Phoebe said as Leo came in with the last of their luggage. His cheeks were reddened with cold and there were snowflakes in his hair. *He* looked amazing, Phoebe thought, swallowing.

Leo smiled. 'I'm glad you like it.'

'Are we alone here?'

'Not quite. Grete and Tobias are the caretakers when the royal family is not in residence.'

'And when they are?'

Leo shrugged. 'Normally they bring an entourage.'

'But you didn't,' Phoebe observed. Christian tugged on her sleeve, desperate to explore more of the chalet.

'I hardly think we want a bunch of dour-faced servants shadowing us,' Leo said lightly. 'Grete is probably rushing around as we speak, making sure everything is in order. I didn't give her or Tobias much warning about our arrival.'

'Actually, I was making *Julestjerner*,' a smiling, grey-haired woman said, emerging from the back of the chalet with a tray of biscuits and cups of hot chocolate, 'and Tobias is outside, making sure the sledges and skates are in order.' She turned to Phoebe, bright-eyed and unaffected. 'It's been a long time since there have been children here.' She set down the tray in front of the fireplace and turned back to Leo. 'It's good to see you, Leo.'

Leo smiled and embraced Grete with a genuine affection. 'And you too, Grete. I'm sorry there was not more warning.'

'For you, we do not need warnings.' Grete laughed.

Phoebe watched this little exchange with both surprise and curiosity. Leo spoke to this woman—a servant—with a warmth and affection she'd rarely heard, and Grete looked at Leo as she might a son. Phoebe wondered if indeed this smiling, red-cheeked woman had been a surrogate mother to Leo.

'I'm happy to meet you,' she told Grete. She glanced around ruefully. 'I'm sure my son, Christian, is around here somewhere.'

'No doubt he's found the games room downstairs,' Grete said comfortably. 'I'm sure he'll return for biscuits—children have a sense about these things!'

Indeed, Christian must have, for a few minutes later he reappeared, talking excitedly about the air-hockey table and the huge TV, not to mention the possibility of skating and sledging.

Grete's husband, Tobias, arrived, and soon they were all seated in front of the huge stone fireplace with its roaring fire, eating buttery *Julestjerner* and sipping cocoa.

Phoebe felt herself relax—fully, properly—for the first time since she'd come to Amarnes.

Christian soon went to explore the games room once more, and Grete led Phoebe upstairs to one of the bedroom suites. As she stepped into the room decorated in deep blues and greens, a fire already crackling in the hearth and the snow falling gently outside, covering the fir trees in soft whiteness, Phoebe felt herself sigh. 'This place is magical.'

Grete smiled. 'Yes,' she agreed quietly, 'it is.'

Phoebe leaned against the window frame, taking in the quiet, peaceful beauty of the trees and mountains, all covered in snow. She was glad they'd come here, she realised. It felt like a respite from the tensions and uncertainty of the palace. A very temporary one.

With Christian settled in the chalet's games room, Phoebe was alone. She tried to read a book or even to nap, but both sleep and activity eluded her. She curled up on the deep window seat and watched the snow fall and the fire snap and blaze. And missed Leo. The conversation with Grete and Tobias had shed an intriguing and welcome light on his character…on the man she wanted to believe in.

The man she *would* believe in, Phoebe thought suddenly. Wasn't love—trust—a choice? A choice she could make, to trust Leo, to trust her own faith in him. To believe in this—them—for her sake, for her child's sake. For Leo's sake.

She wanted to, she realised. She wanted it all: love, passion, happiness. She wanted it with Leo.

Yet even the thought of telling him so—opening herself, not to mention her child, to such vulnerability and pain—made her heart thump with hard, erratic beats and her palms grow damp.

She couldn't.

She couldn't risk so much…and lose. *Hurt*. Not if Leo—that Leo—wasn't real, if it really was all about manipulation, about maintaining the monarchy. Being king.

'Hello.'

Phoebe whirled from the window; Leo stood in the doorway, smiling faintly, a look of uncertainty in his eyes that made her heart beat all the harder.

'Hello. I was telling Grete how magical it is here.' Phoebe paused, sounding, feeling awkward. 'Thank you for bringing us.'

'You're welcome.' Leo strolled into the room, his hands shoved deep into his pockets. Yet, despite his casual pose, Phoebe sensed a tension from him, as if he too was aware of the awkwardness that had sprung between them.

Who are we? What can we be to one another?

She cleared her throat. 'Did you come here very much as a child?'

'Sometimes.' Leo gazed out of the window; the snow had begun to pile up in soft white drifts outside the chalet. 'As often as I could,' he added, and it sounded like a confession.

'You seem close to Grete and Tobias.'

'They are like family to me,' Leo admitted. His lips twisted briefly in a bitter smile. 'Better than family.'

We can be your family, Phoebe wanted to say. Her heart pounded in her chest. *You have me*, she wanted to add, but couldn't. She was too uncertain, too afraid, and perhaps Leo knew it, for, shaking off the mood that had sprung between them—awkward, yet intimate—he smiled wryly and gestured towards the window. 'There's plenty of snow out there. I think it's time to take Christian sledging. Will you come with us?'

Wordlessly Phoebe nodded and slipped off the window seat. At that moment, she felt as if she'd go wherever Leo wanted her to go. If only, she thought, she could tell him so.

CHAPTER ELEVEN

AFTER lunch they all trooped outside, Leo leading them to a rather steep hill piled deeply in snow. Phoebe looked at it a bit dubiously. 'That looks a little dangerous.'

'*Mom!*' Christian exclaimed in outrage.

'He'll be with me,' Leo told her. 'But if you think it's too much…'

Phoebe glanced at Christian, who was hopping up and down in excitement. 'No, no,' she said with a smile, 'I'm sure it will be fine.'

And it was more than fine, she soon saw; it was brilliant. Leo sat on the toboggan, Christian tucked firmly between his legs, and with one push they were shooting down the slope, Christian's shouts of joy echoing through the mountains.

Phoebe watched them trudge back up the hill, Christian's face brightly animated as he gestured to Leo, clearly reliving the highlights of the run. Leo's head was bent, snowflakes glittering in his hair and on his cheeks, smiling as he listened to Christian.

Phoebe's heart contracted. This was too much, too good, all the while knowing it wouldn't last. Couldn't. Yet for the moment she simply pushed away the knowledge that she would be leaving, that Leo would marry her only if she carried his heir and not because he loved her. For now she wanted simply to enjoy the perfection of the day, the sky as brilliant as a pearl, the dense fir trees blanketed in snow, the air so sharp and pure. And Leo. Most of all, Leo.

He smiled at her as they crested the hill. 'Your turn,' he said, a questioning lilt in his voice, and Phoebe started.

'I don't know…' She hadn't been sledging since she was a child, and even then, as a city kid, she'd only gone a few times. And that hill looked *very* steep.

'Come on, Mom,' Christian urged. 'It's *fun*.'

'I'll go with you,' Leo offered, and Phoebe imagined herself sitting snugly between Leo's thighs as he held her around the waist. She swallowed.

'All right.'

A few minutes later she was in that very position, feeling Leo's warmth against her hips and backside, his hands laced around her middle.

'Ready?' he whispered in her ear, and Phoebe's heart began to hammer in a way that had nothing to do with the snowy slope in front of her.

'Yes…'

Leo shoved off and the toboggan began to descend. 'This isn't so bad,' she began cautiously, only to let out a surprised shriek, for the toboggan had picked up speed and they were *flying*.

'Don't worry,' Leo said, his hands still holding her securely. 'I'll keep you safe.'

As the world flew by in a blur of colours, Phoebe knew he would. She leaned her head against his chest, savouring the feel of him holding her, cradling her. Keeping her safe.

All too soon it was over, and the toboggan coasted to a stop at the bottom of the hill.

'That was amazing,' Phoebe said with a little laugh as she dusted herself off. 'Really amazing.' She glanced up at Leo, who was gazing at her with an intensity that dried the breath in her lungs, the laughter on her lips.

'Phoebe…' he began, his voice low, and Phoebe's heart flipped.

'Yes,' she whispered, wanting him to say…something… *Tell me you love me. Please*.

'Come on, you guys!' Christian called from the top of the hill. 'It's my turn next!'

The moment was broken. Almost regretfully Leo shook his head and began to trudge up the hill, dragging the toboggan behind him.

That evening they shared dinner with Grete and Tobias, and, exhausted by the afternoon outside, Christian was soon bundled into bed, while Grete and Tobias had quietly withdrawn to their own quarters.

And Phoebe and Leo were left alone.

The living room was alive with leaping shadows cast by the fire's flames, and outside the world was dark and softened with snow.

'This has been wonderful,' Phoebe said quietly. She was curled up in the corner of one of the big, squashy sofas; Leo sat across from her, his legs stretched out to the fire. 'I wish I could bottle this day up and keep it forever,' she said with a little smile. 'You must have loved it here as a child.'

'I did,' Leo agreed, staring into the fire. He sounded lost in thought.

'Did you go skating and sledging?' Phoebe asked. She tried to imagine him, a dark-haired, sleepy-eyed boy with a mischievous smile. A boy who must have found his happiness here, with people who loved him.

'I spent most of my time outside,' Leo admitted with a quick, wry smile. 'There was some advantage to being the spare.'

'What do you mean?'

Leo shrugged. 'I was allowed a certain amount of freedom.' He paused. 'Anders hated it here. He was never allowed to do anything dangerous, whether it was skate or sledge or even run very fast. I sometimes wondered if that was why…' Leo stopped, his mouth tightening. He shook his head.

'Why he was so jealous of you?' Phoebe finished quietly. She remembered the look Anders had given Leo right before they'd left the palace, and she thought of the times he'd spoken of Leo, with a seemingly unwarranted bitterness.

Leo looked up, surprised. 'I suppose. I never thought…I wish he hadn't wasted his life so much,' he finally said. 'I wish I could have…' He stopped, shaking his head, memories claiming him once more.

'You weren't responsible for Anders.'

'Wasn't I?' Leo didn't give her a chance to respond to this sorrowful statement, for he shifted his position, leaning forward so the light from the fire caught the glints of amber in his hair and eyes. 'But enough of me. I want to know about you.'

'Such as?'

'You mentioned you had a very happy childhood. Tell me about it.'

Phoebe gave a little self-conscious laugh. 'Well, my mother was a potter. She still has a studio in Brooklyn. She's a bit of a bohemian, actually, and when I was growing up we always had artists and writers and poets coming through our house.' She laughed again, remembering. 'To tell you the truth, I don't think any of them were very successful. But they were passionate, at least.'

'So that's where you get it from.'

Phoebe's gaze flew to his, a blush rising. 'What do you mean?'

Leo smiled. 'Your passion…about everything.' There was no innuendo in his voice, yet Phoebe remembered all the same. Remembered the way his lips and hands had felt on her body, and how she'd craved more. She craved it now, longed to close the few feet between them and feel his body on hers once more. *I don't care if you don't love me. I just need to feel you again.*

She swallowed and looked away, not wanting Leo to see the desperate need in her eyes—not wanting him to reject her.

'You have a full life in New York now too,' Leo continued musingly. 'With your own business, friends—'

'What are you saying?' Phoebe asked, although she quickly realised she didn't want to know what he was saying. He sounded all too final, almost as if he were saying goodbye.

Leo shrugged. 'Maybe you're better off in New York…'

'No.' Leo looked at her in surprise, and Phoebe's flush intensified. 'Let's not…talk about that right now.' She took a breath, met his gaze directly. 'Let's not talk at all.'

'Phoebe…'

And then she was closing the distance between them, crossing the carpet until she was kneeling in front of him, her hands sliding along his thighs. Leo closed his eyes briefly, a muscle jerking in his jaw.

'Please, Leo, let's just…be. While we're here. This

place is magical, we don't need to think about anything else. The palace or the future or anything.' She leaned forward and brushed her lips against his jaw, closing her eyes as she inhaled his scent. He smelled so good. 'Please,' she whispered.

Leo's hands came up to tangle in her hair. He turned her head so her eyes met his. 'You're sure?'

'Yes…'

'Just these few days. Just for now.'

He made it so very plain, Phoebe thought. Low expectations. *No* expectations. Well, she would take what she would get. It would have to be enough, for the thought of having nothing was too much to bear. 'Yes.'

Leo nodded, and then his lips claimed hers in a kiss so deep and drugging Phoebe swayed underneath his touch. She'd missed this. She needed this.

The only sound was the crack of the logs settling into the grate and their own ragged breathing as they moved as one, the whisper of clothes sliding to the floor and then the softer sound of skin on skin as their mouths and bodies met again and again, and the desperate craving was finally, gloriously satisfied.

It went too fast. Phoebe knew it would, knew that as soon as she and Leo silently agreed to take these days at the chalet as a time apart, a time together, they would slip by like pearls on a string, so precious and so fleeting. They spent their days with Christian, sledging and skating, building a snowman and having the inevitable snowball fight, revelling in the simplest pleasures.

One day they travelled to a nearby village, a few wooden houses and a tiny Christmas market; Phoebe couldn't resist buying one of the *nissen* on display.

And it was easy to let the cares and worries slip away in a place like this, away from the whispers and rumours, the tension and anxieties of the palace. Here there were no princes or princesses, dukes or duchesses, no heirs at all. They were simply a family, mother, father, son.

Husband, wife. Or as good as. For, while the days were filled with fun, the nights held an even deeper joy as Phoebe learned Leo's body and he hers. Under the cover of darkness, they needed no words beyond a few provocative murmurs: *Do you like this? What about that?* The low, shared laughter of lovers, and the dazzling wonder of shared pleasure, deep and intense.

As she lay in Leo's arms it made Phoebe's heart ache to think it might end. Yet perhaps it wouldn't end. She found herself imagining the child she might be carrying, with her eyes and Leo's hair and smile. She pictured it nestled inside her, protected, cherished…for she wanted this baby, wanted it desperately. She wanted it for itself, a tiny, perfect life, but also as a reason to stay, a reason for Leo to marry her. Perhaps he didn't love her now, perhaps he saw her as only a means to an end, but the last week had shown her he had affection for her, and certainly attraction. Couldn't both grow into love? Could she will Leo into loving her, she wondered, for surely if she could, he would? She'd never wanted anything so much.

Inevitably it all came to an end. The few days they had planned to be away had been extended, and now it had been ten days since she and Leo had first made love; even though he hadn't said anything, Phoebe knew they would soon be returning to the palace, to reality. She would explain to Christian, who had accepted this new life with such amazing ease, that they were going back to New York. Home…except right now it didn't feel like home. This—Leo—did.

That night Phoebe lay next to Leo, one hand resting on his chest, the sheets tangled about their naked bodies. The only light in the room came from the fireplace, where a few orange embers still burned. Outside the world was hushed and expectant; Leo had told her it was meant to snow again.

'I wish we could spend Christmas here,' Phoebe said. The holiday was still over a fortnight away, and by that time Phoebe knew she would most likely be back in New York. Still, she couldn't keep from voicing her wish.

'There are royal duties at Christmas time,' Leo said, and left it at that. His royal duties, Phoebe supposed, not hers. Her hand crept to her middle once more. Unless…

'However,' Leo continued, a slight, surprising note of hesitation in his voice, 'I do have a present for you.'

'You do?' Phoebe heard the blatant surprise in her voice, and obviously Leo heard it too, for he chuckled.

'Is that so shocking? I bought it at the Christmas market in the village.' Leo rolled out of bed and went to the bureau, taking a paper-wrapped package from it. 'It is a small thing, but I thought you might like it.'

'I'm sure I will,' Phoebe whispered as Leo handed it to her. It was a small box, she could tell, with a satisfyingly heavy weight.

'Open it,' he urged when Phoebe remained still, gazing down at the wrapped box. 'That's what you do with presents, you know.'

'I know.' Phoebe smiled, although she felt strangely emotional. Was this a farewell present? she wondered. Slowly she undid the wrapping and opened the box. A necklace nestled inside, a perfect teardrop topaz on a slender gold chain. Phoebe lifted it to the light, which caught the topaz and turned it to fire. 'It's beautiful,' she whispered. 'Thank you.'

Leo shrugged. 'It's a trifle, nothing like any of the crown jewels, but…' He hesitated, and Phoebe, in the act of fastening it around her neck, looked up. 'I thought it would look nice on you,' he finished. 'To bring out the gold in your eyes.'

'My eyes are grey,' Phoebe protested. Leo moved around the side of the bed to fasten the clasp, his fingers lingering on her skin.

'Grey with gold flecks,' he corrected. 'You can only see them up close.' His breath feathered her cheek and, even though they had made love only moments ago, Phoebe found herself weak and dizzy with desire once more. She leaned back against Leo and, the necklace now clasped, he reached around her to cup her breasts in his palms, drawing her closer to him.

They remained that way for a moment, silent, not needing words. The only sound in the room was the hiss and crackle of the dying fire and their own quiet breathing.

Leo bent to kiss her neck, his hands sliding down her navel, fingers teasing, and Phoebe shuddered in response. He knew just how to touch her, knew exactly what made her crazy with need.

And she knew too. She turned around, sliding her legs around his hips, smiling a little as she heard his indrawn breath when she drew him inside her.

They moved slowly, in an exquisite rhythm, never speaking, never taking their eyes off one another, even as the pleasure intensified and Phoebe cried out, their bodies coming together and climaxing as one.

She'd never felt so close to another person, and yet there had been a finality about their lovemaking that made her heart ache. Please, she thought, don't let this be goodbye.

'I have a present for you too,' she said afterwards, as they lay on the bed once more, their limbs tangled so she didn't know where she ended and Leo began.

'You do?' Leo sounded so surprised Phoebe couldn't help but smile.

'It really is a trifle. But…' Suddenly she felt shy, even vulnerable. 'I thought of you when I saw it,' she said, and went to fetch her own package from her handbag by the bureau.

'What could it be?' Leo murmured as he took it, unwrapping the tissue paper. Phoebe nibbled her lip nervously as he undid the paper, staring down at the little hand-carved *nisse*.

'I liked him,' she said after a moment when Leo didn't speak, 'because he looked a bit friendlier than some of the others. Like he wouldn't play tricks on you.' Then, driven by a need she could not name, she reached down and wound a stray lock of Leo's hair around her finger, her thumb caressing his cheek. 'So you must have been a good boy.'

Still Leo didn't speak, and Phoebe wondered if she'd made a mistake. When she'd seen the *nisse* at the Christmas market yesterday, she'd thought of Leo's sorry childhood and wanted to buy it for him. Yet now it seemed wrong somehow, as if she'd been trying to heal a huge wound by offering a sticking plaster.

Finally Leo looked up, his throat working, his eyes suspiciously bright. 'Thank you,' he said, and his voice sounded hoarse. 'It's a wonderful present.'

If she'd had any doubt about whether she loved him—whether he was someone she should love—it fell away in light of the fierce joy of Leo's expression. Suddenly all her doubts and fears seemed ridiculous, irrelevant. Suddenly she was sure.

Leo was that man…the man underneath, the man she'd hoped he was. It was so obvious, had been made apparent in a thousand little ways, from the way he played with Christian, to how he helped Tobias carry in the wood, to the way he'd held her gaze with such certainty as they'd made love.

And she wanted to tell him. She would tell him. Phoebe dropped to her knees, her hands reaching up to cradle his face. 'Leo…'

He stood up, slipping away from her like quicksilver. 'It's late, and we should sleep. Tomorrow we must return to the palace.'

Phoebe dropped her arms, empty and aching. Leo couldn't have been plainer; he didn't want to hear declarations of love from her. He simply wanted to return to the palace. 'All right,' she said dully.

Leo moved to the cupboard and opened a drawer, then handed Phoebe a slim white box. 'I picked this up in the village. You can take it tomorrow morning.'

Phoebe stared down at the pregnancy test. 'It hasn't been two weeks—'

'Apparently you can take them earlier these days,' Leo replied. 'And it's better to know sooner.' His voice was flat, final. Phoebe's fingers curled around the box.

'All right,' she said again, for the fight—the hope—had gone out of her. The magic had ended.

She woke early the next morning, with Leo still asleep beside her, and slipped into the bathroom. She stared at the box with its blazing script: *Test five days early! 99.9% accurate results!*

'What if I don't want to test early?' she muttered. She'd thought she had five more days. Five more days of loving Leo, being with him…

But no. The balance of her life was in this box, and suddenly Phoebe realised she actually wanted to know. Wouldn't it be better to know, to be able to move on with her life sooner, if that was the case?

And if she was pregnant…to begin to build her life with Leo.

She ripped the plastic off the box, her heart thumping. She read the rather simple instructions several times, just to be sure, and then she took the test.

The ensuing three-minute wait was agonising. Phoebe turned the stick over so she wouldn't be tempted to look. She'd brought a watch into the bathroom, and she kept her gaze on the second hand as it moved with tiny ticks around the watch's face. She heard Leo stir in the bedroom, and then knock on the bathroom door.

'Phoebe…?'

'Just a minute,' she called. Literally.

Leo was silent, and Phoebe knew he was also waiting. Waiting for the result, for their future…if they had one.

The three minutes were up. Her heart beating so fast her vision swam, Phoebe picked up the stick and turned it over. She stared at the blazing pink line.

One line. She wasn't pregnant.

'Phoebe?' Leo's voice was low yet insistent on the other side of the door. 'Are you taking the test?'

'Yes…' Desperately Phoebe scrabbled for the instructions in the box: 'One line… One line means you're not pregnant. If you don't get your period, try again in three days.'

Three days! She had three more days at least, just to be sure. The test was early, after all…

'Phoebe,' Leo called again. 'Open the door.'

'All right.' She felt numb, lifeless. Only then did she

realise how much she'd been holding on to that dream, the hope she was pregnant. Now there was no reason to stay, no reason at all.

'Well?' Leo demanded when she opened the door. He searched her face, as if he could find clues in her frozen expression.

'I'm...' Phoebe stopped, started again, her voice toneless despite the misery swamping her heart. 'I'm not pregnant.'

'Not...' Leo repeated in a hiss of breath. His eyes met hers. 'Not,' he said again, and she thought she heard sorrow, regret. 'Well, that's good, then. For the best,' he clarified.

'Yes,' Phoebe managed to say. She couldn't bring herself to tell him about the three-day wait, the possibility of a false negative. Suddenly it didn't matter.

'Not pregnant,' Leo repeated, and Phoebe wondered if he'd been imagining their baby—the reality of their baby—too. He sounded shocked. 'Well.'

'Well. So this is it.' There was nothing more to say, Phoebe thought, yet still they both stood there, staring at each other, wanting...

At least, she wanted. Wanted Leo to take her in his arms, to tell her he loved her as she loved him, that there would be other babies, other opportunities for babies, that they could have a lifetime of living and loving together. She felt the words on her tongue, opened her mouth to let them spill out, when Leo spoke first.

'Phoebe.' She stared at him eagerly, hungrily, waiting. 'Yes...'

Leo gazed at her, his eyes intent on hers, and Phoebe felt the moment stretch and open up between them. Surely, she thought, surely he loves me. Surely he'll tell me now...

Leo opened his mouth, but whatever words he'd been going to speak were drowned by the tinny trill of his mobile phone, his direct line to the palace, and from the sudden blanking of his expression Phoebe knew the moment had passed. She prayed it wasn't gone for ever.

Leo turned away from her and reached for the mobile. He spoke tersely into the phone; Phoebe couldn't understand the rapid-fire Danish. Yet when he turned back to her his expression was so bleak she knew something terrible had happened.

'It is the king,' he told her.

'The king,' Phoebe repeated numbly, and Leo nodded.

'King Nicholas is dead.'

CHAPTER TWELVE

EVERYTHING had changed. It happened so quickly; one minute she and Leo had been in their bedroom, on the precipice of—what? A declaration of love? Phoebe had thought so, had prayed so. She'd almost said those three amazing, life-changing words, *I love you*. And she'd begun to believe that Leo might say them back.

Then, in the next minute, their entire world, as new and fragile and barely there as it was, had been irrevocably changed. Damaged, or perhaps even destroyed…if it had ever existed in the first place. Within minutes of the phone call from the palace, Leo was motivating the household, packing his bags and asking Tobias to bring the car round.

'But Leo,' Phoebe protested, throwing clothes on with haphazard haste, 'it's six o'clock in the morning. Christian—'

'Will adjust,' Leo finished. He wasn't even looking at her, Phoebe saw. He dressed with clinical haste, his expression distant and hard. Thinking of the palace, Phoebe thought. Of himself as king. After the last few days, he was reverting to the old Leo—the Leo she'd hoped wasn't real, true—like a snake sliding into its true skin.

Phoebe had woken Christian, saying only that an emergency back at the palace required them to leave at once.

'What's happened?' Christian asked, blinking sleep from his eyes even as they became shadowed with worry. 'What's wrong?'

Everything, Phoebe wanted to answer. 'It's the king,' she told Christian quietly.

'What happened?'

Phoebe shook her head. 'I don't know what happened exactly,' she prevaricated, not wanting to break the news to Christian without knowing more details. 'We'll find out when we return.'

They drove in silence along the narrow, twisting roads, the world cloaked in snowy darkness. Phoebe sneaked glances at Leo and saw that his hands were clenched tightly around the steering wheel, his knuckles white. She wondered what he was thinking. Feeling. No matter how fraught or damaged the relationship between Leo and Nicholas had been, he was still his uncle, and Leo had lost two close relatives in a matter of weeks.

Phoebe leaned her head back against the seat and closed her eyes. She felt a wave of fatigue—emotional, physical—crash over her. She couldn't bear to think any more. To wonder. She wanted answers. She wanted honesty. Yet she could hardly demand such things from Leo now, when his mind was taken up with matters of state.

Yet still her mind and heart cried out, *Do you love me?* Had he been about to tell her so?

Servants waited outside the palace as Leo drove up in the Land Rover. As soon as he'd parked the vehicle he was out of the door, conferring in hurried, hushed tones with several important-looking officials. Phoebe was left to deal with Christian, and when she turned around again Leo was gone.

She didn't see him again that day. She spent the day in the nursery with Christian, playing with tin soldiers—had they been Leo's once?—and trying not to think. Yet still her mind spun in hopeless circles. What had Leo been going to say? What would he have said if she'd had enough courage to tell him she loved him? *What was happening?*

Frances was tight-lipped for once too, and several times she glanced out of the long, wide windows to the court-yard below, the flag lowered and the gates draped with black crêpe, as if news could be had there.

After an early supper with Frances and Christian, Phoebe settled Christian in bed and then stretched out on a sofa in her suite's little parlour, too tired and dispirited to do anything more.

She should make plans to return to New York, she realised. Arrange plane tickets, pack her bags. They could leave tomorrow, even. There was no reason to stay; Leo had made that abundantly clear by his absence. From the moment he'd returned to the palace he'd been concerned with matters of state, and it was as if she and Christian no longer existed. To all intents and purposes, they didn't.

Phoebe closed her eyes, fighting another wave of sorrow. It was better this way; Leo had shown his true colours. A marriage for convenience's sake would have been miserable, soulless. The life she'd been quietly weaving for herself—a husband, a baby, a family—was no more than a dream or a mirage. False. Non-existent.

Yet even as these thoughts circled sluggishly in her brain, Phoebe knew she could not just lie there and wait for life to happen…or not happen, as the case may be. She would find Leo. She would confront him. She would demand the truth, as cold and hard as it undoubtedly was, and then she would go home.

She rose from the sofa, straightening her hair and clothes before she headed out into the shadowy corridors of the palace in search of Leo.

Leo took off his glasses and rubbed his eyes. He ached with tiredness. He'd been in meeting after meeting that day, with Parliament, with palace staff, with the Press. Always seeking to undo the damage Nicholas's last days had caused, stabilising the monarchy.

His monarchy. He was king. He rose from the desk and moved to the window, gazing out at the palace courtyard now strung with lights. In their eerie glow he could see the lowered flag, the draped crêpe. The king was dead; long live King Leopold.

He turned back to the desk, his heart twisting within him. This was what he'd always wanted, from the moment perhaps when he knew he'd never have it. Yet why, then, was he so unhappy, so empty?

I don't deserve it…

He silenced the voice of his conscience; it didn't matter if he deserved it or not. He was king, he would strive to be a good one, to serve his country and his people with his whole heart.

His country would have his heart, for no one else could claim it. Where was Phoebe? he wondered. Had she gone already, slipped from the palace like a shadow? There would be no need to say goodbye. The time they'd enjoyed at the chalet had been an idyll, separate and finite. And now it was over. She'd made that clear when she'd told him she wasn't pregnant. 'So this is it.' He'd almost—almost— told her he loved her, begged her to stay even if she didn't love him, even if there was no reason. He was glad he hadn't had the chance, for surely Phoebe was better off in

New York, living her full, happy life without the intrigues of the palace, without him.

The door to the study creaked, and Leo looked up in surprise. In the slice of light made by its opening he saw a head of curly hair, the flash of a wide grey eye. Phoebe. His heart lurched in his chest and he straightened, laying his palms flat on the table, knowing what he must do.

'Come in, Phoebe.'

He spoke so flatly, Phoebe thought, so impersonally, as if she was simply one more person—one more problem— to deal with. She slipped into the room, her gaze taking in the scattered papers on Leo's desk, half a dozen newspapers with their blazing headlines: *The King Is Dead. King Leopold Ascends the Throne.*

'Congratulations,' she said, her voice scratchy. Was that what you said to a king? She had no idea.

Leo inclined his head in acknowledgement. 'I will try my best to be a good king to the people of Amarnes.' His voice was still flat.

'Yes. I know you will.' Phoebe's throat ached with the effort of not crying. She wanted to cry, to let all the sorrow and disappointment out, to demand of Leo, *What was last week, then? Did you never love me at all?* She swallowed it back down; surely she didn't need him to spell it out for her, hear his cold rejection of her face to face? She tried to smile and didn't quite manage it. 'So…I thought I should probably book my plane tickets back to New York. Josie, my assistant, must be going crazy.'

'Right.' Leo slipped on a pair of glasses, and the little gesture made Phoebe's heart ache. She didn't know he wore glasses; how many little things did she not know about him? Now she would never find out. 'You can fly back on the royal jet,' he told her. 'It's the least I can do.'

'Thanks.' She swallowed. 'That's very generous of you.'

'It's nothing.'

And, Phoebe thought, considering all they'd shared, it felt like nothing. She stood there, feeling surplus to requirements and slightly ridiculous, but she couldn't bear to go, to end it like this.

'Christian is still your nephew,' she blurted. 'Will you...will you want to see him?'

Leo gazed at her quietly for a moment. 'Do you want me to?'

Phoebe felt a sudden spurt of rage at his obvious indifference. 'You've managed to matter to him these last two weeks,' she said, her voice cold. If she stayed angry, she wouldn't cry. She wouldn't hang on to Leo's sleeve and shame herself by begging him to let her stay.

'He matters to me,' Leo said quietly, so quietly Phoebe almost didn't hear him.

'Does he, Leo?' she asked, and heard the stinging scepticism in her own voice. 'Does he really?'

Leo jerked his head upwards, his eyes flashing. 'Of course he does, Phoebe—'

'Because,' Phoebe cut across him, 'it doesn't seem like it from here. From here it seems like you were just using him the way you were using me.'

Leo's eyes widened, then narrowed, the corners of his mouth turning white. 'Using him?' he repeated dangerously. 'How was I using him, Phoebe?'

'To stabilise the monarchy,' Phoebe retorted, throwing his own words back at him with a bitter, sarcastic edge. 'And the only way to do that is to sit on the throne yourself, right? Except if Christian was named heir, you couldn't, so the next best thing was to be the heir's guardian. Were you hoping to become regent? Control him that way? And then I gave you the best news of all—you could be king!' Tears started at the corners of her eyes, and she bit her lip hard to keep them from sliding down her cold cheeks. 'Only I told you a little too late, and poor you, you had to sleep with me first—'

'Phoebe—'

'What an *inconvenience*,' Phoebe cut him off, one tear escaping to trickle down her cheek.

'Where,' Leo asked in a low voice, 'are you getting these ideas?'

'From you,' Phoebe cried. 'What am I supposed to think, Leo, when you rush us back to the palace at the crack of dawn and then deposit us on the front steps like so much unwanted rubbish? And not a single word all day—nothing! And you know why?'

Leo's eyes glinted with silent menace, his lips compressed in a hard line. 'No,' he said, his voice cold and clipped. 'Why?'

'Because we don't matter to you any more,' Phoebe threw at him. 'Christian is illegitimate and I'm not pregnant, so you're done with us! Isn't that right?' She planted her hands on her hips, giving him a glare of angry defiance even as her heart begged, *Please tell me how wrong I am. Please tell me all these fears are groundless. Don't let me walk out of here…*

'Well.' Leo glanced down at his desk and mindlessly straightened some papers. When he looked up again, his expression was entirely too bland. 'You seem to have worked it all out.'

Phoebe's chest hurt with the effort of keeping all the

emotion inside. Was that all he was going to say? Not one word of explanation or apology? Obviously he had none to give. She drew in a shuddering breath. 'I suppose I have.'

They stared at each other for a long, aching moment; Phoebe felt all the pain and sorrow—the disappointed, destroyed hope—rise up within her, threatening to come out in a howl of misery. She felt it in every aching part of her body, knew it was reflected in her tear-filled eyes. Leo, however, merely looked bland. His eyes and mouth possessed a certain steeliness, making Phoebe wonder if she'd actually *annoyed* him. Nothing more. Finally she spoke.

'I should go.'

Leo's only response was an indifferent jerk of his shoulder; his eyes remained cold. With leaden heart and feet, Phoebe slowly turned around. She walked to the door, hardly able to believe this was goodbye. For ever. After everything—the days and nights they'd shared, the caresses, the whispers and secrets—he was letting her walk out of his life without even saying goodbye. She choked back a cry at the thought, steeling her spine, and put her hand on the knob. Then Leo spoke.

'The reason I was closeted all day with government officials,' he said in a strange, scratchy voice that wasn't like his at all, 'was to keep a coup from taking place.'

Phoebe's hand curled around the doorknob, her back still to Leo. 'A coup?' she repeated in disbelief.

'Yes. You see, no one knew about Christian's birth.'

She turned around slowly. Leo was staring at her with blazing eyes, his face white. Phoebe couldn't tell if he was angry or possessed by some other, deeper emotion. Hurt. 'Why didn't they know?' she whispered. 'Didn't you tell Nicholas?'

Leo hesitated for a fraction of a second. 'No, I didn't,' he said quietly. 'I knew he was dying. It was only a matter of days, maybe weeks. It occurred to me that if he did know, he could make life…unpleasant. For you and Christian.'

Phoebe's heart lurched. 'You mean sue for custody?'

'Something like that. Nicholas is—was—like an old bear, grouchy and mean. He was perfectly capable of making someone's life a misery simply because he could.'

'So when you returned—'

'Nicholas had changed his will,' Leo said, 'and he had enough cronies who would bid for power through Christian if he were king. I had to show Parliament that Christian was ineligible. We had his birth certificate faxed from Paris. His mother was Leonie Toussaint. A waitress like you said, only nineteen years old.' He shook his head. 'Poor girl.'

'Yes,' Phoebe whispered. 'You could have told me—'

'I didn't want you or Christian brought into the limelight,' Leo replied. 'In any case, we handled it with quick discretion, and the stories in the papers will soon be squashed.'

'And you'll be king,' Phoebe finished dully. 'Congratulations. You have everything you've ever wanted.'

Something flashed across Leo's face, streaking through his eyes and tightening his muscles, and when he spoke his voice was terse and strangled. 'Do you think,' he asked, 'that I did all this simply so I could be king?'

Phoebe stared. 'What else should I think?'

Leo gave a short, harsh laugh and turned away. 'I never thought I deserved the throne, Phoebe, and it appears you agreed with me.'

Phoebe's mind whirled with the implications of his

words. 'What are you saying, Leo? Of course you deserve the throne. You're next in line in the succession—'

'An accident of birth does not mean anything,' Leo cut her off. 'You should know that. Look at Anders. He was dismally prepared to be king, so much so that he escaped it the first opportunity he could.'

'So why do you think you don't deserve to be king?' Phoebe asked, and Leo turned back to face her.

'Why do you think I want to be king so much, Phoebe?' Leo returned softly.

'Because…' she shook her head, feeling as if Leo had taken the chessboard of their conversation and scattered all the pieces '…because everything you did was for that. Taking me to Amarnes, asking to marry me—'

'Was to gain control of Christian rather than protect the two of you, keep you from being manipulated, trampled on like my mother was?' Leo filled in. 'What kind of man do you think I am, Phoebe?'

Phoebe flushed. Suddenly her words, so carelessly and angrily spoken, seemed hurtful. Callous, and perhaps even wrong. 'I thought you were a good man,' she whispered. 'When we were at the chalet, and even before…you seemed such a kind man.'

'*Seemed?*' The word was a sneer.

'Yes.' She took a breath, willing herself to continue. Now was the time for total honesty, her last chance, when there surely was nothing left to lose. 'You seemed,' she continued, 'like a man I could fall in love with.' Leo gave a little laugh of disbelief, and Phoebe realised how weak her words sounded. 'I did fall in love with you,' she clarified, her cheeks flushing. 'And I hoped you'd fallen in love with me.'

'So what made you change your mind?'

'What do you mean?'

'Come on, Phoebe.' Leo gestured to the door, still half-open. 'You were about to walk out of here. You came to find me to tell me you needed to buy plane tickets. The truth is, you couldn't wait to leave.'

'No, Leo,' Phoebe returned, shaken, 'that's not true at all—'

'And I don't blame you,' Leo continued savagely, riding over her words, not hearing them. His eyes glittered with pain and anger. 'The only reason I didn't keep you here— get down on my knees and beg you to stay—is that I know how much better off you'd be in New York.'

'What?' Phoebe stared at him in shock and disbelief even as hope was starting to turn crazy somersaults all through her body, making her dizzy. She reached out one steadying hand to his desk. 'Leo—what on earth makes you say that? Think that?'

'I don't deserve you, Phoebe,' Leo said bleakly. He swept an arm to encompass the royal study, the palace, perhaps his entire kingdom. 'I don't deserve any of this.' Phoebe heard a well of despair deep in Leo's voice, a despair that she sensed had been plumbed long, long ago, when he'd been told and shown in a thousand little ways how unneeded he was. How undeserving. And obviously he believed it.

'Leo, *deserving* anything never came into it for me—'

'Well, it should have—'

'Does anyone deserve love?' Phoebe pressed. 'Love simply is. And I love you—'

'You don't know me,' he said in a low voice. He averted his head once more, his face in profile. 'You don't know what kind of man I am, what I'm capable of.'

Phoebe had thought the same thing once, back when

Leo had scared and intimidated her. When she hadn't known what kind of man he was…but she'd found out. She'd discovered it for herself when she'd lain in his arms, when she'd seen him smile at Christian, in so many small ways and instances, treasured memories locked in her heart. She *knew* Leo.

'I think I've come to know you,' she said carefully, 'in the last two weeks—'

'*Weeks*,' Leo dismissed in contempt. 'And if you knew me so well, Phoebe, how could you come down here and accuse me of all the things you did? How could you believe I'd marry you simply to control Christian, make him some kind of puppet ruler?'

Phoebe flushed in shame once more. 'I was angry, and I wanted to make you say something—deny it—'

'And I will deny it,' Leo returned with some heat. 'I intended to marry you to protect you, Phoebe, from Nicholas's machinations, and the machinations of his cronies at court. Even after he was dead…without a protector, Christian would have been vulnerable. Trust me,' he smiled bleakly, 'a boy alone at court is not an easy thing.'

Phoebe's heart ached. 'No,' she whispered, 'I'm sure it's not.'

'But not to control or manipulate him, I swear.' He held up a hand to forestall her argument, even though Phoebe had none. 'I know you believe I manipulated you in trying to get you to marry me. And that is true, in a way. I was kind to you with—with a goal in sight, but also because I wanted to marry you. I wanted to be with you.' He paused, and when he spoke again his voice was ragged. 'I even wanted our child.'

'So did I,' Phoebe admitted with a shaky laugh, and Leo smiled sadly.

'If only…' Why, Phoebe wondered, did he sound so regretful? So final? As if, even now, they couldn't be together?

'Leo…'

'There are other things…' He stopped, shaking his head.

And Phoebe cried, 'What other things, Leo? What do you feel so…so *guilty* about?' He pressed his lips together, saying nothing, and Phoebe continued hesitantly, 'Is it the way you lived before…the women, the parties? The wild lifestyle?' His years as the Playboy Prince. Did he feel so guilty about that after all this time? Leo didn't reply, and Phoebe forced herself to continue. 'Because it was a long time ago and since then—'

Leo gave an abrupt, harsh bark of laughter. 'Do you think this is about a few parties? Or even a few women? Do you think I'm torturing myself over a little wild living?' He sounded so sneeringly incredulous that Phoebe flushed.

'I don't know,' she admitted. 'What is it about, Leo?'

'You want the truth, Phoebe?' he finally said. It wasn't a question; it was a reckoning. 'You want to know what kind of man I am? Then you won't delude yourself into thinking you love me, thinking we could have had anything more than a convenient marriage—than just sex!' His voice rang out, and Phoebe flinched. 'This is the kind of man I am,' Leo said raggedly. He sounded as if he'd been running, as if he was now gasping for air, for life. 'I hated Anders. I always hated him. It wasn't just petty jealousy, some kind of sibling-type rivalry. No,' he said, giving her that terrible smile she remembered from before, 'it's more than that, worse than that. I hated him for all I had to do for him, and all he never did. For all he had and threw away…even you. Especially you.'

'Leo—'

'I hated him so much I was *glad* when he abdicated. I wanted him to walk away. I didn't try very hard to keep him there, did I? Do you remember?' He turned around, took a dangerous step towards her, his eyes glittering. 'There's more than one way to buy someone off, isn't there, Phoebe? You might not have taken money ten years ago, but you would have taken me.' Then, as if he hadn't made it damningly clear enough, he continued, 'I could have seduced you, Phoebe. It would have been all too easy. I could have made you leave him.'

'Then why didn't you?' Phoebe challenged, her face hot with memory and shame.

'Because I wanted Anders to leave.' His voice was a sneer of self-loathing. 'I thought—maybe then—I'd be free. Free of him. But of course I wasn't. I might have been heir, but Nicholas never forgot who was meant to be king. And neither did I.' He turned away, tension and anger—directed, no doubt, at himself—radiating from every taut line of his body. 'So that's the kind of man I am. A man who's been consumed by hatred for far too long, there's no longer any room for love.' He spoke in a flat, final voice that shook Phoebe to the very core.

'Hatred,' she finally said, 'or guilt?'

Leo shrugged. 'It hardly matters.'

'Doesn't it?' Phoebe challenged quietly. She looked at him now, a man in the grips of a horrible memory, an agony of guilt. Guilt, not hatred. At that moment she wondered if Leo had hated Anders at all. She thought of the harsher laws for drunk-driving, the centre for pulmonary diseases. She'd thought they'd been merely the actions of a good king, but Phoebe saw now they'd been something else as well. Atonement. Atonement for a past

Leo had been unable to control, for being the older son but the younger cousin. For wanting to be responsible, and unable to be it…be anything. 'You weren't responsible for Anders, Leo—'

'I was *older*—'

'So?'

'It was my duty—'

'Is that what they told you?' Phoebe guessed. 'You were the one meant to keep Anders's nose clean? And,' she finished, realisation and memory sweeping through her, 'to clean up his messes.' As she had been six years ago…and even two weeks ago. She'd been Leo's job, just another mess to clean up.

'Someone needed to,' Leo said, and Phoebe shook her head.

'Perhaps everyone believed that, but Anders, like anyone else, had to be responsible for his own life. His own mistakes. And he chose his own path, all the way to the end.'

'I never stopped him,' Leo confessed raggedly. 'I should have, God knows I should have, but I never did.'

'You mean,' Phoebe guessed quietly, 'you were never able to stop him.'

Leo shrugged. 'It amounts to the same.'

'I don't think it does.' Phoebe met his gaze directly. Despite the despair in Leo's eyes she felt hope; it coursed through her veins like liquid gold, shining and pure. 'I don't blame you, Leo,' she said. She kept her voice calm and steady, even though it took so much effort. She felt as if she might splinter apart, body and soul, into a thousand agonised fragments of fear. To lose him now—to this! To the past, which was finished, a sorrowful chapter that had ended long ago, even if it had kept Leo in its tortured pages. 'If I were you, I would hate Anders too. And I don't think you hated him as much as you hated what he did, the man he became. The waste he made of his life, when he'd been given so much.'

'I should have helped him,' Leo said after a moment. 'I could have—'

'How? Who would have let you? Not Anders.' She took a breath. 'I think perhaps Anders resented and even hated you.' She felt a jagged shard of sorrow lodge in her soul at the thought of so much bitterness. Baldur and Hod, indeed.

'He did hate me,' Leo said in a low voice, 'because he knew I hated him.'

'Or maybe,' Phoebe countered, 'he hated you because neither of you were ever given the chance to love each other. You were forced into impossible roles as little boys, and there was never any chance for a normal kind of relationship.'

'That's true,' Leo acknowledged after a moment, 'but it doesn't change—'

'The kind of man you are? I *know* what kind of man you are, Leo.' Leo shook his head, an instinctive movement, refusing to accept the hope Phoebe offered. The love. But she wasn't done yet, not by a long shot. She took a step closer to him, even though everything in him was telling her to stay away…everything but the look of hungry desperation in his eyes. 'You know what I think, Leo?' Phoebe asked softly. 'I think everything you've told me makes you a better man, not a worse one. You hated the waste Anders made of his life, and yet you still made a sacrifice of yours.'

'Only because—'

'It doesn't matter *why*,' Phoebe cut him off. 'It doesn't even matter what you thought. Only what you *did*, Leo, for your cousin, for your king. For your mother too. Actions are what count. Love is a verb, after all, isn't it?

And I love you, not just in what I say, but also in what I do. I believe in you. I think you'll make a wonderful king. And…' she took a breath, laying it all out there, needing to, *wanting* to '…and a wonderful husband. And father. If I ever get the chance to know—'

'Oh, Phoebe…' Leo shook his head, his voice breaking.

'Love is an action,' Phoebe continued steadily, 'and it's also a choice. I choose to love you. All of you, all the mess and mistakes and regrets, and all the wonderful parts too.' She was close enough now to touch him, so she did, reaching up to slide her hands along his shoulders and then up to cup his face. 'I love the man you are with my child. I love that you thought about his needs, even when no one asked you to, when no one was looking. I love the way your eyes gleam with laughter when you talk to him…and I love the way you look at me when we're making love. Love,' she emphasised, drawing him closer—so thankful he didn't resist. 'I love you.'

Leo rested his forehead against hers, his breathing ragged and uneven. They were silent for a long moment, breathing each other's air, sharing each other's strength. Phoebe waited; she knew what she wanted from Leo, but she didn't want to ask. She'd trust instead.

'I love you,' Leo finally murmured; it was a confession. Phoebe closed her eyes in relief. 'I love you,' he said again, stronger now, 'but I never thought you could— truly—love me.'

'I do.'

Leo shook his head, pulling away a little bit. 'I can hardly believe it. There's no reason—'

'I told you the reasons.' Phoebe pulled him closer again, and brushed his lips with hers. 'Although I dare say I can think of a few more.'

Leo kissed her back, a slow and lingering kiss, a kiss that swept away the memories and fears, the guilt and regret, and left only its clean, pure beauty.

Phoebe closed her eyes, resting her cheek against Leo's shoulder, felt the solid comfort of his presence, the joy of his love. Outside the sun had set, and moonlight glittered on the snow. The day had ended, a long, endless day, a day that held years of sorrow and pain in it. That day, she thought as Leo claimed her mouth in a kiss once more, was past.

A new day had begun.

EPILOGUE

IT WAS a beautiful April day, the air crisp and clean, the sky washed a perfect robin's-egg blue after the morning rain. Phoebe stood to the left of Leo, her hand clasped with Christian's, smiling through the misty veil of tears. Happy tears.

Christian wriggled, impatient and uncomfortable in his heavy robe. Phoebe sympathised; her own gown was twenty yards of embroidered satin that had been worn by the last eleven queens of Amarnes…the title she was about to assume, as soon as Leo was crowned.

She watched with pride and joy as the archbishop placed the heavy, ancient crown on his head, the sapphires and rubies sparkling in the sunlight. A cheer rose from the crowd in a swell of pride and joy, an outpouring of love for their new king.

Phoebe had seen it these last few months, felt it whenever she'd gone out in Njardvik. Old women pressed her hand and conferred silent blessings; children brought ragged posies of flowers. Everyone was delighted Leo was king. They were ready for a good king, a loving king. They were ready for King Leopold I.

The ancient rite concluded, Phoebe stepped forward to

accept her own crown, glad she'd used her hair-straightening serum for once, even though Leo liked her hair wild and curly. The crown sat on her smooth knot of hair, huge and heavy, yet it was a weight she bore gladly.

As another prayer was offered for the monarchs' long and prosperous reign, Leo's hand found Phoebe's, his fingers twining with hers.

'All right?' he whispered, glancing in concern at the slight swell of Phoebe's belly. She smiled back at him, one hand coming as it had months before to rest on her middle, almost as if she could feel the pulse of new life with her fingers.

'More than all right,' she whispered back. Another cheer rose from the crowd and, as one, Phoebe and Leo turned to greet their people. 'More than all right,' Phoebe repeated as joy swelled inside her. Christian wriggled his way as he often did to be between them, one hand clasped with each of theirs. 'More, even,' Phoebe whispered, 'than wonder-ful.' Leo glanced at her, one eyebrow arched, a smile hovering about his mouth so Phoebe knew he agreed com-pletely.

Yes, more than wonderful, she thought…in fact, just about perfect.

THE SHEIKH AND THE
CHRISTMAS BRIDE

SUSAN MALLERY

Susan Mallery is a bestselling and award-winning author of more than fifty books. She makes her home in the Los Angeles area with her handsome prince of a husband and her two adorable-but not-bright cats.

Prologue

"This is an impossible situation," King Mukhtar of El Deharia announced as he paced the width of his private chambers.

Princess Lina watched her brother, thinking it would be impossible for him to pace the *length* of his chambers—the room was so big, she would probably lose sight of him. Ah, the trials of being king.

Mukhtar spun back unexpectedly, then stalked toward her. "You smile. Do you find this amusing? I have three sons of marriageable age. *Three!* And has even one of them shown interest in choosing a bride and producing heirs? No. They are too busy with their work. How did I produce such industrious sons? Why aren't they out chasing women and getting girls pregnant? At least then we could force a marriage."

Lina laughed. "You're complaining that your sons are too

hardworking and that they're not playboys? What else is wrong, my brother? Too much money in the treasury? Do the people love you too much? Is the royal crown too heavy?"

"You mock me," he complained.

"As your sister, it is not just my privilege, it's my duty. Someone needs to mock you."

He glared at her, but she was unimpressed. They had grown up together. It was hard to find awe in the man when one had seen the boy with chicken pox.

"This is serious," he told her sternly. "What am I to do? I must have heirs. I should have dozens of grandchildren by now and I have not a single one. Qadir spends his time representing our country to the world. As'ad deals with domestic issues so our people have a thriving economy. Kateb lives his life in the desert, celebrating the old ways." Mukhtar grimaced. "The old ways? What is he thinking?"

"Kateb has always been a bit of a black sheep," Lina reminded the king.

Her brother glared at her. "No son of mine is a sheep. He is powerful and cunning like a lion of the desert or a jackal."

"So he is the black jackal of the family."

"Woman, you will not act this way," Mukhtar roared in a fair imitation of a lion.

Lina remained unimpressed. "Do you see me cowering, brother? Have you ever seen me cowering?"

"No, and you are poorer for it."

She covered her mouth as she pretended to yawn.

His gaze narrowed. "You are intent only on your own amusement? You have no advice for me?"

"I do have advice, but I don't know if you'll like it."

He folded his arms across his chest. "I'm listening."

Not according to his body language, Lina thought humorously. But she was used to her brother being imperious. Having him ask for her advice was a big step for him. She should go with it.

"I have been in communication with King Hassan of Bahania," she said.

"Why?"

She sighed. "This will go much faster if you don't interrupt me every thirty seconds."

Mukhtar raised his eyebrows but didn't speak.

She recognized the slightly stubborn expression. He thought he was being protective and concerned, making sure she was kept safe from the evilness of the world. Right. Because the very handsome king of Bahania was so likely to swoop down and ravish her forty-three-year-old self.

Not that she would say no to a little ravishing, she thought wistfully. Her marriage had ended years before when her beloved husband had died unexpectedly. She'd always meant to remarry and have a family, but somehow that had never happened. She'd been busy being an aunt to Mukhtar's six boys. There had been much to do in the palace. Somehow she'd never found the time...or a man who interested her.

Until Hassan. The widower king was older, but vital and charming. Not to mention, he was the first man who had caught her attention in years. But was he intrigued by her? She just couldn't tell.

"Lina," her brother said impatiently, "how do you know Hassan?"

"What? Oh. He and I spent time together a couple of

years ago at a symposium on education." She'd met the king formally at state events dozens of times, but that had been the first occasion she'd had to speak with him for more than five minutes. "He also has sons and he has been very successful in getting them all married."

That got her brother's interest. "What did he do?"

"He meddled."

Mukhtar stared at her. "You're saying…"

"He got involved in their personal lives. He created circumstances that brought his sons together with women he had picked. Sometimes he set up roadblocks, sometimes he facilitated the relationship. It all went well."

Mukhtar lowered his arms to his sides. "I am the king of El Deharia."

"I know that."

"It would be inappropriate for me to behave in such a manner."

Lina held in a smile—she already knew what was coming. "Of course it would."

"However, you do not have my restrictions of rank and power."

"Isn't that amazing."

"You could get involved. You know my sons very well." His gaze narrowed. "You've been thinking about this for some time, haven't you?"

"I've made a few notes about a couple of women I think would be really interesting for my nephews to get to know."

He smiled slowly. "Tell me everything."

Chapter One

Prince As'ad of El Deharia expected his world to run smoothly. He hired his staff with that expectation, and for the most part, they complied. He enjoyed his work at the palace and his responsibilities. The country was growing, expanding, and he oversaw the development of the infrastructure. It was a compelling vocation that took serious thought and dedication.

Some of his friends from university thought he should use his position as a prince and a sheik to enjoy life, but As'ad did not agree. He didn't have time for frivolity. If he had one weakness, it was his affection for his aunt Lina. Which explained why he agreed to see her when she burst into his offices without an appointment. A decision, he would think many weeks later, that caused him nothing but trouble.

"As'ad," Lina said as she hurried into his office, "you must come at once."

As'ad saved his work on the computer before asking, "What is wrong?"

"Everything." His normally calm aunt was flushed and trembling. "There is trouble at the orphan school. A chieftain is in from the desert. He's demanding he be allowed to take three sisters. People are fighting, the girls don't want to go with him, the teachers are getting involved and one of the nuns is threatening to jump from the roof if you don't come and help."

As'ad rose. "Why me?"

"You're a wise and thoughtful leader," Lina said, not quite meeting his gaze. "Your reputation for fairness makes you the obvious choice."

Or his aunt was playing him, As'ad thought, staring at the woman who had been like a mother to him for most of his life. Lina enjoyed getting her way and she wasn't above using drama to make that happen. Was she this time? Although he couldn't imagine why she would need his help at a school.

She bit her lower lip. "There really *is* trouble. Please come."

Theatrics he could ignore, but a genuine request? Not possible. He walked around his desk and took her arm to lead her out of his office. "We will take my car."

Fifteen minutes later As'ad wished he'd been out of the country when his aunt had gone looking for assistance. The school was in an uproar.

Fifteen or so students huddled in groups, crying loudly. Several teachers tried to comfort them, but they, too, were in tears. An elderly chieftain and his men stood by the window, talking heatedly, while a petite woman with hair the color of fire stood in front of three sobbing girls.

As'ad glanced at his aunt. "No one seems to be on the roof."

"I'm sure things have calmed down," she told him. "Regardless of that detail, you can clearly see there *is* a problem."

He returned his gaze to the woman protecting the girls. "She doesn't look like a nun," he murmured, taking in the long, red hair and the stubborn expression on her face.

"Kayleen is a teacher here," his aunt said, "which is very close to being a nun."

"So you lied to me."

Lina brushed away the accusation with a flick of her hand. "I may have exaggerated slightly."

"You are fortunate we have let go of the old ways," he told his aunt. "The ones that defined a woman's conduct."

His aunt smiled. "You love me too much to ever let harm befall me, As'ad."

Which was true, he thought as he walked into the room.

He ignored the women and children and moved over to the tall old man.

"Tahir," he said, nodding his head in a gesture of respect. "You do not often leave the desert for the city. It is an honor to see you here now. Is your stay a long one?"

Tahir was obviously furious, but he knew his place and bowed. "Prince As'ad. At last a voice of reason. I had hoped to make my journey to the city as brief as possible, but this, this *woman*—" he pointed at the redhead still guarding the children "—seeks to interfere. I am here because of duty. I am here to show the hospitality of the desert. Yet she understands nothing and defies me at every turn."

Tahir's voice shook with outrage and fury. He was not

used to being denied and certainly not by a mere woman. As'ad held in a sigh. He already knew nothing about this was going to be easy.

"I will defy you with my dying breath, if I have to," the teacher in question said, from her corner of the room. "What you want to do is inhuman. It's cruel and I won't allow it." She turned to As'ad and glared at him. "There's nothing you can say or do to make me."

The three girls huddled close to her. They were obviously sisters, with blond hair and similar features. Pretty girls, As'ad thought absently. They would grow into beauties and be much trouble for their father.

Or would have been, he amended, remembering this was an orphanage and that meant the girls had no parents.

"And you are…" he asked, his voice deliberately imperious. His first job was to establish authority and gain control.

"Kayleen James. I'm a teacher here."

She opened her mouth to continue speaking, but As'ad shook his head.

"I will ask the questions," he told her. "You will answer."

"But—"

He shook his head again. "Ms. James, I am Prince As'ad. Is that name familiar to you?"

The young woman glanced from him to his aunt and back. "Yes," she said quietly. "You're in charge of the country or something."

"Exactly. You are here on a work visa?"

She nodded.

"That work visa comes from my office. I suggest you avoid doing anything to make me rethink your place in my country."

She had dozens of freckles on her nose and cheeks. They became more visible as she paled. "You're threatening me," she breathed. "So what? You'll deport me if I don't let that horrible man have his way with these children? Do you know what he is going to do with them?"

Her eyes were large. More green than blue, he thought until fresh tears filled them. Then the blue seemed more predominant.

As'ad could list a thousand ways he would rather be spending his day. He turned to Tahir.

"My friend," he began, "what brings you to this place?"

Tahir pointed at the girls. "They do. Their father was from my village. He left to go to school and never returned, but he was still one of us. Only recently have we learned of his death. With their mother gone, they have no one. I came to take them back to the village."

Kayleen took a step toward the older man. "Where you plan to separate them and have them grow up to be servants."

Tahir shrugged. "They are girls. Of little value. Yet several families in the village have agreed to take in one of them. We honor the memory of their father." He looked at As'ad. "They will be treated well. They will carry my honor with them."

Kayleen raised her chin. "Never!" she announced. "You will never take them. It's not right. The girls only have each other. They deserve to be together. They deserve a chance to have a real life."

As'ad thought longingly of his quiet, organized office and the simple problems of bridge design or economic development that awaited him.

"Lina, stay with the girls," he told his aunt. He pointed at Kayleen. "You—come with me."

Kayleen wasn't sure she could go anywhere. Her whole body shook and she couldn't seem to catch her breath. Not that it mattered. She would gladly give her life to protect her girls.

She opened her mouth to tell Prince As'ad that she wasn't interested in a private conversation, when Princess Lina walked toward her and smiled reassuringly.

"Go with As'ad," her friend told her. "I'll stay with the girls. Nothing will happen to them while you're gone." Lina touched her arm. "As'ad is a fair man. He will listen." She smiled faintly. "Speak freely, Kayleen. You are always at your best when you are most passionate."

What?

Before Kayleen could figure out what Lina meant, As'ad was moving and she found herself hurrying after him. They went across the hall, into an empty classroom. He closed the door behind them, folded his arms across his chest and stared at her intently.

"Start at the beginning," he told her. "What happened here today?"

She blinked. Until this moment, she hadn't really seen As'ad. But standing in front of him meant she had to tip her head back to meet his gaze. He was tall and broad-shouldered, a big, dark-haired man who made her nervous. Kayleen had had little to do with men and she preferred it that way.

"I was teaching," she said slowly, finding it oddly difficult to look into As'ad's nearly black eyes and equally hard to look away. "Pepper—she's the youngest—came running into my classroom to say there was a bad man who wanted to take her away. I found the chieftain holding Dana and Nadine in the hallway." Indignation gave her strength. "He was really holding them. One by each arm. When he saw Pepper, he handed Dana off to one of his henchmen and grabbed her. She's barely eight years old. The girls were crying and struggling. Then he started dragging them away. He said something about taking them to his village."

The rest of it was a blur. Kayleen drew in a breath. "I started yelling, too. Then I sort of got between the chieftain and the stairway. I might have attacked him." Shame filled her. To act in such a way went against everything she believed. How many times had she been told she must accept life as it was and attempt change through prayer and conversation and demonstrating a better way herself?

Kayleen desperately wanted to believe that, but sometimes a quick kick in the shin worked, too.

One corner of As'ad's mouth twitched. "You hit Tahir?"

"I kicked him."

"What happened then?"

"His men came after me and grabbed me. Which I didn't like, but it was okay because the girls were released. They were screaming and I was screaming and the other teachers came into the hall. It was a mess."

She squared her shoulders, knowing she had to make As'ad understand why that man couldn't take the girls away.

"You can't let him do this," she said. "It's wrong on every level. They've lost both their parents. They need each other. They need me."

"You're just their teacher."

"In name, but we're close. I live here, too. I read to them every night, I talk to them." They were like her family, which made them matter more than anything. "They're so young. Dana, the oldest, is only eleven. She's bright and funny and she wants to be a doctor. Nadine is nine. She's a gifted dancer. She's athletic and caring. Little Pepper can barely remember her mother. She needs her sisters around her. They *need* to be together."

"They would be in the same village," As'ad said.

"But not the same house." She *had* to make him understand. "Tahir talks about how people in the village are *willing* to take in the girls. As if they would be a hardship. Isn't it better to leave them here where they have friends and are loved? Where they can grow up with a connection to each other and their past? Do you know what he would do to them?"

"Nothing," As'ad said flatly, in a voice that warned her not to insult his people. "He has given them his honor. They would be protected. Anyone who attacked them would pay with his life."

Okay, that made her feel better, but it wasn't enough. "What about the fact that they won't be educated? They won't have a chance. Their mother was American."

"Their father was born here, in El Deharia. He, too, was an orphan and Tahir's village raised him. They honor his memory by taking in his three daughters."

"To be servants."

As'ad hesitated. "It is their likely fate."

"Then he can't have them."

"The decision is not yours to make."

"Then you make it," she told him, wanting to give him a quick kick to the shins, as well. She loved El Deharia.

The beautiful country took her breath away every time she went into the desert. She loved the people, the kindness, the impossible blue of the skies. But there was still an expectation that men knew better. "Do you have children, Prince As'ad?"

"No."

"Sisters?"

"Five brothers."

"If you had a sister, would you want her to be taken away and made a servant? Would you have wanted one of your brothers ripped from his family?"

"These are not your siblings," he told her.

"I know. They're more like my children. They've only been here a few months. Their mother died a year ago and their father brought them back here. When he was killed, they entered the orphanage. I'm the one who sat with them night after night as they sobbed out their pain. I'm the one who held them through the nightmares, who coaxed them to eat, who promised things would get better."

She drew herself up to her full five feet three inches and squared her shoulders. "You talk of Tahir's honor. Well, I gave my word that they would have a good life. If you allow that man to take them away, my word means nothing. I mean nothing. Are you so heartless that you would shatter the hopes and dreams of three little girls who have already lost both their parents?"

As'ad could feel a headache coming on.

Kayleen James stated her case well. Under other circumstances, he would have allowed her to keep the children at the school and be done with it. But this was not a simple case.

"Tahir is a powerful chieftain," he said. "To offend him over such a small matter is foolish."

"Small matter? Because they're girls? Is that it? If these were boys, the matter would be large?"

"The gender of the children is immaterial. The point is Tahir has made a generous gesture from what he considers a position of honor. To have that thrown in his face could have political consequences."

"We're talking about children's *lives*. What is politics when compared with that?"

The door to the classroom opened and Lina stepped inside. Kayleen gasped. "He has the girls?"

"Of course not. They've gone back to their rooms while Tahir and his men take tea with the director." Lina looked at As'ad. "What have you decided?"

"That I should not allow you into my office when you do not have an appointment."

Lina smiled. "You could never refuse me, As'ad. Just as I could never send you away."

He held in a groan. So his aunt had taken sides. Why was he not surprised? She had always been soft-hearted and loving—something he had appreciated after the death of his own mother. But now, he found the trait inconvenient.

"Tahir is powerful. To offend him over this makes no sense," he said.

Lina surprised him by saying, "I agree."

Kayleen shrieked. "Princess Lina, no! You know these girls. They deserve more."

Lina touched her arm. "They shall have more. As'ad is right. Tahir should not leave feeling as if his generous offer has been snubbed. Kayleen, you may not agree with what he's trying to do, but believe me, his motives are pure."

Kayleen looked anything but convinced, yet she nodded slowly.

Lina turned to As'ad. "The only way Tahir can save face in this is to have the children taken by someone more powerful who is willing to raise them and honor the memory of their father."

"Agreed," As'ad said absently. "But who would—"

"You."

He stared at his aunt. "You would have me take three orphan girls as my own?" It was unbelievable. It was impossible. It was just like Lina.

"As'ad, the palace has hundreds of rooms. What would it matter if three girls occupied a suite? You wouldn't have to deal with them. They would have your protection as they grew. If nothing else, the king might be momentarily distracted by the presence of three almost-grandchildren."

The idea had merit, As'ad thought. His father's attempts to marry off his sons had become unbearable. There were constant parades of eligible young women. An excuse to avoid the events was worth much.

As'ad knew it was his duty to marry and produce heirs, yet he had always resisted any emotional involvement. Perhaps because he knew emotion made a man weak. His father had told him as much the night the queen had died. When As'ad had asked why the king did not cry, his father explained that to give in to feelings was to be less of a man.

As'ad had tried to learn the lesson as well as he could. As a marriage of convenience had never appealed to him, he was left with the annoyance of dealing with an angry monarch who wanted heirs.

"But who would care for the girls?" he asked. "The children can't raise themselves."

"Hire a nanny. Hire Kayleen." Lina shrugged. "She already has a relationship with the girls. They care for her and she cares for them."

"Wait a minute," Kayleen said. "I have a job. I'm a teacher here."

Lina looked at her. "Did you or did you not give the girls your word that their life would get better? What are you willing to do to keep your word? You would still be a teacher, but on a smaller scale. With three students. Perhaps there would even be time for you to teach a few classes here."

The last thing As'ad wanted was to adopt three children he knew nothing about. While he'd always planned on a family, the idea was vague, in the future, and it included sons. Still, it was a solution. Tahir would not stand in the way of a prince taking the children. And as Lina had pointed out, it would buy time with his father. He could not be expected to find a bride while adjusting to a new family.

He looked at Kayleen. "You would have to be solely responsible for the girls. You would be given all the resources you require, but I have no interest in their day-to-day lives."

"I haven't even agreed to this," she told him.

"Yet you were the one willing to do anything to keep the sisters together."

"It would be a wonderful arrangement," Lina told Kayleen. "Just think. The girls would be raised in a palace. There would be so many opportunities for them. Dana could go to the best university. Nadine would have access to wonderful dance teachers. And little Pepper wouldn't have to cry herself to sleep every night."

Kayleen bit her lower lip. "It sounds good." She turned to As'ad. "You'd have to give your word that they would never be turned out or made into servants or married off for political gain."

"You insult me with your mistrust." The audacity of her statements was right in keeping with what he'd seen of her personality, but it was important to establish control before things began.

"I don't know you," she said.

"I am Prince As'ad of El Deharia. That is all you need to know."

Lina smiled at her. "As'ad is a good man, Kayleen."

As'ad resented that his aunt felt the need to speak for his character. Women, he thought with mild annoyance. They were nothing but trouble.

Kayleen looked him in the eye. "You have to give your word that you'll be a good father, caring more for their welfare than your own. You'll love them and listen to them and not marry them off to anyone *they* don't love."

What was it with women and love? he wondered. They worried too much about a fleeting emotion that had no value.

"I will be a good father," he said. "I will care for them and see that they are raised with all the privileges that go with being the daughter of a prince."

Kayleen frowned. "That wasn't what I asked."

"It is what I offer."

Kayleen hesitated. "You have to promise not to marry them off to someone they don't care about."

Such foolish worries, he thought, then nodded. "They may pick their own husbands."

"And go to college and not be servants."

"I have said they will be as my daughters, Ms. James. You test my patience."

She stared at him. "I'm not afraid of you." She considered for a second.

"I can see that. You will be responsible for them. Do as you see fit with them." He glanced at his aunt. "Are we finished here?"

She smiled, her eyes twinkling in a way that made him wonder what else she had planned for him. "I'm not sure, As'ad," she told him. "In a way I think we're just beginning."

Chapter Two

Kayleen wouldn't have thought it was possible for her life to change so quickly. That morning she'd awakened in her narrow bed in a small room at the orphanage. If she stood in the right place and leaned all the way over, she could see a bit of garden out of her tiny window, but mostly the view was a stone wall. Now she followed Princess Lina into an impossibly large suite in a palace that overlooked the Arabian Sea.

"This can't be right," Kayleen murmured as she turned in a slow circle, taking in the three sofas, the carved dining table, the ornate decorations, the wide French doors leading out to a balcony and the view of the water beyond. "These rooms are too nice."

Lina smiled. "It's a palace, my dear. Did you think we had ugly rooms?"

"Obviously not." Kayleen glanced at the three girls

huddled together. "But this stuff is *really* nice. Kids can be hard on furniture."

"I assure you, these pieces have seen far more than you can imagine. All will be well. Come this way. I have a delightful surprise."

Kayleen doubted any surprise could beat a return address sticker that said El Deharian Royal Palace but she was willing to be wrong. She gently pushed the girls in front of her as they moved down the hallway.

Lina paused in front of a massive door, then pushed it open. "I didn't have much time to get things in order, so it's not complete just yet. But it's a start."

The "start" was a room the size of a small airport, with soaring ceilings and big windows that let in the light. Three double beds didn't begin to fill the space. There were armoires and desks and comforters in pretty pastels. Big, fluffy stuffed animals sat on each bed, along with a robe, nightgowns and slippers. Each of the girls' school backpacks sat at the foot of her bed.

"Laptop computers are on order for the girls," Lina said. "There's a big TV back in the living room, behind the cabinet doors. There are a few DVDs for the girls, but we'll get more. In time, we can move you to a different suite, one with a bedroom for each of the girls, but for now I thought they'd be more comfortable together."

Kayleen couldn't believe it. The room was perfect. Bright and cheerful, filled with color. There was an air of welcome, as if the space had been hoping for three girls to fill it.

Dana turned around and stared at her. "Really? This is for us?"

Kayleen laughed. "You'd better take it, because if you don't want it, I'll move in."

It was the permission they needed. The three girls went running around the room, examining everything. Every few seconds one of them yelled, "Look at this," because there was so much to see.

A ballerina lamp for Nadine, a throw covered with teddy bears for Pepper. Dana's bed had a bookcase next to it. Kayleen turned to Princess Lina.

"You're amazing."

"I have resources and I'm not afraid to use them," her friend told her. "This was fun. I don't get to act imperious very often and send servants scuttling to do my bidding. Besides, we all enjoyed pulling this together in a couple of hours. Come on. Let's go see where you'll sleep."

Kayleen followed Lina past a large bathroom with a tub big enough to swim in, to a short hallway that ended in a beautiful room done in shades of green and pale yellow.

The furniture was delicately carved and feminine. The bedcovering was a botanical print that suited her much better than ruffles and frills. The attached bathroom was more luxurious than any she'd ever seen.

"It's silk," she whispered, fingering the luxurious drapes. "What if I spill something?"

"Then the cleaners will be called," Lina told her. "Relax. You'll adjust. This is your home now that you're a part of As'ad's life."

Something else that just plain wasn't right, Kayleen thought. How could she be a part of a sheik's life? Make that a sheik *prince?*

"Not a happy part," she murmured. "He didn't want to help."

"But he did and isn't that what matters?"

Kayleen nodded, but her head was spinning. There was too much to think about. Too much had happened too quickly.

"Our bags! Kayleen, hurry! Our bags are here."

Kayleen and Lina returned to the main room to watch as their suitcases were unloaded. The pile had looked so huge at the orphanage, but here it seemed small and shabby.

Lina lightly touched her arm. "Get settled. I'll have dinner sent up. Things will look better in the morning."

"They look fine now," Kayleen told her, almost meaning it. "We live in a palace. What's not to like?"

Lina laughed. "Good attitude." She held out her arms and the sisters rushed to her for a hug. "I will see all of you in the morning. Welcome to the palace."

With that, she was gone. As the door to their suite closed behind her, Kayleen felt a whisper of unease. A palace? How could that be home?

She glanced at the girls and saw fear and apprehension in their eyes. It was one thing for her to worry, but they shouldn't have to. They'd already been through so much.

She glanced at her watch, then looked back at the girls. "I think we need to give the new TV a test drive. Here's the deal. Whoever gets unpacked first, and that means putting things neatly in the armoire, not just throwing them, gets to pick the movie. Start in five, four, three, two, one. Go!"

All three sisters shrieked and raced for their bedroom.

"I can go fastest," Pepper yelled as she crouched down in front of her suitcase and opened it.

"No way," Dana told her. "I'm going to win because you'll pick a stupid cartoon. I'm too old for that."

Kayleen smiled at the familiar argument, then her smile

faded. Dana was all of eleven and in such a hurry to grow up. Kayleen suspected the reason had a whole lot to do with being able to take care of her sisters.

"That's going to change," she whispered, then returned to her room to unpack her own suitcases. Lina had promised that Prince As'ad could be trusted. He'd given his word that he would raise the girls as his own. That meant they were safe. But, after all they'd been through, how long would it take them to feel that way?

The evening passed quickly. Dinner was sent up on an elegant rolling table and contained plenty of comfort foods for lost, lonely children. Kayleen piled everyone on the largest sofa and they watched *The Princess Diaries,* then compared the differences in the movie castle and the real-live palace they'd moved into. By nine all three of them were asleep and Kayleen found herself alone as she wandered the length of the beautiful suite.

She paused by the French doors leading onto the balcony, then stepped out into the warm night.

Lights from the shoreline allowed her to see the movement of the waves as they rolled onto the beach. The inky darkness of the water stretched to the horizon. The air was warm and salty, the night unexpectedly still.

She leaned against the railing and stared into the sky. What was she doing here? This wasn't her world. She could never in a million years have imagined—

The sound of a door opening caused her to turn. She saw a shadow move and take the shape of a man. Fear gripped her then, as quickly as it had come, faded. But she *should* be afraid, she told herself. He could be anyone.

But he wasn't, she realized as he stepped into the light. He was Prince As'ad.

He was as tall and broad as she remembered. Handsome, in a distant sort of way. The kind of man who intimidated without trying. She wondered if she should slip back into her own rooms before he saw her. Perhaps she wasn't supposed to be out here. Then his dark gaze found her.

"Good evening," he said. "You and the girls are settled?"

She nodded. "Thank you. The rooms are great. Your aunt thought of everything to make us feel at home." She looked up at the imposing structure of the palace. "Sort of."

He moved toward her. "It's just a really big house, Kayleen. Do not let the size or history intimidate you."

"As long as none of the statuary comes alive in the night and tries to chase us out."

"I assure you, our statuary is most well-behaved."

She smiled. "Thanks for the reassurance. No offense, but I doubt I'll sleep well for the next couple of nights."

"I hope that changes quickly." He shrugged out of his suit jacket. "If you find my aunt forgot something, let someone on the staff know."

"Sure." Because every palace had a staff. And a king. And princes. "What do we call you? The girls and I. Your Highness? Prince As'ad?"

"You may all use my first name."

"Really? And they won't chop off my head for that?"

One corner of his mouth twitched. "Not for many years now." He loosened his tie, then pulled it free.

Kayleen watched for a second, then looked away. He wasn't undressing, she told herself. The man had the right to get comfortable after a long day of…of…being a prince. This was his balcony. She was the one who didn't belong.

"You are uneasy," he said.

She blinked. "How did you figure that out?"

"You are not difficult to read."

Great. She had the sudden thought she wanted to be mysterious and interesting. Mostly interesting. Like *that* was going to happen.

"A lot has changed in a short period of time," she told him. "This morning I woke up in my usual bed in the orphanage. Tonight I'm here."

"And before you lived in El Deharia? Where did you sleep?"

She smiled. "In the Midwest. It's very different. No ocean. No sand. It's a lot colder. It's already November. Back home the leaves would be gone and we'd be bracing for the first snowfall. Here, it's lovely."

"One of the great pleasures of the most perfect place on earth."

"You think El Deharia is perfect?"

"Don't you think the same of your birthplace?"

Not really, she thought. But they came from very different circumstances. "I guess," she murmured, then felt awkward. "I was a teacher there, too," she added, to change the subject. "I've always loved children."

"Which makes your employment more enjoyable," he said. "I would imagine a teacher who dislikes children would have a difficult time."

Was he being funny? She thought he might be, but wasn't sure. Did princes have a sense of humor? She'd assumed being royal meant being serious all the time.

"Yes, that was a joke," he said, proving she was as readable as he said. "You are allowed to laugh in my presence. Although I would suggest you are sure I'm being humorous. To laugh at the wrong time is a grave mistake most people only make once."

"And we're back to the head-chopping. You're not like anyone I've ever met."

"Not many princes in the Midwest?"

"No. Not even rock stars, which in my country are practically the same thing."

"I have never been fond of leather pants on a man."

That did make her laugh. "You could be considered fashion forward."

"Or foolish."

"You wouldn't like that," she said without thinking, then covered her mouth. Oops.

Something flickered in his gaze. He folded his arms. "Perhaps a safer topic would be the three sisters you insisted I adopt."

"What about them?" Had he changed his mind? She would hold him to his promise, no matter how nervous he made her.

"They will have to change schools. The orphanage is too far away. The American School is closer."

"Oh. You're right." She hadn't thought that part through. "I'll get them registered in the morning." She hesitated. "What do I tell the administrator?"

"The truth. They are my adopted daughters and are to be treated as such."

"Bowing and scraping?"

He studied her. "You're an interesting combination of rabbit and desert cat. Fearful and fearless."

She liked the sound of that. "I'm working to be all fearless. I still have a ways to go."

He reached out and before she realized what he

intended, he touched a strand of her hair. "There is fire in your blood."

"Because I'm a redhead? I think that's just an old wives' tale." She'd always wanted to be a cool blonde, or a sexy brunette. Well, maybe not sexy. That wasn't her style.

"I know many old wives who are wise," he murmured, then released her. "You will be responsible for the girls when they are not in school."

She nodded, wishing they were still talking about her being brave and that he was still touching her hair. Which was strange. Prince As'ad was nothing more to her than her employer. A very handsome, *powerful* employer who could trace his lineage back a few thousand years. She didn't even know who her father was.

"What are you thinking?" he asked.

She told him the truth.

"And your mother?"

Kayleen regretted the change in topic. "I, um, don't really remember her. She left me with my grandmother when I was a baby. She took care of me for a few years, then left me at an orphanage." She gave a little shrug as if the rejection hadn't mattered. "She was older and I was a handful."

In the darkness it was difficult to read As'ad's expression. She reminded herself there was no reason to be ashamed of her past—she hadn't been able to control it. Yet she felt as if she were being judged and found wanting.

"Is that the reason you defended the girls so fiercely?" he asked. "Your own past?"

"Maybe."

He nodded slowly. "They live here now. As do you. You are all to consider the palace your home."

If only. "Easier said than done," she murmured.

"It will be an adjustment. Although it would be best if they did not roller-skate down the hallways."

"I'll make sure of that."

"Good. You will want to learn about the palace. There is much interesting history here. Perhaps you and the girls should take one of the daily tours."

She stared at him. "Tours? People come here and take tours?"

"Only of the public rooms. The private quarters are off-limits. There are security people on duty. You are safe here."

She wasn't worried about being safe. It was the idea of living somewhere grand enough to have tours that made her mouth go dry.

"What does your family think of this?" she asked. "Will anyone be angry?"

He seemed to grow taller. "I am Prince As'ad of El Deharia. No one questions my actions."

"Not even the king?" she asked.

"My father will be pleased to see me settling down. He is anxious for his sons to start a family."

Kayleen had a feeling adopting three American sisters wasn't exactly what King Mukhtar had in mind.

"You said you have brothers," she said.

"I am one of six," he said. "They are in and out of the palace. Kateb lives in the desert, but the others keep rooms here."

Six princes, one princess, one king and her. What was wrong with this picture?

"You will be fine," he said.

"Would you stop knowing what I'm thinking? It's not fair."

He shrugged. "I am gifted. It can't be helped."

"Apparently not." He also seemed to have no problems with his ego. What would it be like to grow up so confident, so sure about everything, including his place in the world?

"Kayleen, you are here because of me," he said, his voice low and mesmerizing. "My name is all the protection you require. It can be used as a shield or a weapon, however you prefer."

"I can't imagine using it as either," she admitted.

"It is there for you. Know that. Know no harm can befall you while you are under my care." He looked at her. "Good night."

Then he turned and was gone.

Kayleen stared after him, feeling as if she'd just had a close encounter with a character from a book or a movie. Who said things like "My name is all the protection you require"? Yet, he was telling the truth. She believed that down to her bones.

No one had ever taken care of her before. No one had ever protected her.

Oh, sure, the nuns had always made sure their charges were safe, but that was different. This was specific.

She hugged her arms across her chest, as if feeling the comforting weight of his protection. As if feeling the strength of the man himself.

It felt good.

As'ad walked into the king's offices the next day and nodded at Robert, his personal assistant.

"Go right in, sir," Robert said with a smile. "The king is expecting you."

As'ad walked through the double doors and greeted his father.

"I hear you have taken in a family," his father said from his seat behind his impressive desk. "Lina tells me you are to adopt three orphans. I did not know you cared for such causes."

As'ad took one of the chairs opposite the desk and shook his head. "It is all Lina's doing. She insisted I go to the orphanage to prevent a nun from jumping off a roof."

"A what from what?"

"Never mind. There was no nun. Only a teacher."

A small kitten who had spit in fury and outrage. He smiled at the memory of Kayleen's determination.

"Three American girls were there," he said. "Their father was born here. When their mother died, he brought them back and then he was killed. Tahir heard of their situation and wanted to take them back to his village."

"Admirable," the king said. "Three orphaned girls would be of no value. Tahir is a good man."

"Yes, well, their teacher didn't share your admiration. She insisted the girls could not be separated, nor could they give up their education to be servants."

"Without family, what choice did the girls have? Tahir would have given them the honor of his name."

"I agree," As'ad said. "Yet that, too, was lost on their teacher. She attacked Tahir."

The king's eyebrows rose. "She lives?"

"She's small and apparently did him no harm."

"She is lucky he didn't insist on punishing her."

"I suspect he was pleased to find a way out of the situation."

"So you solved the problem by taking the girls."

"Yes, and their teacher, who will be responsible for them." He looked at his father. "They are charming girls," he said, hoping it was true. "Almost like granddaughters for you."

The king stroked his beard. "Then I will visit them and their teacher. As'ad, you did the right thing. This pleases me. Obviously you are settling down as you grow older. Well done."

"Thank you, Father."

As'ad kept his voice respectful. Lina was right. Now As'ad would be spared the royal matchmaking for a while.

"What is she like, this teacher?" the king asked. "Is she of good character?"

"Lina thinks so." He was nearly convinced himself. Her sad history could have made her hard or bitter. Instead she led with her heart.

"Have you any interest in her yourself?"

As'ad stared at his father. "In what way?"

"As a wife. We already know she likes children and is willing to face a chieftain to protect her charges. Is she pretty? Would she do for one of your brothers?"

As'ad frowned. Pretty? Kayleen? "She is not unattractive," he said slowly, remembering how she'd looked the previous night with her long hair glowing like fire. "There is a spark in her. A pureness."

Pureness? Where had *that* thought come from?

"I wonder what she thinks of the desert," the king mused. "Perhaps she would do for Kateb."

"She would not," As'ad said sharply, suddenly irritated, although he could not say why. "Besides, I need her to care for my daughters. Find my brothers' brides elsewhere."

"As you wish," the king said easily. "As you wish."

* * *

As'ad stared at the three bridge proposals in front of him. While each provided the necessary access, they couldn't be more different. The cheapest bid offered a utilitarian design while the other two had an architectural element that would add to the beauty of the city. There were—

His phone buzzed. He stared at it a second, then pushed the intercom. "I said I was not to be disturbed."

"I understand, sir. Your orders were very clear." His normally calm assistant sounded…flustered. "It's just, there's someone here to see you. A young woman. Kayleen James. She says she is the nanny for your children?"

The slight rise in Neil's voice probably came from the fact that he wasn't aware As'ad *had* any children.

"I'll explain it all later," As'ad told him. "Send her in."

Seconds later Kayleen walked into his office. As she moved across the open space, he took in the plain brown dress that covered her from the neck to down past her knees, and the flat, sensible shoes. She'd pulled her hair back in a braid. Her pale skin looked bare, and although her eyes were large, she did nothing to enhance her features. Even her earrings, tiny gold crosses, provided little adornment.

He was used to women who took the time and made the effort to be as beautiful as possible. Women who dressed in silk, who showed skin, who smelled of enticing perfumes and glittered with diamonds. Did Kayleen not care for such adornments or had she not had the opportunity to dress that way?

She could, he acknowledged, easily transform herself

into a beauty. The basics were already in place—the perfect bone structure in her face, the large eyes, the full mouth.

Without meaning to, he imagined her wearing nothing at all. Pale and soft, covered only by her long hair, a naked temptress who—

"Thank you for seeing me," Kayleen said, interrupting the erotic image that had no place in his head. "I guess I should have made an appointment."

"Not at all," he said as he came to his feet and motioned toward a sofa in the corner. "How can I help you?"

She sat down. "You're very polite."

"Thank you."

She smoothed the front of her dress. "The palace is really big. I got lost twice and had to ask directions."

"I can get you a map."

She smiled. "For real or are you teasing?"

"Both. There is a map of the palace. Would you like one?"

"I think I need it. And maybe a computer chip implant so security can find me." She looked uneasy as she glanced around the room. "This is nice. Big, but I guess that comes with being a prince."

He couldn't tell if she was just nervous or stalling. "Kayleen, is there a reason for your visit?"

"What? Oh. Right. I enrolled the girls in the American School this morning. It all went well. I used your name."

He smiled. "Bowing and scraping?"

"Some. Everyone was very eager to help. And to have me tell you they helped. That part is weird. You're probably used to it."

"I am."

"The school is great. Big and modern with a real focus

on academics. Not that the orphan school is terrible. If they had more funding…" She sighed. "Asking about that is probably inappropriate."

"Will knowing that stop you from asking?"

She considered for a second. "Not really."

"I will see if funds can be made available."

Her eyes widened. "Just like that?"

"I have made no promises. But I'm sure a few dollars could be found."

"That would be great. We're not working with a big budget over there, so anything would help. Most of the teachers live in, which means the salaries aren't huge."

He doubted they would ever be huge. Teachers didn't choose their profession in an effort to amass a personal fortune. He frowned.

"Why did *you* become a teacher?" he asked.

"Because I couldn't be a nun."

An answer he never would have expected. "Did you want to be a nun?"

Kayleen nodded slowly. "Very much. The orphanage my grandmother took me to was run by nuns. They were wonderful to me. I wanted to be just like them. But I don't really have the right personality."

"Too outspoken?"

"Too…everything. I'm opinionated, I have a temper, I have trouble with the rules sometimes."

She seemed so quiet and mousy in her baggy brown dress, but there was something in her eyes, a spark that told him she was telling the truth. After all, she had attacked Tahir.

He'd never met an almost-nun before. Why would a pretty woman want to lock herself away from the world?

"Our Mother Superior suggested I go into teaching,"

Kayleen continued. "It was a great idea. I love it. I love the children. I wanted to take a permanent position there, but she insisted I first see the world. That's how I ended up here. Eventually, I'll go back."

"To the convent school?"

She nodded.

"What about a husband and a family?"

Kayleen ducked her head, but not before he saw her blush. "I don't really expect that to happen to me. I don't date. Men are… They don't think of me that way."

He recalled his earlier fantasy about seeing her naked. "You would be surprised," he murmured.

She looked up. "I don't think so."

"So there has never been anyone special?"

"A boyfriend?" She shook her head. "No."

She was in her midtwenties. How was that possible? Did such innocence truly exist? Yet why would she lie about such a thing?

He found himself wanting to show her the world she'd been avoiding. To take her places.

Ridiculous, he told himself. She was nothing to him. Only the children's nanny.

Chapter Three

Kayleen backed out of the kitchen, her hands up in front of her, palms out. "No really. I mean it. Everything we have is terrific. I love the food. I've gained three pounds."

When she could no longer see the head chef's furious expression, she turned and hurried to the closest staircase, then ran up to a safer floor.

She'd only been offering to help, she told herself. But her offer of assistance had been taken as an insult.

With the girls gone all day and a kindly worded but clear letter from the orphan school saying it would be too awkward to have her teaching there, now that she was under Prince As'ad's "protection," Kayleen had nothing to do with her time. Sitting around was boring. She needed to keep busy with *something*. She couldn't clean the suite she and the girls lived in. There wasn't even a vacuum in the closet.

She wandered down the main hallway, then paused to figure out where she was. The wide doorways looked familiar. Still, what would it hurt to have a few "you are here" maps to guide newcomers?

She turned another corner and recognized the official royal offices. In a matter of minutes she was standing in front of As'ad's assistant, Neil.

"I really need to see him," she said.

"You do not have an appointment."

"I'm his nanny." It was a bluff. She was staff and she had a feeling that all staff needed an appointment.

"I'm aware of who you are, Ms. James. But Prince As'ad is very particular about his schedule."

Neil was British, so the word sounded like "shed-ule."

The door to As'ad's office opened. "Neil, I need you to find—" He saw Kayleen. "How convenient. You're the one I'm looking for."

Guilt flooded her. "Is it the chef? I didn't mean to insult him. I was only trying to help."

His gaze narrowed. "What did you do?"

She tucked her hands behind her back. "Nothing."

"Why don't I believe you? Come inside, Kayleen. Start at the beginning and leave nothing out."

She glanced longingly at the exit, but followed As'ad into his office. When they were both seated, he looked at her expectantly.

She sucked in a breath. "I went down to the kitchen. I thought I could maybe help out there. I didn't mean anything by it. I'm bored. I need to do *something*."

She stopped talking and pressed her lips together to hold in a sudden rush of emotion. *Need*—there was the word that mattered. She had to be needed.

"You have your three charges," he said. "Many would find that enough."

"Oh, please. They're in school for hours at a time. Someone else cooks, cleans and I'm guessing does our laundry. So what do I do the rest of the time?"

"Shop?"

"With what? Are you paying me? We never discussed a salary. Are there benefits? Do I have a dental plan? One minute I was minding my own business, doing my job, and the next I was here. It's not an easy adjustment."

One corner of his mouth twitched. "If I remember correctly, you assaulted a chieftain. Not exactly minding your own business."

She didn't want to talk about that. "You know what I mean."

"I do. Tell me, Kayleen. What did you teach?"

"Math," she said absently as she stood up and crossed to the window. As'ad's view was of a beautiful garden. She didn't know anything about plants, but she could learn. Maybe the gardener needed some help.

"Advanced?"

"Some."

"You're comfortable with statistical analysis?"

"Uh-huh." What were the pink flowers? They were stunning.

"Then I have a project for you."

She turned. "You want me to do your taxes?"

"No. I want you to work with the education minister. While many girls from the rural villages are graduating from high school and going on to college, the number is not as great as we would like. For El Deharia to grow as

a nation, we must have all our citizens educated and pro-
ductive. I want you to find out which villages are sending
the most girls to college, then figure out what they're
doing right so we can use that information to help the
other villages. Does that interest you?"

She crossed back to the sofa. "You're serious? You're
not just offering me this to keep me busy?"

"You have my word. This is vital information. I trust
you to get it right."

He spoke with a low, steady voice that seemed to pull
her closer. There was something in his eyes that made her
want to believe him.

Excitement grew inside of her. It was a project she could
throw herself into, and still have plenty of time for the girls.
It would be challenging and interesting and meaningful.

She rushed toward him. "I'd love to do it. Thank you."

She leaned forward impulsively, then stopped herself.
What was the plan? To hug him? One did not idly hug a
prince and she didn't go around hugging men.

She straightened and took a step back, not sure if she
should apologize or pretend it never happened. As'ad rose
and crossed to his desk. Apparently he was going to ignore
what she'd almost done. Or he hadn't noticed.

"Then we are agreed," he said. "You'll report your
progress to me in weekly meetings." He opened a desk
drawer and pulled out a credit card. "Use this to get yourself
a laptop and printer. Your suite already has Internet access."

She hesitated before taking the card. No one had ever
offered her a credit card before. She fingered the slim
plastic. "I'll, um, make sure I get a bargain."

"You don't have to. Kayleen, do you have any idea how
wealthy I am?"

"Not really," she admitted.

"You don't need to shop for a bargain."

But she would. She would be responsible with his money, even if he didn't care.

"Okay. I'll get right on ordering one."

He studied her for a moment. "You may also use that to shop for yourself and the girls."

"We don't need anything."

"You will. Clothes wear out. Even my limited knowledge of children tells me they grow and require new clothes."

"You're right." She stared at the card. "You're also very kind."

"I am not. My daughters deserve the best because of who I am."

"You don't have a self-esteem crisis, do you?" she asked, both amused and envious.

"No. I am clear on my place in the world."

Must be nice, she thought longingly.

"You belong here, as well," he told her.

Because he was once again reading her mind? "Not really."

"If I say it is so, it is."

"Thank you" seemed the right response. He was being kind. The truth was, she didn't belong here at all. She was just staff and easily replaceable.

She turned to leave, but he called her back.

"I'll get you information on your salary and benefits," he said. "I should have taken care of that before."

She smiled. "You're a prince. I guess you're not into details."

"You're very understanding. Thank you."

"You're welcome."

His dark gaze caught hers. She told herself it was okay to go now, that they were done. But she couldn't seem to pull away. She felt a powerful need to move closer, to…to… She wasn't sure what, but *something*.

The phone rang. He glanced down and she was able to move again. As much as she wanted to stay, she forced herself to walk out of the office.

"We're making progress," Lina said as she curled up on her bed and held the phone close.

"There is no 'we,'" Hassan told her. "You are in this on your own."

"That's not true. This was all your idea. You're in this as deeply as I am."

"You're a very difficult woman."

"I know." She smiled. "It's part of my charm."

"You *are* charming."

She squeezed her eyes shut and did her best not to scream. Not only wasn't it fitting her position, but she was forty-three. Forty-three-year-old women didn't go around screaming because a handsome man flirted with them on the phone. Even if that handsome man was the king of Bahania.

"Kayleen really likes As'ad," she continued. "She's having a little trouble adjusting to the palace, but who wouldn't? Still, she's doing well. He came and talked to me about making sure she had a salary and benefits. He wants to be generous. That's something."

"You may be reading too much into what he says."

"I hope not. She would be good for him. He always holds back his emotions. I blame his father for that."

"How refreshing," Hassan said dryly. "One usually blames the mother."

She laughed. "Speaking as a woman, I would say that needs to change."

"This is my favorite part of our conversations. The sound of your laughter."

Her heartbeat went from normal to hyperdrive in two seconds. Good thing she was lying down—otherwise, she would have fallen.

"It is as beautiful as the rest of you." He paused. "Have I startled you with my confession?"

"Um, no. It's fine. I mean, thank you."

He sighed. "How much of this awkwardness is because I am a king and how much of it is because I am so much older?"

"None of it is because you're the king," she said without thinking.

His short "I see" had her backpedaling.

"No, no. It's not about your age. I just wasn't sure… We've never really talked about… I thought we were friends."

"We are. Do you wish us to be more?"

Oh, my. Talk about putting it all out there.

Lina clutched the phone and told herself to keep breathing. She was terrified to tell the truth, to admit that she thought about him a whole lot more than she should. What if he wanted to know so he could let her down gently?

"Hassan," she began, then stopped.

"I would like us to be more than friends," he said. "Does that information make things easier or harder for you?"

She exhaled. "Easier. A lot easier. I want that, too."

"Good. I did not expect to find you, Lina. You are a gift for which I will always be grateful."

"Thank you," she whispered, not sure what else to say. "I'm intrigued, as well."

"Intrigued," he repeated. "An interesting choice of words. Perhaps we should explore all the possibilities."

As'ad walked into his suite at his usual time in the early evening. But instead of quiet, dark rooms, he found the living area bright and loud. Dana and Pepper were stretched out on the floor, watching a show on his large television. Nadine swirled and danced by the window and Kayleen stood at the dining room table, arranging flowers.

She looked up when he entered. "Oh, good. You're here. I called Neil to ask him what time you'd be home. He didn't want to tell me." She wrinkled her nose. "I don't think he likes me."

"Perhaps he is just trying to protect me."

"From us?" She asked the question as if it were a ridiculous possibility. "I wanted to have dinner ready, which it is. I have to say, this calling down to the kitchen and ordering food is really fun. We each picked a dish. Which may not have been a good idea. The menu is fairly eclectic."

She paused for breath, then smiled. "We wanted to have dinner with you."

She wore another dress that was ugly enough to be offensive. The dull gray fabric sucked the life from her face and the bulky style hid any hint of curve. Yet when she smiled, he found his mood lifting. He wanted to smile back. He wanted to pull her close and discover the body hidden beneath.

Heat stirred, reminding him how long he had lived only for his work.

He ignored the need and the wanting, the heat that forced blood south, and set down his briefcase. He even ignored that, given her past, Kayleen had probably never been with a man, and instead focused on the fact that she and the girls were in his room.

He had made himself extremely clear. She was to keep the children away from him. They had their own suite and everything they could possibly want or need. He had only taken the sisters to keep them from a less desirable fate. Yet when he started to remind Kayleen of that, he could not seem to bring himself to say the words.

Perhaps because she looked so hopeful as she smiled at him. He did not want to squash the light in her eyes.

"I'll get some wine," he said, moving to the small wine rack tucked in a cabinet. Something stronger might make the evening go more quickly, but he only had wine in his rooms. He did not, as a rule, drink here. Of course he did not, as a rule, have a woman and three children to contend with.

Nadine danced over to him. "Hi, As'ad," she said, her eyes bright with happiness, her mouth smiling. "Did you have a good day? I got every word on my spelling test except one and it was really hard. My new teacher says I'm a good speller. I'm good in all my subjects, except math, and Kayleen is gonna help me with that."

Pepper ran over and pushed in front of Nadine. "Hi! I'm in school, too, and I'm good at math." She stuck out her tongue at her sister, then smiled back at him. "I made a picture and I brought it for you, but you don't have a 'frigerator, so where are we gonna put it?"

Dana stood and joined them. "He doesn't want your picture," she said, then sighed, as only an older sibling can. "She's not a very good artist."

Pepper stomped her foot. "I'm an *excellent* artist. You're just a butthead."

Dana gasped, Nadine looked worried and Pepper slapped her hand over her mouth. Terror darkened her blue eyes and she glanced between him and Kayleen. Apparently saying "butthead" was not allowed.

As'ad rubbed his temple.

Kayleen walked over and looked at Pepper. "You know that's wrong."

Pepper nodded frantically, her hand still over her mouth.

"You need to apologize to Dana."

Pepper, a tiny girl with long, curly blond hair, turned to her big sister. "I'm sorry I called you that."

Dana put her hands on her hips. "That's not good enough. You always call people—"

Kayleen cleared her throat. Dana hunched her shoulders.

"Thank you for apologizing," she grumbled.

Kayleen touched Pepper's shoulder. "Now you help me think of a suitable punishment. What is appropriate for what you did?"

Pepper's eyes filled with tears. "No story tonight?" she asked in a whisper.

Kayleen considered. "That's a little harsh. What if you have to give up your choice on movie night? Dana gets two choices instead."

Pepper shivered slightly, then nodded. "Okay."

"Good." Kayleen smiled at As'ad. "We're healed. You ready to eat?"

He opened the bottle of wine and joined them at the table. When he was seated, before he could pour, Kayleen reached for Pepper's hand and his. He stared at her.

Pepper leaned toward him. "We have to say grace."

"Of course."

He took Kayleen's hand and Nadine's, then lowered his head while Kayleen offered brief thanks for their meal. While she served, he poured two glasses of wine and passed her one.

Kayleen handed him a plate. "I've never been much of a drinker."

"Neither have I." Although under the circumstances, he just might be starting.

This was too much, he thought. More than he'd expected or wanted. There were children at his table. And a woman he did not know and was not going to sleep with, and having sex with her would be the only acceptable reason to have her here. Yet he saw no easy way to escape.

"We go around the table and talk about our day," Kayleen said as she passed Dana her plate. "Everyone has to say one good thing that happened. I hope that's okay."

And if it was not?

He glanced down at the plate in front of him. Lasagna, mashed potatoes, macaroni and cheese and a salad.

"Perhaps some kind of menu would be helpful," he told Kayleen.

"I know. I'll get one made up. But the girls really wanted to order you their favorites."

Dana talked about how she'd finished her homework early and had found a collection of medical texts in the palace's main library. Nadine mentioned her dance class and how well she'd done.

"I hit a boy," Pepper announced cheerfully. "He was teasing these three girls. He's kinda big, but I wasn't scared. So I hit him. The teacher didn't like it but because I'm new, she said she was going to let it go this one time. I heard this other teacher saying that boy needed a good beating and maybe I'm the one to give it to him." She beamed. "That was fun."

Kayleen quickly covered her mouth with her napkin. As'ad saw the humor in her eyes and knew she was hiding a smile. He took a sip of wine to keep from laughing. He liked Pepper—she had the heart of a lion.

"Perhaps hitting boys is not the best plan," he said as he set the glass down. "One day one of them might hit you back."

"I'm tough," she said.

"Still. Violence is a poor strategy."

"What's a better one?"

He hesitated, not sure what to say.

Kayleen grinned. "We're all waiting to be dazzled by your strategy."

"Perhaps you would like to offer a suggestion?" he asked.

"Not really. Go ahead."

Privately he agreed with Pepper's approach, but he doubted it would be successful as she grew.

"We'll talk later," Kayleen said, rescuing him. "I know hitting a bully seems like a good idea, but it's going to get you into a lot of trouble. Not only with the teachers and with me, but as As'ad mentioned, you could get hurt."

"All right," Pepper grumbled. "But sometimes boys are really stupid."

Dana looked at As'ad. "What good thing happened to you?"

"I decided on a bridge. There is to be a new one over the river. After much planning and discussion, a choice was made. I am pleased."

All three girls stared at him. "You're going to build a bridge?" Nadine asked.

"No. I have given my approval and told them what to do. Now they will do it."

"Cool," Dana breathed. "What else can you tell people to do?"

"Can you throw them in the dungeon?" Pepper asked. "Can I see the dungeon?"

"One day."

Her eyes widened. "There's a real one? Here? In the palace?"

"Yes, and sometimes children who do not behave are sent to it."

They all went silent.

He chuckled. "So, Kayleen, what was your one good thing for today?"

This, Kayleen thought as she tried not to stare at the handsome man at the head of the table. This dinner, this moment, with the girls having fun and As'ad acting like they were all part of the same family.

It wasn't real—she knew that. But all her life she'd wanted to be a part of something special, and here it was.

Still, she had to say something. "There are stables nearby," she told the girls. "I found them when I was out walking."

All three of them turned to him. "Horses? You have horses?" Dana asked.

"We love horses," Nadine told him.

"I can ride." Pepper paused, as if waiting for As'ad to be impressed. "I've had lessons."

He turned to Kayleen. "At the orphanage?"

"A former student left several horses to the school, along with the money to pay for them. Many of the children ride."

"Do you?"

There was something about his dark eyes, she thought, knowing she could stare into them for hours and never grow tired of the effect of the changing light.

"Badly," she admitted. "The horse and I never figured out how to talk to each other."

"That's because horses don't talk," Pepper told her, then turned to As'ad. "Kayleen falls off a lot. I try not to laugh, because I don't want her to hurt herself, but it's kinda funny."

"For you," Kayleen murmured.

The main door to the suite opened and a tall, gray-haired man strode into the suite.

"As'ad. There you are. Oh. You're having dinner with your family."

"Father," As'ad said as he rose.

Father? Something nagged at the back of Kayleen's mind, before bursting free. Father? As in the king?

She jumped to her feet and motioned for the girls to do the same. Once they were standing she didn't know what to do next. Bow? Curtsy?

As'ad glanced at her, then the girls. "Father, this is Kayleen, the girls' nanny." Then he introduced each of the sisters. "Ladies, this is my father, King Mukhtar."

Three mouths dropped open. Kayleen kept hers shut by sheer force of will.

The king nodded graciously. "I am delighted to meet all of you. Welcome to the royal palace of El Deharia. May you live long, with happiness and health in abundance. May these strong walls always protect you and provide solace."

Kayleen swallowed. As greetings went, it was a really good one.

"Thank you so much for your hospitality," she murmured, still trying to accept the fact that she was in the presence of a real live king. Which meant As'ad really was a prince.

She knew he held the title, but she didn't think of him as royal or powerful. Yet he was.

The king motioned to the table. "May I?"

Kayleen felt her eyes widen. "Of course, Your Highness. Please. We weren't expecting you, so the meal isn't exactly...traditional."

The king took a seat. As'ad motioned for them to resume theirs. Mukhtar studied the various serving bowls, then scooped some macaroni and cheese onto a plate.

"I haven't had this in years."

"It was my pick," Pepper told him. "It's my favorite. They make it really good here. Sometimes, at the orphanage, Kayleen would sneak us into the kitchen and make the kind in a box. That's good, too."

The king smiled. "So my chef has competition."

"Not really," Kayleen told him. "His food is amazing. I'm honored just to eat it."

As'ad looked at his father. "In an effort to fill her day, Kayleen went down to the kitchen and offered to help. It did not go well."

Kayleen felt herself flush. "He was a little insulted. There was a crash. I'm guessing he threw stuff."

"Was that the night my soufflé was burned?" the king asked.

"I hope not," Kayleen told him.

He smiled. "So what conversation did I interrupt?" he asked.

"We were talking about horses," Nadine told him. "We rode and took lessons at the orphanage."

The king looked at his son. "Horses. I believe we have a stable, do we not?"

As'ad glanced at the girls. "The king is teasing. The palace stables are world famous."

Dana leaned toward him. "Do you have horses that go fast?"

"Faster than would be safe for a novice rider."

She wrinkled her nose. "If we took more lessons, we would be experts."

"Exactly," As'ad told her.

The king nodded. "I agree. All young princesses should know how to ride. I will speak to the head groom myself and arrange lessons." He glanced at Kayleen. "For all of you."

"Thank you," she murmured, because it was expected.

"You do not look excited," As'ad whispered to her.

"Pepper wasn't kidding about me falling. It happens all the time."

"Perhaps you need more personal instruction."

She stared into his eyes as he spoke and found herself getting lost in his gaze. It was as if he had an energy field that pulled her closer. She had the oddest feeling he was going to touch her—and she was going to like him touching her.

"Riding is an enjoyable way to get exercise," the king said.

"Has anyone asked the horse about that?"

She spoke without thinking—something that had often gotten her in trouble back at the convent. There was a moment of silence, then the king laughed.

"Very good," he said. "Excellent. I like her, As'ad. This one may stay."

"I agree," As'ad said, still looking at her in a way that made her thighs feel distinctly weak. "She will stay."

Would she? Kayleen wasn't so sure. She still had her life plan to fulfill and that included leaving El Deharia in a matter of months. A situation complicated by As'ad and her promise to the girls.

Chapter Four

After the king left and dinner was finished, Kayleen sent the girls back to their suite while she lingered behind to speak with As'ad.

"There are just a couple of things I need to discuss with you," she told him when they were alone.

"I'm learning that with you, there always are."

She wasn't sure what he meant by that, so decided to ignore the comment. "It's only about six weeks until Christmas," she said. "We have to start planning. I don't know what happens here at the palace, but this is the girls' first Christmas without either of their parents. We have to do something."

He studied her for a long time. "El Deharia is a very open country. All faiths are celebrated here. No one will object if you wish to set up a tree in your suite."

"It's more than that," she said, telling herself there was

no reason to be afraid, even though As'ad was much taller than her and having to look up to meet his gaze gave her a crick in her neck. "You need to participate."

He looked shocked. "I do not."

She'd had a feeling he would be difficult.

"You've always had family," she pointed out. "Your brothers, your aunt, your father. These girls have no one. The holidays are going to be sad and scary and they're going to feel so alone."

Kayleen spoke from experience. She still remembered waking up on Christmas morning and feeling an ache in her chest. No matter how many presents had been donated to the orphanage, no matter how the nuns tried, there hadn't been *family.*

She hadn't even had the dream that a wonderful couple would find her and want to adopt her. She had plenty of relatives—just no one who wanted her.

"They need traditions, both old and new," she continued. "They need to feel welcome and loved."

His expression tightened. "Then you will take care of that."

"But you're their father now."

"I am someone who agreed to let them live here. Kayleen, these girls are your responsibility, not mine. Do not cross this line with me."

"I don't understand. You were so great with them at dinner. Are you telling me that was just an act? That you don't care?"

"I have compassion. I have honor. That will be enough."

Was he kidding? "That's not enough. It will never be enough. We're talking about children, As'ad. Lost, lonely children. They deserve more. They deserve to be loved."

She wasn't just talking about the children—she was talking about herself. The difference was she'd already given up her dreams.

"Then they will have to find that love in you."

She took a step back. Her throat tightened and her cheeks were hot. "You're saying you don't plan to love them?"

He might as well have said he was going to kill them in their sleep!

"I will honor my responsibilities. In doing so, it is necessary for me to be strong. Emotion is weakness. You are a woman—I don't expect you to understand. Just trust me, it is so. I will see to the girls' needs. You can take care of their hearts."

She didn't know what to say or where to begin to argue with him. "That's the craziest thing I've ever heard," she told him. "Love isn't weakness. It's strength and power. The ability to give means you can be more, not less."

He actually smiled at her. "Your passion is a testament to your caring. That's excellent."

"So it's okay for me to have emotions, but not you? Because you're a man?"

"More than a man," he reminded her. "A prince. I have responsibilities for others. It is my duty to stay strong, to not be swayed by something as changeable as feelings."

"Without compassion, there can be no judgment," she snapped. "Without feelings, you're only a machine. A good ruler feels for his people."

"You cannot understand."

"And you can't mean this."

"I assure you, I do." He took her arm and walked her to the door. "Celebrate Christmas however you wish. You have my permission."

"Can I have your head on a stick instead?" she muttered as she jerked free and walked out into the hallway.

Of all the stupid, annoying things she'd ever heard. He wasn't going to feel anything because he was a prince? But it was okay for her because she was a woman?

"No way," she told herself as she headed back to her own rooms. "Something is going to change around here and it isn't going to be me."

"It's so egotistical," Kayleen ranted the next morning as she paced the length of her living room. "So two hundred years ago. He gets to be in charge because he's a man? What does that make the rest of us? Chattel? I'm so angry, I want to throw him in the dungeon until he begs. I'm smart. I'm capable. And I have a heart. Why can't he see that emotions give us depth? They define us. Are all men so stupid? I have to tell you, Lina, the more I see of the world, the more I long for the convent."

Her friend smiled at her. "Is it possible your energy and intensity on this topic is one of the reasons you *weren't* called to serve in that way?"

"That's what I was always told when I was growing up. I was too passionate about things. Too willing to go my own way. It's just when I see an injustice, I can't stop to think. I act."

"As you did with Tahir."

Kayleen remembered the tall chieftain who had wanted to take the girls. "Exactly."

"Life does not always move on your timetable," Lina said. "You need to be patient."

"Don't act impulsively," Kayleen said, knowing she'd heard the same advice a thousand times before.

"Exactly." Lina patted the seat next to her. "As'ad is a product of his world. His father taught all his sons to avoid emotion. To think logically. While my brother grieved after his wife died, he chose not to show that to the boys. In front of them, he went on, as if unmoved by her passing. In my opinion it was the wrong lesson."

Kayleen agreed. "Because of that, As'ad won't care?" She didn't wait for an answer. "He's not stupid. Why can't he see the truth all around him?"

"He has been trained for a specific purpose. His is a life of service, in a way, but with ultimate power and ego. You haven't met his brothers, but they are all like him. Strong, determined men who see little virtue in love. It's probably why none of them have married."

"But love is strength and a great gift," Kayleen said as she sat on the sofa. "He has to love the girls. They need that. They deserve it. He would be better because of it. Happier. Besides, there's a ticking clock here."

Lina frowned. "You're still leaving?"

"I can go back on my twenty-fifth birthday. That's less than four months away."

"But you have the girls now."

"I know." Kayleen hadn't worked that part out. "They'll get settled and then As'ad can bring in someone else."

She spoke bravely, but the words sounded a little feeble, even to her.

"I'm surprised," Lina admitted. "When you asked As'ad to adopt the girls, I thought you were taking on the responsibility with him. This isn't like you, Kayleen. To retreat from the world."

"The world isn't always a fun place. I want to go back

to where I belong." Where she'd grown up. It was the only home she'd ever known. "I can teach there." That was the deal. She had to stay away until she was twenty-five. Then she could return to the convent school forever.

"You can be a mother here."

"Not really. It's just a game. When the girls are older, As'ad will have no use for me. Besides, if he doesn't want to get involved, maybe I can take them with me."

"I assume my nephew doesn't know about your plan to leave."

"I haven't mentioned it."

"When will you?"

"Soon. It's not as if he'll miss me or anything."

Kayleen had always wondered what it would be like to be missed by someone. By a man. To be cared for. Loved, even.

"Things change," Lina told her. "You have a responsibility to the girls."

"I know."

"Would you walk away from them so easily?"

Kayleen shook her head. "No. It won't be easy. Sometimes I do think about staying." She didn't know what was right. Her plan had always been to go back. Being here with the three sisters had changed everything.

Was Lina right? Did she, Kayleen, have a responsibility to the children? Should she give up her dreams for them? Could she go back later? When the girls were older?

Three weeks ago, she'd known all the answers and now she knew none. Her instinct was to go talk to As'ad about all this. But that made no sense. He was a man who didn't listen to his heart and she had always believed the truth could be found there.

"My head is spinning. Enough about this. Let's change the subject."

"All right." Lina smiled slowly. "Hassan is coming here."

Kayleen stared at her friend. "The king of Bahania? The one you've been talking to all this time?"

"I can't believe it, either. I just… We were talking and he said he liked the sound of my laughter and now he's coming here."

Kayleen hugged her. "That's wonderful. I'm so happy. You've been shut up in this palace for years. Good for you."

"I'm scared," Lina admitted. "I thought my life was all planned out. I helped my brother raise his sons, I have my charity work. I was waiting to be a great-aunt. Suddenly there's this wonderful man offering me something I thought I'd lost. There are possibilities. Am I too old for possibilities?"

"Never," Kayleen said fiercely. "The heart is never too old. At least it isn't in all those romantic movies."

"I hope not. I married young and I was so in love. Then he was killed and I never planned to love again. I'm the sister to the king. It's difficult to date. After a while, I stopped wanting to. Then Hassan and I started talking and suddenly I'm alive again." Lina took Kayleen's hands. "I want this for you. I at least experienced falling in love when I was young, but you've never had that."

Kayleen squirmed. "I'm not good with men."

"You don't try. How many dates did you go on before you gave up? Five? Six?"

Kayleen cleared her throat, then pulled her hands free. "One and a half."

"You're too young to lock yourself away in that convent school of yours."

"Because I would meet so many men here at the palace?"

"You'd meet some. More than you would there. There are many young men in the palace. I would be happy to introduce you to one or two of them."

"I don't know…. I work for As'ad. As nanny to his children."

"Why would he mind you dating?"

"He wouldn't." Not that she enjoyed admitting that truth.

"Then think about what I said. Wouldn't it be wonderful to fall in love?"

As'ad looked up as his brother Qadir walked into his office. "I must speak with Neil about keeping out people who don't have appointments."

Qadir ignored that. "I am back from Paris, where the city is still beautiful, as are the women. You should have come with me. You have been locked up here working for far too long."

As'ad had spent two sleepless nights unable to rest for the need burning inside. Worse, when he closed his eyes, the woman he saw satisfying his ache was Kayleen. An impossible situation. The nanny and a virgin?

"You are right, my brother," he said as he rose and greeted Qadir. "I should have gone with you. There have been changes since you were last here."

"I heard." Qadir settled on a corner of his desk. "Three daughters? What were you thinking?"

"That I had been placed in an impossible situation and this was the easiest way out."

"I find that hard to believe. There had to be another solution."

"None was presented."

Qadir shook his head. "To raise children that are not your own. At least they are girls."

"There is the added advantage of our father now believing I am occupied with my new family and therefore cannot be expected to look for a wife."

"Lucky bastard."

"Indeed. Perhaps now he will focus more of his attention on you."

"He has already begun," Qadir grumbled. "There is to be a state function in a few weeks. Several likely candidates are to be paraded before me, like very attractive cattle."

As'ad grinned. "I, of course, will be busy with my family."

As'ad turned the corner to walk to his rooms and saw all three girls huddled by his door. They wore riding clothes and boots. When they saw him they ran to him.

"You have to help!" Dana told him.

"It's terrible. Please!" Nadine begged.

Pepper simply cried.

He stared at the three of them. "What happened?"

"We went riding," Dana told him, her blue eyes wide and filled with fear and guilt. "We might have been gone longer than we were supposed to, but we were fine. We were only a little late. But Kayleen got worried and came after us, even though we had a groom with us. She went out by herself and she's not back yet."

Pepper brushed her hand across her face as she tugged on the bottom of his suit jacket. "She's not a very good rider. She gets thrown a lot. What if she's hurt and it's all our fault?"

As'ad's first thought was that he regretted that whoever had let Kayleen go out by herself could not be flogged. Sometimes he missed the old ways. His second was the low-grade worry at the thought of a defenseless young woman alone in the desert. It was not a place to be traveled lightly.

The girls crowded close, as if seeking comfort from him. Although he had no time for this, he resisted the urge to push them away and instead awkwardly patted them on their shoulders.

"All will be well," he told them. "I will find Kayleen and return her to you."

"Promise?" Pepper asked, her lashes spiky from her tears.

He crouched down until he could look her in the eye. "I am Prince As'ad of El Deharia. My word is law."

Pepper sniffed. "Promise?"

He gave her a slight smile. "I promise."

Ten minutes later the girls were settled with Lina and he was in the garage, sliding into an open Jeep. The desert was a vast space and in theory, Kayleen could be anywhere. But in truth, an inexperienced rider would stick to trails and not get far. Unless she had been thrown.

He did not allow himself to consider that option. He would find her and if she were hurt, he would deal with the situation as it arose.

He found the riding trail easily. He had been taking it all his life. As it bent to the left, he considered how far Kayleen might have traveled, then accelerated. A mere ten miles into the desert was the permanent outpost of a local tribe. If Kayleen kept to the trail, she would end up there.

He drove slowly, checking the area for signs of any

accident, or a woman walking without a horse, but found nothing. At the outskirts of the outpost he saw a cluster of people gathered around a petite woman with flaming red hair. She was holding on to a horse and gesturing wildly.

As'ad eased the Jeep to a stop and picked up the satellite phone. When he was connected with his aunt, he informed her he had found Kayleen and that she appeared fine.

"Will you be coming right back?" Lina asked.

As'ad considered. "I believe we'll stay for dinner."

"That's fine. I'll put the girls to bed. Thanks for letting me know. They were worried."

He disconnected the call and parked, then walked toward the crowd.

Kayleen saw him and excused herself from the group, then raced toward him. When she was close enough, she launched herself at him.

He caught her and held her against him as she trembled in his embrace.

"You came," she breathed. "It's the girls. They're gone. They were late and we had no way to get in touch with them and I was so worried, so I took a horse out myself. I found this village, but no one speaks English and I can't tell if they've seen the girls. What if something happened to them? I'll never forgive myself."

She was distraught and panicked and surprisingly beautiful. Her hazel eyes darkened with emotion and her cheeks were flushed. Impulsively, he bent down and lightly brushed her mouth with his.

"They're fine," he told her. "All three of them returned unharmed. You are the one who is missing."

"What?" She drew in a breath. "They're all right?"

"Perfectly fine, although suffering from guilt for

causing you distress. Kayleen, the girls are good riders. The head groom took them out himself to confirm that. They also had someone with them. Why did you feel it necessary to go rescue them yourself?"

"I don't know. I was worried and I acted."

"Impulsively."

She glanced down. "Yes, well, that's an ongoing problem."

"So it seems."

She looked around and noticed the villagers gathered close. "Oh." She pulled back.

As'ad let her go, but only reluctantly. She had felt good in his arms. He wanted to kiss her again—but thoroughly and without an audience. He wanted to push aside her unattractive clothing and touch the soft skin beneath. Instead he stepped back and turned to greet Sharif, the village chieftain.

"She is your woman?" Sharif asked.

Kayleen spun toward the old man. "You speak English? You stood there, pretending not to understand and you speak *English?*"

"They don't know you," As'ad told her. "They were being cautious."

"What about desert hospitality? What about claiming sanctuary or asylum or something?"

"Did you?" he asked.

Kayleen pressed her lips together. "No. I was asking if they'd seen the girls. They wouldn't answer and they weren't speaking English."

As'ad glanced at Sharif. "She is mine."

"Then you are both welcome. You will stay and eat with us?"

"It is an honor."

"Arrangements will be made."

"Arrangements?" Kayleen asked. "What arrangements? And what's all this about being your woman? I'm your nanny. There's a really big difference."

He took her by the elbow and led her to the Jeep. "It makes things easier if they think you belong to me. Otherwise you would be fair game for every man here. You're very exotic. They would find that tempting."

Kayleen didn't know what to say to that. She was so far from exotic that if they put her picture on that page in the dictionary, it would have a circle with a line drawn through it over her face. She couldn't imagine a man ever being tempted by her.

It was the hair, she thought with a sigh. Bright red hair tended to call attention to itself.

"Fear not," As'ad told her. "I have claimed you. You are safe."

She shivered slightly, but not in fear. It was more from the memory of the brief kiss he'd given her when he'd first arrived. An unexpected and warm touch of his lips on hers. She'd been shocked by the contact, but not in a scary way. More surprised, but pleased.

"We're staying for dinner," he said.

"I got that."

"It's the polite thing to do."

She looked around at the tidy camp. "I don't mind. I like it here, out in the desert. Although it would be nice if they didn't pretend not to understand me."

"They are private people. You rode in from nowhere, babbling about missing children. They were cautious."

She narrowed her gaze. "I do *not* babble."

He raised an eyebrow.

"Not often," she amended. "I was scared. I thought the girls were lost."

"You were not equipped to find them, yet you went after them."

"Someone had to."

"Perhaps one of the grooms. Or you could have called me."

Oh. Right. "I didn't think of that. I'm not used to having resources."

"Perhaps next time you will consider that you do."

It would take some getting used to. "You came after me yourself," she said. "*You* could have sent one of the grooms."

"The girls were most distressed to think they were the cause of your being gone. Coming after you myself seemed the quickest way to allay their fears."

"It was a little impulsive. You have resources, too."

"You mock me?"

"Maybe."

"A dangerous path."

"I'm not afraid."

Something flashed in his eyes. Something dark and primitive that made her heart flutter. She didn't know if she should throw herself at him or run into the desert, so she stood her ground.

"So what do you think is for dinner?"

The women of the village prepared a rich stew with lots of vegetables and a flat bread that smelled so good it made Kayleen's mouth water. She did her best to be friendly and polite, helping with the cooking as much as the women in the camp would let her.

Zarina, Sharif's oldest daughter, was the only one who would speak to her in English.

"Am I really that scary?" Kayleen asked quietly as she stirred the stew.

"You are different. From the city and from another country. You do not know our ways."

"I could learn."

Zarina, a dark-haired beauty with a flashing smile, laughed. "Give up your comforts to roam the desert? I do not think so."

"Comforts don't matter to me," Kayleen told her. She would give up many things to belong somewhere.

"Yet you live in the palace with the prince."

"It's a long story and I don't live with him. I take care of…" She shook her head. "It's a really long story."

Zarina glanced at As'ad where he sat with the leaders of the tribe. "The prince is handsome. If I were not happily married, I might try to steal him from you."

Kayleen started to say he wasn't hers to steal, but figured there was no point. "He's nice."

Zarina laughed. "Not nice. No man worth having is nice. As'ad is a desert warrior. He takes what he wants, but then he protects those he claims. He is a strong man. A powerful husband. You have chosen well."

A lion of the desert? As'ad? He was strong and powerful and he did seem to take care of those around him. His presence here was proof of that. But a dangerous animal? She didn't believe that. As for her choosing him…as if.

He looked up and met her gaze, then rose and approached. "What troubles you, Kayleen?"

"Nothing. I was just thinking. Zarina says it's good she's happily married, otherwise she would steal you from me."

He laughed. "She is a beautiful woman."

Kayleen didn't like that answer. "You and I don't have that kind of relationship."

"So you would not mind if she and I…"

"No," Kayleen said carefully, even as a knot formed in her stomach. It was hard and hot and made her feel uncomfortable. "You have a family now. You should be with someone."

"You suggest Zarina?"

"She's already married."

"I am Prince As'ad of El Deharia. I can have whomever I choose."

How annoyingly arrogant. "I don't think so. You're just a man. There are women who would say no to you."

He moved closer. "Who would that be?"

She stood at straight as she could, tilted her head back and glared at him. "Me, for one. I'm not interested."

His smile was slow, sexy and confident beyond measure. "You think so."

"Absolutely."

"I see."

He reached toward her. Before she knew what he intended, he pulled her close and kissed her.

Chapter Five

Kayleen had almost been kissed once in her life, on a date with a young man in college. He had been nice enough, but she was so inexperienced that just being around him had made her nervous. At the end of their awkward evening, he'd moved in for a kiss and she'd bolted for the safety of her dorm room.

But there was no bolting from As'ad. With his arms around her, she had nowhere to go. Not to mention the fact that she didn't want to run.

She'd wondered about kissing, had wondered if she was the last innocent in a world where even twelve-year-olds seemed to know more about men and sex than she did. She'd wondered how it was possible to enjoy someone being so close, pressing his mouth against hers. Worse, using his tongue in some intimate way.

Would she feel trapped, uncomfortable, violated?

The short answer was no, she thought as As'ad moved his mouth gently against hers, teasing, caressing, but not taking. Even though his arms were around her, she didn't feel trapped. Instead she felt protected and wanted.

The wanting was new, as was the odd hungry sensation inside of her. She needed to be closer, although she couldn't say why.

She put her hands on his shoulders, feeling the strength and heat of him. As'ad would keep all in his world safe, she thought, distracted by the pressure of his lips. It would be nice to feel safe.

She inhaled the masculine scent of him, liking the fragrance. She enjoyed the feel of his body so close to hers. She grew bolder and slipped her arms around his neck, bringing her front in contact with his.

He increased the pressure of his mouth on hers. His strong hands traveled up and down her back. When he stroked his tongue against her bottom lip she gasped in shock, then felt the soft, erotic touch of his tongue against hers.

Fire shot through her. The unexpected heat made her tremble as she almost expected to go up in flames. Sensations exploded everywhere, especially in places that were usually without them. Her breasts ached in a way they never had before. Her legs felt funny—trembly and weak. She stood frozen, unsure, awkward, yet willing him to keep on kissing her.

Fortunately As'ad seemed more than capable of reading her mind. He explored her mouth with his tongue, making her tingle and want to lean into him. She ached, but couldn't say for what. She clung to him, and at last, tentatively, slowly, carefully, touched her tongue to his.

A low, masculine groan burst from him. The sound filled her with a sense of sensual power she'd never experienced before. She touched his tongue again and felt a reaction in her own body. A clenching. A wanting. A hunger.

She let herself get lost in the touching, the intimate kiss. It was heaven. She could do this for hours. She liked how her body turned to liquid. She liked everything about kissing him.

But instead of reading her mind again, he put his hands on her shoulders and eased her away from him.

"What?" she breathed.

"Perhaps another time," he said calmly. "When we are alone."

Alone? What was he…

Kayleen bit her lower lip and turned her head. While much of the village had gone about their business, there were still several obviously interested people observing their kiss. As she looked at them, they grinned. A couple waved. A few of the women laughed knowingly.

"Now no one will question that you are mine," he told her.

They arrived back at the palace shortly after ten. Kayleen met Lina in the suite she, Kayleen, shared with the girls.

"We're back," she said. "Thanks for staying with them."

"It was fun," Lina told her. "So how was your evening?"

Kayleen did her best not to blush, although she could feel heat on her cheeks. "It was fine. Good. I really liked meeting everyone in the village. They're wonderful people. Dinner was good. They let me help a little with the cooking. Everyone was friendly." She realized she was babbling and pressed her lips together, then blurted, "Nothing happened."

Lina slowly raised her eyebrows. "Excuse me?"

"Nothing happened. With As'ad. In case you were, you know, wondering. Nothing happened."

"I see." Lina smiled. "You're protesting an awful lot, especially when you consider I never asked if anything happened."

"Oh." Kayleen shifted. She needed to stop talking now or Lina would find out about the kiss. Not that Kayleen regretted it—on the contrary, it was a delicious secret she wanted to keep to herself.

Lina waited another few seconds, then walked to the door. "I'll see you later, then."

"Uh-huh. Thanks again for staying with the girls."

"Anytime," Lina said, and then left.

When she was alone, Kayleen tiptoed into the girls' bedroom. All three of them were asleep. She smoothed covers, adjusted the nightlight, then went into her own room. When she had shut the door behind her, she sighed with happiness, spun in a slow circle, then sank onto the bed.

She'd been kissed. Really kissed and it had been wonderful. Better than she could have imagined.

She'd liked everything about kissing As'ad…the taste of him, the heat, the way he'd held her. She wanted to kiss and be kissed again. Unfortunately, it wasn't the sort of thing she could simply ask him to do. Worse, she wasn't sure *why* he'd kissed her. Had he wanted to, or had he just been proving a point in the village? And why did it suddenly matter which?

* * *

Several days later As'ad returned to his rooms to find Kayleen sitting at his dining table in front of a sewing machine. Fabric covered every available surface. She'd pulled over a floor lamp for additional light and didn't notice his arrival.

His reaction was as powerful as it was instantaneous. Not about the fact that she'd once again ignored his request that she take care of all things involving the girls. Instead his body recognized the woman who had most recently brought him to his knees with a single kiss.

A virgin's kiss, he reminded himself, still annoyed and aroused at the sight of her. What should have been meaningless, done only to prove a point, had instead started a fire within him that still burned hot and strong. He'd been hungry before kissing her—now he was starved.

He hadn't been able to sleep for wanting Kayleen. The kiss had shown him potential where he'd seen very little. She'd felt right in his arms—all soft curves and innocence. Yet there had been heat in her, an instinctive passion that had matched his own.

The event should have meant nothing. He should have been able to walk away without thinking of it again. Instead it was all he could do not to cross the room, pull her to her feet and kiss her over and over until she surrendered. He wanted her wet, naked and begging. He wanted all of her.

She looked and saw him. "As'ad." She smiled. "You're back." She stood and held up both hands. "I know what you're going to say. This is a big mess. I'm sorry. I meant to get it cleaned up before you got home. I lost track of time."

Her mouth. He couldn't seem to look away from it. The

shape, the hint of white teeth and nimble tongue. His brother Qadir was right—he *should* have gone to Paris and spent the week mindless in an unknown woman's bed. Now the opportunity was lost. He had a bad feeling it would be some time before he could use someone else to forget the appeal of Kayleen.

"What are you doing?" he asked, pleased his voice was so calm. Nothing of his turmoil must show.

"Making costumes for the Christmas pageant. All three girls are in it. I want the costumes to be a surprise."

"The school will not provide them?"

"I suppose they could. They asked if some of the parents could help out. I said I would. Lina found this machine for me. It's fabulous and practically sews on its own. You should see the instruction manual—it's as thick as a dictionary. But I'll figure it out."

He fingered a length of fabric. "I am sure there are employees in the palace who could do this for you."

She looked as if he'd slapped her. "But I like sewing. Besides, it'll matter more if I make the costumes for the girls."

"As you wish."

"I'm going to guess you're not into crafts."

He allowed himself a slight smile. "No."

"I learned to sew in the orphanage. I could make more clothes for a lot less. You probably don't do anything like that here."

"We do not."

She tilted her head and her long, red hair tumbled over her shoulders. His fingers curled toward his palms as he ached to touch her hair, to feel it in his hand, dragging along his chest, across his thighs.

"Did your mother sew?" Kayleen asked, jerking him back to the present.

"I don't know. She died when I was very young. I don't remember her."

The light faded from her eyes. "Oh. I'm sorry. I knew she was gone. I didn't know how old you were when it happened. I didn't mean to remind you of that."

"It is of no consequence."

"But it's sad."

"How can it be sad if the memory is gone?"

She frowned. "That is the loss of what should have been."

"I am not wounded, Kayleen. Share your concerns with someone who needs them."

"Because you feel nothing?" she asked. "Isn't that what you told me? Emotion makes you weak?"

"Exactly." Any emotion. Even passion. His current condition proved that.

"What about trust?" she asked.

"Trust must be earned."

"So many rules. So many chances to turn people away. It must be nice to have so many people in your life that there are extras."

She sounded wistful as she spoke, which made him want to pull her close and offer comfort.

Kayleen, who wanted to belong, he thought, realizing her concern for the girls came from having lived in an orphanage herself. She was all heart and would bruise easily in a harsh world. Their backgrounds couldn't be more different.

"It is a matter of control," he told her. "To need no one is to remain in charge."

She shook her head. "To need no one is to be desperately alone."

"That is not how I see it."

"That doesn't make it any less true. There's nothing worse than being alone," she told him. "I'll get this cleaned up now, and get out of your way."

Kayleen walked through the palace gardens. While she loved the beauty of the rooms inside, they were nothing when compared with the opulence of the lush gardens that beckoned just beyond her windows.

She chose a new path that twisted and turned, and once again reminded herself that she wanted to find a book on flowers in the palace library. She'd grown up gardening, but in the convent, all extra space had been taken up with vegetables. With money tight and children to feed, the nuns had not wasted precious earth on flowers.

Kayleen plucked a perfect rose and inhaled the sweet scent, then settled on a stone bench warm from the sun. She needed a moment to close her eyes and be still. Maybe then the world would stop turning so quickly.

So much had happened in such a short time. Meeting As'ad, moving here with the girls, getting ready for the holidays, kissing As'ad.

The latter made her both sigh and smile. She longed for another kiss from him, but so far there had been no opportunity. Which made her wonder if the kiss had been as interesting and appealing to him. Maybe he'd found her inexperience disgusting. Maybe he'd been disappointed.

Did it matter? There shouldn't be any more kissing between them. She had her life plan and As'ad had his.

They wanted opposite things—she needed to connect and he claimed connection didn't matter. She just wasn't sure she believed him.

She heard footsteps on the path and turned toward the sound. She expected to see one of the many gardeners. What she got instead was the king.

"Oh!" Kayleen sprang to her feet, then paused, not sure what she was supposed to do.

King Mukhtar smiled. "Good afternoon, Kayleen. I see you are enjoying my garden."

"I enjoy wandering," she said with a slight bob she hoped would pass for a curtsy and/or bow. "Have I stepped into off-limits space?"

"Not at all. I welcome the company. Come, child. Walk with me."

It didn't sound like a request.

Kayleen fell into step beside the king and waited for him to start the conversation. She was just starting to sweat the silence when he said, "Are you settled into the palace? Does it feel like home?"

She laughed. "I'm settled, but I'm not sure anywhere this magnificent will ever feel like home."

"A very politically correct answer," he told her. "Where did you grow up?"

"In an orphanage in the Midwest."

"I see. You lost your parents at an early age?"

She shrugged. "I don't know anything about my father. My mother had me when she was really young. She couldn't handle a baby so she left me with her mother. When that didn't work out, I went to the Catholic orphanage, which turned out to be a great place to grow up."

She was used to telling the story in a upbeat way that

avoided making anyone feel awkward. There was no reason for the king to know that her mother had abandoned her and that her grandmother hadn't wanted to be stuck with another child to raise. No reason to talk about what it had felt like to be left on the doorstep of an orphanage on her fifth birthday, knowing no one in her family wanted anything to do with her. King Mukhtar wouldn't know what it felt like to never belong anywhere.

"So you don't remember your mother at all?" he asked.

"No." Which was fine with Kayleen.

"Perhaps you'll meet again one day," the king said.

"I would like that very much," Kayleen lied, knowing it was what the king wanted to hear.

Growing up, she'd been taught that it was her duty to forgive her mother and grandmother for abandoning her. She'd made peace with what had happened, but that didn't mean she wanted to be close now. Perhaps there *were* circumstances that, if explained, would help her understand. In truth, she wasn't interested enough to find out.

"So your past is the reason you were so against the three sisters being split up," the king said.

"Absolutely. They only have each other. They need to stay together."

"Because of you, they will."

She smiled. "Actually As'ad gets all the credit. He's the one who saved them. I'll always be grateful to him."

The king glanced at her. "I heard you rode into the desert and met with some of the villagers who live there."

"I did. I liked them a lot. It's an interesting way of life. Carrying one's roots wherever one goes."

"Most young women would be more interested in the elegant shops on our boulevards than in the desert."

She wrinkled her nose. "I'm not much into shopping." She'd never had the money for it to be serious sport and she doubted the stores the king spoke of had much in the way of bargains.

"Perhaps As'ad will take you one day," the king said.

"That would be fun, but it's not necessary. He's given me so much already."

"So you like my son?"

"Of course. He's a wonderful man. Charming and kind and patient." And a great kisser, but she wasn't going to mention *that* to the king.

"I am pleased to hear you are getting along," King Mukhtar told her. "Very pleased."

Chapter Six

Kayleen waved at Neil, As'ad's assistant, and when the man didn't lunge for her, walked past him and into the prince's office.

As'ad glanced up from his computer. "You have so intimidated my assistant that he has given up trying to stop you."

She laughed. "If only that were true. I won't stay long, I just…" She walked to the desk, started to sit down, then stopped. "I spoke with the king."

As'ad looked at her as if waiting for her point.

"Your father is a king," she said.

"Yes, I know."

"I don't. I can't be speaking with a king. That sort of thing doesn't happen to people like me. It doesn't happen to anyone. It's not normal."

"You live in the royal palace. What did you expect?"

"Not to be living here," she admitted. "It's too crazy. You're a prince."

"Again, information I have already obtained."

She sighed and sank into a chair. "You're not taking me seriously."

"You have given me no reason to. My father and I are who we have always been."

She nodded slowly. He'd grown up this way. It was impossible for him to grasp the incredibleness of the situation for her.

"I shouldn't have made you take the girls," she told him. "I didn't think the whole thing through. How they would change things for you."

He rose and walked around the desk until he was standing in front of her and she had to look way, way up to meet his gaze.

"You did not *make* me do anything."

She waved that away. "You know what I mean."

"Indeed, I do not. I was aware that adopting three American sisters would make things different and still I went forward."

Which made her wonder why he hadn't just dismissed her like an annoying gnat. Isn't that what princes did?

"I don't belong here," she told him. "I'm not used to this sort of thing."

He took her hand and pulled her to her feet. "I say who belongs and who does not."

"Off with my head?"

"That is not what I had in mind."

She knew he was going to kiss her even before he bent toward her and brushed his mouth against hers. She couldn't say how she knew, only that anticipation tightened her stomach and she forgot to breathe. Nothing else mattered but the feel of his lips on hers and the nearness of his body. He put his arms around her and drew her close.

It was like going home. The sense of belonging and safety. She'd never experienced that before and the sensation was so sweet, so perfect, she never wanted to be anywhere else. Then his mouth was moving on hers and she got lost in the kiss, the feel of his hands moving up and down her back. The heat of them. The way they pressed against each other, her body melting into his.

She put her hands on his upper arms and explored his muscled strength. When the pressure on her lips increased, she parted and was rewarded by the sensual sweep of his tongue across hers.

Somewhere along the way she must have remembered to breathe again because she moaned low in her throat. She felt tense and relaxed at the same time. She wanted this to never stop and she wanted more.

Without thinking, she rose on tiptoe, so she could press herself against him more fully. She tilted her head and kissed him back, teasing his tongue with hers.

His hands moved more urgently. One slipped to her rear, where he squeezed her curves. The contact shocked her, but excited her, too. Instinctively she arched forward, bringing her lower body in contact with his. He squeezed again, then moved his other hand to her waist before sliding it higher.

Anticipation chased away any hint of apprehension. His large hand settled on her breast with a confidence that allowed her not to be afraid. She broke the kiss so she could lean her forehead against his shoulder while he cupped her breast in his hand.

His touch was gentle and slow, but more wonderful than anything she'd ever experienced before. It was as if he knew the best way to touch her, to stroke her. When he moved his fingers across her nipple, she gasped and clung to him.

He moved his free hand to her chin, raised her head, then kissed her again. She held on to him as the room began to spin faster and faster. When he finally stepped back, she wasn't sure she could stay standing.

His eyes were dark as night, but bright with a fire that burned as hot as the one flaring inside of her. She'd never seen sexual need on a man's face before, but she recognized it now. Recognized it and knew that somehow she had caused it.

He wanted her. It was magic and filled her with delight and wonder and a sense of feminine power. Now if only she knew what to do with it.

"Kayleen."

He'd spoken her name dozens of times before, but never with his voice so heavy and rumbling. She wanted this, she thought happily. She wanted this and so much more.

Somewhere in the distance she heard people talking. She remembered they were in his office and she had interrupted his day. The realization made her unsure of what to do next.

"I should, ah, probably go," she told him, wondering if he would ask her to stay.

"Do not worry about the king," he said instead. "My father is very pleased with you."

"How do you know? Have you talked to him?"

"I have no need. You are exactly what he wants you to be."

What? But before she could ask for an explanation,

As'ad's phone rang. He glanced at his watch. "A teleconference with the British foreign minister."

"Right. Okay. I'll see you later."

She walked back to her room, wondering what it all meant. The kiss, the intimate touch, As'ad's comment that she was what the king wanted her to be. Did that mean a good nanny? A tidy guest?

Yet more reminders that this was a foreign world and not one she was likely to be comfortable in. She should be eager to escape. Yet there was a part of her that wouldn't mind staying for a very long time.

"You summoned me?" Lina asked as she breezed into the room. "And don't say you didn't. There was a definite command in your message."

"I won't deny it," As'ad told her, motioning to the sofa in the corner and joining her there.

"Am I to be punished?" she asked, a twinkle in her eye.

"You are my aunt and the woman who raised me. I have great respect for you."

"So I'm in *serious* trouble."

She didn't sound worried, but then why should she? He would never do anything to hurt her. Despite what she'd done, he had trouble being angry with her. Not that he would let *her* know that.

If he was annoyed with anyone, it was with himself for being too blind to see what was happening. It had been obvious from the beginning and he hadn't noticed.

"Shall you go first or shall I?" Lina asked.

"I called you here."

"I know, but that doesn't mean I don't have an agenda."

He nodded. "Please. Begin."

"I spoke with Zarina the other day. You claimed Kayleen as your own."

"For the moment. She created a stir in the village. I did not wish things to get awkward."

"You kissed her."

That damn kiss, he thought grimly. It had created nothing but trouble. The second kiss had been worse. Now he knew the passion between them had not been brought on by too many nights alone. It flared as bright and hot as the sun. He ached to claim Kayleen's body. But her innocence and position in his household made the situation complicated.

"To make a point," he said with a casualness he didn't feel.

"So that explains it," Lina murmured. "You have no feelings for her yourself."

None that he would admit to. "No."

"So if I wanted to introduce her to a pleasant young man, you would be agreeable?"

"I would," he lied, picturing himself ripping off the man's head. "But it will not be an issue."

"You're saying I don't know any young men, but you are wrong. I know several. One is an American. I mentioned Kayleen to him and he thought he would like to meet her. Did you know it's nearly Thanksgiving?"

"Nearly what?"

"Thanksgiving. It's an American holiday. I had forgotten myself, but the young man in question mentioned getting together with Kayleen that evening. They would both be missing home and could connect over that."

Missing home. Kayleen would, he thought, and so would the girls. They would miss the traditional dinner.

"I will arrange it," he told his aunt.

"Kayleen's date?"

"Of course not. Thanksgiving dinner for her and the girls. A traditional meal. I'll speak with the head chef right away." He turned his attention back to his aunt. "As for your young American, I doubt he exists."

"Of course he does."

"Perhaps, but he is not intended for Kayleen. You have other plans for her."

"I have no idea what you're talking about. But while we're on the subject, Kayleen is lovely, isn't she? I met her the first time I volunteered at the orphanage. She'd been here all of two weeks and yet had already settled in. I was impressed by her intelligence and her dedication to the children. She has many fine qualities."

"I will not marry her."

Lina narrowed her gaze. "No one has asked you to." Her voice was level enough, but he saw the temper in her eyes.

"You would not ask," he told her. "But you have gone out of your way to throw her in my path. Tell me, was Tahir a part of your plan? Did you arrange for him to come to the orphanage and set the events in motion?"

"I have no idea what you're talking about, but if I did, I would point out Kayleen would be a good mother. Her sons would be strong. You have to marry someone. Why not her?"

Why indeed? A case could be made for his aunt's logic. Kayleen may not have been born royal, but sometimes that was an advantage. She had an inner strength he respected—it was her heart that made him wary.

"She cares too much," he told his aunt. "She is too emotional."

"She's a woman."

"She leads with her heart. She deserves someone who can appreciate that."

Lina studied him for several seconds, then nodded. "All right. That's the one answer I can respect. It's too bad. I think she would have been good for you. Then we'll just have to find her someone else."

"She is the children's nanny."

"She deserves more than just a job. You were right, there's no young American man, but I'll find her someone." She rose and smiled. "Don't worry, As'ad. While I'm finding Kayleen a husband, I'll find you another nanny. You won't be inconvenienced."

Those should have been the words he wanted to hear, but something about them bothered him. Something he couldn't define but that created a knot in the middle of his chest.

"What is it?" As'ad asked, staring at the thick, flat cutout.

Dana grinned. "It's a turkey."

He eyed the layers of paper. "It is a turkey that has met with some unfortunate circumstances."

She giggled, then pulled the top over, creating a three-dimensional paper turkey. "It's a decoration," she told him. "They delivered a whole box of 'em. We can put them on the table and hang them from the ceiling." She glanced up at the curved, fifteen-foot ceiling. "Okay, maybe not the ceiling. But we'll put them all around."

"This is tradition?" he asked.

"Uh-huh. Along with the leaves."

The box with the flat paper turkeys had also included festive garlands in fall colors, along with silk leaves in red, brown and gold.

Pepper leaned over and grabbed a handful of leaves. "I'll put these on the table. We can make a line down the center of the tablecloth. It'll be pretty."

Nadine trailed after her younger sister, picking up the leaves that drifted to the floor. As'ad took a length of garland and followed them to the table.

"This will go on top of the leaves?" he asked.

Pepper grinned. "Uh-huh. And we need to have candles. Really tall ones. They're the prettiest." She set down her leaves, put her hands on her hips and looked at him. "How come you don't know this?"

"We don't celebrate Thanksgiving here."

Her blue eyes widened. "But you have to."

"They weren't discovered by pilgrims," Nadine told her. "America was the new world. It had to be found."

"It was lost?" Pepper asked.

"In a manner of speaking," As'ad said. "It's a celebration unique to your country. Although I believe the Canadians also celebrate Thanksgiving, but on a different day."

He waited while the two girls straightened out the leaves, then he set the garland on top. It was attractive, he thought. Very festive. Kayleen would like it. The surprise would make her happy.

He imagined her throwing herself at him, and him pulling her close. Then the vision shifted and changed so they were both naked and he was pushing his way inside of her as they—

"As'ad, what traditions do you have here?" Dana asked.

He forced his attention back to the present. This was not the time to explore sexual fantasies with the girls' nanny.

"We have many celebrations. There is the day the El Deharian armies defeated the Ottoman Empire. We also celebrate Christmas, although it is not as big a holiday here as it would have been for you back in the States."

Pepped sighed. "I worry about Santa being able to find us here."

"He'll find you and he'll enjoy the large fireplace in your room," As'ad told her. "It won't be so hard for him to get inside."

Her eyes widened. "Santa comes to the palace?"

"Of course."

"So I can write him a letter? I've been very, very good this year."

"Yes. You can write a letter. We'll arrange to have it sent through the royal post office, so it gets priority treatment."

The little girl beamed at him.

"Will there be snow at Christmas?" Dana asked as she set yet another paper turkey on the bookcase.

"We do not get snow here."

"I didn't think so." She shrugged. "I miss snow. We grew up in Michigan and we always had a white Christmas. We used to made snowmen and snow angels. Mom always had hot chocolate and cookies waiting."

"I don't remember her much," Pepper said in a whisper.

"Sure you do," Nadine told her. "She was tall and pretty, with blond hair."

There was a wistful, sad quality to her voice. It tugged at something in As'ad. Like Pepper, he had minimal memories of his mother. Perhaps his older brothers had more. He had never asked. Instead he'd been raised by a series of nannies when he'd been young and tutors when he was older. Then he'd been sent away to school. It was the expected life of a prince.

"I don't remember her," Pepper insisted, her eyes filling with tears.

He crouched in front of her. "You remember snow, don't you?"

She nodded slowly. "It's cold and white and it makes my nose red. I want snow for Christmas."

"It seems unlikely," he told her. "We live in the desert, on the edge of the ocean. This is not a cold climate. But it can still be very beautiful."

"We'll be fine," Dana told him bravely. "You'll see. It's just the change. Change is hard. For all of us."

"Agreed, but you are here now. This is where you will stay. Didn't Kayleen tell you?"

The girls exchanged glances, then looked at him.

"We don't know what we're going to do," Pepper told him. "We're supposed to stay here, with you, but what happens when Kayleen leaves?"

He straightened. "What are you talking about? She's not going anywhere."

"Yes, she is. She told us a long time ago." Dana drew in a breath. "She'll be twenty-five soon. When she's twenty-five she gets to go back to teach at the convent school where she grew up. It's what she always wanted. What we don't know is if we go with her or stay here with you."

Lina hovered by the front of the palace, not an easy thing to do when there were tour groups lining up, official visitors arriving and she was well recognized. She supposed it would make more sense to wait in her rooms until she was notified that King Hassan was in residence.

But she couldn't stand the thought of being confined right now. It was far easier to walk the length of the entryway—a distance of about two hundred feet—than walk back. If nothing else, she was getting her exercise for the day.

Part of the problem was she hadn't slept for a week. She'd barely dozed the previous night and had been wide awake at four in the morning. It had taken nearly a half hour with chilled gel packs on her eyes to reduce the puffiness. Then there had been the issue of what to wear.

She'd gone through her considerable wardrobe more than once over the past few days. A dress seemed too formal, slacks too casual. In the end she'd settled on a black skirt and a silk blouse. She'd fussed over her makeup, her hair, her jewelry. It was like being sixteen again, but with all the baggage that comes with middle age. It was exhausting.

As she paced, smiled at visitors and did her best not to be recognized by the tour group moving into the palace, she told herself it was ridiculous to be so nervous. Officially she'd known King Hassan for years. But this was the first time he was coming to El Deharia to see *her*.

"It's not a date," she murmured to herself, grateful the vast entryway was finally almost empty. "It's a...a..." She sucked in a breath, not sure what his visit was.

A large SUV drove into the courtyard, followed by a dark Mercedes. Another SUV parked behind it.

Guards stepped out, looking stern in their business suits and sunglasses. One of them moved to the rear of the Mercedes and opened the passenger-side door.

Lina walked toward the car, telling herself to be calm, to smile and speak with at least the pretense of intelligence. King Hassan stepped out into the afternoon.

He was a man of medium height and strong build. His hair was gray, as was his neatly trimmed beard. He had handsome features and an air of confidence and power about him. There were no outward symbols of his rank, yet just looking at him, it was easy to guess he wasn't like everyone else.

Lina hesitated. Normally she curtseyed when she greeted a monarch, yet that now seemed strange. Still, protocol and her upbringing won out.

But before she could offer the gesture of respect, Hassan stepped toward her, took both her hands in his and smiled at her.

"My dear Lina. You are more beautiful than I remember."

He gazed into her eyes. She stared back, seeing pleasure and humor, along with something very much like interest. Her stomach continued to flop around, but the reason changed from nerves to anticipation. A warmth stole through her and she smiled.

"Welcome, sir. All of El Deharia is pleased at your visit. Me, most of all."

He pulled her close and tucked her hand into the crook of his arm. "Hassan," he said. "You must call me Hassan. Do you forget how you mocked me in your e-mails? You can't be formal now."

They walked into the palace. "I never mocked you," she told him, liking the feel of being next to him, close to him.

"You called me a crazy old man who was too concerned about his cats."

She laughed. "I did not. You're making that up."

"Perhaps."

He smiled at her, making her heart beat wildly and her

throat get dry. It had been so long since any man had affected her, she thought happily. So long since she'd let herself notice a smile, a voice, a touch.

They walked along the main corridor, toward the elevators that would take them up to the guest floors.

"How is your first project coming?" he asked. "Has As'ad noticed the lovely Kayleen?"

"Absolutely." Lina grinned. "She got lost in the desert and ended up with some local tribesmen. As'ad went after her and claimed her for his own. He says it was to keep her safe, but I think there was more to it than that. When they got back, Kayleen specifically told me nothing had happened. She was so intent on telling me that, I knew something had."

"So you are a success."

"Not yet, but I hope to be soon."

They rode up three floors and exited onto a wide, open hallway.

"Your suite is just down here," Lina told him. "It is the one you stayed in before."

When they reached the double doors, she opened one and led the way in. The rooms were large, elegantly furnished and only used for kings and heads of state.

Fresh flowers filled several vases and a large fruit basket sat on the dining room table.

"I thought we could go out to dinner tonight," she said. "There are a couple of really nice restaurants in the city with private rooms. I can give the names to your head of security so he can check them out in advance. There are a few plays we could take in and a visiting European symphony, depending on what interests you most. My brother would be delighted if you would care to ride any of his horses and I—"

Hassan crossed to her and pressed his finger to her mouth. "You can stop talking now."

She drew in a breath, then pressed her lips together. "All right."

"I am not here to be entertained or to go riding. I am here to spend time with you. You have charmed me, Lina. I had not thought that would happen again in my lifetime and I am delighted to be wrong. I sense many possibilities."

Oh, my. The man had simply put it out there. Of course, he was a king and that could have something to do with his confidence level. If only she could say the same about herself.

"I, ah…" She swallowed. "Me, too."

He laughed, then pulled her close. "So let us see where this all leads."

And then he kissed her.

Chapter Seven

As'ad watched as several members of the kitchen staff set up the dinner. There was a large turkey, along with dishes of stuffing, yams, vegetables, mashed potatoes, gravy and several pies.

"I'm starving," Pepper whispered to Dana. "Can I have just a bite?"

"No," her sister told her. "We're waiting for Kayleen, remember? It'll just be a few more minutes."

Kayleen had phoned to say she'd received the message telling her to come to As'ad's room for dinner and would be right up.

As'ad did his best to focus on the girls, on how Pepper kept sniffing the air and how Nadine gracefully danced from foot to foot in impatience.

His plan had worked perfectly—the room was decorated, the meal prepared and Kayleen would be able to celebrate her country's holiday. Yet despite the success, he couldn't shake the deep sense of outrage that stirred within him.

She was leaving in a few months? Just like that? She hadn't said anything to him, hadn't hinted. He had hired her to be nanny to the three girls *she* had insisted he adopt and now she was going to disappear?

Equally insulting was the fact that Dana said she didn't know if the sisters were staying or going. As if it was their decision to make. He was Prince As'ad of El Deharia. *He* decided who would stay and who would leave. How dare Kayleen think she could simply walk away without speaking to him.

He took out his anger on the bottle of Chardonnay he'd chosen for their dinner, jerking out the cork with more force than necessary.

Did Kayleen think it was acceptable to leave the girls so soon after bringing them to the palace? Did she think they could bear another upheaval in their lives? What about him? Was he to raise them on his own?

He didn't know what annoyed him more—the fact that she'd been making plans without consulting him or the reality that she'd been considering leaving in the first place. Not that he personally cared if she went. His outrage was all for the girls, and perhaps for the violation of her position. She was the nanny. She reported to *him*.

Apparently she was not impressed enough with his position and power. Obviously he needed to show her what it meant to deal with someone in the royal family.

He poured himself a glass of wine and drank it down. Even more annoying was her desire to cut herself off from the world. She did not belong in drab clothes, teaching at a convent school. What would happen to her there? Her bright spirit and fresh beauty would wither and die. She would grow old before her time.

It was up to him to change that. As her employer, he had a duty to protect Kayleen, even from herself. He knew best. At least here, in the palace, she would *live* her life. So how to convince her that she must stay, must serve him and be nanny to the girls?

He could order her, he thought as he poured a second glass of wine, then dismissed the idea as quickly as it formed. It pained him to admit the truth, but Kayleen was not one to take orders well, even from a prince. So he must convince her another way. He must make her see that there was more to her future than the high walls of a convent school. That there was much she would miss.

It would be one thing if she wanted to leave to live, he told himself. Perhaps to marry, although the idea of her with another man was irritating. Who would be good enough for her? Who would be patient with the unexpected virgin? Who would teach her the—

The thought formed. A solution. Perhaps unorthodox, but workable. He considered the possibilities and knew that it would be successful. A sacrifice, he thought, but not a hardship.

In time, she would thank him.

Kayleen walked into As'ad's rooms with her mind still on her work. She'd been making a lot of progress on the report he'd requested and had found out a lot of interesting information about the various reasons why some villages sent a lot of young women to college and some didn't. She wanted to discuss it all over dinner after they—

She paused, noting the room was especially dark, which didn't make sense. There had been lights in the corridor. Had she accidentally gone into the wrong room?

She reached for a switch on the wall, only to have all the lights come on, the three girls jump out from behind furniture and yell, "Surprise!"

Kayleen took a step back. "What are you up to? What's the surprise?"

And then she saw the paper turkeys covering every surface in the room. The festive fall garland, the leaves decorating the perfectly set table.

"It's Thanksgiving," Pepper said, rushing up and grabbing her hand. "We're having a real Thanksgiving dinner."

As'ad appeared. "The kitchen staff have done their best. They have never had a Thanksgiving dinner, so they apologize in advance if they didn't get everything exactly as you would have it."

Thanksgiving? Here? She'd willed herself not to think about the holiday, but it had been difficult and much of the day she'd felt sad. To walk into this was more than she could have imagined.

Dana and Nadine moved next to her. Kayleen crouched down to hug all three girls. Still holding them close, she looked up at As'ad.

"Thank you," she said, delighted by the surprise and feeling oddly emotional. "You're very thoughtful."

"I cannot take all the credit. Lina reminded me of the holiday and the girls helped with the preparations. Are you pleased?"

She rose and smiled at him. "Very. Thank you."

She'd never expected the gesture. As'ad wasn't who or

what she'd expected. There was a kindness in him, a caring and sensitivity she hadn't thought possible. He was the classic handsome prince, yet he wasn't indifferent or selfish. He could have chosen to spend his life going to parties and hanging out with models and stars. Instead he worked hard and took in orphans.

It occurred to her that he was a good man, the sort of man she admired. The kind of man the Mother Superior had told her to look for when she left for college. Kayleen hadn't found anyone remotely fitting that description during her four years away. How odd she should find him now…here in El Deharia.

As'ad poured her a glass of wine as the girls dragged her to the table. "What are you thinking?" he asked, passing her the glass.

"That you're very unexpected."

"I could say the same about you."

His low voice made her insides quiver.

They served themselves from the buffet and then settled at the table. Kayleen said grace, then took her first bite of turkey.

"It's delicious. Dana, what do you think?" She looked at the girl and was surprised to see tears in her eyes. "What's wrong?"

"Nothing. This is nice. Thank you." A tear rolled down her cheek.

Pepper was crying, as well, and Nadine was sniffing into her napkin.

"I miss my mom and dad," Nadine whimpered. "I want to go home and be with them."

"Me, too," Dana said, and turned her gaze to As'ad. "You're the prince. Can't you do something?"

Kayleen felt helpless. What could she possibly say to make the situation better? She felt awful for the girls, because she understood what they were going through. Holidays were always a mixed blessing—she'd loved the specialness of the day, but it had also reminded her of how alone she was. How she had no family, no one who loved her best.

As'ad put his arm around Dana, then kissed the top of her head. "If only I could," he said quietly. "I know your pain and can tell you with time, it will get better."

"You can't know that," the preteen told him, her voice thick with bitterness. "You can't know anything about it."

"I lost my mother when I was very young. Kayleen grew up with no family. We understand exactly what you are feeling."

Dana seemed to deflate. "That doesn't help. I know it should, but it doesn't. I want to go home."

As'ad stared at her for a long moment, then said, "When I was about your age, I ran away. I was angry at my father for not recognizing that I was growing up, practically a man. I was tired of being sent away to school every year, of being different. A prince. You'll find that out as you grow. To be royal defines one."

"I'm not royal," Dana told him.

He smiled at her. "You are now. You are my daughter."

Dana fiddled with her fork. "What happened when you ran away?"

"I decided to become a camel dealer."

All three of the girls stared at him. Kayleen tried not to laugh. "Really?" she asked.

"Yes. I thought I could make a good living selling camels. I took several from the royal stable, thinking I would use them to start my business."

Her lips twitched, but she was determined to be serious. "There's a royal camel stable?"

His dark gaze settled on her, seeming to caress her with a warm, tender touch. "Of course. There is a royal everything."

Pepper took a bite of turkey and chewed. "Can I see the royal camels?"

"Certainly."

"Do they look different than regular camels?" Nadine asked.

"They wear very small crowns."

Dana grinned. "They do not."

As'ad laughed. "You're right. But they are a special breed. And they are extremely stubborn. I did not know this when I first took them, but soon they were leading *me* into the desert, rather than the other way around."

Nadine giggled. Dana joined in. "What happened?" she asked.

As'ad wove a funny tale about a boy and four stubborn, angry camels, a lost night in the desert and many disasters. By the time he was done, all three sisters had finished their dinner, gotten seconds and were eyeing the pie. The tears were gone, as were the bad memories.

This is what they would remember about their first Thanksgiving in El Deharia, Kayleen thought as she tucked them in and kissed them good-night. As'ad's story would be a part of their history and they would remember it and him for the rest of their lives.

He'd escorted them down to their suite and had waited while they got ready for bed. As she walked back into her living room, she saw he'd started a fire in the fireplace and made himself at home on the large sofa across from the flickering flames.

"It's not exactly chilly outside," she told him, knowing it made sense to sit next to him, but suddenly feeling shy.

"I thought you would appreciate the ambience. More memories of home, but happy ones I hope."

She walked over to the sofa and sat down at the far end. "There are a lot of happy ones," she said, then turned to him. "Thank you for tonight. For the surprise and for helping the girls through a difficult time. This is their first holiday season without their parents and it's going to be hard for them."

"They will need both of us to get through," he said.

"I agree." She was a little surprised that he saw it that way, though. "I didn't think you wanted much to do with them."

"They are charming girls with much potential. I find I enjoy spending time with them."

"I'm glad."

"And you?" he asked, his dark gaze seeming to see into her soul. "What do you think of them?"

"I adore them. Why do you ask?"

"Because you plan to leave them."

She opened her mouth, then closed it. Embarrassment made her stare at the fire. She battled guilt, as if she'd done something wrong. She knew she should have talked to him before—so he learned of her plans from her and not someone else. But she'd been afraid of what he would think of her.

"They told you," she murmured.

"Dana said you planned to return home on your

twenty-fifth birthday. That you would lock yourself away and teach at the convent school."

When he said it, her dreams seemed small and point-less. "As you say, it's my home."

"A place we cannot always return to. What of your commitment to the girls?"

"I don't know," she admitted. "I haven't really thought anything through. This was planned a long time ago. I didn't expect to be their nanny."

"You are the one who insisted I adopt them. You *are* the most stable adult presence in their lives. Would you subject them to more upheaval by leaving them so soon after they came to be here? Are they nothing to you?"

"No. Of course not." She hated what he was saying. "I don't know what I was going to do. Of course I'd help you hire someone else. Someone to replace me."

"Would you? Or was your plan to take them with you?"

She ducked her head. "I thought of that, too."

"Did you think that would be allowed? This is El Deharia. No one may take royal children from the country without their parents' permission. I will not give it."

Kayleen could only stare at him. Of course. Thanks to her, he *was* their father and his rules applied. She hadn't thought that part through, either.

"It's all a mess."

"No decision has to be made now," he said. "We will find a solution together. Do you have any other secrets you are keeping from me?"

"What? No. Never. And I would have told you about leaving." She leaned toward him. "As'ad, I wasn't trying to trick you about anything. I was desperate for Tahir not to take the girls back to his village."

Somehow he wasn't at the far end of the sofa anymore, she thought as he reached out and lightly stroked her cheek. "I believe you."

"Good, because it's true. I just…" She had a hard time stringing words together. His touch was very distracting. "I love your country. It's beautiful. I love the modern city and the wildness of the desert. I love your people, the kindness of them. You were right about Tahir only wanting to do the right thing, even if I don't agree with him. I've been learning so much about the villages while researching my project for you. This is an amazing place."

"But it is not home?"

She shook her head slowly. "I feel safe at the convent. That probably sounds stupid to a man like you."

"Feeling safe is important, especially when one did not grow up with that benefit. But there is so much more for you to experience than what you will find behind the convent walls."

"I like the convent walls."

"They lock you in."

"They shelter you."

He smiled gently. "From life. That is not a good thing."

Getting back had been her goal from the moment she'd been told she must leave and live in the world. Those words had broken her heart. It was like being thrown out of her home.

"Those walls protect me," she told him.

He looked at her intently. "*I* will protect you."

Then he leaned in and kissed her.

It was as if she'd been waiting for his kiss all her life. The second his mouth touched her, she felt both relief and an odd tension.

His lips were warm and firm, asking rather than taking, making her want to give all that he asked and more. He brushed against her, exploring, remembering perhaps. She remembered everything about their heated kiss in the desert. The feel of his body against hers, the hard planes and strength of him. The way he'd held her so tenderly, the taste and heat of him.

Those memories combined with the wonder of his kiss to make her strain forward, as she eagerly waited to experience it again. She parted without being asked and was rewarded when he licked her bottom lip before slipping inside.

He kissed her deeply, exploring all of her. She put her hands on his shoulders, as much to steady herself as to touch him, then kissed him back, stroking, dueling, dancing. It was magical, something more wondrous than she'd ever imagined. It was as if she were melting from the inside out.

Again and again he kissed her, taking his time, making her feel as if the magic could go on forever. He stroked her back, moving up and down. Oddly, that touch made her want to squirm in place. If only he would touch her breasts again, she thought hazily. If only he would put his hands there, like he had before.

And because that's what she wanted and because she trusted him fully, she let him ease her onto the sofa, until she was nearly lying down.

He pulled back and stared into her eyes. "You are so beautiful," he murmured before kissing her cheekbones, her nose, her forehead, then her jaw.

Beautiful? Her? She'd seen her reflection a thousand times. Sometimes she thought she might be pretty, but other times, she knew she was just like everyone else.

"Your skin is so soft and pale," he continued as he nibbled his way down her jaw to her neck. It both tickled and aroused, so she stayed very still, wanting him to continue forever.

"Then you blush and the fiery color delights me."

"I'm a redhead," she whispered. "Blushing comes with the package."

"It is a glorious package." He touched her hair. "So cool to the touch. I have fantasies about your hair."

"Seriously?"

"Seriously."

He kissed her again and she kissed him back, but all the while she was wondering what fantasies he could have about her hair? It was just hair, wasn't it? Long and wavy and very red.

He kissed her chin, then trailed down her neck. She'd never thought about a man's lips on her neck and was unprepared for the electric sensations that shot through her, making her toes curl and her insides tighten.

He put his hand on her belly. Even through the layers of clothing, she felt the warmth and each individual finger. He moved up slowly, so slowly. Her breath caught in anticipation.

Touch me there, she whispered to herself, closing her eyes and waiting until he finally settled his palm on her breast.

The feeling was exquisite. She wanted more of that, but didn't know how to ask. He kissed her ear, which was a distraction, then nipped her earlobe, which was delicious. Everything felt so good that she barely noticed when he unbuttoned the front of her dress and eased the fabric open.

She supposed her first instinct should have been to cover herself, but she didn't want to. She wanted to know what it would feel like to have his hand there, on her breast, with only her bra between them.

And then she knew. He touched her gently, almost teasing, fingers lightly brushing her skin. He moved against her tight nipple. She groaned. It wasn't a sound she'd ever made before and she wanted desperately to have reason to make it again.

He explored both breasts, then reached behind her to unfasten her bra. He eased his hand under the cup and touched her again. This time bare skin on bare skin.

It was amazing, she thought, her body practically shaking. She hadn't known she was capable of such sensations. More. She wanted more. More touching, more naked, more kissing, more everything.

As'ad drew back and stood. She opened her eyes and wondered what she'd done wrong. Why was he stopping? Then he bent down and picked her up in his arms. He cradled her against him and kissed her, even as he began to walk across the rug toward the bedroom.

It was the most romantic moment of her life. As they stepped into the darkness of her bedroom, she knew that she wanted to be with him, to experience making love with him. Perhaps there should have been questions or fears, but her mind was free of both. She only knew that her body seemed to recognize him and welcome him. He made her tremble and feel and she wanted more of that.

He lowered her to her feet, then closed the door behind them and turned on a bedside lamp. The light was dim, which was probably better, because as much as she wanted more, she was a little nervous about being naked. People did get naked when they made love, didn't they?

She thought about asking, but then he was kissing her

again and speaking seemed really unimportant. His hands were everywhere, gently easing her dress from her shoulders so it puddled at her feet, then removing her bra.

Even as he stroked her tongue with his, he put both his hands on her breasts, cupping the curves and teasing her nipples with his thumbs. It was good—better than good. It was amazing.

Her body was suddenly a great unknown to her. She didn't have any idea about what she would experience next, but she wanted it all.

When he bent his head down and took her breast in his mouth, she gasped, then grabbed him to help herself stay standing. Fire roared through her, settling between her legs where the heat grew.

She knew the mechanics of what went on between a man and a woman, but she'd never imagined it could be so *good*. He moved back and forth between her breasts, licking them with his tongue, sucking until she wanted to scream. It was amazing and arousing and intriguing.

When he moved them to the bed, she went eagerly, wanting to know what else there could be, what other experiences she could have. He removed the rest of her clothes and she shocked herself by not minding that she was naked. Not when he stared down at her with a fire even she could see in his eyes.

"I want you," he breathed. "All of you. Kayleen, I want to touch you and taste you and be inside of you. But I will not take what isn't offered."

He had her at "I want you." She reached out to touch his hand, then gently tugged until he knelt next to her.

"You are eager?" he asked quietly.

"I'm shameless. I want you to touch me." She couldn't

say the other stuff, but she was thinking it. She wanted to know what it was like to be with a man—to be with *him*.

He removed his shoes and socks, then shrugged out of his shirt. His chest was broad and muscled, with a light dusting of hair she itched to touch. Then he stretched out next to her and smiled.

"I will go slowly," he told her, tracing the shape of her mouth with his finger. "Tell me if anything frightens you or hurts you and I will stop."

"I know it's going to hurt when you, um, well, you know."

His smile faded. "It will, for a moment. Do you wish to stop?"

She shook her head.

"Good. Neither do I."

He took her hand in his and brought it below his waist. She felt the hard thickness of him.

"This is what you do to me," he told her. "This is what touching you does to me."

His words and his arousal filled her with a feminine power she'd never experienced before. It hadn't occurred to her that a man could *want* her that way. Or any way. A shiver raced through her as desire and anticipation both grew.

He leaned in and kissed her again. His hand settled on her stomach, an unfamiliar weight. She told herself not to think about it, but then he was moving down her belly to the apex of her thighs.

His touch was light and gentle, more teasing than insisting. When he reached the curls only slightly darker than her hair color, she wasn't sure what to do.

A single finger eased between the curls. It explored her, which was really sort of nice. She wouldn't mind him touching her more if he—

He brushed against the very center of her. She'd heard about that place, of course, but had wondered how she would ever know if she was touched there. Stupid question, she thought happily as delicious, erotic fire raced through her. She knew. How could she not know?

He moved against that place again and her legs fell open of their own accord. She found it difficult to breathe.

He continued to touch her there, moving lightly across that single spot, rubbing it, circling it, making her body tremble and heat and strain. She barely noticed when he stopped kissing her because his touch was so exquisite. She closed her eyes and let herself get lost in the sensation.

Around and around. He moved against her, going faster now. She found herself pulsing her hips in time with his touch. She strained but wasn't sure toward what. He bent down and took her nipple in his mouth. The combination of sensations made her gasp.

It was too much. A direct connection between her legs and her breasts. She grabbed at the sheets, trying to push herself toward…toward…

Her body tensed. She felt every muscle clench, which probably wasn't a good thing, but what he was doing felt too good for her to stop. Then time seemed to pause as she hovered on the brink of—

The wave of sensation caught her off guard. It was unlike anything she'd experienced before. Liquid pleasure poured through her as her muscles contracted. It was frenzied and amazing and she was terrified if she did anything at all, it would end suddenly.

But the moment went on and she lost herself in what she realized was her first orgasm. She allowed herself to breathe and the bliss continued. Tension faded, muscles relaxed, until she felt content and satisfied and more than a little shocked such a thing was possible.

As'ad moved his fingers away. She opened her eyes and stared up at him.

"I want to do that again," she told him.

He laughed. "So you enjoy the lovemaking?"

"Who wouldn't? Can that happen again? Can it happen now?"

He rose onto his hands and knees. "As you wish, Kayleen. We will try another game. But a gentle one. I don't want you to hurt later."

Later was a long time away, she thought as he settled between her legs and gently parted her curls.

It was obvious he was going to kiss her *there,* which was shocking and something she probably should refuse. Except what he'd done before had been so amazing. Could this be as good?

She sank back onto the bed and closed her eyes. A soft whisper of breath was her only warning, then his mouth pressed against her and his tongue touched her more intimately than she'd ever thought possible.

It was like kissing, but a billion times better, she thought as all the air rushed from her lungs. The steady flick of his tongue was impossible to resist. She gave herself over to the sensation, to the tension that quickly tightened all her muscles. Despite the awkwardness of the position and her lack of experience, she found herself pushing toward the pleasure goal.

She wanted that experience again. She wanted the waves, but this time from his tongue. She wanted him to push her higher and closer and she wanted it now!

She found herself digging her heels into the bed as she

pushed her body against him. Impatience battled with arousal. The journey was exquisite, but the destination was—

He slipped a finger inside of her. The action was shocking enough to make her gasp. She waited for pain or pressure, but there was only the need to push down on that finger, to have him fill her.

He continued to lick her, making her body tense more. Then he moved his finger in and out, matching the rhythm of his tongue, taking her up and up and up until she had no choice but to crash back to earth.

The second journey down was even better than the first. She felt herself cry out and tried to stifle the noise. Her body shuddered as her release filled every cell and pleasured every nerve. It was too much. She hadn't known that anything like this was possible.

As'ad straightened, then moved next to her. He touched her all over, caressing, but perhaps reassuring. She stared into his dark eyes.

"I didn't know," she whispered.

"There is more."

That made her laugh. "Not possible."

"I will show you."

Would he? Could they explore this together? "I'd like that."

He stroked her face. "What is your wish, Kayleen? For me to leave now? You remain an innocent."

"Technically," she murmured, although she knew a whole lot more than she had an hour ago. She gathered her courage and put her hand on his bare chest. His skin was smooth, his muscles hard. "Be in me."

"You are sure?"

She smiled. "Very."

He pulled her into a sitting position, then stood beside the bed. After removing his slacks and briefs, he stood in front of her.

She'd never seen a man naked before. Art really didn't count. He was bigger than she'd expected.

She stroked the length of him, liking the velvety smoothness of the skin and the way he felt like a rock underneath.

"You're not going to fit," she told him as she wondered if women did to men what he had done to her. Touching with their mouths. Would that be nice?

He chuckled and reached for his slacks. "It will fit."

He removed a square of plastic, then sat on the bed. She was going to ask what he was doing, then remembered that the act itself had consequences. He was making sure she had nothing to worry about.

She was about to ask him why he had a condom in his pocket, then he eased her onto her back and slipped between her legs.

The position felt a little strange and she didn't know what to do with her feet or her hands. Did she just lie there? Was she supposed to move? Should she keep quiet or did people talk?

"This will hurt a little," he warned. "You are prepared?"

She nodded and braced herself.

He smiled. "Perhaps you could pretend you are excited."

"What? Oh, sorry. I'm just nervous."

"Perhaps I can distract you."

He reached between her legs and began to rub her again. She immediately relaxed as the familiar tension started. If he kept that up for very long, she would come again.

But before she could get far along the path, he stopped and she felt something hard pushing against her. She took a deep breath as he slowly, slowly filled her.

The pressure was unfamiliar and a little uncomfortable, but not bad. There was more and more until at last he said, "I am in."

She opened her eyes and smiled at him. "I'm wild now."

He smiled in return. "It will take a little more for you to be wild, but this is a start. I would like you to touch me."

Oh. "All right," she murmured, not sure where or how.

She stroked the length of his arms, then put her hands on his back. He withdrew and pushed in again. This time she tilted her hips slightly, taking him more easily.

By the fifth time, she didn't have to think about the touching—it just happened on her own. And there was a subtle tension between her legs. Different from what happened before, but still compelling.

She closed her eyes and lost herself in the rhythm of him making love to her, filling her, pushing deep inside of her, making her ache and want. He moved faster and his breathing increased. More and more until he groaned and was still.

He murmured her name as he held her. She wrapped her arms around him, feeling the weight of him, a stretch in her hips, and knew that everything had changed forever.

Chapter Eight

Kayleen spent the following morning not sure what to think. Her evening with As'ad played over and over in her mind like a very naughty movie. Every time she remembered him touching her, she felt all squishy inside.

She hadn't expected to sleep, but after he'd gone back to his room, she'd fallen into her bed and the next thing she knew it was morning. She'd awakened happy and sore and just a little out of sorts. She didn't regret what had happened, but she certainly felt…different.

As'ad had been so great, she thought as she waved to the girls as they climbed into the Town Car that took them to school each day. He'd been gentle and patient and funny and sexy. He'd been everything she could have imagined a man being. More, she reminded herself. He was *better* than anything—or anyone—she could have imagined.

And the whole being together thing had been amazing. Who had thought that up? Why hadn't she understood before? Was this what her Mother Superior had meant about getting out in the world?

Kayleen covered her mouth. She doubted that was exactly what the other woman had meant. Still, she understood now that there were possibilities. Things she'd never known about. Did she want to give up that kind of a relationship forever? Did she want to get married and have a family? Did she—

"Good morning, Kayleen. How are you?"

She looked up and saw Lina walking toward her. Kayleen had the sudden thought that the other woman knew. That everyone knew. It had to be obvious, didn't it? Could they tell? Was her appearance different? Was there something in her eyes?

The crash of guilt was as powerful as it was unexpected. Yes, her night with As'ad had been wonderful and exciting, but what was she thinking, giving herself to a man like that? They weren't in love. She wasn't sure she knew what being in love with a man felt like. So she'd just given herself to him? Why? Because he'd made her feel good? Would she give herself to anyone who asked?

"Kayleen?" Lina frowned. "What's wrong? Are you ill?"

"I'm fine," she said, trying to act normal, which was difficult. She suddenly couldn't remember what normal was.

"What happened? You're flushed. Are you sure you feel all right?"

Kayleen ducked her head. Guilt quickly turned to shame as she realized she was not the person she'd always thought. "I'm not sick. It's nothing. I just... I can't... I have to go. Please excuse me."

She turned and ran, but no matter how fast she went, she couldn't escape herself.

As'ad finished with his tie and reached for his jacket. The door to his suite burst open and Lina stepped inside. He raised his eyebrows.

"I did not hear you knock," he said mildly, in too good a mood to mind the intrusion. Last night he had shown Kayleen the possibilities. She would quickly realize that returning to the convent school was not the right path for her. She would want to stay in the world—in *his* world. All would be well and very shortly she would come and thank him.

Perhaps they could continue to be lovers, he thought absently. He had enjoyed his time in her bed. She had been passionate and responsive. Just thinking about her soft cries made him want her again. They could pleasure each other and—

"I can't believe it," Lina said, stepping in front of him, her expression stern. "I can't believe you did it."

He shrugged into his jacket. "Did what?"

"You slept with Kayleen."

He shrugged. "It is not for you to criticize."

"What?" Her voice was high-pitched and carried a tone that warned him there was danger ahead.

He decided to change tactics. "Kayleen is nearly twenty-five. While it is very kind of you to be concerned about her welfare, she is more than capable of taking care of herself."

Lina put her hands on her hips. "Are you kidding me? That's it? That's all you have to say? As'ad, you are a prince. You defiled a virgin under the king's roof. You don't get to escape by telling me she's an adult and therefore responsible for her decisions."

Defiled a virgin? Did she have to say it like that? He shifted uncomfortably. "I did not take anything that wasn't offered."

"Oh, there's an excuse."

"Lina, you will not speak to me this way."

"Of course I will." She glared at him, her outrage clear. "As'ad, I am Kayleen's friend. I brought her into this house. I'm responsible for her."

"You wanted me to marry her."

"I considered it a possibility. I thought you would be a good match. You weren't supposed to take her virginity. She was raised by nuns. She's nearly twenty-five and has had what, a dozen dates?"

He refused to feel guilty. He was Prince As'ad and because of that, whatever he chose to do was the right thing. And yet there was a nagging voice in the back of his head that pointed out he hadn't thought things through.

"She planned to return to the convent school," he told Lina. "She was going to bury herself there."

"So you decided to change that? If you don't want her, who are you to destroy her life?"

"Her life is not destroyed." He resented the implication. "I honored her."

"Oh, please. It was never for you to decide what she did with her life. It was never for you to judge. You took the one thing she would want to give her husband. Now she can't go back to the convent school and you'll have no use for her. Then what? She's ruined, As'ad, and you did it. Kayleen isn't the type to take that lightly. She had choices before. You've taken them away from her."

He turned from his aunt and walked to the French doors leading to the balcony. While Lina made things more dramatic than they needed to be, he understood her point.

He'd wanted Kayleen and he'd taken her. It had happened before—dozens of times. Hundreds. Women were always delighted to be with him. But there was a large difference between them and Kayleen. The women he enjoyed were experienced. They understood how the game was played. Kayleen didn't even know there was a game.

She had given herself eagerly, sensually. She'd enjoyed their lovemaking. He'd opened her eyes to the possibilities, but he had also taken something that couldn't be returned.

His aunt's words echoed in his head. That he had defiled a virgin under the roof of the king. There was a time when, prince or not, such an offense would result in his death. Virginity was a prize to be given to a husband. It was a gift of honor. Something she had no more.

He turned back to Lina, intent on explaining, once again, that he'd only had Kayleen's best interests in mind. That it was important that she not lock herself away and ignore the world. But was that his only motivation?

Had there been some part of him that had wanted to be her first time? Some part of him that had wanted to claim her for himself because he knew he could?

"I will marry her," he said firmly, the words surprising him. He paused, waiting for the sense of being trapped to rise up inside of him. Waiting for the protests he must feel, but there was nothing.

It occurred to him that because he did not plan to love his wife, Kayleen was an excellent choice. As good as any other he could think of. He already liked her. She was spirited and beautiful, he enjoyed her company. She was good with children and had a sharp mind. While she knew nothing of the lifestyle of a royal bride, she would learn quickly. She would provide him with strong sons. And just as important, she was not the type to make unreasonable demands. She would be grateful for his proposal and treat him with respect.

Lina stared at him. "You'll what?"

"I will marry her. I accept my responsibility in what has occurred. Kayleen deserves more than having her gift taken in a thoughtless manner. While she gave herself to me willingly, I do not believe she had thought through the ramifications of our night together."

"That's why they call it 'swept away,'" Lina murmured, then nodded slowly. "You are sure?"

"I will speak to her this morning. I have a meeting in fifteen minutes, but after that I will explain what has to be done. She is a sensible woman. She will understand the great honor I bestow upon her and be pleased."

"How I wish I could be there for that conversation."

"Why do you say that?" he asked.

His aunt smiled at him. "I would tell you to phrase things differently, but you won't listen. For what it's worth, I think you have chosen well, As'ad. I hope things work out the way you want them to."

"They will. I am asking Kayleen to marry me. What more could she want?"

Lina's smile widened. "I can't think of a single thing."

Kayleen ran and ran until she found herself outside. The bright, sunny morning seemed to be mocking her as she wandered through the curving paths. How could everything here be so beautiful when she felt so awful inside?

What had she done? How could she have slept with As'ad? A few kisses and she'd given in? What did that make her?

She found a bench and sat down. The stone was warm to her touch, almost as if it were trying to offer comfort. Her eyes burned as she longed for someone to talk to. Someone to advise her. But who? She didn't feel comfortable discussing something so personal with the other teachers she'd worked with. Especially after moving to the palace. She was too ashamed to call her Mother Superior back home. Normally she would go to Lina, but how to explain to her what she'd done? As'ad was Lina's nephew.

Besides, Kayleen couldn't bear to see disappointment in her friend's eyes.

All the regrets she'd been so happy not to feel seemed to crash in on her. Not regret for what she'd done, but for the consequences, which made her horribly weak. Her regrets were about her future, not her past.

How could she return home now? How could she walk into that place where she'd grown up and had longed to return, knowing she had given in to the first man who asked? It wasn't that she feared punishment, it was that she didn't know who she was anymore.

She stood abruptly and started walking. An odd sound caught her attention.

She turned toward it and saw a large cage filled with doves. They were beautiful, so white and lovely in the sunlight. She watched them hop from perch to perch.

Her dream was gone, she thought. Her plans, her hopes. Now she was trapped here. Nanny to the girls until they were too old to need her or until As'ad replaced her. She was at his mercy. And then what? Another job? Where? Doing what?

She didn't know who she was anymore. What she wanted. What she should do.

Impulsively she leaned toward the cage and opened the door. The doves chirped in excitement, then in a rush, flew out and up, disappearing into the brilliant blue sky.

"Fly away," she whispered. "Fly and be free."

"I do that myself."

Kayleen jumped and turned toward the speaker. She was stunned to find the king standing on the path.

Horror swept through her. She'd just set free royal doves. "I… I…"

King Mukhtar smiled kindly. "Don't worry, child. It's difficult to resist setting them loose. There is no need for concern. They always return. It is their nature. This is their home. They can't escape their destiny."

She knew he meant the words to be reassuring, but they cut through her. Yesterday she had known her own destiny, but today she was less sure. What was her place? Where did she belong? What happened now?

"Are you enjoying living at the palace?" the king asked. "You are treated well?"

His question nearly made her laugh. But she was afraid that if she started to laugh, she wouldn't stop and then she would start crying. Hysterics would lead to a lot of questions she didn't want to answer.

"Everything is lovely," she said, doing her best to keep her emotions in check. "The palace is beautiful. I've been studying the history of the building and of your people. There is a long tradition of bravery in battle."

"The desert runs in our blood. We were warriors long before we were rulers."

"It must be difficult to leave the desert," she told him. "The beauty, the wildness, the tradition. The nomads live as they always have."

"With few modern conveniences," he said with a smile. "Much can be endured if one has excellent plumbing."

She gave a little giggle, which seemed to take a sharp turn at the end. She swallowed the sound. "But to walk in the steps of those who have gone before would be a fair compensation."

"So says the woman who has not experienced desert life. Spend a week with my people and then we will have this conversation again."

She nodded. "I would like that."

She spoke the truth. There was something appealing about simplicity right now. About having the rules of one's life spelled out. Too many choices could be complicated.

If she had never left the convent school in the first place, she wouldn't have met As'ad and none of this would have happened. Yet was it equally wrong to hide from the world? To take the safe and, therefore, easy road? To never test herself? Is that what she'd been supposed to learn?

"I just don't know," she said.

The king looked quizzical. "What troubles you, child?"

"Nothing." She felt tears burning in her eyes. "I... I'm sorry. I don't feel well. Please excuse me."

She gave a little bow, then hurried away. When she'd taken a turn in the path and knew she was out of sight, she began to run. The only problem was there was nowhere else to go.

* * *

As'ad walked to Kayleen's suite, knocked, then entered. He found her in her room, curled up on the bed, sobbing as if her heart was broken.

He stared at her for a moment, feeling both compassion and a sense of certainty that his good news would erase her tears. He allowed himself to anticipate her sweet kisses when he proposed. How she would be so excited and grateful. Perhaps they would make love again. He was more than ready, although he would have to be careful so that he did not hurt her. She was new to the sensual world and too much attention in too short a time would leave her sore.

He walked to the side of the bed. "Kayleen."

"Go away."

"I will not. Sit up. I wish to speak to you."

"No. I don't want to talk. This isn't your problem."

"Of course it is. I caused it."

She continued to cry, which surprised him. She'd seemed fine when he'd left her last night. A woman should not be left alone with her thoughts. It only created trouble.

"Kayleen—"

"Go *away*."

He considered the situation, then sat on the edge of the bed and pulled her upright. She ducked her head, refusing to look at him. He drew her against him.

"It is not as bad as all that."

"Of course it is." Her body shook with the force of her sobs. "I have betrayed everything I believe in. I'm not the person I thought. I gave myself to you without thinking it through. I barely know you. I don't love you. You're just some guy. What does that say about me?"

Some guy? He was Prince As'ad of El Deharia. He was royal and a sheik. Women *begged* him to claim them for just a single night.

"I honored you," he told her curtly.

"It wasn't an honor to me."

What? He pushed away his annoyance. She was emotional, he told himself. She wasn't thinking clearly.

"Kayleen, we share a connection with the girls. You see me as a friend and someone you can trust. It is natural you would turn to me easily."

She looked at him, her eyes swollen and red. "It's not natural to me. I'm supposed to wait until I'm in love and married."

"Sometimes it is difficult to resist the pull of sensual need."

She hiccuped. "You're saying I gave in because I wanted to do it and you just happened to be there? That's supposed to make me feel better?"

Why was she deliberately misunderstanding him? "Not at all," he said through gritted teeth. "I'm saying that I am an experienced man. I know what to do to awaken that part of a woman."

"So you tricked me? While I appreciate the effort, it's not working. I have a responsibility in this. I have to deal with what happened, what I did and what it says about me."

"I did not trick you."

She shifted away and stood. "Whatever. You can go now."

"I am not leaving," he said as he rose to his feet. "Kayleen, you are missing the point of my visit."

She wiped her cheeks with her fingers. "What's the point?"

Not exactly the opening he'd imagined. He cleared his throat. "It occurs to me that you were not in a position to consider the ramifications of what happened to us. You were lost in the moment, not realizing that by giving in to me you were destroying your most precious gift and—"

Fresh tears filled her eyes. "How could you?" she breathed and ran into the bathroom, slamming the door behind her.

He stared in disbelief. She'd walked away from him?

He followed her to the closed door. "Kayleen, please come out here at once."

"Go away. I have to figure this out and you're not helping."

He opened the door and stepped into the bathroom. "You will listen to me. I am here to make this better. I am here to fix your problem."

She shook her head. "You can't fix anything. I've lost everything I wanted."

"You have lost nothing. You are not a woman to be locked away. You deserve more than that and I am going to give it to you. Think of being married, of having a family to fill your day, children of your own." He paused to give her a chance to brace herself for the honor he would bestow upon her.

"Kayleen, I will marry you."

He smiled at her, waiting for her tears to dry. Instead more fell. Perhaps she did not understand.

"You will be my wife. You will live here, with me. In the palace. I have taken your virginity, therefore I will return your honor to you by marrying you. You will carry my name."

He waited, but she said nothing. She didn't even look at him.

"All right. I see you are having trouble understanding all this. It is unlikely you ever allowed yourself to dream of such a life. In time you will be able to believe this has truly happened. Until then, you can thank me and accept. That is enough."

She raised her gaze to stare at him. Something hot and bright burned in her eyes, but it wasn't happiness or gratitude.

"Thank you?" she repeated, her voice high and shrill. "*Thank* you? I'm not going to thank you. I wouldn't marry you if you were the last man alive."

He was so stunned that when she shoved him, he took a step back. The bathroom door slammed shut in his face and he heard the bolt shoot home.

Chapter Nine

"Take another drink of tea," Lina said soothingly.

Kayleen wrinkled her nose. The brew was a nasty herbal concoction that tasted like wet carpet smelled, but her friend assured her it would help. At this point, Kayleen was open to any suggestions.

She finished the mug and set it on the table, then grabbed a cookie she didn't want to get the taste out of her mouth.

"Better?" Lina asked.

Kayleen nodded because it was expected. In truth she didn't feel better, she felt awful. She still couldn't get herself to understand what had happened or how she'd so quickly and easily lost her moral compass. Yes, As'ad was handsome and charming and an amazing kisser, but she should have been stronger than that.

Lina sighed. "I can see by the look on your face that

you're still beating yourself up. You need to let it go. Men like my nephew have been tempting women since the beginning of time."

"It's not that I don't appreciate the information," Kayleen murmured. "It's just…"

"It doesn't help," Lina said kindly.

"Sort of. I feel so stupid and inexperienced."

"At least you're more experienced than you were."

Despite everything, Kayleen smiled. "That's true. I won't fall for that again. Next time, I'll resist."

Assuming there was a next time. Her last meeting with As'ad had ended badly. He had to be furious.

"He was serious about marrying you," Lina told her. "Don't dismiss that."

"I didn't have a choice. He didn't propose—he commanded, then he expected me to be grateful. I know he's part of your family and you love him, but that wasn't a proposal, Lina. He's just so…"

"Imperious?"

"Among other things."

And it hurt, Kayleen admitted to herself. That he would talk to her that way. If he'd come to her with compassion, truly understanding what she was going through, she would have been appreciative of what he offered. She might have been tempted to say yes. At least then her world would have been set right. But to act the way he did?

"I understand," Lina said. "As'ad is like most princes—used to being impressive. He handled the situation badly and violated your romantic fantasy at the same time."

Kayleen frowned. "I don't have a romantic fantasy."

"Don't you?"

An interesting question. She'd never really thought about getting married and having a family, so she'd never really thought about a proposal. But if she had, it would have been different. Flowers and candlelight and a man promising to love her forever.

The image was clear enough to touch, she thought ruefully.

"Okay, maybe I did. Maybe I didn't allow myself to believe it would ever happen, but deep down inside, I wanted more than instructions and an order to feel grateful."

Lina winced. "That bad?"

"Oh, yeah. The only good news is I slammed the bathroom door in his face. I don't think that happens to As'ad very much." She touched her stomach, as if she could rub away the knot that had formed inside. If As'ad was angry enough, he could send her away and she might never see the girls again. "How mad is he?"

"He's less angry and more confused. From his perspective, he did a wonderful thing."

Kayleen resisted the need to roll her eyes. "I'll write a thank-you note later."

"His world is a different place," Lina said quietly. "Like his brothers, he has been raised to know that he will be expected to serve his country, that his life, while privileged, comes with a price. Growing up it was difficult for him to know who truly wanted to be friends because they liked him, and who wanted to be friends with a prince. He made mistakes and slowly learned whom he could and could not trust."

Kayleen could relate to the pain of not having real friends, of wanting to find a place that was safe.

"But he had his brothers."

"Yes, and that helped. Still, as he got older, there were many girls, then women, willing to do anything to make him fall in love with them. Or at least sleep with them."

Kayleen felt heat on her cheeks. "Like me."

"Not like you at all. You didn't throw yourself at him or pretend to be interested. You were caught up in circumstances. As'ad shares blame in what happened. I'm simply saying he has a different perspective. While his proposal was meant to be the right thing, he handled it badly. As'ad isn't skilled in dealing with emotion. His father saw to that. He was taught that emotions make a man weak. He avoids them."

Kayleen had heard that from him and still found it hard to believe anyone could think of love as a weakness. Love gave a person infinite power and strength.

"Is there any part of you that wants to marry As'ad?" Lina asked.

The question was unexpected. Kayleen considered her reply. "It seems the easy way out."

"Which does not give me an answer."

Did she want to marry As'ad? In truth, the idea wasn't horrible. He was a nice man and the thought of spending every night in his bed was thrilling beyond words, which probably meant she was in even worse shape than she'd first thought.

But there was more to marriage than the physical, she thought. There was a lifetime of connection. Did she want to have children with As'ad? Be a true mother to the three girls? Live in El Deharia forever?

The swell of longing surprised her. The need to belong—to have roots and a home—swept over her until it was difficult to breathe. She'd been on the outside looking in all her life. To be inside now was more than she'd ever dreamed. But to marry without love?

"I'm tempted," she admitted. "Marrying As'ad would give me so much. But I'm not in love with him."

"Practical marriages are a time-honored tradition," Lina reminded her.

"I'm not royal. He's a prince. Doesn't that matter?"

"The old ways have changed. Now a prince may pick his bride. You have qualities such as honor, intelligence and kindness that make you everything I could want for As'ad."

The gentle praise made Kayleen want to cry again. "Thank you," she whispered.

"There is more to consider," Lina said. "As the wife of a prince, you would be in a position to do good on a grand scale, both here and in the world. You could devote yourself to many worthwhile causes, assuming you have time after you and As'ad start to have children."

Lina painted a picture that was difficult to resist. "Allow me to use some of the intelligence you claim I have to point out you're manipulating me."

Lina smiled. "Perhaps a little, but not as much as I could. If I truly wanted to convince you against your will, I would tell you that As'ad needs you. He needs someone who will love him unconditionally and teach him how important love is."

"I don't love him."

Lina's smile never wavered. "Perhaps you are right, but I'm not convinced. I know you, Kayleen. You wouldn't give yourself lightly to a man. I think you have feelings for As'ad and it won't take much for them to grow. Everyone deserves love. Give him his and in time, he will give you yours."

The idea of being loved was much more powerful than the fantasy of being a princess. Yes, the palace was lovely, but Kayleen would be content to live in a trailer at the ends of the earth if she could be with a man who truly loved her.

Was Lina right? Did she, Kayleen, have feelings for As'ad? Did he need her to care for him?

"What are you thinking?" Lina asked.

"That I don't know what to do."

"Then we are in a good place to start finding that out."

Kayleen forced herself to go to As'ad's office because it was the right thing to do. She knew that he had only been trying to help and the fact that he'd done it so badly didn't excuse her behavior or take away his intent. Still, it was embarrassing to face him again after her emotional outburst. She'd slammed a door in his face, both figuratively and literally. He might not be so happy to see her.

She walked into his office. Neil, his assistant, didn't immediately throw her out, which she considered a good sign.

"Is he available?" she asked.

"Perhaps. Just a moment." Neil buzzed As'ad and announced her. There was a pause before Neil said, "You may go in."

Kayleen nodded, then braced herself and opened the door.

The prince rose as she entered. He wore a suit, which was typical, yet everything about him seemed different.

Maybe it was because she *knew* him. She'd touched his

bare skin, had been as intimate with him as it was possible to be. She knew his heat, his taste, his sound. She knew what he could do to her and how she could make him react. Nothing was as it had been and she wondered if it would ever be the same again.

"Kayleen."

His voice was low, his dark eyes unreadable.

Their last meeting was a blur. She'd been beyond upset, still reeling from the reality of what she'd done. While she'd tried to explain that her feelings were about herself and not him, she wasn't sure he'd understood or believed her. Oddly, she didn't want him to feel bad.

She crossed her arms over her chest, then dropped her hands to her sides. The silence stretched between them. It occurred to her that he might be feeling a little awkward after the way she'd rejected him.

Was that possible? Did a prince get upset when his proposal of marriage was thrown back in his face? She couldn't decide if As'ad was too arrogant to feel rejection or if the lack of it in his life left him unprepared for the sensation.

"I'm sorry," she told him, meeting his gaze. "You came to me in good faith and made a generous offer. I handled the situation badly. I know you meant well and I should have acknowledged that. You were trying to do the right thing."

"I was," he agreed. "But I have blame, as well. I could have phrased things differently and not been so…"

"Imperious?" she offered.

"That is not the word I would have chosen."

"And yet it fits perfectly."

His gaze narrowed slightly. "Your apology seems to be lacking humility."

"Humility has never been a strength for me. Yet another flaw."

"You have much to recommend yourself, Kayleen. That is what I should have told you before."

Had he always been so good-looking? she wondered as she got caught up in his eyes. His features were perfectly balanced and his mouth...just looking at it made her remember kissing him over and over again.

Weakness invaded her legs, making it suddenly difficult to stand. Fortunately As'ad took her arm and led her to the sofa at the far end of his large office. When she was seated, he settled next to her.

He smiled. "You challenge me."

"Not right now."

"True, but let's give it a minute. You have done well with the girls."

"They mean a lot to me."

He touched her cheek. "I do not want to see you lock yourself behind convent walls. In my arrogance, I chose to make that decision for you. I chose to seduce you so that you couldn't return. It was wrong of me and I apologize."

She opened her mouth, then closed it. He'd planned it? All of it? "You slept with me on purpose? You weren't caught up in the moment?" The information stunned her and hurt quite a bit.

"I was more than caught up," he told her. "You bewitched me."

"I don't think so."

He cupped her chin, forcing her to look at him. "I assure you, my desire for you remains as fiery as ever."

There was a light in his eyes, a need she recognized.

Her insides clenched and she found herself wanting to be with him again. The hurt faded.

"I took away your choices," he told her. "I decided for you and that is wrong."

"An apology is enough," she muttered, wishing she could look away from his intense gaze.

"It is not."

"Marriage is a pretty high price to pay for poor judgment."

One corner of his mouth lifted. "I said I was wrong to decide *for* you. I never said there was anything wrong with my judgment."

"What?"

He released her chin only to take her hand in his. "Kayleen, I am a man in need of a wife. I need someone who understands what it is to give with her whole heart, who will love the girls and El Deharia and my people. I need someone who cares more about what is right than the latest fashions or how many pieces of jewelry she has in her possession. A woman I can respect, who will stand up to me and yet be by my side. I need *you*."

She heard the words. Her heart was still beating, she could hear that, too, and feel his hand on hers. And yet it was like she'd left her body and was watching the moment from somewhere else. Because there was no way this was really happening to her. Princes didn't propose to her. Normal guys didn't even want to *date* her.

"But…"

"Do you doubt my sincerity?" he asked. "I cannot promise to be the most perfect husband, but I will try to be all you wish me to be. I need you, Kayleen. Only you."

Need. The word was magic. To be needed meant to

never be abandoned. She would have a home, a husband, a family. As Lina had pointed out, she could help people and make a difference in the world. Her—some no-name kid whose only family had dumped her on the steps of an orphanage and left her forever.

"I can't be a princess," she blurted without thinking. "I don't even know who my father is. What if he's in prison or worse? I told you about my mother. She abandoned me. My grandmother didn't want me, either. What if there's something hideously wrong with me?"

"There is not. There never could be." As'ad drew her hand to his mouth and kissed her fingers. "I know *you*," he told her. "That is enough. I know your character and you are more than I could ever wish for. I would be proud to have you as my wife. Marry me, Kayleen. Marry me and adopt the girls. We will be a family together. We need you."

There was only one answer, she thought as her eyes filled with tears. Happy tears, she reminded herself as she nodded.

"Yes," she whispered. "Yes, I'll marry you."

"I am pleased."

He leaned in and kissed her. She started to respond, but then he straightened and removed something from his jacket pocket. Seconds later, he slipped a massive diamond ring onto her finger.

She stared down at the center stone. It was nearly as big as a dinner plate. It glittered and shimmered and was unlike anything she had ever seen.

"Do you like it?" he asked.

"I don't know if I can live up to it," she admitted. "I think the ring is a little too smug for me. What if it calls me names behind my back?"

He chuckled. "This is why you delight me."

"Seriously, As'ad. I own two pairs of earrings, a cross necklace and a watch. I don't think I can wear this."

"What if I told you I picked that stone specifically and had it set for you? The diamond belonged to an ancestor of mine. A queen known for speaking her mind and ruling both her people and her husband with wisdom and love. She was admired by all. She lived a long time and saw many grandsons born. I think she would have liked you very much."

As he spoke, the ring seemed to glow a little brighter. The last of Kayleen's fears faded and she knew she had finally found the place she was supposed to be.

As planned, As'ad went to Kayleen's suite after work that evening. She and the girls were waiting, although only Kayleen knew the nature of the announcement.

He walked in to a domestic scene, with Dana and Nadine both absorbed in their homework and Pepper on Kayleen's lap. The little girl read aloud.

As'ad took in the moment, thinking how it looked like a styled photograph. They were his responsibility now— all of them.

His gaze settled on the woman he would marry. Over the years he hadn't given much thought to his bride and he never would have imagined someone like Kayleen. But now that she was here—in his life—he knew he had made an excellent choice. She would suit him very well.

As for the sisters—he had grown fond of them. With Kayleen he would have sons, but the girls would always be special, for they had come first.

He smiled as he imagined facing Dana's first boyfriend. It would not be easy to meet a prince on a first date, but having to deal with him would be an excellent test of character for any young man.

Kayleen looked up first. "As'ad, you're here."

"So I am."

She took the book from Pepper, then set the girl on the sofa next to her. After she rose, she paused, as if not sure what to do. They were engaged now—some greeting was required. Obviously she did not know what.

He crossed the room to her and pulled her close, then kissed her. Behind him, he heard the girls murmuring. They were not used to such displays of affection, but they would become accustomed to them. He enjoyed being with a woman and having Kayleen in his bed would be one of the perks of married life.

When he stepped back, he kept his arm around her.

"We have something to tell you," he said.

All three girls huddled together, their eyes wide and apprehensive.

Kayleen smiled. "It's a good thing. Don't worry."

"Kayleen and I are to be married," As'ad said. "Nothing has been formally announced so you'll need to keep the information a secret for now, but I wanted you to know."

The girls stared at each other, then back at him. "What about us?" Dana asked, sounding worried.

Kayleen knelt down and held out her arms. "You're staying right here. With us. We'll both adopt you. This will be your home forever."

Nadine and Pepper ran into her embrace. Dana looked at him. Her smile was bright and happy, her eyes wide with excitement.

"I'd hoped this would happen," she admitted. "I wanted you to figure out you were in love with Kayleen. You look at her the way Daddy used to look at Mommy."

Love? Not possible, As'ad thought, dismissing the very idea. Kayleen kept her head down. Dana rushed to her.

"Do you have a ring?" the girl asked.

Kayleen removed it from her pocket and slipped it on her fingers. The girls gasped.

"That's really, really big," Pepper said. "Is it heavy?"

"I'm getting used to it."

As'ad watched in contentment. All had turned out well, thanks to his aunt. She had given him advice on the best way to approach Kayleen. While he didn't usually agree with taking advice from a woman, in this case she was the acknowledged expert.

She had told him about Kayleen's desire to be needed. It was a position he could respect. Having a place to belong was far better than worrying about a fleeting emotion like love.

Kayleen stood. The girls rushed at him and he found himself embracing them all. He bent down and gathered Pepper into his arms, then straightened and settled her on his hip.

"I'm a real princess now," she said. "I want a crown."

"A princess wears a tiara," he told her.

"Then one of those. Does this mean the next time I hit a bully I won't get into trouble?"

"Hitting anyone is never a good idea," Kayleen told her.

Pepper sighed and looked into his eyes. "But you're the *prince*. Can't you change that?"

She was delightful, as were her sisters. He smiled. "I will see what I can do."

"You shouldn't encourage her," Kayleen told him.

Perhaps not, but he suddenly wanted all that was possible for the girls. He wanted to give them everything, show them everything, and always keep them safe.

An odd pressure tightened in his chest. It was a feeling he didn't recognize, so he ignored it. But it was there.

Fayza St. John arrived the next morning exactly on time for her prearranged meeting with Kayleen. She was a fifteen-year veteran of the protocol office, something she shared with Kayleen immediately upon their meeting.

"I'll be in charge of the wedding," Fayza said as she stretched her thin lips into what Kayleen hoped was a smile.

Everything about the woman was thin—her body, her face, her legs, her hair. She was well-dressed, but more than a little scary-looking, although elegant. Kayleen had the feeling that the other woman already knew her dress had been bought at sixty percent off at a discount outlet and that the patch pockets had been added after the fact to cover a stain that wouldn't come out.

"You're our first bride in decades," Fayza went on. "Princess Lina was the last, of course. With the princes getting older, we knew it was just a matter of time, so we've been doing a lot of prep work, just in case. Now you'll have to deal with a lot of decisions yourself, but much of the wedding will be handled out of my office. You can request things like colors, but everything will have to be vetted. While this is your happy day, it is also a state occasion." She paused. "Any questions?"

Kayleen shook her head. A question would require a functioning brain, which she didn't have at the moment.

Marrying As'ad was unexpected enough, but to find out the event would be a state occasion?

"Obviously no serious work can get done until we have a date," Fayza continued. "The king mentioned a spring wedding."

"Uh-huh."

"With a formal announcement right after the holidays?"

Kayleen nodded.

"All right. That gives us time, which, believe me, we won't have enough of. You'll start working with one of our people right away. She'll help you learn the culture and traditions of El Deharia. You'll need instruction in the language, deportment, current events, etiquette and a hundred other things I can't even think of right now. Oh, I'll need your personal list for the announcements and the wedding. What family are you inviting?"

Kayleen had to consciously not grab her head to keep it from spinning. This wasn't anything she'd imagined. All she wanted was to marry As'ad and get on with her life.

"Does it have to be like this?" she asked. "Can we just go away and get married quietly?"

Fayza laughed. "He's a prince, dear. And the first one to marry. You're going to be on the cover of *People* magazine."

The idea made her want to throw up. "What if I don't want to be?"

"Sorry—this will be the social event of the spring. We'll try to keep the number of guests down. Anything over five hundred is a nightmare."

F-five hundred? Five? As in five hundred?

Kayleen stood and walked to the window. The need to

run was as powerful as her instinct to keep breathing. None of this felt right, probably because it wasn't. Not for her. But this was As'ad's world. This was what he expected. If she was to be his wife, she would have to learn his ways. He believed in her and she wouldn't let him down.

"Your family? About how many?" Fayza asked again.

What family? Not her own—they had abandoned her. Why would she want them at her wedding? Would any of the nuns she knew back home make the journey?

"I'm not sure I have any," she admitted.

"Something we'll deal with later. Now, you're going to have to be a little more careful when you go out. You must be escorted, either by Prince As'ad or Princess Lina. If neither of them are available, you'll have a security person with you. You already have one in the car when the girls go to and from school, so that helps. You will not be allowed to be alone with a man who is not attached to the palace. No friends even. Brothers are fine, cousins squeak in."

"That won't be a problem," Kayleen told her as she stared down into the garden.

She wanted to marry As'ad, she thought. She wanted to be with him, his wife, the girls' mother. But like this? Why couldn't he be a regular man? Even the camel dealer he had joked about on Thanksgiving.

She told herself she was being ungrateful. That her hardships were nothing when compared with those in the world who truly suffered. She should be grateful.

"We won't be making an announcement for a few months," Fayza continued. "It's unlikely there will be any media leaks, but it would be best if you didn't wear your engagement ring outside the palace. Just to keep things quiet."

Kayleen nodded, but she wasn't really listening anymore. Instead she stared at the cage in the garden. The one that had held all the doves. Even though the door was open, the space was full again. They had all returned home.

Products of their destiny, she thought. Trapped. Just like her.

Chapter Ten

"**I**'m not sleeping at all," Lina complained as she sat on the stone bench in the garden.

"Thank you."

It took her a moment to realize what Hassan meant. She laughed. "All right. Yes, you're a part of my exhaustion, but not the only part. Playing matchmaker is hard work. I feel guilty in a way. I started all this. I brought them together."

"You introduced them and then removed yourself from the situation. You did not lock them in a room together and insist they become intimate. They chose that course themselves."

"I agree, in theory. But I planned this from the beginning. I thought Kayleen would be good for As'ad and that she secretly longed for more than teaching at the convent school. But what if I was wrong? What if I messed up both their lives?"

Hassan leaned in and kissed her. "You worry too much."

"I'm very good at it."

"Perhaps it is not a gift one should cultivate."

She smiled. "You don't actually expect me to change, do you?"

"Not really."

"Good." Her smile faded. "I just wish I knew I'd done the right thing."

"Why would it be otherwise? As'ad proposed and Kayleen agreed. Now they will be thrown together even more. Who knows what might happen."

He was so confident the outcome would be positive, but Lina wasn't so sure. What if As'ad couldn't open his heart to Kayleen? What if she stopped falling in love with him?

"I can see I do not have your full attention," Hassan complained. "I forbid it to be so."

She laughed. "You are not king here, sir. You are my guest."

His dark eyes brightened with humor. "I have enjoyed being your guest. Spending time with you makes it difficult for me to consider going home. But I must."

She didn't want to think about that. "You have many sons to rule in your place."

"For a time, but the ultimate responsibility is mine. I must also consider my people. I do not want them to believe I have abandoned them."

"I know." She didn't want to think about that. She didn't want Hassan to leave, but couldn't ask him to stay. She looked at him. "I will miss you."

"As I will miss you." He squeezed her hand. "I suppose it would be presumptuous to ask that you could come with me to Bahania."

She steeled herself against hope. "As a visit?"

He smiled. "No, my love. Not as a visit. It has been so long, I'm doing this badly." He kissed her. "Lina, you are an unexpected treasure in my life. I did not think I would find love again. I certainly never expected to find such a beautiful, enticing woman such as yourself. Your physical perfection is only matched by the gloriousness of your spirit and your mind. You have bewitched me and I wish to be with you always. I love you and would be most honored if you would consider becoming my wife."

Kayleen stood frozen on the garden path. She'd been walking as she did each morning, only to accidentally stumble into a personal moment.

At first she'd only heard the low rumble of voices and had thought nothing of them. There were often other people in the garden. Then she'd heard King Hassan say something about his people. The next thing she knew, he'd proposed.

Now she held her breath and looked desperately for a way to escape so they could be alone. She turned slowly, intent on creeping away, when Hassan spoke again.

"Tears are unexpected, Lina."

"They're happy tears. I love you so much. I never dreamed, either, that I could fall in love."

"So you will be my queen."

"Oh, dear. A queen. I never thought of that."

"My people will adore you nearly as much I do. I have the added delight of knowing every part of you."

There was a soft giggle and silence. Kayleen took advantage of their attention to each other and quietly moved away.

So Lina and the king had fallen in love. She was happy

for them. The thought of her friend moving to Bahania was a little sad, but also exciting. Kayleen had never known a queen before.

She made her way back to her suite. As she climbed the wide staircase leading to the second floor, she paused, remembering the king's emotional proposal and how happy Lina had been. Even from several feet away, Kayleen had felt the love they shared.

"I want to be in love," Kayleen whispered. "With As'ad."

She wanted to love the man she would marry and she wanted him to love her back. Could it happen? Was it possible? Or was she like a child, hoping to catch the moon?

As'ad walked into the suite Saturday morning. "Are you ready?" he asked.

The girls all called out that they were, while Kayleen hovered behind them. For some reason, she felt shy with As'ad. How strange. She'd never felt awkward with him before. Perhaps it was because they were engaged now. Everything was different, yet it was oddly the same.

"You never said what we were going to do," Dana told him.

"I know. It's a surprise."

He crossed to Kayleen and smiled at her. "You are quiet."

"I'm caught up in the moment."

"You don't know what the moment will be."

"I'm sure it will be wonderful."

"Such faith." He captured her hand in his, then glanced down. "You do not wear my ring."

She pulled her hand free and hid it behind her back. "I, um, thought it was best. After talking to Fayza and all."

"Who is Fayza?"

"From the protocol office. I think that's where she's from. She wanted to talk to me about the wedding and how to behave, now that I'm going to be, you know, a princess."

She could speak the word, but it was hardly real to her. It was the same as saying she was going to wake up an aardvark. A princess? Her? Not possible.

"I see," As'ad murmured. "What were her instructions?"

Kayleen tried to remember them all. "I shouldn't go out by myself. I shouldn't talk to any man who isn't staff or a member of the royal family. I shouldn't wear my ring until the engagement is officially announced. I shouldn't talk to the press, dress inappropriately." She paused. "There's more. I wrote it all down."

He touched her cheek, then lightly kissed her. "It seems there are many things you should not do. Perhaps it would have been easier to give you a list of what is allowed."

"That's what I thought."

His dark gaze settled on her face. "Kayleen, you may do whatever pleases you. In all things. I would ask that you not travel outside of the palace walls without a bodyguard, but you may come and go as you wish. You are my fiancée, not my slave."

She liked the sound of that. "But Fayza was very insistent."

"I assure you, she will not be again. Would it please you to wear your engagement ring?"

She nodded. Somehow wearing the ring made her feel as if she belonged.

"I would like you to wear it, as well."

She went into her bedroom and slipped on the ring. When she turned, she found As'ad behind her. He pulled her close and settled his mouth on hers.

His kiss was warm and insistent, with just enough passion to make her breath catch. She liked the feel of him next to her, the way he held her as if he would never let her go. She liked the taste and scent of him, the fire that burst to life inside of her.

"What are they doing?" Nadine asked in what Kayleen guessed was supposed to be a whisper.

"They're kissin'," Pepper told her.

As'ad straightened. "There are issues with children I would not have guessed," he told her. "Such as privacy."

She smiled. "It's because they're excited about the surprise. You never said what it was."

"You're right. I did not." He led her back into the living room and faced the girls. "We are going shopping. All three of you need new wardrobes, now that you are to be my daughters."

Nadine spun in place. "Pretty dresses and party shoes?"

"Of course. Riding clothes, as well. Play clothes and whatever else Kayleen thinks you require."

"I want a crown," Pepper announced.

As'ad laughed. "I am not sure the store carries crowns, but we will ask."

Kayleen laughed. "Maybe we can make one here." She turned to him. "Thank you. The girls will love getting new things. They're all growing so quickly."

"You will be shopping, as well," he told her.

"What? I'm fine."

"You need a wardrobe that befits your new position." He shook his head. "What you have will not do."

She felt herself flush and tried to tell herself that it made sense a prince wouldn't be impressed by her plain, inexpensive wardrobe.

"I've never been much of a shopper," she admitted. Growing up, she'd made do with hand-me-downs and donations. When she started working, she'd never made a lot of money and her clothing budget had been modest at best.

"You will have to learn," he told her. "You are a beautiful woman and you deserve to wear beautiful things. Silks and lace with jewels that glitter. You will sparkle like the stars in the sky."

She'd never heard him talk like this before, she thought happily. She liked it.

The store was like nothing she'd ever seen before. It was on a quiet street with pale buildings that had striped awnings at all the windows. There was no sign overhead. Just discreet gold lettering on the door.

"I have called ahead," As'ad told her as they got out of the limo. "Wardrobes have been collected for each of the girls."

"How did you know the sizes?" she asked, wishing she'd had something nicer to wear into the store. She felt frumpy.

"Neil phoned the laundry and asked them to check. A selection has been made for each of them but the final decision is yours. If something has been forgotten, it will be ordered."

Kayleen had a feeling this was going to be a different experience than the sixty-percent-off sales at the discount stores she usually frequented.

A tall, slender woman greeted them graciously. She was beautifully dressed and smiled as she bowed to Prince As'ad.

"Sir, you are always welcome here. How delighted we are to be of service."

"Glenda, this is Kayleen James, my fiancée. These

three young ladies are my daughters. Dana, Nadine and Pepper, this is Miss Glenda."

The girls smiled shyly and stayed close to him.

"A perfect family," Glenda told him. "Although a son would be a lovely addition."

"You speak as my father does," As'ad told her. "You are prepared?"

"We have dozens of things to show everyone. I think you will be pleased." She turned to the girls. "Come on. I'll show you." Glenda took Dana's hand and introduced her to the clerks who were hovering. Each gathered a girl and led her off. Then Glenda turned to Kayleen.

"Such beautiful hair," she said with a sigh. "And a natural color." She slowly walked around Kayleen. "Good structure, excellent posture, clear skin. Prince As'ad, you're a fortunate man."

"I think so."

"All right. Let the fun begin. The dressing rooms are this way." She glanced back at As'ad. "You will find magazines, drinks and a television waiting for you."

"Thanks." He smiled at Kayleen. "Enjoy yourself."

Kayleen nodded because she couldn't speak. Nothing about this experience was real to her. None of it had any basis in reality. In her world, boutique owners didn't act this way. They weren't so accommodating or friendly. At least, Kayleen thought the woman was being friendly. She could have just been acting nice because of the money that would be spent, but Kayleen hoped not.

She followed Glenda to the dressing room where the girls were giddily trying on clothes.

"I have socks with kittens!" Pepper yelled. "Can I have socks with puppies?"

"Yes," the woman helping her said with a laugh. "We even have giraffes."

"I *love* giraffes."

For Nadine there were dance clothes and frilly dresses, for Dana, clothes that were slightly less girly, but still pretty. Pepper ran to Kayleen and thrust kitten socks in her hand.

"Aren't they the best?" she asked breathlessly.

"They are."

"I love shopping!"

"So you're starting them young," Glenda murmured.

"Apparently."

She was taken into her own dressing room where dozens of items hung. There were dresses and jeans and blouses and skirts and suits. In the corner, three towers of shoe boxes stood nearly four feet high.

"We'll start with the basics," Glenda told her. "The prince mentioned you didn't have much of an appropriate wardrobe." She laughed. "Hardly something he had to mention. Not many of us have clothing fit for royal duty. Of course you'd be starting over. And isn't that the best place to be?"

Kayleen fingered her plain dress. "I've never been into fashion before."

"That is about to change. Fortunately you can learn a lot fairly quickly. Pay attention to what looks good on you rather than what's in style, go with classics and coordinates. And expect to be tortured by pretty shoes on formal evenings. All right, dear, let's see what you've got."

Glenda waited patiently until Kayleen figured out she was expected to undress.

Kayleen reluctantly unzipped her dress and stepped out of it. Glenda nodded.

"Excellent. Not too curvy, so you can dazzle in evening wear. That's good. No offense, dear, but you have very ugly underwear. If you're going to marry a prince, you need sexy and pretty. You want to keep him interested."

She began making notes, then motioned to the rack on the right. "We'll start there."

An hour later Kayleen realized she'd underestimated women who shopped for sport. It was exhausting. Trying on, walking out for As'ad's approval, then getting pinned and poked so everything fit perfectly, finding the right shoes, walking around in them, getting another nod from As'ad, then starting the whole thing over with a different dress.

She was zipping up a simple day dress when Dana walked into the dressing room.

"We're finished," she said. "As'ad said to tell you Aunt Lina is coming by to take us to the movies."

Kayleen smiled. "Are you as tired as I am?"

Dana nodded. "It was fun, but work."

"I didn't get to see half of what any of you bought. We'll have to have a fashion show when the clothes are delivered."

But instead of agreeing, Dana moved close, put her arms around Kayleen's waist and started to cry.

Kayleen sat down and pulled the girl onto her lap. "What's wrong?"

"I miss my mom and my dad," she said as she cried. "I know it's wrong, but I do."

Kayleen hugged her tight. "It's not wrong to miss them. Of course you do. This is all new and different. You want to share what's happening and you want the comfort of what's familiar. I don't blame you at all. You've been so brave, sometimes I forget you're not all grown-up."

"I get scared."

"Because all this is different?"

Dana buried her face in Kayleen's shoulder. "We don't want you to go away."

"I won't."

"Promise? Not ever? No matter what?"

"We will always be together. As'ad and I are getting married. We're going to be a family."

Dana looked at her. "If you leave him, you'll take us with you?"

Kayleen smiled. "I'm not leaving."

"You could. People leave."

"I won't, but if something happens and I do, I'll take all three of you with me. I promise."

Dana wiped her face. "Okay. I trust you."

"Good, because I love you."

Dana sniffed. "Really?"

"Really. You and Nadine and Pepper. I love you all so much. I always wanted girls and now I have three."

Dana hugged her hard. Kayleen held her, willing her to feel safe, to know she, Kayleen, would always protect her. At last Dana straightened.

"I'm better," she said as she slid to her feet.

"I'm glad. I'm always here, if you need to talk or anything. Just tell me. Okay?"

Dana nodded and left. Kayleen stood and smoothed the front of the dress. "We know it wrinkles," she said to herself.

As'ad stepped into the dressing room. He stood behind her and put his hands on her shoulders.

"I heard your conversation with Dana," he told her, meeting her gaze in the mirror.

"Do you disapprove?" she asked.

"Not at all. You reassured her and she will reassure her sisters." One corner of his mouth turned up. "Perhaps you could have hesitated before agreeing you would probably leave me."

"I never said that. I won't. Marriage is forever for me."

"As it is for me," he told her, then turned her to face him. "You are an excellent mother. That pleases me. For the girls and the sons to follow."

"You do realize that you're technically responsible for the gender of any children we have. That if I have girls, it's your fault?"

He smiled. "Yes, I know. Although I would remind you I am one of six brothers. So the odds are in my favor."

She wanted to mention that a healthy child should be enough, regardless of gender. But what was the point? As'ad was a prince and a sheik. He was arrogant, but he was also kind and charming and she didn't want to change anything about him.

"Are you enjoying shopping?" he asked.

"It's a lot of work. I'm not really used to this level of service."

"You will become accustomed to it."

"Maybe. Do I really need all these clothes? It seems excessive."

"You are my wife."

"I get that, but still…"

"You represent El Deharia. The people have expectations."

Oh. Right. How long would *that* take to get used to? "Then it's fine," she told him.

"So you will do what is necessary for my people but not for me."

"Pretty much."

He bent down and kissed the side of her neck. Her insides clenched in response.

"I see I have to teach you to respect me," he murmured, his mouth moving against her skin.

He wrapped his arms around her waist and drew her back against him. He was warm and hard and she loved the feel of him so close.

She wanted this to be real—all of it. The girls as her family and As'ad as the man she loved more than anyone else. She wanted him to feel the same way. She wanted to make him weak at the knees and be all to him. If only...

He turned her to face him. "When we return to the palace I wish to discuss finances with you," he told her. "You and the girls will always be taken care of. Even if something should happen to me, you will be financially secure. The palace will always be your home, but should you wish to live elsewhere, money would be made available."

He didn't have to do that. She wasn't marrying him for the money. "I don't want anything to happen to you."

"Neither do I. Regardless, you are protected. Now that we are engaged, I have opened a bank account for you. As you spend money, more will be provided. I will give you credit cards, as well." He touched her face. "I want you to be happy, Kayleen. Go shopping as you like."

"I don't need much."

"Then you will be embarrassed by your excesses. Life is different now. You are different."

He kissed her, his mouth moving lazily over hers. When she parted, he slipped his tongue inside, teasing hers until she couldn't catch her breath.

She wanted him to touch her everywhere. She wanted

them to make love. She wanted to know the wonder of a release, his body so close to hers, their hearts beating together.

He pulled back slightly. "Although I would prefer you didn't change too much," he whispered as he lowered the zipper on her dress.

She felt his hands on her bare skin. He pulled the dress down to her waist, then moved aside the cup of her bra. His fingers were warm on her breast. He brushed against her hard nipple, making her gasp, then lowered his head and sucked on her.

Aware they were in a dressing room with a very flimsy door, she did her best to keep quiet, but it was difficult as his tongue circled her. Heat blossomed between her legs. Heat and an ache that made her squirm for more.

"So impatient," he whispered, then unfastened her bra.

She pushed the scrap of lace away and ran her hands across his head, then his shoulders. More. She needed more.

He chuckled before moving to her other breast and teasing it until her breath came in pants.

She felt one of his hands on her leg. The material of her dress was drawn up and up, then he moved between her legs.

She knew she should stop him. The girls were gone, but there were other people out there. Clerks and Glenda and maybe customers. They couldn't do this.

Except she didn't want him to stop. Not when he pushed down her panties and urged her to step out of them. Especially not when he slipped his hand between her thighs and began to rub.

He found her center immediately. Back and forth, back

and forth, the steady pressure of his fingers on her slick flesh. She was so ready, she thought as she held in another groan. He eased her backward, then raised her leg until her foot rested on the bench.

"Lean on me," he whispered.

She did as he asked because to do otherwise was to risk him stopping. He supported her with one arm around her waist and eased the other under her dress, back between her legs.

She clung to him as he carried her higher and higher. The pleasure was so intense, she could think of nothing else. He knew exactly how to touch her, how to push her closer and closer until her release was in sight.

She felt the tension in every part of her body. She began to shake, holding on to him to keep from falling. Her breath came in pants. Suddenly she was there…on the edge and aching for him to push her over.

He circled her once, twice, and then she was coming and coming and it was as intense and glorious as she remembered. He leaned in and kissed her, silencing her gasps. He continued to touch her, flying with her, down and down, as the ripples of release eased through her. She was still shuddering in aftershocks when he swore softly and let her go.

"What's wrong?" she whispered.

"This was supposed to be for you," he muttered as he bent down and grabbed her bra. "Here. Put this on."

"I don't understand."

He looked at her, passion flaring in his eyes. "I must take you back to the palace at once. To my bed. We will finish the shopping later."

She smiled. "That's a good plan."

* * *

It was nearly midnight when Kayleen dialed the familiar number and, when the call connected, ask to speak to the woman in charge.

"Kayleen? Is that you?"

Kayleen smiled. "Yes. It's been too long since I last called. I'm sorry."

"If you've been off having adventures, I forgive you at once. How are you? How is life at the palace? You must tell me everything."

The familiar voice, rich with affection and a life energy that inspired those around her, made Kayleen wish to be back in the convent, sitting in the room with her Mother Superior, instead of half a world away.

"I'm well. Very busy. I... The girls are adjusting well." She'd already called and talked about As'ad adopting the girls and her becoming their nanny.

"I worry about them. There have been so many upheavals. So much pain for those so young. You're with them and that must help."

"I hope so." Kayleen cleared her throat. "I have something to tell you. I'm not sure what you'll think." She drew in a deep breath. "It's about Prince As'ad. He arranged for us to have a Thanksgiving dinner a few weeks ago. It was lovely. But then..."

The Mother said nothing. Kayleen suspected she had long ago learned that silence was powerful motivation for the other person to keep talking.

"It was late and we were alone," Kayleen said, then told her everything. When she'd finished explaining about the proposal, she paused, waiting for whatever judgment might follow.

"He is a good man?" the other woman asked at last.

It wasn't the question Kayleen had expected. "Um, yes. A very good man. A little too used to getting his way, but that must come with being royal."

"He takes care of you and the girls?"

"Yes. Very well."

"Can you love him?"

An interesting question. "Yes, I can. I want to."

"Then I am pleased. I always wanted a husband and a family for you, Kayleen. I know you longed to return here, to the familiar, but sometimes we find our happiness in unexpected places. To love and be loved is a great blessing. Enjoy what you have and know I am always thinking of you."

"Thank you," Kayleen whispered, feeling the words wash over her like a blessing.

"Follow your heart and you will never be led astray. Follow your heart, child."

Kayleen nodded. She could already feel her heart drawing her toward As'ad. As he was the man she would marry, it was a journey she longed to make. To a place where she would finally belong.

Chapter Eleven

Kayleen looked at all the designs spread out on the large dining room table. "You're kidding," she said.

"This is only from today's mail," Lina told her with a sigh. "I never thought anything I did would make designers notice me. I certainly buy nice clothes, but I'm not that into fashion. Besides, I gave up being trendy years ago. But the second Hassan announced our engagement, I started getting calls." She flipped through the sketches of wedding gowns. "He was supposed to wait, you know. He promised." She sounded more exasperated than actually annoyed.

"He said he couldn't stand to keep his happy news a secret," Kayleen told her with a smile. "I saw the news conference. He was giddy."

Lina grinned. "Don't tell him that. He'll explain that a king is never giddy."

"He was this one time. I'm glad you're so happy."

"Me, too." Lina sighed. "I've really liked my life. I've been blessed. Even though I lost my husband so early, I had my brother's sons to fill the void. I was okay with that. I was going to grow old taking care of their children. Now, suddenly, I'm in love and engaged. I still can't believe it."

Kayleen glanced at Lina's ring—the diamonds glittering on the platinum band made her engagement ring look like a tiny toy. "You're going to have to start exercising more if you're going to carry that around all day."

Lina laughed. "I know. It's huge. So not my taste, but if you'd seen the look on Hassan's face when he put it on my finger. He was so proud. How am I supposed to tell him I'd like something smaller than a mountain?"

"If it doesn't really matter to you, you don't."

"You're right." Lina picked up a design and studied it. "You're going to have to go through all this as soon as your wedding is announced."

"Hopefully on a much smaller scale," Kayleen told her, knowing being royal was going to take a lot of getting used to. "I only ever wanted to belong to a family. Now I have a whole country."

"There are perks."

"I'm not that interested in the perks."

"Which is why I'm glad As'ad picked you," Lina told her. "I know you're not in it for the money." She set down the design and picked up another. "I'll admit I'm hoping you'll fall in love with him."

Kayleen felt herself blush. "I've thought about it," she admitted. "He's a good man. Thoughtful and kind. He really cares about the girls. He takes care of things. He makes me feel safe. I know I like him, but love? What does that feel like?"

"Like you can hold the stars in the palm of your hand," Lina said, then laughed. "I sound foolish."

"You sound happy."

"I am. Hassan is my world. Oh, I know that will change, we'll settle into something more normal. But for now, I'm enjoying the magic. The way my heart beats faster when he walks in a room. The way he can take my breath away with a simple kiss. I only want to be with him."

"So I'm boring you?" Kayleen teased.

Lina laughed. "Not exactly. But I think about him all the time. It was different before. When I was young. I loved my husband, but I didn't appreciate what I had. Now that I'm older, I understand how precious love is. How rare." She turned to Kayleen. "I think you already know that, because of how you grew up."

"I know it's something I want. It's important to me. I want to love As'ad. I already love the girls."

"Then you're halfway there. Just give things time."

"We have that," Kayleen murmured.

"You have your life. After you're married, you can start having children of your own."

Kayleen touched her stomach. A baby. It had always been her secret dream. The one she wouldn't allow herself to think of very often.

Lina sighed. "I'd love to get pregnant. I'm a little old, but I'm going to try."

"Really?"

The princess nodded. "I always wanted children. While my nephews have been a source of endless delight, I confess I still have the fantasy of my own child. Hassan is willing to try. We'll see. If it is meant to be, then it will happen. If not, I still have the man of my dreams."

"I'm nervous," Kayleen told As'ad as they walked into the auditorium at the American School. "I've been working with the girls. I know in my head they'll be fine, but I'm still terrified."

"Yet they are the ones performing."

"I want them to do well so they'll be happy," she said. "I don't want them to feel bad."

"Then you should have faith in them. They have practiced. They are ready."

"You make it sound so logical."

"Is it not?"

"No, it's not. It's horrible. I think I'm going to throw up."

As'ad laughed and pulled her close. "Ah, Kayleen, you delight me."

"By vomiting? Imagine how excited you'll be when I get a fever." She grumbled, but in truth she enjoyed the feel of his arm around her and the heat of his body next to hers. Not only for the tingle that shot through her, but because the sensation was familiar. She'd leaned against him enough to know it was him. She would be able to pick him out blindfolded—by touch or scent alone. She'd never been able to think that before.

They took seats toward the front, by the aisle. Kayleen was vaguely aware that people were looking at them, but she was too nervous for the girls to notice or feel uncomfortable. A thousand horrible scenarios ran through her mind. What if Dana forgot her lines or Nadine tripped or Pepper decided to teach some bully a lesson?

As'ad took her hand and squeezed her fingers. "You must breathe. Slowly. Relax. All will be well."

"You don't *know* that."

"I know that your panic will in no way influence the outcome and it will only make you more uncomfortable."

"Again with the logic. It's really annoying."

She glanced at him and he smiled. She smiled back and felt something tug at her belly. Something that felt a lot like a connection. It startled her and made the rest of the room fade away. In that moment, there was only As'ad and she didn't want anyone or anything else.

A few minutes later, the orchestra began and the curtains parted. The pageant went from the youngest students to the oldest, so it wasn't long before Pepper appeared on stage with her class. They did a skit about a frog family snowed in for the holidays. Pepper was the mother frog.

Kayleen mouthed the girl's lines along with her, only relaxing when she left the stage at the end of the skit.

"A flawless performance," As'ad murmured. "You worry for nothing."

"Maybe my worrying is what made it perfect."

"You do not have that much power. Nadine is next. I believe she will dance. That will be enjoyable to watch."

Sure enough, Nadine and several of her classmates danced to music from *The Nutcracker.* Kayleen willed her to hold her positions exactly long enough and exhaled when the music ended and the girls were still.

"You will wear yourself out," As'ad told her.

"I can't help it. I love them."

He looked into her eyes. "Do you?"

"Of course. How could I not?"

Something flashed through his eyes—something she couldn't read. "I was most fortunate to find you. Not that I can take total credit." He smiled. "We must send Tahir, the desert chieftain, a gift of thanks."

"Maybe a fruit basket."

"I was thinking more of a camel."

"That can be tricky," she told him. "Don't you hate it when all you get in a year is camels?"

"You mock me."

"Mostly I'm mocking the camel."

Another class took the stage, then Dana's group appeared. Once again Kayleen held her breath, willing the preteen to get through all the lines without messing up.

Partway through the performance, As'ad took her hand in his. "You may squeeze my fingers, if that helps."

She did and felt a little better. When Dana finally left the stage, Kayleen slumped back in exhaustion.

"I'm glad we only have to do that a few times a year," she said. "I couldn't stand it."

"You will grow more used to this as the girls are in more performances."

"I don't want to think about it. I'm not sure my heart could take it."

"Then brace yourself. There is one more surprise yet to come."

She turned to him. "What are you talking about?"

"You'll see. All will be revealed when we leave here."

Kayleen really wanted to whine that she wanted to know *now,* but managed to keep quiet. She fidgeted until the last song ended, then followed As'ad out of the auditorium. Only to step into an impossible-to-imagine scene of snow.

It fell from the sky, cold and wet and delightful. The children were already outside, running and screaming. Kayleen held out her hands, then laughed as the snow landed on her palms.

"It's real," she said.

As'ad shrugged. "Dana mentioned missing snow, as did the other girls. I thought they would enjoy this."

It was only then that Kayleen noticed the roar of the large snow-making machine off to the side of the parking lot.

"You arranged it?" she asked, stunned by the thoughtful gift.

"Neil arranged it. I simply gave the order."

It wasn't just simple, she thought. As'ad had thought about the girls, about how this time of year would be difficult for them, and he'd done his best to make it better.

Dana came running up to them. "It's snowing! I can't believe it."

She flung herself at As'ad, who caught her and held her. Then Nadine was there and Pepper and he was holding all of them.

Kayleen watched them, her eyes filling with happy tears. It was a perfect moment, she thought.

Her chest ached, but not in a scary way. Instead it seemed that her heart had grown too big to hold all her emotions. Light filled her until she was sure it poured from her body.

The world around them shrank until there was only As'ad and the children he held. She wanted to hold that moment forever, to never forget the image or the feelings.

The director of the school came up to greet them and the spell was broken. Dana crossed to Kayleen and hugged her.

"Isn't this the best?"

"It's wonderful," Kayleen told her. "All of it. You did really well. I was scared, but you didn't seem nervous at all."

"It was fun," Dana said. "I've never been in a play before. I like it. I think I want to go into drama next year." She raised her face to the snow. "Can you believe this?"

Kayleen looked at the tall, handsome prince who had asked her to marry him. The man who spoke of their life together, of children and who made it snow in the desert because it brought a smile to a child's face.

"No, I can't," she admitted, even as she realized she now knew exactly what it felt like to be in love.

As'ad watched the children play in the snow and was pleased with his gift. All was going well. Lina had told him to pay attention to the females in his life—that for a small amount of effort, he would receive much in return. She had been right.

He heard Kayleen's laughter and found her in the crowd. With her hair like fire and her hazel eyes, she was a brightly colored flamingo in a flock of crows. He was proud to have her as his bride. She would provide him with strong, healthy sons and serve the people of his country well. She would keep him satisfied at night and, if the emotions he'd seen in her eyes earlier told the truth, love him.

He knew it was important for a woman to love her husband. That life was much easier for them both when her heart was engaged. He had hoped Kayleen would come around and she had. She would be content in their marriage, as would he. He could not ask for more.

"I'm exhausted," Kayleen said as she slumped in the back of the limo. "All that worrying, then the snowball fight. If this keeps up much more, I'm going to have to start working out."

"I do not wish you to change anything about yourself," As'ad told her.

Words to make her heart beat faster, she thought as he pulled her into his arms and kissed her.

At the first brush of his mouth, her entire body stirred in anticipation. She was eager to taste him, touch him, be with him. Unfortunately the trip back to the palace was only a few minutes.

"Perhaps later," he murmured, kissing her mouth, her cheeks, her jaw.

"Yes," she whispered. "I am very available."

"An excellent quality."

Far too soon, they arrived at the palace. A royal guard opened the passenger door and As'ad stepped out. He held out his hand to her. As she took it, she saw King Mukhtar in the courtyard. He seemed very pleased with himself as he spoke with a woman Kayleen had never seen before.

"Who is that?" she asked.

"I do not know."

The woman was of average height, with platinum-blond hair teased and sprayed into a curly mass. Heavy makeup covered her face, almost blurring her features. She wore a too-tight sweater and jeans tucked into high-heeled boots. Inappropriate clothing for someone visiting a palace.

Kayleen had never seen her before but as she walked toward the king and his guest, she got an uneasy feeling in the pit of her stomach.

King Mukhtar saw her and beamed. "My dear, you are

back. Excellent. I have a surprise." He put his hand on his companion's back and urged her forward. "Do you remember when we were walking in the garden shortly after you arrived? You mentioned your family. Specifically how you did not remember your mother and did not know her whereabouts."

Kayleen jerked her attention back to the badly dressed woman and wanted to be anywhere but here. It wasn't possible. Nothing that horrible could really be happening.

"I have found her," the king said proudly. "Here she is. Kayleen, this is your mother. Darlene Dubois."

The woman smiled broadly. "Hi, baby. Why, Kayleen, you're just so pretty. I knew you would be. Let me look at you. You're all grown up. How old are you now? Nineteen? Twenty?"

"Twenty-five."

"Oh, my. Well, don't go telling people that. They'll think I'm getting old. Although I was only sixteen when you were born." She held out her arms. "Come on, now. I've missed you so much! Give your mama a hug."

Trapped by the manners instilled in her by caring nuns, Kayleen moved forward reluctantly and found herself hugged and patted by the stranger.

Could this woman really be her mother? If so, shouldn't she feel a connection or be excited? Why was her only emotion dread?

"Isn't this fabulous?" Darlene asked as she stepped back, then linked arms with Kayleen. "After all these years. You won't believe how shocked I was when that nice man on the king's staff called and invited me to El Deharia. I confess I had to look it up on a map." She smiled at the king. "I had to leave high school when I got pregnant. Since then, I've been pursuing a career in show business. It hasn't left much time for higher education."

Or contact with her family, Kayleen thought bitterly, remembering standing alone on the steps of the orphanage while her grandmother told her that no one wanted her and that she would have to stay with the nuns.

"But what about my mommy?" Kayleen had cried.

"You think she cares? She dumped you with me when you were a baby. You're just lucky I put up with you all these years. I've done my duty. Now you're on your own. You'll grow up right with those nuns looking after you. Now stop your crying. And don't try to find me or your mama again. You hear?"

The memory was so clear, Kayleen could feel the rain hitting her cheeks. She knew it was rain because it was cold, unlike the tears that burned their way down her skin.

"Kayleen, would you like to show your mother to her rooms?" the king asked. "She is on the same floor as you and the girls. The suite next to yours. I knew you would want to be close."

Kayleen was happy that one of them was sure of something. She felt sick to her stomach and caught by circumstances. She looked at As'ad, who watched her carefully.

"What girls?" Darlene asked. "Do you have babies of your own?"

Darlene sounded delighted, but for some reason Kayleen didn't believe her. The other woman didn't seem the type to be excited about being a grandmother.

"They're adopted," As'ad told her. "My children."

Kayleen introduced them, using the chance to disentangle herself from her mother.

"A prince?" Darlene cooed. "My baby marrying a

prince. Does that just beat all." She smiled at the king. "You have very handsome sons, sir. They take after you."

Mukhtar smiled. "I like to think so."

Kayleen couldn't believe this was happening. It didn't feel real. She looked at As'ad and found him watching her. There was something quizzical in his expression, as if he'd never seen her before.

What was he thinking? Was he looking at her mother and searching for similarities? Was he uncomfortable with the living reminder that she didn't come from a socially connected family? That she would be of no use to him that way?

"Your mother must be tired from her journey," the king said. "Let us keep you no longer."

"I'll arrange to have your luggage sent up," As'ad told the other woman. "Kayleen, I'll see you later."

She nodded because she had no idea what to say. Both the king and As'ad left, abandoning Kayleen to a stranger with greedy eyes.

"Well, look at you," Darlene drawled when they were alone. "Who would have thought my baby girl would grow up and land herself a prince. I'm so happy for you, honey." She grabbed a strand of Kayleen's hair and rubbed it between her fingers. "God, I hate that color. Mine's exactly the same. It costs a fortune to keep it bleached, but it's worth every penny. Men prefer blondes. Although you're carrying the color off great and the prince obviously likes it." She looked Kayleen up and down. "You could pass for Vivian's twin."

"Who's Vivian?"

"My sister. Your aunt. You had to have met her before, when you were living with my mama." She looked around at the vast entrance hall. "Did you get lucky or what? I couldn't believe it when that guy who works for the king called and asked if you were my daughter. After all this time, I had no idea what had happened to you." She smiled. "Imagine my surprise to see what you've become. My little girl. Come on. Show me what life is like in the palace."

Kayleen led her down the hallway. Her head hurt. This couldn't be happening. Not after all these years. Not *now,* when she was engaged to As'ad.

Then she scolded herself for not being happier to see her mother. The woman had given birth to her, after all. Then abandoned her. But shouldn't she be able to forgive that?

Rather than try to decide now, Kayleen talked about the history of the palace. She took Darlene to the room next to hers and walked inside.

The other woman followed, then breathed a sigh of sheer pleasure as she took in the view of the Arabian Sea and the elegant furnishings filling the large space.

"Oh, I like living like this," Darlene said. "How did you get from that convent to here?"

Kayleen looked at her, trying not to notice that under the layers of makeup, they had the same eyes. "You knew about that? Where they sent me?"

"Sure. Mama kept complaining about how much trouble you were. I got tired of hearing it and told her to take you there. I knew, ah, you'd be cared for real well. So how'd you get here?"

"I took a teaching job at the convent school here. I'm a teacher."

Darlene looked amused. "Seriously? You teach children? Interesting."

Kayleen watched her move around the room. "Your last name is Dubois?"

Darlene nodded without looking at her. She lifted up a small Waterford clock, as if checking the weight and the value.

"Is that my last name?"

Darlene glanced at her. "What are you talking about?"

"I never knew. When my grandmother dropped me off at the orphanage, I didn't know my last name. Everyone in the house had a different one. Grandmother wouldn't say which was mine. I had to make one up."

Darlene grinned. "I made mine up, too. What did you pick?"

"James. From the King James Bible."

"I prefer Tennessee Williams myself." Darlene started opening cabinets. "Can you drink in this place?"

"Yes. Right there." Kayleen pointed to the carved doors hiding the fully stocked wet bar.

Darlene found the ice and fixed herself a vodka tonic, then took a long drink. "Better," she said with a sigh. She walked to the sofa and sat down, then patted the seat next to her. "You're going to start at the beginning and tell me everything."

Kayleen stayed where she was. "About what?"

"The story here. You're really engaged to that prince?"

"Yes. There will be a formal announcement in a few weeks and a wedding in the spring."

Darlene took another drink. "So you're not pregnant. I'd wondered if you were."

Kayleen tried not to be insulted. "I didn't have to trick As'ad into marrying me."

"Of course not. I didn't mean to imply you would. Still,

you have to be sensible. Do you have a prenuptial agreement? How many millions is he offering? Do you have an attorney? I wonder if you could get one to fly out and help."

Kayleen took a step back. "I don't need an attorney. As'ad has promised the girls and I will be taken care of."

"And you believe him? You're lucky I'm here."

Kayleen doubted that. "Why *are* you here?"

"Because I finally found my long-lost daughter."

"You knew I was in the convent all those years. That's hardly lost."

Darlene shrugged. "You're much more interesting now, honey."

"Because of As'ad." It wasn't a question.

"Partly. Oh, Kayleen, life was hard for me when you were young. I couldn't take care of a baby, I was just a baby myself. You're grown-up. You can see that. Then I lost track of you. But now we're together."

Kayleen found it difficult to believe she would have been so hard to find.

Darlene stood. "I'm your mother. I want what's best for you. If you really expect this prince to marry you, you're going to have to keep him interested. I can help you with that. Otherwise, some rich socialite will steal him away. We don't want that, do we?"

"I find it hard to believe you care anything about me," Kayleen said, feeling both anger and guilt. What was she supposed to believe? "You never did before."

"Don't say that. Of course I cared. But I had a career. You were better off with those nuns. They took real good care of you."

"How would you know?"

"It's the kind of people they are. Am I wrong?"

"No," Kayleen told her. "They're exactly who you'd think they would be."

"Then you should thank me." She walked to the bar and fixed a second drink. "I'm not leaving, Kayleen. The king thinks he's done you a big favor, finding me and bringing me here. I, for one, agree with him. You're my baby girl and that means something to me. We're going to get to know each other, you and I. Now run along. I need to rest. We'll talk about this more later."

Kayleen left. Not because she'd been told to, but because she couldn't stand to be there anymore.

She didn't know what to think about Darlene. She'd never really allowed herself to imagine what her mother was like—it hurt too much to think about all she'd lost. But this woman wasn't anyone's fantasy.

Then Kayleen thought about what the Mother Superior would say about judging someone so quickly. Maybe Darlene *was* sorry about their lost relationship. Maybe they could at least learn to be friends. Didn't Kayleen owe her to give her a chance to prove herself?

Chapter Twelve

Kayleen returned to her suite, but she couldn't seem to settle down. Not with her mother so close. Just a wall away.

It was her own fault for lying, she reminded herself. If she'd told King Mukhtar the truth, none of this would have happened. But she hated talking about how her mother didn't want her and her grandmother abandoned her. It sounded sad and pathetic. So she'd made up a more comfortable version and now she was stuck with it.

She walked to the French doors and started to open them, then remembered her mother was right next door. She didn't want another run-in with her. She turned back to pace the room when someone knocked.

Kayleen froze, afraid of who would be there. The door opened and As'ad stepped inside.

Without thinking, she ran to him. She wrapped her

arms around him, wanting to feel the warmth of him, the safety that came from being close.

"That bad?" he asked as he hugged her.

She nodded.

"I take it my father's surprise was not a pleasant one."

She looked at him. "I don't know," she admitted. "I don't know what to think or what I feel. She's not like mothers on television."

"Few are." He touched her cheek. "Are you all right?"

She sighed. "I will be. It's just strange. I don't know her. I've never known her and now she's here and we're related and I can't figure out what it all means."

"I should probably tell you that getting to know her will take time, that it will get easier, but I am not sure that is true." He smiled at her. "So perhaps I bring you good news."

"Which is?"

"Do you remember your unexpected visit to the desert? Sharif, the chieftain there, has heard of our engagement and invites us to join him and his people for dinner."

"I thought the engagement was supposed to be a secret."

"There are those who find a way to know everything. He is one of them."

"He probably saw light reflecting off my diamond ring. It's like a beacon."

As'ad chuckled. "Perhaps. I have spoken with Lina. She is pleased to take the girls if you would like to go."

Kayleen bit her lower lip. "Is it too rude to leave my mother on her first night here?"

"I think she will be exhausted from her journey. Perhaps you can leave a message on her phone and see her another time."

Kayleen was more than up for that. She left the message, then changed into a comfortable dress for her evening in the desert and met As'ad downstairs.

They walked out front where a Jeep was waiting. "You will need to learn to ride," he told her. "Eventually you will want to go into the desert with the girls."

"I know." She settled in beside him and fastened her seat belt. "Maybe I'd do better on a camel. Horses and I don't get along."

"A camel is not a comfortable ride. Trust me. You would much prefer to be on a horse."

"Maybe." She would have to try a camel first.

It was late afternoon. The sun sat in the west, giving everything a rosy, golden glow. The air was warm with the promise of a cool night to follow.

"I wonder what it's like to live in the desert," she said as she stared out the window. "Traveling with a tribe, connected to the land."

"No plumbing, no heat or air-conditioning, no closet."

She laughed. "I can't see you worrying about a closet."

"I would not, but what about you?"

"I like plumbing and closets." She didn't have a lot of things, but she did like to have her few treasures around her.

"My brother Kateb lives in the desert," he said. "He has always preferred the old ways, when life was simple and a man lived by his wits and his sword."

"You're serious? He's a nomad?"

"It is how he prefers it. When each of us reached the age of thirteen, my brothers and I were sent into the desert for a summer. It is considered a rite of passage—a test of manhood. The tribes were not cruel, but we were shown no preference because of our stature. I enjoyed my time, but had no interest in changing my future because of the experience. No so Kateb. He spoke of nothing else when he returned. Our father insisted he complete his education and Kateb agreed. But when he graduated from university in England, he returned here and went into the desert."

It sounded romantic, Kayleen thought, if she didn't think about the reality of the life. Weren't there sand fleas? And the heat in summer would be devastating. Still, the wilderness had some appeal. Not answering to anyone. Except one would have to answer to the tribe. There would have to be rules for the greater good.

"Will I meet him?" she asked.

"Not tonight. Kateb lives deep in the desert. Once or twice a year he returns to the palace, to meet with our father."

As'ad watched as Kayleen stared out into the desert. "It's all so beautiful," she said. "I can see why your brother would want to make it his home. Even without running water."

She spoke almost wistfully, as if she meant what she said, which she most likely did. He had learned that Kayleen's word was truth—an unusual trait in a woman. But then Kayleen was not like other women he'd known.

Now that she had a wardrobe of designer clothes, she dressed more like someone engaged to a prince, but there was still an air of…freshness about her. She blushed, she looked him in the eye when she spoke, she never considered hiding her emotions. All things he liked about her. He hoped she would not develop a hard edge of sophistication. He enjoyed her candor and down-to-earth ways.

A surprise, he thought, knowing he had always preferred women of the world. Of course, those women had been companions for his bed, not anyone he would consider to be the mother to his children. He remembered a conversation he'd had years ago with his aunt. Lina had told him that there were different women in this world. That he should have his fun but save his heart for someone unlike his playthings.

She had been right—not that he would give her the satisfaction of telling her. At least about marriage. His heart remained carefully unengaged, as it should in situations as important as these.

He pulled up by the edge of the camp and parked. Kayleen drew in a deep breath.

"They are so going to laugh at me," she murmured.

"Why would they do that?"

She looked at him and said, "Good evening. Blessings to you and your family," in the old tongue of El Deharia. Then added in English, "My pronunciation is horrible."

"You are learning our language?"

"It seemed the right thing to do. Plus, last time almost no one would talk to me in English. It's their country, right? One of the maids is teaching me on her lunch hour. She's taking night classes and I'm helping her with her calculus."

He stared at the hazel-eyed beauty who sat next to him. In a few months, they would be married and she would be a princess for the rest of her life. Her blood would mingle with his and their children would be able to trace their lineage back a thousand years.

She had a vault of jewels to wear whenever she liked, a bank account that never emptied; she lived in a palace. Yet did she expect humble people of the desert to speak her

language? Did she hire a tutor? Have a linguistic special-
ist summoned? Not Kayleen. She bartered with a maid and
learned an ancient speech not spoken outside the desert.

In that moment, as he stared into her eyes and saw their
future, he felt something. A faint tightness in his chest. A
need to thank her or give her something. The feeling was
fleeting and unfamiliar, therefore he ignored it.

Or tried to.

There could be no softer emotions. With them came
weakness, and strength was all. But he could be grateful
that she had stumbled into his life and changed everything.

He reached for her hand. "I am glad we are to be
married," he told her.

Happiness brightened her eyes and her whole face took
on a glow. Love, he thought with satisfaction, knowing all
would be well.

"I am, too," she whispered.

Sharif and Zarina greeted them as they arrived, then the
other woman pulled Kayleen aside.

"I see you managed to keep him all to yourself," Zarina
teased as she picked up Kayleen's left hand and stared at
the ring there. "You have chosen well."

"I think so."

Zarina laughed. "I recognize that smile. You are
pleased with As'ad."

"He's wonderful."

"What every bride should think about her groom."

She led Kayleen toward a group of women and introduced her. Kayleen recognized a few of them from her last
visit and greeted them in their native language. There
were looks of surprise, then two of them started talking

to her, speaking so quickly she caught about every tenth word.

"I have no idea what you're saying," she admitted in English. "I'm still learning."

"But you are trying," Zarina said, sounding pleased. "You honor us with your effort."

"I was hoping we could be friends," Kayleen told her.

Zarina smiled. "We are. But we will have to remember our places. Once you are a princess, things will change."

"Not for me." Kayleen wasn't interested in position or money. She wanted more important things.

"Then we will be good friends," Zarina told her. "Come. We are fixing dinner. You can keep us company. We will teach you new words. Perhaps words of love to impress your future husband."

"I'd like that."

Kayleen settled in the open cooking area. The women gathered there, talking and laughing. She couldn't follow many of the conversations, but that was all right. She would get more fluent with time.

She liked the way the women all worked together, with no obvious hierarchy. How the children came and went, dashing to a parent when they felt the need for attention. How easily they were picked up and hugged, how quick the smiles.

The tribe was an extended family—in some ways similar to her experiences in the orphanage. The group pulled together for the greater good. The difference was one would always belong to the tribe.

Roots, she thought enviously. Roots that traveled along. What would that be like?

She thought about her mother, back at the palace.

They were supposed to be family, but Darlene was a stranger to her. Kayleen only had vague memories of her aunts and her grandmother, but then she'd forgotten on purpose. What was the point of remembering long days of being left alone, of being hungry and frightened?

She heard giggles and saw Zarina whispering to one of the young women. There were gestures and the next thing Kayleen knew, she was being pulled into a tent.

"We don't do this very much," Zarina told her. "It is only to be used on special occasions. With power comes responsibility."

"I have no idea what you're talking about."

Zarina opened a trunk and dug around, then pulled out several lengths of sheer veil.

"The trick is to maintain the mystery," Zarina told her as she passed over the fabric. "It's about confidence, not talent. No man can resist a woman who dances for him. So you can't feel self-conscious or worry about how you look. You must know in your heart that he wants you with a desperation that leaves him weak. You are in charge. You decide. He begs and you give in."

Kayleen took a step back. "If you're saying what I think you're saying…"

"After dinner, we will send As'ad to a private tent. You will be there. You will dance for him." Zarina smiled. "It's a memory he'll hold on to for the rest of his life."

As much as Kayleen wanted to be accepted by the women of the tribe, she was terrified at the thought of trying to seduce As'ad.

"I don't know how to dance. I'm not good at this."

"You are the woman he wishes to marry. You know

all you need to. As for the dancing…it is easy. Come, I will show you."

Zarina tossed the fabric onto a pile of pillows, then shrugged out of her robes. Underneath she wore a sleeveless tank top and cropped pants. A simple, modern outfit that would work perfectly in the desert.

"Lower your center of gravity while keeping your back straight. Rock your hips until you feel the movement, then begin to rotate them."

Zarina demonstrated, making it look easy. Kayleen tried to do as she said, but felt awkward.

But she didn't give up and after a few minutes, she had the hip movement down. Next she learned to hold her arms out to the side, moving them gracefully.

"Very good," Zarina told her. "Now turn slowly. You want to dance for a minute or two, turn, then remove one of the veils."

Kayleen skidded to a stop. "I can't dance naked."

"You won't have to. No man can resist the dance of the veils. You will remove two, maybe three, then he will remove the rest."

"What if he thinks I look stupid?"

"He won't. He'll think he's the luckiest man alive. Now let us prepare you for the evening."

Unsure she was really going to be able to do this, Kayleen followed Zarina to another tent where there were several women waiting. She was stripped down to her underwear and sat patiently as henna was applied to her hands and feet.

"It's the temporary kind," Zarina told her. "A sugar-based dye that will wash off in a week or so."

Kayleen stared at the intricate design and knew she wouldn't mind if it lasted longer.

Next she was "dressed" in layers of veils. They were wound around her, woven together until they appeared to be a seamless garment. They were sheer, but in enough volume to only hint at what was below.

Zarina applied makeup, using a dark pencil to outline Kayleen's eyes and a red stain on her lips.

"Better than lipstick," the other woman told her. "It won't come off."

Her hair was pulled back and up through a beaded headpiece. Dozens of bracelets fit on each wrist. The final touch was a pair of dangling earrings that nearly touched her shoulders.

When they were finished, Zarina led her to a mirror. Kayleen stared at the image, knowing it couldn't possibly be her. She looked *exotic*. She'd never been exotic in her life. She also looked sexy and mysterious.

"I will leave you here for a few minutes to practice, then come for you," Zarina told her. "Believe in yourself. With this dance, you can snare As'ad's heart so that he can never be free again. What wife doesn't want that?"

Good question, Kayleen thought when she was alone. Nerves writhed in her stomach, but she ignored them. Having As'ad respect her wasn't enough. She wanted more—she wanted him to love her.

He had to see she was more than just someone to take care of the girls or an innocent he'd slept with. Their engagement might have begun due to circumstances other than love, but it didn't have to stay that way.

She'd already given him her heart—now she had to claim his. Which meant being equal to a prince.

Could she? Kayleen had spent her whole life in the

shadows, lurking in the background, not making waves, desperate for what she wanted, but afraid to step up and take it. It was time to be different. If she wanted to love a prince, she would have to claim him. She would have to show him she was so much more than he imagined. Her upbringing had given her an inner strength. She would use that power to achieve her heart's desire.

With a last look at herself, she walked to the front of the tent to wait for Zarina. She wasn't afraid. She was going to bring As'ad to his knees and make him beg. And that was just for starters.

While As'ad enjoyed the company of Sharif, he was disappointed in the evening. He'd brought Kayleen to the desert so they could share the experience. But she had been whisked away and a polite guest did not ask why.

As the strong coffee was served at the end of the meal, he glanced at his watch and calculated how long he would have to wait until they could politely take their leave. Perhaps he and Kayleen could go into town for a couple of hours. There were a few nightclubs that were intimate and had small, crowded dance floors. He liked the idea of holding her close.

Zarina approached and bowed. "Prince As'ad, would you please come with me?"

As'ad looked at his host. "Do I trust your daughter?"

Sharif laughed. "As if I know her plans. Zarina, what do you want with the prince?"

"Nothing that will displease him."

As'ad excused himself and followed her. Night had fallen and the stars hung low in the sky. He thought briefly of his brother Kateb, and wondered when he would next return to the palace. If he came in time, he could attend the wedding. As'ad would like to have all his brothers there for the ceremony. And to point out that he would no longer have to listen to their father's complaints that they had yet to all find brides.

Zarina wove her way through the tents, pausing at one in the back, almost on its own.

"In here, sir," she said, holding open the flap. "I wish you a good evening."

As'ad ducked inside. The tent was dim, with only a few lights. There was an open space covered with rugs, and a pile of cushions in front of him.

"If you will please be seated."

The request came from a dark corner. He recognized Kayleen's voice. A quiet tent, seclusion and the company of a beautiful woman, he thought as he lowered himself to the cushions. The evening had improved considerably.

Music began. The melody was more traditional than contemporary, as were the instruments. An interesting choice, he thought, as Kayleen stepped out of the shadows. It was his last rational thought for a very long time.

She wore veils. Dozens and dozens of sheer lengths of fabric covered her body. Yet there were flashes of skin— her waist, her legs, a bit of arm.

Her face looked the same, yet different, with her eyes suddenly dark and intriguing. Jewels glittered from her wrists and her ears; her skin shimmered in the dim light. She was the woman he knew yet a woman he had never known. Even before she began to move, he wanted her.

She moved her arms gracefully. He saw the henna on her skin and dropped his gaze to her bare feet. It was there, as well. The patterns were oddly erotic on her fair skin.

She moved her hips back and forth, turned and a single veil dropped to the rug.

It showed him nothing more. She was too well-wrapped. But when it hit, his chest tightened. Blood heated and raced through him, heading to his groin, where it settled impatiently. The desire was instant, powerful and pulsing.

He knew of the dance, had heard it described, but had never experienced it himself. He'd heard men talk of the power of being seduced in such a way by a woman and had privately thought them weak. But now, as Kayleen danced in time with the music, he knew he had been wrong. There was something primal in her movements, something that called only him.

She turned again and another veil fell.

It was all he could do to stay seated. He wanted to jump to his feet, pull her close and take her. He wanted to be inside of her, feeling her heat, pleasuring them both. Heat grew until he burned. And still she danced.

Her hips moved back and forth, her arms fluttered. This time when she turned, he knew the veil would fall, anticipated it, looked greedily to see more of her. A tug and it fluttered to the ground.

She turned back. He saw a hint of curve, the lace of her bra, and he was lost. He sprang to his feet and crossed to her. After he grabbed her around the waist, he pulled her against him and kissed her.

He told himself to hold back, that she wouldn't appreciate his passion, but despite his forceful kiss, she met him with the same intensity. She plunged her tongue into his mouth, taking as much as she gave.

Kayleen was shaking, both from nerves and from need. Zarina had been right. Despite her uncertainty, she'd managed to bring a prince to his knees. Or at least his feet, which was just as good.

She'd seen the need in As'ad's eyes, had watched him get aroused. He was already hard and straining. Even as they kissed, he pulled at the veils covering her, swearing with impatience when one tangled and would not budge.

"How many are there?" he asked, his voice thick with frustration and sexual arousal.

"A lot."

She reached for his shirt and began to unbutton that.

"Too slow," he told her and ripped the shirt open, then shrugged out of it. Seconds later he'd removed the rest of his clothes. Then he was naked and reaching for her.

His eagerness thrilled her. She was already damp and swollen, ready to be taken. To show him, she reached between them and stroked his arousal. He groaned as his maleness flexed in her hand.

"I want you," he breathed in her ear. "I want you now."

His words turned her to liquid. "Then take me."

He stared into her eyes. "Kayleen."

"I am to be your wife, As'ad. Take me."

He lowered her to the cushions and pushed the veils aside. After pulling down her panties, he slid his fingers between her legs.

"You want me," he told her as he rubbed against her swollen center.

"Always."

He smiled, then continued to touch her. She pushed his hand away.

"Be in me," she told him. "Claim me."

His breath caught, then he did as she asked. He settled between her knees and pushed inside of her.

She always forgot how large he was, how he filled her and made her ache with need. Normally he was slow and gentle, but tonight he pushed inside as if driven. The passion excited her.

He thrust deeply, groaning, his arousal moving her in a way she'd never experienced before. Her muscles began to tense and she closed her eyes to enjoy the ride.

He took her hard and fast, as if daring her to keep up. She accepted him easily, letting each plunging, rubbing pulse take her higher and higher. She pulled her knees back, then locked her legs around his hips, drawing him in deeper.

Faster and more, pushing and straining until her release was only a heartbeat away.

He spoke her name. She looked up and saw him watching her.

"You are mine."

Three simple words, but they were enough to send her spiraling out of control. She lost herself in her release, screaming as the pleasure claimed her. He pushed in twice more, then groaned the end of his journey.

The waves of their pleasure joined them and they clung to each other until the earth stopped moving and their bodies were finally at rest.

Kayleen let herself into her suite shortly after midnight. She felt happy and content and as if she could float. Or do the whole veil dance again!

Rather than turn on a light, she crossed to the balcony and stepped out into the night. The air had a slight chill, but she didn't care. All she had to do was think about how much As'ad had wanted her and she got all hot inside.

The evening had been magical and she didn't want to forget any part of it. If there were—

The sound of a chair moving caught her attention. She turned and saw something sitting in the shadows. The light from a cigarette glowed briefly.

"Well, well, aren't you a bit of surprise." Her mother's voice was low and tight with something Kayleen didn't recognize. "I thought you were just a silly girl who'd gotten lucky, but I was wrong. You just have a different game you play."

Kayleen faced her. "I don't know what you're talking about."

"That innocent, country-mouse act is a good one. I'll bet your prince fell for it in a heartbeat."

"I'm not acting. All of this is real."

Darlene laughed. "Don't try to play me. I invented the game. I'm saying I respect your tactics. They wouldn't work for me, but they obviously work."

"I have no idea what you're talking about. It's late. I'm going to bed."

"You've already been to bed. What you're going to do this time is sleep. Am I wrong?"

"I'm not discussing this with you." She wouldn't allow the other woman to turn her amazing evening into something ugly.

"You made one mistake, though. Falling in love with him makes you vulnerable and that means you can make a wrong move. It's better to stay detached. Safer."

"I'm marrying As'ad. I'm supposed to love him."

Her mother laughed again. "Just don't go expecting him to love you back. Men like him don't. Ever." She inhaled on her cigarette. "That's my motherly advice to you. A little late, but no less valuable."

"Good night," Kayleen told her and walked back into her room.

Her good mood had faded, which she hated, but worse were the doubts. Was her mother right about As'ad? Kayleen needed him to love her. She hadn't realized it mattered, but it did. And if he couldn't…

She walked into her bedroom and sank onto the mattress. If he couldn't, how could she marry him?

Chapter Thirteen

Kayleen huddled in the chair in Lina's living room and did her best to keep breathing. She'd recently discovered that terror and anxiety tended to make her hold her breath. Then she ended up gasping, which was not attractive or likely to make herself feel better.

"She's hideous," she moaned. "Isn't it enough that she abandoned me when I was a baby? Does she have to show up now?"

Lina patted her hand. "I am so sorry. My brother thought he was helping. Truly."

"I know. I've already mentally flogged myself for not telling the truth, but I just hate talking about my biological family. It's pathetic to be abandoned twice. What does that say about me?"

"That you rose above your circumstances. That you

have great character and inner strength. That we are lucky to have you marrying into our family."

Kayleen smiled. "You're good."

"Thank you. It's a gift. Now about your mother…"

Kayleen's smile faded. "I don't want to think about her, but I have to. She's everywhere. Lurking. She constantly shows up without warning. She has totally terrified the girls. Last night she made Pepper cry when she told her she was going to have to be smart in life because she wasn't that pretty. Pepper wanted to hit her and I almost let her. Who says that to a little girl? Pepper's adorable. I can forgive her being mean to me, but to little kids? Never."

"Do you want me to tell her to leave the country?" Lina asked. "I will. I can be very imperious. We can ship her back on the next plane."

Kayleen was tempted. Very tempted. "I can't tell you how much I want to say yes. It's just…she's my mother. Shouldn't I try to have a relationship with her? Don't I owe her?"

"Only you can answer that. Although I must ask what you owe her for. Giving birth? You didn't ask to be born. That was her choice. And with having a child, comes responsibility. If she didn't want to be bothered, she should have given you up for adoption."

"I wonder why she didn't," Kayleen said. What would her life have been like if she'd been raised by a couple who wanted a child? She couldn't begin to imagine.

"Who knows. Perhaps the paperwork was too complicated for her tiny brain."

Kayleen grinned. "I like that. But it still leaves me with the issue of what to do with her. While I appreciate your offer to get rid of her, that doesn't feel right to me.

I think I have to try and make a real connection with her, no matter how different we are. I'll deal with her for another week. If we can't find some common ground and she's still acting awful, then I'll take you up on your offer."

"You're giving her more chances than I would, but you have a kinder heart."

"Or more guilt." She sighed. "You don't suppose As'ad thinks I'm anything like her, do you?"

"Of course not. We can't pick our relatives. Don't worry—he doesn't blame you for your mother."

"I hope not." She rose. "All right. I need to go make good on my word and try to spend time with Darlene."

"Let me know how it goes."

"I will."

Kayleen walked down a flight of stairs to her suite. She paused at the door, then moved to the next one and knocked.

"Come in."

She walked into her mother's suite and found her at the dining room table, sipping coffee. There was a plate of toast and some fruit in a bowl.

Breakfast, she thought, trying not to judge. It was after eleven.

"Oh, there you are," Darlene said by way of greeting. "I just received the most delightful note from the king. I'm invited to a formal party. Something diplomatic. It sounds fabulous. I'll need something to wear. Can you take care of that?"

Kayleen sat across from her at the table. "Sure. One of the boutiques is sending over some dresses. If you give me your size information, I'll have them send over some for you."

Darlene smiled. "I like the service here."

Despite the fact that she hadn't been up very long, Darlene was perfectly made-up, with her hair styled. She wore a silk robe that clung to her curves. She looked beautiful, in a brittle sort of way.

"I thought maybe we could spend some time together," Kayleen told her. "Get to know each other. Catch up."

Darlene raised her eyebrows. "What do you want to know? I got pregnant at sixteen, left you with my mother and took off for Hollywood. I landed a few guest spots on soaps and a few prime-time shows, which paid the bills. Then I met a guy who took me to Las Vegas. You can make a lot more money there. Which I did. But time isn't a woman's friend. I need to secure my future. I wasn't sure how that was going to happen, when I heard from your king. Now I'm here."

Kayleen leaned toward her. "I'm your daughter. Don't you want to at least be friends?"

Darlene studied her for a long time. "You have a very soft heart, don't you?"

"I've never thought about it."

"You took in those girls. Now you're adopting them. You're going to be exactly the kind of wife As'ad wants."

"I love him. I want him to be happy."

Darlene nodded slowly. "You like it here? In El Deharia?"

"Of course. It's beautiful. Not just the city, but out in the desert. I'm learning the language, the customs. I want to fit in."

Darlene lit a cigarette. Her gaze was sharp, as if she were trying to figure something out. "The king is nice."

"He's very kind and understanding."

"Interesting. Those aren't the words I would have used." Her mother sipped her coffee. "Yes, Kayleen, I *would* like us to be friends. I just showed up here, which had to have been a shock. I've only been thinking of myself. I'm sorry for that."

"Really?" Kayleen was surprised, but pleased to hear the words. "That's okay. You've had a difficult life."

"So have you. But a better one than you would have had if you'd gotten stuck with my family. I know you probably don't believe that, but it's true." She rose. "Let me shower and get dressed. Then, if you have time, you can take me on a tour of the palace. It's a beautiful building."

"It is. I've been studying the history. I want to know everything about As'ad and his people."

Darlene's expression tightened. "I'm sure he appreciates that."

As'ad took Kayleen's hand in his and kissed her fingers. "What troubles you?"

They were having lunch together in his office. She smiled at him. "Nothing. I'm just thinking."

"Obviously not about how you consider yourself blessed above all women for being engaged to me."

She laughed. "No. Not that. I'm thinking about my mother."

"I see."

She looked at him. "You don't approve of her?"

"I do not know her. What matters to me is your feelings."

"I'm not sure of anything," she admitted, wondering when everything had gotten so complicated. "I told her I thought we should get to know each other and try to be friends."

"And?"

"It's better," she said slowly. "I just don't know if I believe her. Then I feel horrible for saying that. I asked, she agreed and now I'm questioning that? Shouldn't I trust her?"

"Trust must be earned. You have a biological connection, but you don't know this woman."

"You're right. I'm so uncomfortable about everything." Especially Darlene's statements that she was in El Deharia to find a rich man to secure her future. Kayleen was torn between keeping her emotional distance and wanting to have family.

She'd always been taught to see the best in people, to believe they would come through in the end. So thinking her mother was using her violated what she knew to be right and what she felt in her heart. But assuming all was well violated her common sense.

She glanced at him. "You know I'm not like her, right?"

He smiled. "Yes, I know."

"Good."

Darlene hummed as she flipped through the dresses on the rack. "I could so get used to this," she murmured as she picked out a low-cut black gown that glittered with scattered beads. "The work is incredible. The details are hand-done. Have you looked at these prices? Twenty-three thousand dollars. Just like that." She put the black dress in front of her and turned to the full-length mirror set up in Kayleen's living room. "What do you think?"

"It's beautiful." Kayleen thought the dress lacked subtlety, but what did she know about fashion?

Darlene laughed. "Not your thing?"

"Not exactly."

"You're young. You'll grow into black." She carried the dress over to the tray of jewelry on the dining room table. "I'm thinking the sapphire-and-diamond-drop earrings and that matching pendant. Or the bracelet. As much as I want to wear both, less is more. Are you wearing that?"

Kayleen held up a strapless emerald-colored dress. The style was simple, yet elegant. It wasn't especially low-cut, but it was more daring than anything she'd ever worn. Still, she wanted to be beautiful for As'ad.

"I love it," she admitted. "But it makes me nervous."

"It's all in the boning. That dress is couture. It should have the support built right in. Don't worry—you'll stay covered." Darlene put her dress back on the rack, then returned to the jewelry tray. "Something surprising. Young, but sophisticated. Let's see."

She picked up an earring, then put it down. She handed another to Kayleen. "Here."

Kayleen took the piece and studied the curving shape. The free-form design was open and sparkled with white and champagne diamonds.

"Really? Not the emeralds?"

"Too expected with the dress," Darlene told her. "And just the earrings. No necklace or bracelet. You're young and beautiful. Go with it. When you start to fade, you can add the sparkle. Someone's going to do your hair, right? You'll want it up, with long curls down your back. And you don't wear enough makeup. It's a party. Use eyeliner."

Kayleen put in the earring, then held her hair away from her face. "You're right."

"Thanks. I've been around a long time and I know

what men like. Now let's see how I look in this black dress."

She stripped down to her lingerie and then stepped into the black gown. Kayleen helped with the zipper.

"Perfect," Darlene said as she stared at herself in the mirror. "I've already met the Spanish ambassador earlier in the garden. He's very charming. A little older, but that's good. I can be his prize."

Kayleen didn't know what to say to that. "Have you ever been married?"

Darlene held her hair up, as if considering the right style. "Once, years ago. I was eighteen. He was nobody. But I was in love and I told myself money didn't matter. Then the marriage ended and I had nothing. I learned my lesson. Something you should learn."

"What are you talking about?"

"As'ad. You get starry-eyed when he's around. It's embarrassing for all of us."

Kayleen flushed. "We're engaged."

"I don't see how that matters." Darlene stepped out of the dress and put it back on the hanger, then reached for her own clothes. "I know this sounds harsh, but believe me, I have your best interests in mind. Men like As'ad don't have to bother with love. You're setting yourself up for heartache. Take what you can get and move on."

"So no one matters. No one touches your heart."

"Life is easier that way," her mother told her.

"You're wrong," Kayleen said. "Life is emptier that way. We are more than the sum of our experiences. We are defined by our relationships. The people we love and those who love us in return. In the end, that matters more than money."

"So speaks the girl who has never been hungry and without a home."

Kayleen stiffened. "I *have* been without a home. My grandmother dumped me at an orphanage because she couldn't be bothered. But then why should she when my own mother walked out on me?"

Darlene pulled on her shirt and buttoned it. "Here we go," she said, sounding bored. "Poor you. Nobody loves you. Get over it. Life is hard, so make the best of it."

"You mean use other people to get what you want."

"If necessary." Darlene seemed untouched by the comment. "Maybe it seems cruel to be tossed aside, but sometimes it's worse to be kept. Your grandmother wasn't exactly a loving parent. There's a reason I left."

"I was your daughter. You should have taken me with you."

"You would have only dragged me down."

"So you left me to the same fate?"

Darlene shrugged. "You got lucky. She didn't bother with you. Trust me, if she had, it would have been a whole lot worse."

Kayleen didn't want to believe the words, but it was impossible not to. "You don't care about me at all."

"I'm proud of what you've accomplished."

"Catching a rich man?"

"Every woman's dream."

"Not mine," Kayleen told her. "I only wanted to belong."

"Then consider the irony. You have what I want and I've turned down a thousand of what you want. Life sure has a sense of humor."

The battle between Kayleen's head and her heart

ended. She walked over to the tray of jewelry and shook it. "This is why you're here. This is why you're pretending we can be friends. Let me guess—if you land the Spanish ambassador, you'll be gone and I'll never hear from you again. Until you need something."

Darlene shrugged. "I didn't come looking for you, honey. I was living my life, minding my own business. You're the one who set all this in motion. I'm just taking advantage of the ride."

Kayleen had always tried to hate her mother. It had been easier than being disappointed and heartbroken over being thrown away. But it was impossible to hate someone so flawed and unhappy.

"It won't matter if you end up with the Spanish ambassador," Kayleen told her mother. "You'll never feel like you have enough. There's not enough money in the world to fill that hole inside of you. It's going to take more. It's going to take giving your heart."

"Spare me." Darlene waved her hand dismissively.

"I can't. You can only spare yourself. But you won't listen to me because you think you already know everything you need to. You can't use me anymore. You can stay for the party, but then you have to leave."

Her mother glared at her. "Who the hell are you to tell me whether or not I can stay?"

Kayleen drew herself up to her full height. "I'm As'ad's fiancée."

Kayleen was determined to enjoy her first formal event despite feeling uneasy about her mother. Darlene had been friendly, as if nothing had happened. As if she wasn't planning on leaving. Kayleen was determined to handle the situation herself, so she didn't mention anything to As'ad.

He came to her door a little past seven, looking tall and handsome in a black tuxedo and white shirt.

Dana let him in after insisting Kayleen needed to make an entrance.

"You're so pretty," the girl told her. "He needs to see all of you at once."

Kayleen did her best not to fidget as As'ad walked toward her, his dark eyes unreadable. He paused in front of her.

"You are perfection," he murmured as he lightly kissed her. "I will have to keep you close or you will be stolen away."

"Not likely," she told him with a laugh. She turned in a slow circle. "You like the dress?"

"Yes, but I adore the woman who wears it."

Her heart fluttered.

She'd taken Darlene's advice on her hair, asking the stylist to put the top part up and leave the rest in long curls. The gown fit snugly and seemed secure enough for her to relax. She wore the champagne-and-white-diamond earrings, along with a simple diamond bracelet. Her high-heeled sandals gave her an extra four inches and would be excruciating by the end of the evening, but they looked fabulous.

"When do *we* get to go to formal state parties?" Pepper asked with a whine. "I want a new dress and fancy hair."

"When you are thirteen."

"But that's forever away."

He touched her nose. "You will get there soon enough."

"I only have to wait a year and a half," Dana said happily. "Then I can go."

"Three pretty girls," As'ad told Kayleen. "We're going to have to watch them closely. There will be boys at these parties."

"Am I pretty, too?" Pepper asked. Her eyes were big and she sounded doubtful, as if expecting a negative answer.

Kayleen remembered Darlene's harsh assessment and wanted to bonk her mother on the head for it.

As'ad crouched in front of the little girl. "You are more than pretty. You are a classic beauty. Never doubt yourself. You are to be a princess."

Pepper smiled widely. "When I'm a princess can I chop off people's heads if they're mean to me?"

As'ad choked back a laugh and straightened. "No, but you will have other powers." He took Kayleen's hand. "We must leave. Be good tonight."

"We will," Nadine told him.

Kayleen waved as they left. This being a palace, there was always someone to babysit.

They walked the length of the long corridor, then went down a flight of stairs. Once on the main floor, they joined the milling crowd walking toward the ballroom.

While Kayleen had toured the palace many times, she'd never seen the ballroom anything but empty. She was unprepared for the thousands of lights glittering from dozens of massive chandeliers or perfectly set tables set around a large dance floor.

The room was like something out of a movie. Well-dressed couples chatted and danced and sipped champagne. She'd never seen so many jewels in her life. Each dress was more beautiful than the one before, each man more handsome. As they walked into the ballroom, she waited for the sense of not belonging to sweep over her. She waited to feel awkward or out of place. Instead there was only contentment and the knowledge that she belonged here.

The burst of confidence bubbled inside of her, as if she'd already had too much champagne. She enjoyed the sensation, knowing this was her world now. She would marry a wonderful man and together they would adopt the girls. In time she would have children of her own.

As'ad led her to the dance floor, then pulled her into his arms. "Now what are you thinking?" he asked.

"That I'm Cinderella and I've finally arrived at the ball."

"So you leave me at midnight?"

She stared into his eyes. "I'll never leave you."

He stared back. "Good. I do not wish you to go. I need you, Kayleen. I will always need you."

Happiness filled her until she felt as if she could float. The music was perfect, as was the night. They danced until the king arrived, then As'ad led her around and introduced her to several of the guests.

The sound of loud laughter caught her attention. She turned and saw Darlene leaning against a much older, heavyset man. The man's attention seemed locked on her barely covered chest.

"The Spanish ambassador?" Kayleen asked As'ad.

"Yes. Do you wish to meet him?"

"Not especially."

He watched Darlene. "So that is who she has chosen?"

"Apparently."

"He's very rich, but alas, he is married. His wife does not accompany him when he travels."

Married? Kayleen looked at her mother. Did Darlene know?

"I should tell her," she said.

He frowned. "Why?"

"Because she's looking for security in her old age and he's obviously not the way to find it."

"Do you care what happens to her?"

"She's my mother. I can't not care." Which didn't mean she'd changed her mind. She still wanted her mother gone. Not that she'd figured out how to make her go.

"I think it is time I dance with my new sister."

Kayleen turned and saw Qadir, As'ad's brother, standing next to her.

"Assuming you don't mind," Qadir told As'ad.

"One dance and don't flirt."

Qadir laughed. "I flirt as easily as I breathe. Are you so worried that I will steal her away?"

"A man always guards what is precious to him."

Kayleen held in a sigh. "Flirt away," she told Qadir. "My heart belongs to your brother."

"Then he is a lucky man." Qadir led her to the dance floor. "You are beautiful tonight."

"Just tonight? Am I usually a troll?"

He laughed. "So this is what has charmed my brother. There's a brain."

"I have all my organs. Unusual, but there we are."

He laughed again. They chatted about the party and the guests. Qadir told her outrageous stories about several people, including a rumor about an English duchess who complained about not being allowed to bring her dog to the event.

When the dance was finished, Kayleen excused herself.

Qadir was nice enough, but not the person she wanted to spend the evening with.

She walked around the edge of the room, and saw As'ad speaking with her mother.

"That can't be good," she muttered to herself and crossed the room to where they were standing.

"You will leave," As'ad said as Kayleen approached.

"I'm not so sure about that," Darlene told him. "The girl is my daughter. Who are you to come between her and her family?"

"A man who is willing to pay you to leave."

Kayleen caught her breath. No. As'ad couldn't do that. It wasn't right. She moved forward, but neither of them noticed her.

"You will not see her again," he continued. "If she contacts you herself, that is fine, but you will not have contact with her directly without her permission."

"So many rules." Darlene smiled. "That'll cost you."

"I would think a million dollars would be enough."

"Oh, please. Not even close. I want five."

"Three."

"I'll take four and you'll consider it a bargain."

The room went still. Oh, sure, people were dancing and talking and Kayleen was confident the orchestra kept playing, but she couldn't hear anything except the conversation of the two people in front of her.

"I'll wire the money as soon as you get me an account number," he said.

"I can give it to you tonight." Darlene patted his arm. "You really care for her. That's sweet."

"She is to be my wife."

"So I hear. You know she's in love with you."

Kayleen's breath caught.

"I know." As'ad spoke quietly, confidently.

"I'll bet that makes things real easy for you," Darlene said.

"It does."

Her mother tilted her head. "You think she's foolish enough to think you love her back?"

"You are not to tell her otherwise."

"Of course not." Darlene smiled again. "But I think I should be allowed to keep the dress and the jewelry then. As a token of goodwill."

"As you wish."

"Then she'll never hear the truth from me."

Chapter Fourteen

Kayleen didn't remember leaving the party, but she must have. When she finally looked around, she was in the garden—the one place she always seemed to retreat to. It was mostly in shadow, with lights illuminating the path. She wandered around, her body aching, her eyes burning, neither of which compared to the pain in her heart.

As'ad didn't love her. While he'd never specifically said he cared, she'd allowed herself to believe.

"I'm a fool," she said aloud.

He'd dismissed feelings as nothing more than a convenience. He'd admitted that their marriage would be easier for him, because of her feelings. He was using her. Nothing about their engagement mattered to him. *She* didn't matter to him.

She hurt. Her whole body ached. Each breath was an effort. She wanted to cry, but she was too stunned.

Her hopes and dreams continued to crumble around her, leaving her standing in a pile of dusty "what could have been." She'd thought she'd found where she belonged, where she could matter and make a difference. She'd thought so many things. But in As'ad's mind, she was little more than a comfy ottoman, where he could rest his feet. Useful, but not of any great interest.

She turned, trying to figure out where to go, what to do. Light caught her engagement ring and made it sparkle. She'd been such a fool, she thought bitterly. So stupidly innocent and naive about everything. Her mother had been right—why on earth would a man like As'ad be interested in a country mouse like herself? She'd wrapped herself in the fantasy because it was what she wanted to believe. Because it was easier than accepting the truth.

She heard a sound and looked up. One of the doves shifted in its cage. Willingly trapped because they either didn't understand they could be free or weren't interested. They took the easy way out, too.

Anger joined a sadness so profound, she knew it would scar her forever. Because whatever mistakes she'd made, she truly did love As'ad. She always would. But she didn't belong here. She couldn't stay and marry a man who didn't love her.

That decided, she made her way into the palace. Her mother's door stood partially open. Kayleen stepped inside without knocking to find her mother supervising two maids who were packing her suitcases. Darlene had already changed out of her evening gown into an elegant pantsuit. When she saw her daughter, she smiled.

"Oh, good. You stopped by. That saves me writing a note. Look, I'm leaving—just like you said I should. I've had a great time. I'm sorry we didn't get a chance to get to know each other better. Next time you're back in the States, you'll need to look me up."

Everything about her was false, Kayleen thought emotionlessly. From her bleached hair to her fake smiles.

"You're leaving because As'ad is paying you four million dollars," Kayleen told her. "I heard the conversation."

"Then you know I got what I came for. A secure future. It's not a fortune, but I know how to invest. I'll live well enough and maybe find someone to supplement my excesses. It doesn't compare with your haul, of course, but we can't all be that lucky."

Lucky. Right. To fall in love with a man who didn't care about her.

"When do you leave?" Kayleen asked.

"There's a plane waiting at the airport. I love the truly rich." Darlene frowned. "You're not going to want an emotional goodbye, are you?"

"No. I don't want anything from you."

With that, she left and returned to her own suite. The babysitter greeted her.

"They were all so good tonight," the young woman said.

"I'm glad. Thank you."

The other woman left and Kayleen was alone.

Despite the pain, she felt almost at peace. Maybe it was finally seeing the world as it was, and not as she wanted it to be. Maybe it was knowing the truth.

The truth was she would never have the kind of relationship with her biological family that she wanted. She could keep trying and maybe in time, things would improve, but there was no rescue there. There was no happy ending.

The same was true with As'ad. He'd proposed out of duty and maybe with the belief that she would be a good wife. He'd told her he didn't believe in love and she hadn't listened. She'd created a different story because it was what she wanted to believe.

But he didn't love her and he had no intention of loving her. So her choices were clear. She could stay and marry him, live life as a princess, or she could walk away. Darlene would tell her the money, the prestige, the palace, were worth nearly everything. But Kayleen remembered reading once that when a woman marries for money, she earns every penny.

She didn't want to marry for money—she wanted to marry for love. She wasn't like the doves—trapped even though the door was open, she was free to leave.

After looking in on the girls, she returned to her own room. She undressed and pulled on a robe, then sat in a chair by the French doors and stared out at the night.

The only part of leaving that bothered her was knowing how much she would miss As'ad. Despite everything, she loved him. Would she ever be able to love anyone else?

Because that's what she wanted. A real life, with a family and a man who cared. She wasn't going to run back to the convent school. She was going to make her way in the world. She was strong—she could do it.

As'ad found Kayleen in her suite. She'd changed out of her ball gown and pulled on a robe. She sat in the living room, a pad of paper on her lap.

He walked in and stared at her. "You left the party. I looked everywhere and you were gone."

She glanced up at him. "I didn't want to stay any longer."

That didn't sound right, he thought warily. She'd left without talking to him? "Are you ill?"

"I'm fine."

"You came back here to make notes?"

"Apparently." She set the paper and pen on the coffee table, then stood. "Have you transferred the money to my mother?"

He swore silently. "You spoke with her?"

"Not about that. Don't worry. She didn't tell me anything, so she gets to keep the dress and jewelry, right? I mean, that *was* the deal. Along with the four million. A generous offer. I'd already told her to leave, but you didn't know that. She made out well."

"I do not care about the money," he said, trying to remember exactly what he and Darlene had discussed. Obviously Kayleen had been in a position to overhear their conversation.

He felt badly—he guessed she was hurt and his intent had been to avoid that.

"I know," Kayleen said. "But she does, so it works out well for both of you."

He tried to read her expression, but he had no idea what she was thinking. Was she angry?

"Once she is gone, all will be well," he said, willing it to be so.

"I'm not as sure." She stared into his eyes. "This is just a marriage of convenience for you. I'm surprised you'd pick me. I'm sure there are women with better pedigrees out there. Women who understand what it's like to be a princess and who won't have foolish expectations."

"I am pleased to be marrying you. I want you to be the mother of my sons. I respect you, Kayleen. Isn't respect and admiration more important, more lasting, than a fleeting emotion like love? I will honor you above all women. That must have value."

"It does. But love has value, too. Maybe it's a peasant thing."

She was calm and he didn't like it. Screaming and crying he could understand, but not this quiet conversation. What did she want from him?

"I take a lot of the blame," she said, her gaze steady. "I took the easy way out. You told me that after we slept together, and you were right. I want to hide, first at the convent school and then here, with you. I was never willing to really strike out on my own. I was afraid and I let that fear rule me. I thought by staying close to what I knew, I would be safe and belong. Even when I went halfway around the world to your country, I huddled in the orphan school, terrified to take a step."

Her reasoning sounded correct, but he had a bad feeling about what she was saying.

"Now you have chosen a different path," he pointed out. "So you are making changes. That is as it should be."

"I am making changes, As'ad. Big ones." She removed her engagement ring and held it out to him.

"No," he told her, shocked by her actions. "You have agreed to marry me. Changing your mind is not permitted."

"*You* don't get to decide that. I won't marry a man who doesn't love me. I'm worth more. I deserve more. And so do you. I know you believe love makes you weak, but you're wrong. Love makes you strong. It is powerful and the reason we're here. To love and be loved. You need that,

As'ad. I love you, but that's not enough. You have to be willing to love me back. Maybe I'm not the one. Maybe there's someone else you can love."

She gulped in a breath and tried to smile. Her lips trembled. "It hurts to say that. It hurts to think of you with someone else. But I can't make you love me."

She didn't mean this, he told himself. It was the emotion of the moment. She would get over it.

"I will not accept the ring back."

"That's your choice." She put it on the coffee table. "Either way, I'm leaving."

"You cannot go. I won't permit it. Besides…" He prepared to say the one thing that would change her mind. "I need you."

She nodded slowly. "You do. More than you realize. But that's not enough."

He frowned. It had worked before. Lina had told him Kayleen wanted to be needed above all. "I need you," he repeated.

"Maybe, but you can't have me." She sighed. "It's late, and you should go."

Somehow he found himself moving to the door. Then he was in the hallway. He stood there a long time, fighting the strangest feeling that he'd just lost something precious.

No, he told himself. Kayleen wouldn't leave him. She couldn't. She belonged here. To him and the girls. She would be fine. In the morning they would talk again. He would make her understand that she belonged here. With him. It was what he wanted. And he was Prince As'ad of El Deharia. He always got what he wanted.

As'ad gave Kayleen plenty of time to think about what she was considering, which turned out to be the one flaw in his plan. For when he returned to her suite close to midday, she and the girls were gone.

Their closets were empty, the toys missing, the dining room swept clean of homework and books. The only thing lying there was the engagement ring he'd given her.

He had expected a fight or tears or even an apology, but not the silence. Not the absence of life. It was as if they'd never been there at all.

He walked through the rooms, not truly accepting the truth of it. She had left him.

Him! A prince. After all he'd done for her, all he'd given her. He'd rescued her and the children, started the adoption process for the girls. He'd given them a home, had proposed to Kayleen. What more did she want?

He burst into his aunt's office and glared at her. "This is all your fault," he told her sternly. "You created the problem and you will fix it."

Lina's office was small and feminine, overlooking the garden. Normally he would tease her about the frills and ruffles, but not today. Not now when she had ruined everything.

Lina poured herself some tea from a pot on a silver tray. "I have no idea what you're talking about."

"Of course you do. Kayleen is gone. She left and took the girls. Those are my children. El Deharian law states royal children cannot be taken from the country without their royal parent's permission."

"You're not the royal parent yet. Your petition for adoption has not been approved, nor is it likely to be. Custody will be given solely to Kayleen. She's already spoken to the king."

As'ad stared at her, unable to believe what she was saying. "That is not possible."

"It's very possible. You only took the girls because I suggested it as a way to solve the problem with Tahir. You never actually wanted them."

This was *not* happening, he told himself. "I did not know them. I know them now and they are my daughters."

"Not really. Kayleen is the one who loves them."

"I provided snow for their pageant."

"Which was great and I know they enjoyed it. I'm not saying you didn't care about them, As'ad. But love? You don't believe in it. You've told me yourself. Your father understands completely. Don't forget, these aren't royal children who grew up like you did. They expect their parents to love them. Kayleen will. They're leaving El Deharia. All four of them."

Leaving? Permanently?

"I will not allow it," he told her. "I insist they stay."

"They will through the holidays, then Kayleen is taking the girls back to the States. It will be easier for them to start over. Your father has offered to help financially. Kayleen is being her usual sacrificing self. She will allow him to help her with the girls until she gets established, but then she'll handle things. She's going to let him pay for college, though. Especially for Dana. Apparently she wants to be a doctor."

"I know that," As'ad said through ground teeth. "And Nadine will dance and Pepper has yet to decide, but she's only eight and why should she? This is ridiculous. My father will not support my children. It is my responsibility and my right. You have meddled, Lina. You have ruined everything."

"Actually, you did that all yourself. Kayleen is a wonderful woman. She adored you and would have made you very happy. She was yours to lose and you did. But don't worry. She'll find someone else. I'm a little more worried about you."

He wanted to rant and yell. He wanted to throw her antique desk through the large window. He wanted to crush her teapot with his bare hands.

"None of this is acceptable," he growled.

"I'm sorry you see it that way, but I think it's for the best. Kayleen deserves a man who will love her. Or don't you agree?"

He glared at his aunt. "You seek to trap me with your words."

"I seek to make you understand that you don't deserve a woman like Kayleen."

Her words cut him in a way no words had before. He stared at her for a long moment as the truth settled into the wound. She was right—he did not deserve Kayleen. All this time he had assumed he was doing her a favor when, in truth, the situation was reversed.

He left Lina's office and retreated to his own. He told Neil he would not be disturbed. Then he stood alone in the silence and wondered what had gone wrong.

Two days later he understood the real meaning of the words *living in hell.* Only there was no living for him, only reminders of what he had lost.

He had always enjoyed life in the palace, but now every room, every corridor, was a reminder of what was missing. He turned, expecting to see one of the girls. But they weren't there. He thought of a thousand things he should tell Kayleen, but she wasn't around to listen. He ached to hold her, touch her, kiss her, and there was no one.

She had left him. Willingly, easily. She had walked away and not come back. She, who had claimed to love him.

While he knew in his heart her affection for him had not had time to fade, in his mind he grew angry. But she was not there to fight with.

He spent the night in her rooms, wandering, sitting, waiting, remembering. He arranged to go to Paris to forget her, then canceled his plans. He, who had never allowed himself to care, to need, to love, had been broken. Prince As'ad of El Deharia reduced to a shell of a man because his woman had left.

He hated that. Hated to be weak. Hated to need.

He hurried to see his father, walking in on the king without knocking. His father looked up from his morning paper. "As'ad, what is wrong? You do not look well."

"I am fine. Kayleen has left."

"Yes, I know."

"You must not give her permission to leave the country, or take the girls with her. Those are my children. The law is clearly on my side."

His father frowned. "Kayleen said you did not love the girls. That they would be better off with her. Was she wrong? What do you wish?"

Love. Why did it always come back to that? As'ad walked to the window and stared out at the horizon.

What *did* he wish?

"I want her back," he said quietly. "I want her here, with me. I want the girls to return. I want…"

He wanted Kayleen smiling at him, laughing with him, close to him. He wanted to see her stomach swell with their baby, he wanted to ease her discomfort when she was sick. He wanted to see the girls grow and learn and prepare for college. He wanted to walk each of them down the aisle, only after terrifying any young man who would claim one of them as he had claimed Kayleen.

What if Dana was in a love with a man who did not love her back? What would he do?

Kill him, he told himself. He would kill the suitor in question, then take his daughter home where she belonged. He would insist she not be with anyone who did not love her desperately. Because that was what she deserved. What they all deserved. He could not let them go under any other circumstances.

Didn't Kayleen deserve the same?

He already knew the answer. He believed it. But if it was true, then shouldn't he let her go to find such a man?

No!

The roar came from deep within him. He faced his father. "No. She is to have no one but me. I am the one who first claimed her and I will not let her go."

His father sighed. "We have let go of the old ways. You will not be allowed to claim a bride who is not interested in marrying you."

"I will convince her."

"How?"

"By giving her the one thing she wants."

The king looked doubtful. "Do you know what that is?"

As'ad finally did. "Where is she?"

Mukhtar hesitated. "I am not sure…"

"I am. Where is she? I know she has not left the country. Lina told me. Where is she hiding?"

And then he knew that, as well. "Never mind. I'll find her myself."

* * *

Kayleen did her best to smile. The puppy was adorable, as was Pepper as the two of them tumbled together on the rug by the fire. Dana and Nadine were off with the older girls. Despite the sudden change from a palace to a desert camp, the sisters had adjusted well. They thought they were on a fun adventure.

Kayleen wished she could share their excitement and flexibility. While she appreciated that Sharif and Zarina had taken them in, she longed to be back at the palace. While life under the stars offered a level of freedom she'd never experienced before, it was difficult to even breathe without thinking of As'ad.

She ached for him every minute of every day. She knew she had to stay strong and she was determined not to give in to the need to see him, but there were times when the pain overwhelmed her.

Zarina hadn't asked any questions when Kayleen had shown up with the girls. Instead she'd offered a comfortable tent and acceptance by the villagers. But it was a temporary situation—in a few days the tribe would return to the desert and Kayleen would have to find temporary housing until she could leave El Deharia.

Perhaps in the city somewhere. A small house. Lina had promised it would only take a couple of weeks for her paperwork to be pushed through the legal channels. There were advantages to a royal connection.

Thank goodness As'ad hadn't been interested in hurrying the adoption. If he had she wouldn't have been able to leave. Royal children could not be taken from El Deharia without the royal parent's permission.

She touched her belly and remembered the last time

they'd made love. If she was pregnant, she would be trapped forever. Imagine the irony if she at last had the baby she'd long desired.

"I will not think of that," she whispered to herself. "I will stay strong."

She might not know the future, but she was confident she could handle whatever life threw at her. She'd stood up for what she believed, she'd faced As'ad and turned down the half life he'd offered. She'd been willing to lose everything to gain her heart's desire. There was some peace in knowing she'd been true to herself. Unfortunately peace did not seem to ease pain.

She stood and walked to the fire, where tea always boiled. After pouring herself a mug she stared up at the clear sky. Only two days until Christmas. They would celebrate out here, under the stars, then return to the city.

She turned back to the tent, only to stop when she saw a man riding toward the camp. For a moment her heart jumped in her chest, but then she realized he wore traditional clothes. One of the young men who came and went, she thought, looking away. Someone's husband.

Several of the tribespeople called out to each other. Kayleen tried to figure out what they were saying, but they were speaking quickly, yelling and pointing. Was there a problem?

Then she looked back at the man and recognized him. As'ad. But he was unlike she'd ever seen him before. He looked determined, primal. This was no prince in a suit—this was a sheik.

She stood her ground, reminding herself she had nothing to fear. He couldn't hurt her worse than he had when he'd admitted he didn't love her and that her love for him was a well-timed convenience. She shook out her long hair, then raised her chin. Pride and determination stiffened her spine. She didn't move, not even when he rode his horse right up to her.

Their eyes locked. She had no idea what he was thinking. Despite everything, she was happy to see him, happy to drink in the male beauty of his hard features. She wanted to touch him and kiss him and give herself to him. So much for being strong.

"I have claimed you," he told her sternly. "You cannot escape me."

"You can't hold me against my will. I'm not your prisoner."

He dismounted and handed the horse off to one of the young boys who had run up. Then he stalked over to her.

"You're right, my heart. I am yours."

She blinked. What had he called her? And what did he mean that he was her prisoner? What?

He touched her face with his fingertips. "I have missed you. Every second of every day since you left me has been empty and dark."

She swallowed. "I don't understand."

"Nor do I. My course was set—the plan clear. I would marry appropriately, father sons, perhaps a daughter or two, serve my people and live my life. It was arranged. It was my destiny. Then one day, I met a woman who leads with her heart, who is fearless and giving and kind and who bewitched me."

She couldn't breathe, but that didn't seem to be such a big deal. This was all good, right? He was saying good things. Maybe, just maybe, she could hope.

"Kayleen, I was wrong," he told her. "Wrong to think I knew so much more, that I was in charge. You swept into my life and nothing was the same. It was better—so much better. I miss you desperately. You and the girls. I need to see you smile every day. All of you. I need to hear your voices, your laughter. You cannot take my daughters from me and you cannot take yourself."

She ached for him. Giving in seemed the only option. But how could she?

"I won't live in a loveless marriage," she told him, fighting tears, fighting the need to surrender. "I deserve more."

"Yes, you do. I was wrong to suggest such a thing before. You deserve to be loved, to be worshiped. To be the best part of your husband's life."

He took her hands in his and kissed her knuckles, then turned her wrists and kissed her palms.

"Let me be that man," he said quietly. "Let me show you all the ways I love you. Let me prove myself again and again, then, when you are sure, continue to test me." He stared into her eyes. "I will not fail, my heart. I will never fail. Because I love you. Only you. I did not think it was possible, yet here I stand. Humbled. Needing. In love. Can you find it in your heart to forgive me? To give me another chance?"

"Say yes."

The words were whispered from behind her. She sensed all three of the girls standing there, willing her to give As'ad the second chance he asked for.

"Yes," she whispered, then threw herself into his arms.

He caught her and pulled her close, saying her name over and over, then kissed her and held her as if he would never let her go.

He felt so right, next to her, she thought, nearly bursting with happiness. Then there were more arms and he pulled back only to let the girls into their circle of love.

He picked up Pepper and put his arm around Nadine. Kayleen pulled Dana against her and they held on to each other…a family at last.

"I'm so happy," Kayleen told him.

"As am I. Perhaps not as quick a learner as you would like."

"You figured it out."

"Only because you had the strength to leave me. You will always do the right thing, won't you?"

"I'll try."

He kissed her again, then frowned. "Why do you cry?"

"I'm not."

She touched her cheek and felt wetness. But it was cold, not warm and wasn't a tear.

Pepper shrieked. "It's snowing. As'ad, you brought the snow machine to the desert!"

"I did not. There is no way to power it out here."

Kayleen looked up. Snow fell from a clear sky. Perfect snow. Miracle snow. Christmas snow.

He set Pepper on the ground. She joined her sisters and the other children, running around, trying to catch snowflakes in their hands and on their tongues. As'ad pulled Kayleen close.

"You must promise to never leave me again," he said. "I would not survive it."

"As you will never leave me."

He laughed. "Where else would I want to be? I have you."

"For always," she told him.

"Yes," he promised. "For always."

Love burned hot and bright in his eyes. Love that filled the empty space inside of her and told her she had finally, *finally* found her way home.

* * * * *

CHRISTMAS IN HIS ROYAL BED

HEIDI BETTS

An avid romance reader since junior high school, **Heidi Betts** knew early on that she wanted to write these wonderful stories of love and adventure. It wasn't until her freshman year of college, however, when she spent the entire night reading a romance novel instead of studying for finals, that she decided to take the road less travelled and follow her dream. As well as devoting her time to reading, writing and creating romance, she is the founder of her local Romance Writers of America chapter. She also has a tendency to take injured and homeless animals of every species into her Central Pennsylvania home.

Heidi loves to hear from readers. You can write to her at PO Box 99, Kylertown, PA 16847, USA, (a SASE is appreciated, but not necessary) or e-mail heidi@heidibetts.com.

And be sure to visit www.heidibetts.com for news and information about upcoming books.

In loving memory of Helen Brown. When she passed away this time last year after a long and valiant battle with breast cancer, I lost a friend, and the romance world lost a dedicated fan. We miss you, Helen. And if Heaven is any kind of Heaven at all, it will be filled with romance novels for you to enjoy.

And with much appreciation to loyal reader Jennifer Yates, who, when I challenged readers to help me out, came up with many of the names used in this story. Thanks, Jennifer!

One

*O*nly she would do.

Prince Stephan Nicolas Braedon of Glendovia watched the ebony-haired beauty from afar. Tall and lithe, with an hourglass figure, she had silky black hair that fell in a straight curtain to her hips. He was too far away to know the color of her eyes or see the full pout of her lips, but he trusted the feeling in his gut that told him both would be just as alluring as the rest of her.

Cocking his head toward the tall, suited man

at his side, he said in a low voice, "Find out her name."

His bodyguard followed the direction of his gaze, then gave a stiff nod before moving away. Nicolas didn't need to ask how Osric intended to get the information, nor did he care.

A few minutes later, his bodyguard returned, standing at attention at Nicolas's side.

"Her name is Alandra Sanchez, Your Highness. She is in charge of the organization of this evening's event."

Alandra. A beautiful name for a beautiful woman.

She floated around the large, crowded ballroom, smiling, chatting with guests, making sure everything was running smoothly. The full-length lavender gown she wore shimmered in the muted lighting every time she moved, and fit her perfect feminine curves like a glove.

Nicolas hadn't attended this fund-raising dinner in hopes of finding a lover, but now that he'd seen her, he knew he wouldn't be leaving the United States without making arrangements for her to become his next mistress.

It was true that he was the member of the royal

family in charge of overseeing Glendovia's charitable organizations, but his duties did not extend to attending charitable events outside of his own country. That, he usually left to his sister or one of his two brothers.

But though his sister, Mia, had been scheduled to make the trip to the States and attend this dinner to raise funds for a new children's wing at a central Texas hospital, she'd had to cancel at the last minute. Since Nicolas was to meet with very wealthy oilmen to discuss fuel for his country, he decided to attend.

Until a few minutes ago, he had been resenting the interruption of his own life and plans, and all but cursing his sister for being the cause. Now, however, he was considering sending Mia a bouquet of flowers or a box of her favorite truffles. He wanted to thank her for putting him on a path to what could turn out to be an extremely pleasurable experience.

Smiling so brightly the muscles in her cheeks ached, Alandra Sanchez moved around the room, making sure everything was running smoothly. She'd been working to set up this gala for months now, in hopes of raising both awareness and money for the new children's hospital wing.

Unfortunately, things weren't going quite as well as she'd hoped, and Alandra knew she had only herself to blame.

Everyone in the room seemed to be watching her. She could see their curiosity. Sense their condemnation.

All because she'd had the dreadful misfortune to get mixed up with the wrong man.

Of all the things that could have happened to put a damper on this evening's event, this was the worst. A hurricane, a flash flood, even the hotel catching on fire…

Those were all disasters she could have handled. They barely would have caused a blip on her radar. But instead, she was being personally attacked, her reputation besmirched.

It served her right for ever getting involved with Blake Winters in the first place. She should have known the minute she met him that he would end up causing her nothing but trouble.

And now everyone in this room—everyone in Gabriel's Crossing, the great state of Texas and

possibly the entire United States of America—
thought she was a home-wrecking adulteress.

That's what the newspaper gossip columns
were saying about her. Her picture, along with
Blake's and that of his wife and two children, had
been plastered everywhere, with glaring, slander-
ous headlines.

Ignoring the stares and whispers she knew were
aimed in her direction, Alandra held her head high
and continued wending her way through the ballroom, acting as though nothing was wrong. As
though her heart wasn't racing, her face wasn't
flushed with humiliation and her palms weren't
damp with anxiety.

Nothing that had happened in the week since
the story of her affair with Blake Winters broke had
led her to believe the fund-raising dinner wouldn't
still be a complete success. None of the invited
guests had cancelled, making excuses for why they
couldn't attend. No one from the hospital benevo-
lence society had called to complain about the
scandal she found herself suddenly embroiled in,
or to voice concerns about her name being linked
to the organization.

All of which led her to believe everything would be fine. That even though reporters were camped out on her front lawn, the rest of her life continued to run smoothly.

Now, though, she wasn't so sure. Now, she thought perhaps every seat in the room was filled because the cream of central Texas high society wanted an up-close-and-personal glimpse of one of their own who had so recently fallen from grace.

She might as well have a scarlet letter pinned to her chest or a piece of spinach stuck in her teeth, for all the attention being focused on her every move.

The attention—even negative attention—she could handle. What concerned her more than the stares and whispers was the impact her newly sullied reputation might have on the amount of money collected this evening.

She'd worked so hard to put this event together, was so passionate about her philanthropy, giving of both her time and money to support the causes she felt most strongly about. And she had always been quite successful in convincing others to give to those causes, too.

Usually, by this point in the evening, she would

already have collected a dozen extremely generous checks slipped to her by those in attendance, with more to follow at the end of the night. Tonight, however, her hands—and the hospital's coffers—were still empty.

Because she'd had the misfortune of meeting Blake Winters at another fund-raiser last year, and hadn't been wise enough to turn him away when he'd started asking her out, those who were most in need could very well end up going without.

The prospect broke her heart, and she pressed a hand to the snug satin stays sewn into the lining of her gown in an attempt to settle the nervous caterpillars squirming and wiggling in her belly.

She would act as though nothing was wrong, nothing was out of the ordinary—and pray like the dickens that the crowd got over their curiosity and remembered their true purpose for being here before the evening was over. Otherwise, she had a sneaking suspicion her personal bank account would be taking a hard hit when she attempted to single-handedly make up for what the children's wing fund should have earned tonight. And probably would have, if not for her bad luck and some of the poor decisions she'd made recently.

Once she'd made her loop through the crowd to be sure every seat was filled, every guest served and everything was running as smoothly as possible, she returned to her own place at the front of the room, where a raised dais had been set up for the event's organizers. She made small talk with the women on either side of her and choked down her meal, barely tasting a bite.

Next came a speech from the organization's president, and a short ceremony where plaques were given to several members who had gone above and beyond in the past year. Even Alandra received one, for her continued dedication to raising money for the hospital.

Finally, the evening drew to an end, and she breathed a sigh of relief. She was now holding a few generous checks, and had received promises for more. Not as many as she'd collected in the past, and she had definitely noticed a distinct difference in the way people had treated her throughout the evening. But at least things were looking a bit brighter than they had when the night began.

She made a final round of the room, nodding farewells to guests as they exited the ballroom, and making sure no one left anything behind before the hotel staff started cleaning up.

Gathering her own small, beaded clutch and shawl from her seat, she found her mind racing ahead to what she needed to do the next day—thoughts that were interrupted when she heard a low, masculine voice call her name.

"Miss Sanchez?"

Turning, she found herself dwarfed by a wide-shouldered, dark-haired mountain of a man.

She swallowed once before pasting a smile on her face and tipping her head up, up, up to meet his gaze.

"Yes?"

"If you have a minute, my employer would like to speak with you."

He inclined his head, drawing her attention to the back of the room, where a lone gentleman sat at one of the now-cleared round tables.

From what she could see at this distance, he was quite handsome.

He was also staring at her.

"Your employer?" she asked.

"Yes, miss."

So much for gaining more information about who, exactly, the mountain's employer was.

But if he had attended tonight's dinner, then he was likely a current or potential donor, and she always had time to speak with a contributor. Especially one who could afford his own bodyguard, or CIA agent, or professional wrestler....

"Of course," she said, maintaining her bright, upbeat demeanor.

Turning sideways, the giant gestured for her to move ahead of him, and then escorted her across the nearly empty room. Around them, dishes clinked and stacked chairs clattered as the kitchen and cleaning staff worked to disassemble what had taken all day to set up.

As she approached the man who wished to speak with her, he lifted a flute of champagne and took a long sip.

He wore a smartly tailored jacket of navy blue, cut quite differently than most of those she'd seen throughout the night. He definitely was not a local.

She also noticed that her earlier perception of

him being "quite handsome" was a gross inaccuracy. He was movie-star gorgeous, with dark hair and startling blue eyes that seemed to bore into her like laser beams.

Holding out her hand, she introduced herself. "Hello, I'm Alandra Sanchez."

"I know," he replied, taking her hand and refusing to let it go as he tugged her gently forward. "Have a seat, won't you, please."

Letting her shawl fall lower on her bare back, she slid onto the chair beside him. "Your…employee said you wanted to speak to me."

"Yes," he replied slowly. "May I offer you a glass of champagne?"

She opened her mouth to refuse, but the hulk was already pouring and setting a glass in front of her.

"Thank you."

Though they both had drinks now, and the evening's event was clearly over, the man seated beside her still didn't speak. The silence made Alandra shift uncomfortably, and caused gooseflesh to break out along her arms.

"What did you need to speak with me about,

Mr.…." she finally pressed, careful to remain as polite as possible.

"You may call me Nicolas," he replied.

His voice carried a slight accent. Perhaps the hint of a British lilt, but Alandra couldn't place it.

"Nicolas," she repeated, because he seemed to expect it. Then she continued in her attempts to get to his reason for wanting to speak with her.

"Were you interested in making a donation to the fund for the new children's cancer wing of the hospital?" she asked. "If so, I would be happy to accept a check tonight. Or if you'd prefer, I can put you in touch with someone from the organization you can speak with, to make your contribution personally."

For a moment after she finished, he simply continued to study her, his lapis-blue eyes sharp and commandingly intense.

After taking another sip of the expensive champagne, he slowly said, "I would be happy to give to your little…cause. However, that is not why I invited you over here."

Alandra's eyes widened fractionally at that, but she did her best to hide her consternation.

"I am staying in a suite of rooms here in this hotel," he informed her. "I'd like for you to return there with me. Spend the rest of the evening in my bed. If things go well and we are…compatible, perhaps we can discuss further arrangements."

Alandra blinked, but otherwise remained frozen in place, her entire body mannequin-stiff and unmoving. She couldn't have been more stunned if he'd lifted a hand and slapped her across the face.

She didn't know what to say. Didn't know what she *should* say.

This certainly wasn't the first time she'd been propositioned. Young or old, rich or poor, men had always been attracted to her, and she'd had more than her share of invitations to dinner, the theater, even romantic jaunts to private island hideaways.

And, yes, she was well aware that every single one of those men had hopes that dinner, the theater and tropical getaways would help him to seduce her into his bed.

But never—*never*—had any of them been so bold, so brash, as to flat-out ask her to sleep with him.

This was all because of the scandal, she realized

suddenly, her spine snapping straight with offense. Those bloody articles had labeled her an immoral home wrecker. And this man had obviously gotten wind of that and decided she wouldn't be averse to an indecent proposal.

Well, she was averse. She was disgusted and thoroughly insulted.

Pushing her chair back, she rose to her feet, rearranged her shawl across her back and arms, and tightened her fingers on her small clutch purse. Concentrating on her breathing, she stood perfectly rigid, looking down at him.

"I don't know what kind of woman you think I am. But I can assure you I'm *not* the kind to go to bed with a man I've just met."

She cut a quick glance at the bear standing at attention a yard or two away. "Maybe your bodyguard can find someone a little more willing and a lot less discriminating to go back to your room with you tonight. That is, if you're utterly incapable of finding her on your own."

With that, Alandra turned on her heel and marched out of the ballroom to the elevator.

Just who the hell did the man think he was?

Two

Who did she think she was to speak to him in such a manner?

Nicolas had never been turned down like that before.

He blinked once, slowly, searching his memory for a similar incident that might have taken place during his lifetime.

No, he didn't think he'd been turned down *ever*.

Had she actually implied that he was incapable of finding his own female companionship? Or that he had to order Osric to *pay* a woman to spend time with him?

He shook his head, still not quite believing what had just taken place. Behind him, Osric shuffled closer, looming over his right shoulder.

"Your Highness, shall I go after her and bring her back so that you may finish your conversation?"

Nicolas could picture his oversize bodyguard, who closely resembled a brick wall, tackling Miss Sanchez to the ground and carting her back to him…and the fuss the lady would kick up if he so much as tried.

"No, thank you, Osric," he replied. "I believe I'll be returning to the suite alone this evening."

Placing his hands on the tabletop in front of him, he stood and straightened the front of his jacket, then started out of the ballroom, with his trusty security guard close on his heels.

He should be upset, Nicolas thought, as they made their way through the hotel to his private, luxurious suite on the thirty-third floor.

Ironically, he was more intrigued than ever by the ebony-haired beauty. It was her face and figure that had first caught his attention, and seeing her up close hadn't changed his mind about having her in his bed.

He would have expected a dressing-down such as she'd given him to turn him off, to make him realize he didn't want to sleep with a woman who possessed such a sharp tongue. Instead, her spirit fired his blood.

If anything, he found himself wanting her more. She was lovely and fierce, and he could only imagine how passionately those qualities would translate between the sheets.

Alandra Sanchez might think she'd gotten in the last word downstairs, when she'd all but told him to take his offer and go straight to the devil. But Prince Stephan Nicolas Braedon was used to getting his way, getting what he wanted.

And he wanted *her*.

So he would have her. He only had to figure out how.

One week later...

"Pop? Alandra? Is anybody here?"

Alandra heard her sister calling from downstairs,

and was more than happy to take a break from the event plans she'd been working on all afternoon.

Since Elena had moved out of their father's house and into her own with her new husband, Chase, Alandra didn't get to see her as often as she used to.

Abandoning her desk, she found her sister looking slightly frazzled as she flipped through a pile of mail stacked beside a large arrangement of fresh flowers on the round table in the center of the foyer. When she heard Alandra's approach, Elena raised her head and rolled her eyes.

"A reporter tried to follow my car through the security gate," she snapped, waving a hand over her shoulder in the direction of the front door. "He was camped out front, waiting."

Alandra frowned, moving closer to give her sister a gentle squeeze. "I'm so sorry. I really thought they'd have lost interest by now and moved on to something else."

"It's not your fault," Elena said with a sigh, returning Alandra's hug. "And eventually they *will* lose interest and move on."

"So what are you doing here?" she asked distractedly, her mind still on the reporter. It was one thing for *her* to be harassed and annoyed because of her own foolish actions, but it was another for her family to be dragged into this mess.

"Since Chase won't be home for dinner because of a late meeting, I thought I'd stop by to say hello, see how you and Pop are doing, and grab a bite to eat. Not to mention picking up any stray mail," she added, stuffing a few letters into the side pocket of her handbag.

Her sister had married and moved out last year, but the change-of-address process took time, and the odd letter or piece of mail showed up for her occasionally.

"Well, dinner will be served at seven, as usual, and as far as I know, everything is fine around here. Pop is still at the office, and I've just been working on the plans for that fund-raiser for the animal shelters."

"Will Chase and I be invited?" Elena asked.

"Of course."

"Looks like you got something important," her sister said, nodding toward the letter left on top of the stack.

Alandra picked up the thick envelope and read the return address, which was embossed in dark blue, fancy raised script on parchment-quality stationery. "H.R.H. Prince Stephan Nicolas Braedon, Kingdom of Glendovia."

"His Royal Highness?" Elena asked. "Really? You got a letter from a prince?"

"It appears so." She opened the envelope and skimmed the official-looking letterhead and neatly typed text of the top page. Then, heart stuttering, she read it again. "Oh, my God," she breathed.

"What?"

"This Prince Stephan wants me to come to his kingdom and oversee all of their fund-raising organizations."

Both sisters scanned the letter. It touched on Alandra's past fund-raising accomplishments, which the prince claimed were very impressive, and stressed how much Glendovia could use her assistance. He even went so far as to enclose copies of a contract for her employment that he hoped she would peruse and strongly consider signing.

Lifting the cover sheet, Alandra read the one-page agreement. It briefly outlined her duties and obligations, if she chose to accept the royal family's offer, as well as their obligations to her.

"Do you think this is legitimate?" Elena demanded.

The Braedon name did ring some bells. "I guess it would be easy enough to check out," she replied.

The two of them went into Alandra's office, where she started going through her guest lists, and her sister did a quick search on the Internet.

"Huh," Elena said when they discovered at almost the same moment that Stephan Nicolas Braedon was, indeed, a bona fide prince, and the island of Glendovia really did exist. According to Alandra's records, another member of the Braedon royal family—a Princess Mia—had attended one of her recent fund-raisers.

"What are you going to do?" Elena asked.

"Well, I'll reply, of course, and thank him for the generous offer, but I can't possibly accept. I'm already knee-deep in organizing my next event, and Christmas is a month off. I don't want to be away from my family over the holidays."

"I don't blame you, but you have to admit it's a flattering offer."

Extremely flattering, Alandra thought, glancing once again at the raised script of the letterhead. She almost wanted to reach out and run her fingertips over the prince's name. Her letter of refusal definitely wouldn't be an easy one to write.

"But maybe…"

Alandra glanced at her sister. "What?"

"I was just thinking that maybe this position in Glendovia is exactly what you need."

Alandra frowned. "What?"

"Well, things are anything but simple around here for you right now. You've got a reporter camped outside the house, that jerk Winters still calling you, and…well…" Her gaze skittered away and her voice softened slightly. "I heard that last week's fund-raiser didn't go as well as your events usually do."

Alandra took a breath, trying not to let the pain of having her shortcomings pointed out by her own flesh and blood overwhelm her.

Running a supportive hand down her arm, Elena continued. "I was just thinking that if you got away for a while, where no one could find you, this would all blow over. And when you came back, you could get on with your life as though none of it had ever happened."

"But I would be away from you guys," Alandra murmured. "Over Christmas."

"You could come back before then. But even if you didn't, it's only one holiday. There's always next year." Wrapping an arm around her shoulders, her sister added, "I don't necessarily *want* you to go, I'm just saying that maybe you should think it over and do what's best for you. I think Pop would agree."

"I'll consider it," Alandra said, realizing her sister was making a good point. Perhaps the best way to leave all this scandal behind *was* to fly off to a foreign country.

Three

Less than a week later, the Saturday after Thanksgiving, Alandra arrived on the island of Glendovia, hoping against hope that she'd made the right decision.

Her flight had been uneventful. And a limousine had been waiting at the airport for her, as promised in the itinerary that had been faxed to her as soon as she'd accepted Prince Stephan's offer.

Staring out the window as the car sped through the countryside, Alandra was swept away by the beauty of the tiny island country. Located in a northern area of the Mediterranean, it was postcard perfect, with a clear azure sky, rolling emerald hills, and the sprawling blue-green of the sea visible in the distance.

Even what she assumed to be the center of the capital seemed more quaint and clean than anywhere she'd traveled in America or Europe. The buildings were tall, but not mammoth. The streets were busy, but not crowded and harried.

Things seemed more tranquil here, and for the first time since scrawling her name across the bottom of that employment contract, she thought she might actually be glad she'd agreed to come.

Her family had supported the decision wholeheartedly, wanting her to be happy and get away from the scandal they knew was causing her such pain. She had accepted the position in order to protect them from a part of her life that had gotten ugly, in hope it would not spill over onto them.

The limousine slowed and waited for a tall, antique iron gate to slide open. They drove up a long, winding lane that ran among pristine, well-manicured lawns and gardens.

The house—*palace* was a better word—was somewhat historical in design, but looked updated and modern. Eggshell-white, with pillars and balconies and a myriad of floor-to-ceiling windows, it stood atop a small rise overlooking the splashing waves of the Mediterranean.

As the driver opened the door and helped her out of the vehicle, she couldn't tear her eyes away from the breathtaking view. Alandra continued to gawk while the driver removed her bags from the trunk and escorted her to the front door.

A butler opened it and invited her inside, where a handful of maids dressed in matching gray uniforms collected her luggage and trotted off with it.

The butler said, "The prince has requested you be brought to him immediately upon your arrival, Miss Sanchez. If you'll follow me."

Feeling as though she'd just stepped into a fairy tale, Alandra did just that, taking in every detail of the foyer as they passed.

The floor was of highly polished marble in squares of black and a mottled gray-white. A chandelier the size of a small bus hung overhead, with thousands of dangling crystals twinkling in the natural light. Directly across from the front entrance stood a wide staircase leading halfway to the second level before branching off to either side.

The butler led her to the right of the foyer and down a carpeted corridor lined with priceless art-work. He paused at one of the closed doors and knocked. When a low, muffled voice bade him enter, he stepped inside, announced Alandra's presence and then moved aside for her to pass.

The personal office was decidedly masculine, with a dark area rug, built-in bookshelves lining three of the four walls, and a large cherrywood desk taking up a good portion of the room.

Dragging her gaze from the impressive sur-roundings, Alandra turned her attention to the man sitting behind that desk…only to feel her eyes go wide and her mouth fall open.

"You."

"Miss Sanchez." He rose and regally rounded the desk until he stood directly in front of her. "How good of you to accept my offer and come to work for our family."

"You're Prince Stephan—"

"Nicolas Braedon of Glendovia, yes. You may call me Nicolas."

Nicolas. The same Nicolas who had asked her over for a glass of champagne and then invited her to sleep with him.

Her mouth went dry with shock, her stomach clenching and her pulse kicking as though she'd just run a marathon.

How could this be happening?

"I don't understand," she said, her voice faint as she struggled to put her thoughts into words. "Why would you invite me to work for you after the way we parted? All you wanted from me then was…"

Realization dawned.

"You did this on purpose. You lured me here under false pretenses so that I would sleep with you."

"My dear Miss Sanchez," he replied, standing straight as a sword, with his hands clasped behind his back, "Glendovia is very much in need of someone to organize its charitable foundations. And, after seeing you in action, I decided you would be the perfect person for the job."

"And you've changed your mind about wanting me in your bed?" she challenged.

Nicolas studied the woman in front of him, struggling not to smile at her forthright manner and the fury snapping in her brown, almond-shaped eyes. It was a sight to behold, and only made him more certain of the wisdom of the campaign he'd put in motion.

Her rejection of him during his stay in America hadn't dulled his desire for her at all. He had decided, not long after, that since the direct approach hadn't worked, perhaps he needed to go about attaining his goal in a more subtle way.

When it came to Alandra Sanchez, it seemed a bit of seduction was in order.

It had taken him a few days after returning home to land on the idea of asking her to his country for an extended stay. He knew she wouldn't accept if he merely invited her…or if she knew he was extending the invitation, for that matter.

But because they had philanthropy in common, he knew that was the one motive that had a chance of catching her attention. There was also the rather generous bonus he'd included in the employment contract as an added incentive—two hundred and fifty thousand dollars to be donated by him to a charity of her choosing once she'd fulfilled her part of the bargain.

And now she was here, exactly where he wanted her.

Not that she looked even remotely willing to jump into bed with him at the moment. But as with everything else, that would come.

He would see to it.

"I wouldn't say that," he murmured, replying to her question about whether or not he'd changed his mind about wanting her in his bed. "But I am certainly capable of separating business from pleasure."

Without giving her a chance to argue, he continued. "Come. I'll show you to your room, where you can unpack and perhaps rest before supper."

Dropping his arms to his sides, he stepped around her and crossed the room to open the door.

"Don't bother," she replied curtly behind his back. "I'm not staying."

Half turning to face her once again, he maintained a neutral expression. "Don't be ridiculous. Of course you are. You signed a contract."

"Contract be damned." She started for the door, her demeanor icy.

He waited for her to pass, then caught her arm as she marched down the empty hallway. "Are you really willing to deprive one of your favorite charities of a quarter of a million dollars?"

The reminder stopped her in her tracks, and he pressed his advantage. "If you leave, reneging on the agreement, you forfeit the bonus. Stay through the month of December and you will not only be paid the agreed-upon wage, but will also earn a hefty sum to bestow as you see fit."

He could almost hear the gears turning in her head as she weighed her options. Leave, and she would be safe from him; he would have no opportunity to try to lure her into his bed. Stay, and she would be all but walking into the lion's den, but would also end up earning a quarter of a million dollars to fund one of her pet projects. It was a compelling enticement.

The seconds ticked by while she stood in the middle of the hall, wracked with indecision. Once again, he chose to give her a small nudge in the direction he wished her to go.

Moving closer, he placed a hand at the small of her back. She stiffened and pulled away just enough to break the contact.

"Please," he said diplomatically, "allow me to show you where you'll be staying if you elect to remain and fulfill your contract. The family will gather in the dining room for dinner at eight o'clock. I'd like you to be there, if you would, to meet everyone. After that, if you still wish to return to the United States…"

He paused, choosing his words carefully. "I won't say I'll let you go without penalty, but I will be willing to discuss the situation further."

For a moment, he thought she would continue her retreat. And then the rigid line of her spine relaxed slightly and her shoulders lifted as she inhaled a deep breath.

Without turning around, she said, "Fine. I'll stay through dinner."

"Excellent. Come along, then," he replied, careful not to let his satisfaction show as he stepped around her and walked the rest of the way down the hall.

He led her through the foyer and up the curved staircase, toward the west wing. There were more hallways and a second set of stairs before they reached the suites of rooms reserved for guests.

The royal family's quarters were located in the east wing, on the opposite end of the palace. But that was for the best. If his plan to seduce Alandra succeeded, their relationship could be kept almost completely secret, thanks to the relative privacy of the west wing and the fact that she would be the only person in residence there for the next month.

Reaching her suite, he opened the heavy, carved mahogany door, standing just inside to allow her to enter ahead of him. Briefly, he showed her the sprawling sitting room, with its large-screen plasma television and DVD library. Nicolas hadn't known her personal tastes, so he'd ordered the room to be stocked with a variety of choices, any of which she could exchange in the family's entertainment room whenever she liked.

Glancing through the bedroom door, Nicolas was happy to note that Alandra's things had already been unpacked and put away. She was carefully observing her surroundings, and if she was offended that the palace staff had handled her belongings, she didn't say so. She looked pleased with the accommodations, her expressive eyes taking in every detail of the beautifully decorated rooms.

"I'll leave you alone now, to rest or take a tour of the grounds, whatever you like. One of the staff can show you to the dining room when you're ready."

Turning on his heel, he left her standing in the middle of the bedroom.

Alandra watched him go, still seething at his manipulation, and yet not so angry that she failed to notice the handsome, regal picture he made as he exited.

She supposed she should be flattered that a prince wanted her in his bed. Most women would be, she imagined.

The problem was that he hadn't seemed interested in *her*, in getting to know her or starting a relationship with her. His request when they'd met in Texas was to take her to bed for a night—or perhaps a handful of nights. And because of who he was, he expected her to simply acquiesce.

Even if she might have been attracted to him otherwise, that fact turned her off entirely. She didn't want to be some playboy prince's temporary intimate diversion.

With a sigh, she began to explore her rooms,

checking to see where all her things had been stored. Dresses, blouses and slacks hung in the wardrobe. More casual tops and pants had been folded and stacked in the dresser, along with her underthings. And her toiletries had been lined up on the bathroom counter or tucked into the available drawers. Even the books and folders she'd brought, for work and for leisure, had been neatly stacked on a small desk set before one of the windows overlooking the balcony.

She hadn't made up her mind yet about whether she planned to stay, but had to admit that if she *did* decide to fulfill her bargain with the Prince of Lies, the view alone would make her visit feel less like manipulation and more like a paid vacation.

Stepping onto the wide stone balcony, she moved to the railing and gazed out at the ocean beyond. Waves rolled to the shore, bringing with them a gentle lulling sound that could soothe even the most restless soul.

Glancing at her watch, Alandra saw that she still had a couple of hours before she needed to start getting ready for dinner with the royal family. The thought of meeting them caused her stomach to dip dizzily.

But she would deal with that when she had to. For now, she would call home to let her father and sister know she'd arrived safely, and to maybe get Elena's advice about her current situation.

Should she stay or should she go? Should she tell the prince just what he could do with his devious, conniving contract, and walk away from the chance to gift a quarter of a million dollars to a charity that could dearly use the money? Or should she swallow her pride and do what she had to to get through the month?

Four

At five minutes to eight that evening, Alandra followed the maze of hallways on the palace's second floor and found her way to the main staircase. The maid who had come to check up on her earlier had given her general directions to the dining room, and Alandra thought she could find it on her own.

But she needn't have worried. As soon as she reached the stairs, she found Nicolas standing at the bottom, waiting for her.

He was dressed in a dark suit, which made her feel better about her own outfit. She hadn't known quite what to wear to her first dinner with a royal family, so had opted for a simple blue silk dress.

"Good evening," Nicolas said in greeting, watching her intently as she descended the stairs.

Alandra felt a skittering of awareness as his gaze swept her from head to toe. No doubt about it, this man was dangerous. If she decided to stay, she would have to be very careful not to let those blue eyes and his handsome face lure her in and make her do something she wouldn't normally do.

"Good evening," she replied, pausing at the bottom of the stairs.

"May I?" he asked, offering his arm.

She hesitated only a second before accepting, lightly slipping her hand around his elbow.

"You look lovely," he told her as they crossed the marble floor. The chandelier had been turned on, sending bright, twinkling light throughout the foyer and beyond.

"Thank you."

She was saved from having to make further conversation as they reached the dining room. Nicolas opened one of the tall double doors, ushering her inside.

The room was as opulent as the rest of the palace. A long, narrow trestle table ran the length of it, surrounded by heavy, high-backed chairs with seats embroidered with what must be the Braedon family crest. Light trickled down from another chandelier hanging over the table, and glowed from many wall sconces.

The queen and king were already seated at the table, which held intricate place settings laid out for six guests. Nicolas guided her forward, stopping near what she assumed would be her seat.

"Mother, Father, I'd like you to meet Alandra Sanchez. She's from the United States and will be our guest for the next month while she works to help us better organize Glendovia's charitable foundations. And hopefully increase their profit margin. Alandra, this is my father, King Halden, and my mother, Queen Eleanor."

The older man rose and came halfway around the table, taking her hand and pressing a soft kiss to her knuckles. "Welcome to Glendovia, my dear.

We appreciate the work you'll be doing on behalf of our country."

"Thank you, Your Highness," she replied, only slightly intimidated by meeting and speaking with a real live king. "It's a pleasure to meet you."

Turning toward the queen, Alandra noticed that she'd remained seated. And when Alandra approached, she didn't offer to shake her hand.

"Your Highness," Alandra murmured politely and respectfully, pausing before the older woman.

She was greeted with a rather stiff nod, giving her the uncomfortable feeling that she wasn't as welcome as Nicolas and his father would have her believe.

"Please be seated," the queen told her. "Dinner will be served soon."

Returning to Nicolas's side, Alandra allowed him to hold her chair for her before he made his way around the table to the place directly across from her.

A second later, the dining room doors opened again and another couple swept in. It was obvious to Alandra that the gentleman, at least, was related to Nicolas. He had the same build, coloring and facial structure as Nicolas and the king.

The woman had similar physical traits, but Alandra didn't want to assume anything for fear she was a wife or girlfriend rather than a sister.

"Good evening, everyone," the man boomed, smiling easily.

"Mother, Father," the young woman intoned, removing any doubt of her relation to the others. "Nicolas," she added, laying her hands on his shoulders and leaning in to press a kiss to his cheek.

"Menace," he replied, one corner of his mouth quirking up in a grin before he shifted his attention back to Alandra. "I'd like you to meet my younger brother, Sebastian, and my sister, Mia, the baby of the family."

Princess Mia gave a short, harried sigh. "I hate it when you introduce me that way," she told him.

"I know. That's why I do it," he countered. Alandra didn't miss the affectionate sparkle in his eyes or the amusement that lingered on his sister's face as she strolled around the table to take the seat to Alandra's left.

"Our eldest brother, Dominick, is out of the country right now, but hopefully you'll meet him before you leave."

Shaking out the napkin on her plate and placing it neatly in her lap, Mia said, "It's nice to meet you, Alandra. Nicolas mentioned that you would be coming. He says you have brilliant ideas about increasing the amount of funds taken in by non-profit organizations."

Alandra's gaze flashed to Nicolas, flattered by his indirect praise, but he was looking at his sister.

"She's done terrific work with several charities back in the States," he announced.

From his seat across the table, Sebastian said, "That's good. We certainly have our share of worthy causes here on the island that could use a bit of a boost. And it helps that she's quite the beauty." Glancing in her direction, Sebastian winked.

For a moment, Alandra was startled by his brash behavior—in front of his family, no less. Then she realized this must simply be his personality. He was the youngest son, the one furthest in line from taking over the throne, and from the looks of it, a bit of a playboy, to boot.

She returned his good-natured smile before noticing the scowl on Nicolas's face. Her enjoyment fled immediately, replaced by a strange sensation in the pit of her belly. She didn't know whether to be concerned or intimidated, or even amused.

He had brought her here to be his mistress; she knew that. Under the pretense of working for his family, perhaps, but that didn't change the fact that he wanted her in his bed.

However, that didn't explain why he would look so cross at his brother's harmless comment and teasing.

Unless Nicolas and Sebastian had fought over— or perhaps shared—women before. Was Nicolas concerned that his brother would catch her eye before he'd had a chance to seduce her himself?

Oh, that was an interesting twist. And it would serve him right for spinning such a web of deceit to bring her here in the first place.

Servants arrived then to pour glasses of water and rich red wine. When the salad course was served, conversation turned to family and Glendovian affairs. Alandra ate in relative silence, finding the topics interesting, but having few comments of her own to add.

During dessert, Mia and Sebastian asked her about her own family and life back in Texas. She was only too happy to answer, but avoided any mention of the scandal that had driven her away.

"And what are your plans now that you're here?" Mia inquired. "Where do you think you'll begin with the charities?"

Before Alandra could answer, Nicolas interrupted. "That's something I intend to discuss with her at great length, but she's just arrived and I haven't had the chance to fill her in yet on everything she'll need to know." Pushing back his chair, he rose to his feet. "In fact, if you'll excuse us, I'd like to get started on that now."

He came around to her side of the table, taking her arm and giving her little choice but to leave with him. She said her good-nights and followed him across the room.

"Nicolas," the queen called out as he reached the door. "I'd like a word with you."

"Certainly, Mother," he replied in a respectful tone. "As soon as I see Alandra to her rooms, I'll return to the library. We can speak there."

His mother offered an almost imperceptible nod and they left.

With his hand once again at the small of her

back, he guided Alandra to the main stairwell, and they started slowly up the steps. She didn't miss his continued attempts at familiarity. And while his fingertips warmed her through the material of her dress, sending tiny shocks of desire through her system, she had to wonder if it was merely the first phase of his orchestrated attempts at seduction.

Even if it was, it wouldn't work.

She was stronger than that. Nicolas might be charming and gorgeous, his status as a prince alluring, but he had brought her here under false pretenses, and she was not going to be won over.

"So," he began, his voice low and persuasive, "have you had a chance to look over the files I left in your room?"

He had, indeed. A pile of colored folders had been left on the desk, each summarizing a different Glendovian charity she assumed she would be working with if she decided to stay.

"I glanced at them," she said.

"And…"

"You have some interesting organizations set up."

"They're not running as well as they should," he said.

"I noticed."

"Do you think you can fix them?"

That was the problem—she did. Even looking over the files for a few minutes before she'd started getting ready for dinner, she'd had a dozen ideas for improvements. Not to mention raising awareness and drawing in larger amounts of funding.

They were concepts she was excited about and eager to put into effect. But in order to do that, she would have to remain in Glendovia and fulfill the terms of her contract.

"I have some ideas," she replied guardedly, as they turned down the hall that led to her suite.

"Excellent." He waited a beat before continuing. "Does this mean you've decided to stay and work here?"

"I'll stay," she told him. "I'll stay through the month, as agreed in the contract, and at the end of the month you'll give me the bonus you promised."

"Of course."

He might have said more at that point, but she cut him off. "And no matter what your reason for bringing me here, no matter what you expected to happen, I will *not* be sleeping with you. You can cross that little item right off your Christmas wish list."

At that, she turned the knob, spun on her heel and disappeared into the suite.

Five

The door to the library was open when Nicolas arrived. His mother was sitting in one of the armchairs before the fireplace, sipping a glass of sherry and staring at the flames leaping in the hearth. Closing the door behind him, he moved to the sideboard and poured himself a drink before joining her.

"You wanted to speak with me?" he asked, leaning back.

Typical of his mother, she got right to the point. "What is she doing here, Nicolas?"

He didn't pretend to misunderstand the question. "As I told you at dinner, I hired her to help with our charities. She's very good at what she does. I think she'll be a boon to the organizations."

"And that's the only reason," his mother said shortly, eyeing him over the rim of her glass. "Nothing else?"

He took a sip of his brandy. "What other reason would there be?"

"Come now, Nicolas. I may be your mother, and therefore not your first choice of confidante about your love life, but I'm well aware of your... leisure pursuits. Are you sure you didn't bring her here to be your next conquest?"

While his personal relationships were no one's concern but his own, it was hard—not to mention foolish—to tell the queen to mind her own business. Even if she was his mother.

So he did what he and his siblings had done many times while growing up. He looked her straight in the eye and lied.

"Of course not. I take my responsibilities to our country very seriously. As soon as I saw what Alandra had done with the event I attended in

America, I knew she would be a great benefit to our own charitable causes."

His mother narrowed her gaze momentarily, as though gauging the truthfulness of his statement. "I'm glad to hear that. You understand, I'm sure, that it wouldn't do for your little associations to become public this close to announcing your engagement. We both know that you haven't been celibate since you agreed to wed Princess Lisette, but it's important that you keep up pretenses and do nothing to upset her or her family. This marriage will create a very important bond between her country and ours."

A brief second passed, and when she spoke again, both her tone and expression were sharper. "We can't jeopardize that association simply because you can't keep your hands off some American commoner."

Letting another swallow of brandy warm its way through his system, Nicolas consciously unclenched his jaw and forced himself to remain respectful.

"I know my duties, Mother. You needn't worry about me causing any problems with Lisette.

Alandra is a lovely woman, but she's no threat to my engagement, believe me."

"That's good to hear. But just in case you change your mind, or Miss Sanchez suddenly begins to look like an amusing diversion while she's visiting, I have something I think you should see."

With that, she reached between the side of her chair and the cushion and removed a folded piece of paper. She handed it to Nicolas and then sat back, every inch the queen as she awaited his reaction.

Unfolding the page, he found himself staring at a printout of a newspaper article with Alandra's picture. On either side of her photo were two others with jagged edges.

The headline accused Alandra of coming between the man and woman depicted, of being the ruin of a happy home and marriage. He scanned the write-up, which made Alandra sound like a selfish, devious trollop with no compunction about carrying on a torrid affair with a married father of two.

"She isn't one of us, Nicolas," his mother intoned. "She created a scandal in the States and brought shame upon her own family with her promiscuousness. We don't need her here, doing the same to us."

Nicolas tensed in response to both the content of the article and his mother's high-handed warning, then relaxed. This revelation about Alandra surprised him, but didn't concern him. And it certainly didn't change his mind about wanting her in his bed, despite his mother's cautionary warning.

"I appreciate your trepidation, Mother, but I think you're making too much of Alandra's visit. She's only here for a month, and only to help with the charities. Nothing more."

The queen arched a brow, but remained silent, making it clear she doubted his claims. But his life was still his own, and until he had actually taken his wedding vows with Princess Lisette, he owed no explanation to anyone.

Refolding the printout and slipping it into the front pocket of his jacket, he pushed himself to his feet and returned his empty glass to the sideboard before crossing to his mother's chair and leaning down to press a kiss to her cheek. "Good night, Mother. I'll see you in the morning."

* * *

Alandra was up early the next day, ready to get to work and start putting some of her strategies into action.

She also hoped to see more of the island and get *away* from Nicolas. He was dangerous to her peace of mind, and the less time they spent together during her stay, the better.

Carrying a briefcase stuffed with papers, she arrived in the dining room. The family was already gathered and eating. A plate was quickly set before her, and Alandra enjoyed her breakfast until the queen inquired about her plans for the day. Alandra still had the distinct feeling Nicolas's mother didn't like her.

"After studying the notes Nicolas gave me, I thought the local orphanage would be the best place to start," she answered. "I've got an idea directly connected to the holidays that I think will be quite successful, but since Christmas is right around the corner, it's important to get things moving as soon as possible."

If the queen was pleased with Alandra's response, she didn't show it. Instead, Nicolas replied. "I'll have a car brought around to take us to the children's home," he said, pushing back his chair and moving toward the dining room's double doors.

"You're…coming along?" Alandra asked, her words stumbling over themselves as her heart thudded. She really, *really* didn't want to spend the day with him.

He stopped at the door and turned back to face her. "Of course."

Swallowing past the lump in her throat, she tried to ignore the heat suddenly licking its way through her insides. "That isn't necessary."

"But it is," he replied softly. "Glendovia's national charities are my responsibility. I take that duty seriously and intend to work quite closely with you over the next month. I hope you don't mind."

He added the last, she was sure, for the benefit of his family, all of whom were watching and listening attentively. Because it was clear that even if she did mind—which she did—it would make absolutely no difference.

If they had been alone, she might have argued,

but she certainly wasn't going to put up a fuss in front of the royal family.

Forcing the words past her tight throat, she said, "No, I don't mind at all."

His lips curved in a smile that told her he knew exactly how much it had pained her to acquiesce. "I'll meet you at the car, then," he murmured, before walking out of the room.

Ten minutes later, they were seated in the back of a luxurious black sedan, driving away from the palace. According to the map of the island she'd studied the night before, the orphanage was nearby.

She was happy to simply gaze out the window at the passing scenery and mentally review what she hoped to accomplish at the children's home. But she should have known Nicolas would never allow her to keep to herself for long.

"So tell me about this holiday idea you have for the orphanage. I'm surprised you've begun to devise a plan already, without even having visited."

Keeping her fingers tightly wrapped around the folders on her lap, she tore her gaze away from the view and turned to face him.

"The files you supplied gave me a general impression of the home, and the type of event I have in mind is something I've been a part of before. It seems to go over well and is usually successful in getting the community involved."

"Sounds promising," he intoned. "What is it?"

"Basically, we throw a small party where Santa Claus visits the children and hands out gifts, and we invite the press and locals to attend. The goal is to draw attention to the orphanage, reminding people that the children are alone and in need not only over the holidays, but year-round."

Nicolas nodded, his mouth pursed in thought. "Interesting. And who provides the presents for the children, given that your fund-raising efforts haven't yet been put into effect?"

She smiled. "You do."

He raised a brow, and she hurried to elaborate. "Or rather, the royal family does. We'll be sure to mention that to the press, throwing your family into a very positive light. In fact, if this goes over as well as I think it will, you may want to consider sponsoring the event every year. Back home, we've made the visit from Santa an annual event, and it goes over extremely well."

Inclining his head, he said, "I'm sure that's something my family would be willing to consider."

The car eased to a stop in front of the children's home. A second later the driver came around to open Nicolas's door. He stepped out, and a bevy of flashbulbs immediately began going off in his face.

Alandra had slid across the seat to exit behind him, but rather than reaching for his hand, which he held out to her, she lifted an arm to shield her eyes from the blinding onslaught.

"Who are all these people?" she called to him.

He leaned in a bit closer to keep from having to raise his voice. "Just members of the press you were speaking of. They tend to follow members of the royal family wherever we go."

Reaching for her hand again, he said, "Come along. It's time to go in, and you'll get used to the attention."

She wasn't so sure of that. Where she had been happy a moment ago, and eager to get to work, she now dreaded having to step outside the vehicle into the crowd of photographers circling like vultures. She'd had quite enough of that back in Texas.

She'd come to Glendovia to get away from the

media. Now here she was, smack in the middle of the frenzy once again.

Of course, she wasn't the center of their attention this time, which she considered a blessing. But that didn't mean she appreciated having her picture taken without her permission here any more than she had back home.

Drawing a breath, she pushed aside the anxieties swirling in her chest as best she could, then placed her hand in Nicolas's and let him help her from the car.

She stared straight ahead, at the redbrick building they were about to enter. The fingers of her left hand tightened almost desperately on the handle of her briefcase, while she concentrated on keeping those of her right loose and relaxed. She didn't want to give Nicolas a single sign of just how disturbed she was by the reporters crowding around, still snapping pictures and calling out to the prince.

Nicolas smiled and gave a polite wave, but otherwise ignored them as he led her forward. The sea of photographers parted at his approach, and finally they were inside.

Releasing her pent-up breath, she let go of his

hand and stepped away, leaving a safer distance between them. When she lifted her gaze to his, she found him watching her, an amused glint in his eyes.

The move had been an act of self-preservation, and he knew it.

Dammit, he must sense that she was attracted to him, and he probably took it as a sign that he was that much closer to his objective: seducing her into his bed.

"Your Highness," a voice called, and footsteps clacked as an older woman came forward to greet them.

She offered him a small curtsy and smiled at Alandra. "I'm Mrs. Vincenza, administrator of the children's home. We're delighted to have you visit us. I hope you'll find everything to your liking, and we'll happily do everything we can to help you with your efforts."

"Thank you, Mrs. Vincenza," Nicolas replied with a small bow. "This is Alandra Sanchez. She'll be handling the fund-raising plans."

"Where *are* the children?" Alandra asked, scanning the open space, with its center stairwell leading to the upper floor.

"The older ones are in school, of course, and the younger ones are upstairs in the nursery. Would you like to meet them?"

"I'd love to," she answered.

She followed Mrs. Vincenza up to the second floor, with Nicolas behind them.

They toured the nursery, where Alandra played with the babies and toddlers for a bit, then met a few other members of the staff. From there, Mrs. Vincenza showed them the children's bedrooms, dining hall, playroom and reception area.

The reception area, Alandra realized as soon as she saw it, would be the perfect place to set up the Santa Claus event. It was large enough for all the children, the media and any number of guests they might invite. There was even a lovely tree already set up and decorated in the far corner.

She jotted down notes as fast as she could, her mind racing ahead to everything that would need to be done. At the same time, she shared her plans with Mrs. Vincenza, whose eyes lit up at the prospect.

Behind them, standing tall and straight in the doorway, Nicolas listened silently. Alandra assumed that meant he approved of the project so far. She was certain he'd let her know if he objected to anything.

An hour later, she'd finalized the initial plans with the administrator and had a list of tasks to deal with herself. After thanking the woman for her time and enthusiasm, she and Nicolas made their way back outside, through the throng of reporters still hovering on the sidewalk, and into the backseat of the waiting car.

The vehicle had barely started rolling away from the curb before Nicolas faced her and asked, "How do you feel it went?"

"Very well," she answered, flipping through the pages of her spiral pad and reviewing some of the notations she'd made. "Mrs. Vincenza is eager to help us because she knows it will ultimately help *her*, and even though there's a lot of work to do, I think we've got enough time to set everything up so it goes smoothly."

A small smile touched his lips. "I have to admit, I was quite impressed with what you said to her. You're very good at describing your visions so that others can see them clearly."

Her cheeks flushed with pleasure at his compliment and she nodded a silent thank-you.

"Allow me to buy you lunch at one of our local eateries to show my appreciation for all your hard work. We can discuss what else needs to be done to have everything ready by the week before Christmas."

Although she was starting to feel hungry and certainly could have used a bite to eat, she didn't think it was a good idea to spend any more time with him than absolutely necessary. It would be better to go back to the palace and ask for something to be sent to her rooms, where she could hide out and get some work done *away* from Nicolas.

Without meeting his gaze, she said, "Thank you, but no. I'd prefer to go back and get straight to work."

His eyes narrowed slightly at her refusal, and she almost expected him to argue. But then he turned to look forward and said, "Very well. You should remember one thing, however."

"What's that?"

His eyes returned to hers, bright blue and blazing. "You can't avoid me forever."

Six

For the third time in ten minutes, Nicolas checked his watch. He was standing at the bottom of the main stairwell, awaiting Alandra's arrival, while everyone else was gathered in the dining room, ready for dinner.

But the minutes continued to tick by, and still there was no sign of her.

Spotting a maid leaving the dining room, he motioned her over. "Would you please run up to

Miss Sanchez's room and find out why she's running late for dinner?"

"I'm sorry, sir, but she called down earlier to make her excuses and ask for a tray to be brought to her room."

"Is she ill?" he asked, his brows knitting with genuine concern.

"I'm not sure, sir. She didn't say so."

"Thank you," he said, nodding to dismiss the maid.

As soon as the maid disappeared around the corner, he turned and started up the stairs. Minutes later, he was knocking on Alandra's door.

He heard her call that she was coming, and then the door swung open. She was standing there in a short, turquoise-blue nightgown and a matching robe in some slinky material that made his mouth go instantly dry. Her hair was pulled up and twisted into a loose knot at the crown of her head.

Her lovely chocolate-brown eyes went wide with surprise for a second before narrowing with annoyance.

Noticing that his gaze was inexorably drawn to

the shadowed valley between her breasts, she raised a hand to close the edges of her robe.

"May I help you?" she asked in a tone that surely wasn't often directed toward someone of royal lineage.

Biting back his amusement, he kept a straight face and linked his hands behind him. "I heard you weren't coming down to dinner and wanted to make sure you were feeling well. Is everything all right?"

Her expression softened at his inquiry. "I'm fine, thank you. I just decided to have my meal in my room so I could continue to work."

"You've been working since we returned from the children's home," he said, more of a statement than a question.

"That *is* why you hired me," she replied with a tiny smile.

Her grip on the front of her robe loosened and he caught another quick glimpse of cleavage. His body immediately went tight and hot.

Clearing his throat, he struggled to make his brain work past the thought of stripping her bare and having her writhing beneath him. When he couldn't seem to manage that, he gave a curt nod and headed back the way he'd come.

It took him the full length of both hallways and the staircase to regain his reason and decide on a course of action.

First, he strode into the dining room, where the rest of the family had already been served, and told them he wouldn't be sharing dinner with them. Then he went to the rear of the palace and entered the kitchens, asking that two trays be made up and taken to Alandra's suite rather than only one.

He waited while that was done, and then accompanied the servant as the young man delivered the cart. Alandra answered the door when he knocked, a frown marring her brow when she noticed Nicolas trailing behind. To her credit, she held her tongue as the cart was wheeled into the center of the sitting room.

Glancing toward Nicolas, the servant waited to be told where they wished their meals to be served.

"That's fine, Franc. I'll take it from here. Thank you."

The young man inclined his head and quickly

made his way from the room, closing the door behind him and leaving Nicolas and Alandra alone.

Her gaze skated from the cart, with its silver-domed platters and bottle of wine, to him. "You're not planning on eating with me?" she asked, not bothering with even a modicum of civility as she crossed her arms beneath her breasts and tapped the red-tipped toes of one bare foot impatiently.

"We have a lot to do, as you've said, and I agree that taking dinner in your rooms is a good way to make rapid progress. We'll eat on the balcony," he added, pulling the cart out onto the terrace. "You'll like it out there. Bring some of your files, if you like, and we can discuss them while we eat."

She didn't say anything, but he wouldn't have stopped if she had. Giving her the chance to respond was only inviting a refusal, and he had no intention of being put off.

She followed him to the French doors, still without uttering a word, but stopped before actually stepping onto the balcony.

It was still light outside, edging into dusk, and the bright shades of sunset could be seen on the far horizon. The temperature, normally quite comfortable at this time of year, was even warmer than usual, giving him no qualms about inviting her out in little more than a thin slip of satiny material.

And if she got cold…well, he could think of several ways to heat things up quickly enough.

He moved to the round, glass-topped table outside, and pretended not to be watching her as he transferred their dinner from the cart. In reality, however, he kept track of her in his peripheral view. He saw her fingers twisting nervously on the frame of the open double doors, and her bare toes curling on the threshold rather than taking the step that would bring her out onto the balcony.

"Maybe I should change," she said in a soft voice.

Though he was careful not to let it show, he felt a flash of triumph. She had apparently accepted that arguing or asking him to leave was futile. He was here for dinner, and he meant to stay.

Raising his head, he once again looked directly at her. He wanted her sitting across from him just like that, with her legs bare and the turquoise fabric bringing out the sparkle in her dark eyes.

"What you're wearing is fine," he replied. "This is a casual meal, and we'll be talking about the charities most of the time. In fact, I'll join you in getting more comfortable."

Shrugging out of his suit jacket, he hung it neatly over the back of his chair, removed his tie and rolled up his shirtsleeves. "How's that?" he asked, giving her a moment to study his appearance. "I can remove more of my clothing if you like, but I have a feeling you would consider that a bit *too* casual. Am I right?"

He cocked a brow, silently challenging her to deny it. If he had his way, they would both be naked before the night was over.

For a second, she returned his look with a steady, rebellious one of her own, then spun around and disappeared into the bedroom.

At first, he thought she'd gone to cover herself in battle armor. But she reappeared a moment later, still wearing the same nightgown and robe, and not a stitch more. She was also carrying a legal pad and small stack of folders.

She took a seat and pulled her chair closer to the table, acting as though she was sitting down to a business lunch in a full business suit. But he certainly wasn't going to complain now that he had her exactly where he wanted her.

Following her lead, he lifted the silver covers from both plates and set them aside, then took his own seat across from her. He uncorked the bottle of wine, from one of Glendovia's own vineyards, and poured a healthy portion for each of them.

Nicolas made small talk while they ate. And though Alandra's side of the conversation was stilted at first, eventually she relaxed and spoke to him as easily as she would anyone else.

They'd just begun discussing the plans for the children's home when a knock sounded at the sitting room door.

"That will be dessert," Nicolas announced. Rising to his feet, he slung his jacket over his arm. "Let's move things into the other room, shall we?"

He strolled in that direction, leaving her to follow with her stack of files.

Before the waiting servant had a chance to knock a second time, Nicolas pulled the door open, gestured for him to enter and instructed him to serve the coffee and dessert at the low, square table in front of the fireplace.

While that was being taken care of, Nicolas

lowered the lights, then proceeded to build a small fire in the hearth.

Alandra watched from the bedroom doorway, chagrined to find herself admiring the broad expanse of the prince's back. The narrow span of his waist. The ripple of muscles beneath his crisp white shirt and dark trousers as he moved.

She swallowed hard, feeling a flush of heat flow over her chest, up her neck and into her cheeks.

Noticing Nicolas's considerable physical attributes was the last thing she should be doing. Finding him attractive at all, in any way, would be the kiss of death. A risk she could not afford.

And yet she couldn't seem to tear her eyes away from him.

"Isn't it a little warm for a fire?" she asked as the servant finished his task and slipped silently from the room.

"I thought you might be chilly," the prince replied, turning from the flickering flames and glancing in her direction.

His attention lingered on her bare legs, she noticed, and it took all her willpower not to shift uncomfortably or attempt to cover herself. The only thing that kept her from doing either was the knowledge that he'd noticed the tiny goose bumps beginning to break out on her arms and legs earlier. She was unaccountably touched by his consideration, which was *not* what she wanted to be feeling.

"We won't get too close," he said, dragging the table back from the hearth a few more inches before taking two cushions from the sofa. "Come, have a seat."

He lowered himself onto one of the cushions on the floor and sat cross-legged, leaving the other for her. Instead of sitting across from each other, they would now be much closer, with only one small corner of a rather small table between them.

It wasn't the typical setup for a business meeting. But then, her attire wasn't exactly typical, either. None of this was.

Striding across the room in her bare feet, she set her files aside and curled her legs beneath her as she sat down.

Nicolas poured coffee from a brightly polished silver carafe while Alandra studied the dessert. A fluffy, golden pastry was sliced into layers and

filled with large, juicy strawberries and a decadent amount of rich cream. Her mouth watered
just looking at it.

Because this situation could easily begin to take
on a romantic feel, Alandra immediately started
back on the topic of Christmas at the orphanage,
and didn't stop until they'd made it through the
pastries and a cup of coffee each. To his credit,
Nicolas stuck with the conversation, never trying
to change the subject or insert a level of intimacy
that didn't belong.

His enthusiasm and participation delighted her.
She'd expected him to put in only a minimum
amount of effort, to convince her he'd brought her
to his country for legitimate reasons rather than
simply to become the latest in what she was sure
was a string of lovers.

But he was taking their conversations and the
business of organizing these fund-raisers seriously.
Taking *her* seriously.

It was a welcome change after being made the
butt of any number of jokes and cruel jibes back
home once the rumors had spread that she'd been
sleeping with a married man.

Despite the cup of coffee she'd just consumed, Alandra found herself blinking tired eyes and covering her mouth to stifle a yawn. And maybe she was off her game, maybe her defenses were down, because it seemed sensible, almost natural, to join Nicolas when he moved closer to the fire.

She reclined beside him, letting the flickering flames and the opulence of her surroundings lull her. Keeping company with a gorgeous prince didn't hurt, either, even if she had to steel herself against his charms, his looks, the spicy scent of his cologne.

And he was about as handsome as a man could be. If he weren't already a prince, she would think he should be. A prince or perhaps a movie star.

"What are you thinking?" he asked softly from only inches away.

He had a nice voice, too. Low and slightly husky, it rumbled up from his chest and straight down her spine, causing her bare toes to curl.

If he wasn't a royal, constantly being followed by paparazzi, and if she hadn't recently been slandered and torn apart by vicious rumor and innuendo, she might just be willing to throw caution to the wind and sleep with him, after all. Not become his mistress—that was a bit beyond even her—but spend one passionate, sure-to-be-glorious evening making love with a man who had the power to turn her knees to jelly.

Thank goodness he didn't know that. Thank goodness he couldn't tell exactly what she *was* thinking. Otherwise all her good intentions, her insistence that her presence here was purely business, with no possibility of pleasure being thrown into the mix, would drift away like a wisp of fog on the ocean breeze.

Thank goodness.

"Only that this is nice," she replied. "Relaxing. I should still be working, but I think I'm too tired."

He turned, and she found her own shimmery image reflected in his pupils.

"Would you like to go to bed?"

It was on the tip of her tongue to say, "Yes, very much," before her hazy brain identified the danger his question posed.

"Clever," she said with a chuckle, feeling just tranquil enough to find his attempt to trap her amusing. "But while I would like to go to bed… eventually…I won't be doing it with you."

"What a shame. Although there's always to-morrow."

There it was again, that calm, cajoling tone. The voice that thickened her blood and sent warm, tingling sensations to areas she'd rather not have tingling in his presence.

"I didn't come here for that," she replied quietly.

He was only an inch away now, his heated breath dancing over her cheeks and eyelashes. His mouth looked incredibly inviting, sexy and about seven kinds of sinful.

Surely one little kiss wouldn't hurt anything. One tiny peck to satisfy an overwhelming curiosity.

It wasn't smart. Was, in fact, ludicrous.

Before she had a chance to decide if she could afford a momentary lapse of sanity, Nicolas made the decision for her.

Seven

Oh, my.

He tasted of wine and the strawberries and cream that had been part of their dessert, with a hint of the coffee he'd sipped afterward. Sweet and tart and smoky all at the same time.

It was a heady mixture, but nothing compared to the feel of his tongue sweeping into her mouth, tasting, stroking, claiming.

His hands gripped her shoulder and the side of her face, gently pulling her up. She wasn't sure how it happened, had no conscious memory of moving, but suddenly she was on her knees, pressed chest to chest with Nicolas and kissing him back with equal vigor.

While his hands kneaded and caressed her upper arms, hers clutched at his shirt, desperately holding on and pulling him closer. Her breasts were squashed between them, but she could still feel her nipples beading. Heat gathered and pooled low in her belly, and her heartbeat was a thunderbolt blasting in her ears.

She'd been wrong about keeping her distance, wrong about trying to convince herself she wasn't interested in this man. He was hard and strong and self-assured, and brought to life emotions she'd never felt before, at least not to this degree.

Her fingers trailed upward to tangle in the short strands of his silky hair. The two of them were already mouth to mouth, body to body, as close as they could be while still clothed, but that didn't keep her from exerting a small amount of pressure at the back of his skull and—if it was possible—taking the kiss even deeper.

With a groan, Nicolas moved his hands to skim

the undersides of her breasts. He cupped them in his palms, measuring their fullness and weight before letting his thumbs slide up and over the tight peaks of her nipples.

The caress, made even more erotic by the thin layer of cool, slick material between her flesh and his fingers, gave her shivers.

As she wriggled in his grasp, her knee bumped into the coffee cup she'd set aside earlier. The rattle of the porcelain on the saucer startled her out of the haze of passion and arousal she'd been lost in.

She pulled back slightly, breaking the kiss even though her body cried out for more. Her lungs heaved, straining for breath. Her arms and legs quivered, overcome with a lassitude she couldn't remember ever feeling before.

Good Lord, what had she almost done? How could she have gotten so wrapped up, so swept away by a single kiss?

His hands remained at her breasts, his fingers lightly brushing the rigid peaks. His eyes blazed a deep, dark sapphire in the firelight, no less heated than a moment ago.

Did he not realize she'd pulled away, or was he as blinded by desire as she'd been?

Regardless, she had to stop this, had to make it clear to him that what had just taken place between them was a mistake. A mistake of monumental proportions that could not, *would* not happen again.

"Stop," she gasped.

"What's wrong?" he asked in a ragged voice. Though he dropped his arms to his sides, he clenched his hands, betraying the tension vibrating through him.

"This is not going to happen," she said, though her tone was less firm than she'd have liked. Still on her knees, she inched away, afraid that he might reach for her again and she wouldn't have the conviction to fend him off.

One dark eyebrow hitched upward. "I thought we were off to a fairly adequate start," he replied.

Without looking at Nicolas, she rose to her feet. "I told you before that I didn't come to Glendovia to become your latest conquest. I'm here strictly for business purposes. That kiss was a mistake. It never should have happened, and it won't happen again. Things only got as far as they did because I'm tired and let my guard down."

But Nicolas wasn't ready to walk away, not quite yet.

He also got to his feet, then touched her elbow, stroking the satin fabric of her sleeve. "I could stay," he whispered smoothly, seductively. "Make sure the rest of your evening is both restful and enjoyable. Infinitely enjoyable."

The spark in her eyes let him know he'd overstepped his bounds. She shrugged out of his hold and moved passed him. Wrenching open the door, she stood back, body rigid, and glared.

"Good night, Your Highness," she said, her tone only a shade shy of disrespectful.

If he weren't such a patient man, intent on his goal, he might have taken exception.

But he *was* a patient man, and he knew that pushing Alandra was not the way to win her over, not the way to lure her into his bed. Better to take things slowly, to woo and seduce her properly.

"I'll see you in the morning, then," he said politely, moving to stand before her, giving no indication that her attitude or demands disturbed him in the least.

Though she remained stiff, he took her hand and lifted it to his mouth, pressing a soft kiss to the back of it.

"Thank you for being such a lovely dinner companion, and for all of your hard work on behalf of the children's home. I knew bringing you here was the right thing to do."

With a swift grin, he left the room and strode casually down the hall. A few seconds later, he heard her door close with a slam, and his smile widened.

Alandra Sanchez was a fiery, passionate woman with a temper to match. She thought she was brushing him off, holding him at bay, but her reluctance merely intrigued him all the more.

For the next two weeks, Alandra did her best to avoid Nicolas whenever she could, and treat him with cool professionalism whenever she couldn't.

Nicolas, meanwhile, did *his* best to get her alone as often as possible, to touch her hand, her arm, her cheek on a regular basis, and to romance her into letting down her guard and inviting him into her bed.

So far, she'd remained firm in her commitment

not to be seduced. But she had to admit, at least to herself, that it had been no simple feat.

Nicolas was nearly irresistible. He was attractive and charming, and if he hadn't approached her to sleep with him before getting to know her—which she found gallingly arrogant—she very well might have fallen into bed with him by now.

Sad but true, and rather ironic. If he'd gone about courting her in a more traditional manner, he'd have likely gotten lucky.

Alandra might be considered beautiful by many—a fact of life that was sometimes a blessing and sometimes a curse for her—but she was anything but compliant.

And then there was the continued guilt and humiliation over the scandal that still clung to her name back in Texas.

She'd phoned home numerous times since arriving in Glendovia, and each time she'd asked her sister about the scandal she'd been running away from. Elena had admitted that people were still talking, but the reporters had finally stopped camping out at the house.

But even though the attention had died down,

Alandra knew she'd been right to leave town when she had. She was also even more determined never to leave herself open to disgrace again.

She reminded herself of this, firmly and repeatedly, as she made her way down to the foyer.

In the time she'd been a guest of the royal family, the palace's decor had gone from tidily opulent to brimming with holiday cheer.

The banister had been strung with long, twisting garlands of holly and ivy. Giant wreaths hung on both the outside and inside of all the main doors. And in the center of the foyer was a towering evergreen tree, covered with gold ornaments. A golden angel perched gloriously at the very top.

The holiday decorations were helping Alandra feel more at home. She missed her family terribly, and it broke her heart to think that she wouldn't be spending Christmas with them. But she found it soothing to be surrounded by all this cheer.

She was smiling when she reached the front door, where Nicolas was waiting. Tonight was the Evening with Santa event at the children's home, and he had insisted on accompanying her, despite the fact that she had to be there early. The rest of the royal family would arrive later.

Even Nicolas's mother, Queen Eleanor, had reluctantly approved of Alandra's efforts to aid the local orphanage. She hadn't come right out and complimented her on all of her hard work, or changed her attitude, but the few remarks she'd made about tonight's event had been mainly positive.

Alandra didn't let it go to her head. She knew the queen still disapproved of her.

As soon as she drew close, Nicolas took her elbow, offering a small smile. He was dressed in his princely finery, complete with a red sash running from shoulder to hip, and a number of important-looking medals pinned to his chest.

Alandra's dress was a sumptuous red velvet gown that hugged her curves and left her shoulders and arms bare. She wore classic, understated diamonds at her ears and throat.

"Shall we go?" Nicolas asked, and escorted her out of the palace into the slightly chilly evening air. It wasn't yet dark, but the sun was setting and dusk was well under way.

She had purposely scheduled tonight's affair so

that it could be both a fun party for the children and an opportunity for the adult guests to mingle. Especially since she had invited some very wealthy, influential individuals, whom she hoped would make generous donations.

When Alandra and Nicolas arrived, a crowd of photographers was already gathered outside the orphanage, snapping pictures. Inside, the home was decorated festively. There was a tree in the main entranceway, covered with ornaments handmade by the children. Holiday music filled the air.

After Alandra settled a few last-minute issues, she started mingling with the arriving guests.

The appearance of the rest of the royal family caused quite a stir. Voices hushed, heads turned and people stood frozen as they watched the king and queen.

Leaving Nicolas with his family, Alandra made her way to the other rooms. She began wandering around, double-checking that everything was running properly.

All in all, it looked as though the evening was progressing perfectly. She released a sigh, praying no accidents or crises cropped up to mar an otherwise successful occasion.

Turning back to survey the reception area, she immediately spotted Nicolas striding toward her. Tall and imposing, he seemed to tower over the crowd.

The air caught in her chest. She would have liked to blame her sudden inability to breathe on the tightness of her form-fitting dress, but knew it was all due to Nicolas.

Nicolas, who could stop her heart with a glance.

Nicolas, who made her palms damp and her stomach quiver.

Nicolas, who made her want to rethink her decision not to get any closer to him than necessary during her stay.

Be strong, she told herself, swallowing hard and making a concerted effort to keep her knees from quaking as he came closer.

When he reached her, he gave a small bow and took her hand, his eyes holding hers the entire time.

"Dance with me," he murmured softly.

His tone and princely manner made it more of a command than a request, but she did her best to argue. "I don't think Christmas music is exactly conducive to dancing," she said, glancing about the room. Although there were several couples taking the floor.

"Of course it is."

He tipped his head, as though paying extra attention to the slow strains of a holiday classic. Tightening his grasp, he tugged her behind him as he headed to the clear space at the center.

"Besides, it's my royal duty to set a good example for others, and we want everyone to enjoy themselves, don't we? Isn't that your goal, so that guests will feel more generous when it comes time to start writing checks?"

She could tell from his expression that he was taking pleasure in teasing her, tossing her own ambition back at her in an attempt to get what he wanted. His lips twitched and the corners of his eyes crinkled as he tried to keep his amusement in check.

She might have continued protesting, but it was too late. They had reached a small empty stretch of the hardwood floor, and Nicolas had his arm around her waist, pulling her against him.

He splayed his fingers at the small of her back, holding her in place and guiding her as they swayed in small circles. And just as he'd predicted, others began to follow their lead and joined them, dancing to the holiday carols being piped through the building.

This hadn't been part of her plans for the evening, but it did seem to be having a positive effect. Alandra hoped Nicolas didn't notice, or she might have to swallow her pride and tell him he'd been right.

The song came to an end and they stopped moving, but instead of releasing her, he continued to hold her, staring down into her eyes until her mouth went dry and butterflies decided to take up tap dancing in her belly. Her chest was too tight to draw a full breath, which made her head begin to spin.

She thought, for a brief moment, that he was going to kiss her. Right there, in the middle of a roomful of people.

And she was chagrined to realize that her mouth had opened slightly, that she was both anticipating the kiss and looking forward to it. Yearning for it, even.

With his gaze still locked on hers, he leaned in another inch, until she could feel his warm breath dancing across her skin.

"I can't kiss you here and now, the way I'd like, but I promise to rectify that before the night is through." His voice was low and mesmerizing, washing over her.

Dropping his hand from her waist, he smiled, gave a small bow and then turned and walked away, as though he hadn't just set every nerve ending in her body on high alert.

She watched him go, trying to regain control of her senses. And control of her limbs, which seemed incapable of movement, even as she struggled to get her brain to send the correct signals.

It wasn't until she noticed people beginning to stare that she shook off whatever spell had overtaken her, and was able to take step after measured step to the refreshment table. She poured herself a glass of punch and drank it down in nearly a single gulp.

This was bad, so very bad. He was wearing her down, eroding the last of her defenses.

She was very much afraid that she wouldn't be able to evade him for much longer.

Eight

It was late by the time the evening wound to a close, but as Alandra watched the guests filing out, she was delighted to see that the majority of them had smiles on their faces. Better yet, Mrs. Vincenza had happily reported that she'd received several generous contributions throughout the night, with promises of more to come.

Watching Santa Claus hand out presents to the children had obviously turned a number of hearts—exactly what Alandra had been hoping for. She'd seen more than a few eyes turn misty during the gift-giving ceremony, and many follow the children out of the room and up the stairs at bedtime.

While it hadn't been her main goal, Alandra hoped that tonight's event would result in some much-needed adoptions, as well as added donations.

Stifling a yawn behind her small clutch purse, she watched the door close behind the last guest a moment before she felt Nicolas come to stand beside her.

Although she wasn't surprised that she could sense his presence even before she saw him, it did disturb her. She didn't *want* to sense him. Didn't want to believe that they might be growing that close in such a short time, especially when she'd spent most of the last three weeks avoiding him.

Not that she'd been terribly successful. Nicolas, she was learning, had a way of being everywhere she was, whether she wanted him there or not.

She had to admit, though, that he'd been a definite asset this evening. Not only had he gotten everyone in the room to relax enough to dance to Christmas music, but he'd spent the rest of the night circulating through the crowd to shake hands, kiss cheeks and talk up the orphanage as an extremely worthy charity—or write-off, depending on who he was conversing with.

And she admired him for it. For caring about the children's home and about what he could do to make the fund-raiser a success.

Glendovia was his country, and she had been hired to do a job for it. But he seemed to know that she took her work of organizing charitable events and raising funds for worthy causes very, very seriously. Seemed to know…and in his own way, care.

That touched Alandra more than a dozen roses, a hundred glasses of champagne or a thousand romantic dates ever could have.

He might have taken a wrong first step with her by inviting her into his bed before even getting to know her, but he had taken a few right steps since. Redeeming right steps.

When he took her elbow now, she felt a familiar tingle in every millimeter of skin his fingers came in contact with.

"Ready to go?" he asked.

She nodded and let Nicolas adjust her wrap

around her shoulders before guiding her outside and into the waiting limousine.

Despite the late hour, there were still plenty of paparazzi gathered to snap more pictures upon the royal family's departure. The camera flashes burned her eyes and blinded her vision. She was only too happy to have the car door slam behind her, blocking out the pesky photographers.

When they arrived home, the family said their good-nights before heading for their respective bed-chambers. Alandra wished them all a good night, as well, before turning toward her own rooms.

"I'll walk with you," Nicolas said, catching up with her and once again slipping her arm through his.

She started to tell him it wasn't necessary, but thought better of it with his parents and siblings still within earshot. Instead, she inclined her head, tightened her hold on his arm and murmured, "Thank you."

They walked to her suite without speaking, and she was surprised to find it a comfortable silence. Perhaps because it had been such a long and busy day, and she was too tired to worry about what she should be saying or doing. She couldn't find it in her to be concerned about what Nicolas might say or do, either.

When they arrived, he opened the door, then stood back for her to enter. Crossing the dark sitting room, she turned on a small table lamp, which bathed the space in a yellow-gold light.

Alandra straightened and turned, and nearly bumped into Nicolas, who had followed her silently and was standing mere inches away. For a moment, her mind went blank. Her breath hitched and her heart leaped at finding him so near.

She swallowed nervously and opened her mouth to speak, though she didn't have a clue what she planned to say.

Not that it mattered. Before she could utter a sound or get her brain to function properly, Nicolas had lifted a hand to the back of her neck and threaded his fingers into the loose hair at her nape. He tugged her forward, and she went easily, willingly, like a puppet on a string.

Their eyes met, and in that brief second, she saw passion and fire and desire. Those same emotions caused her stomach to tumble to her toes, and made her feel suddenly light-headed.

Then he bent and lowered his mouth to hers.

The minute their lips met the earth seemed to rock on its axis. Alandra had never felt such heat, such electricity, such an amazing and overwhelming need.

Nicolas's fingers at her nape tightened, while his other hand grasped her hip. Her own hands were on his shoulders, gripping and clawing. She couldn't seem to get close enough.

His scent filled her nostrils, spicy and masculine. As his tongue swept through her mouth, he tasted the same.

She kissed him back with equal fervor, delighting in the way contact with him flooded her senses.

Just when she thought she might expire from pleasure, Nicolas broke the kiss. "Say no," he whispered raggedly against her lips. "Tell me to go. Tell me you don't want this."

He kissed her again, hard and swiftly. "Go ahead, Alandra," he taunted softly, "tell me."

She knew what he was doing. He was challenging her to stick to her declaration that she wouldn't sleep with him during her visit. That she wouldn't allow herself to be seduced.

But, God help her, she couldn't. She wanted him too much to deny it any longer.

To deny him.

Wrapping her arms around his neck, she pressed her mouth to his. The same smoldering heat washed over her again and, with a sigh, she whispered, "Don't stop. Don't go. I do want this."

She expected him to smile—a cocky, self-important response to show her he'd known all along he would win their little cat-and-mouse game.

But he didn't smile. Instead, his eyes flashed with fire, a second before narrowing dangerously.

Bending slightly, he scooped her up, ball gown, high heels and all. His determined strides carried them to her bedroom, where he kicked the door closed and crossed to the wide, four-poster bed.

The room was dark, with only a hint of moonlight shining through the diaphanous curtains on the French doors. It took a moment for her eyes to adjust, but as Nicolas deposited her on the mattress, then stood back to unbutton his jacket, she decided it didn't matter. She could see him just well enough, and in a few minutes she would be touching him everywhere. Feeling him everywhere.

He stripped off his jacket and kicked off his shoes, then loosened the first few buttons of his shirt, keeping his gaze locked on her the entire time.

Not wanting to be a mere bystander, Alandra rose to her knees and pulled off her strappy heels, tossing them aside. She reached behind her for the zipper of her dress.

"No."

Nicolas's low, stern voice stopped her. He took two steps forward to the edge of the bed and ran his hands seductively down her bare arms.

"Let me."

Her stomach muscles clenched as his fingers ran over her abdomen and around her sides, to her lower back. Slowly, he slid his palms up the line of her spine.

His touch burned through the velvet of her gown as his hands trailed upward, and then drew the zipper down. The quiet rasp of the tiny metal teeth parting accompanied their harsh breathing.

When the zipper was lowered, her dress fell open, helped along by Nicolas's large, strong hands. She shrugged and shifted slightly; he pulled it away and dropped it unceremoniously at his feet.

Alandra knelt at the edge of the king-size mattress in her cherry-red bra and panties, and a pair of sheer, thigh-high stockings. Her heart was racing out of control, her nerves skittering like a million angry ants. Licking her dry lips, she remained perfectly still, watching Nicolas and waiting.

He stood equally still, his blue eyes riveted on her face. And then he reached for his shirt, undoing the buttons and pulling the tail from his slacks.

His movements weren't hurried, but they weren't patient, either. He made short work of removing the garment, letting it flutter to the floor while he reached for the front of his pants. There was no belt to slow him down, and with a flick of his wrist, he released both the catch and zipper.

Half-naked, he was impressive enough. But fully naked, he was the stuff of dreams and naughty female fantasies. His arms and chest were beautifully sculpted. A tight, flat abdomen flowed to narrow hips and long legs corded with muscle.

Alandra's pulse skittered and her mouth went dry as she focused her gaze to the area between his thighs. He was impressive there, too.

She didn't know what to say or how to act, so

merely sat where she was and waited for him to make the first move.

It didn't take long. With a single stride, he was with her, cradling her in his arms, while his mouth devoured hers.

Their lips meshed. Their tongues tangled. And everywhere their skin touched, she sizzled.

Alandra curled her fingers into his shoulders, her nails gently scraping. Behind her, she felt him fiddling with the clasp of her bra, and then it came free. She released him long enough to allow him to remove the garment.

Rather than wrapping his arms around her again, Nicolas reached for her breasts, cupping them in his palms, toying with the tight, beaded nipples. All without breaking their kiss.

She moaned into his mouth, pressing even closer. Her own hands roamed over every inch of hot, hard flesh she could reach—his arms, his back, his pectorals and the slim, sensitive sides of his waist.

It was his turn to make a ragged sound of longing when she ran her fingertips over the taut twin globes of his rear, then raked her nails back up to the base of his spine.

She almost smiled. She could feel the desperation rippling through him as he tightened his grasp on her breasts, deepening their kiss, pressing himself against her belly.

Without warning, he tugged her legs out from under her, so that she fell flat on her back on the bed. He followed her down, covering her completely as he trailed his lips across her cheeks, over her eyelids, along her jaw and behind her ear.

At the same time, his hands worked to remove her stockings, rolling them slowly down her thighs and calves, and over her feet. Next went her panties, and she lifted her hips to help him, until she was blessedly naked, rubbing against him in all the best places.

His mouth was at her throat now, licking and sucking and humming, sending little trills of sensation straight to her core. He cupped her buttocks, bringing her flush with his arousal and turning her insides liquid with longing.

"You're so beautiful," he murmured, still kissing everywhere he could reach. "Lovelier than I imagined. And much better than anything I've dreamed of these past weeks."

She smiled, running her fingers through his hair and enjoying his husky declaration, even if he'd said it to a million other women before. This wasn't about commitment or honesty. It was about lust and desire and untold pleasures, fleeting though they might be.

"You're not so bad yourself," she replied, remembering the multitude of erotic dreams that had revolved around him since she'd moved into the palace.

Grinning, he raised his head to gaze down at her. He leaned in to kiss her, hard and fast, then pulled back, his expression serious. "Tell me you want me," he demanded.

She studied him for a long moment, her eyes locked with his. He was more handsome than any man deserved to be, and when he focused his attentions on her, she felt like the only woman in the world. The only woman he was interested in, at any rate.

And right now, that was all that mattered.

"I want you," she whispered, wrapping her arms and legs around him and holding him tight. "Make love to me, Prince Stephan Nicolas Braedon."

No one had called him by his first name in years, not since he decided to go by Nicolas, after years of his sister referring to him as Nico. He held her gaze for another split second, then pressed his lips to hers. The kiss was hot enough to suck all the air from her lungs and from the room, and she kissed him back with equal enthusiasm.

His hands raked her sides. Then he was caressing her thighs, both outside and in.

His knuckles brushed the triangle of curls between her legs as he began to explore. He stroked and teased, groaning when he found her already damp.

She writhed beneath him as he used two fingers to plumb her depths. She was panting now, and her breathing grew more shallow as he traced his fingertips over the tiny nub of pleasure hidden within her folds.

He touched her there, and she exploded. The orgasm washed over her like a wave of heat.

His smug, satisfied smile greeted her when she opened her eyes. Her cheeks heated at his close scrutiny, and she felt suddenly self-conscious about her wanton response to his touch.

"You blush beautifully," he told her, kissing the corner of her mouth.

He didn't give her a chance to respond, but immediately began caressing her again, his hands filled with magic as they danced across her flesh, leaving no part of her unsatisfied.

The tip of his erection pressed against her opening, and she spread her legs wider, inviting him in. Little by little, he entered her, his heat and hardness filling her. The deeper he went, the more she responded, any signs of discomfort overpowered by the delight shivering through her.

But when he thrust forward in one powerful motion, what had been a minor tenderness turned to a sharp stab of pain that had her gasping aloud.

Nicolas jerked back, brows knit and eyes narrowed as he scowled down at her.

"Alandra," he said, his breathing slightly labored as he held himself perfectly still. "You're a *virgin?*"

Nine

She was a *virgin?*

How in the name of all that was holy could she be inexperienced?

Nicolas's mind raced back over everything he knew about Alandra. All the times he'd been with her, spoken with her, observed her from across a room without her knowledge. Nothing in her demeanor so much as *hinted* that she was an innocent.

And what about the scandal she'd been involved in back in the States? His mother had been only too pleased to share the details of Alandra's indiscretion—a love affair with a married man.

A love affair with a married man that had left her a *virgin?* Nicolas could feel his brow furrowing, the skin of his face tightening as he continued to study her. And all the while he was powerfully aware of their physical connection, of the fact that he still ached and throbbed inside of her.

"How can you be a virgin?" he demanded, his tone brittle and more accusing than he'd intended.

Alandra's eyes grew wider, but passion still filled them. "Forget about my virginity and finish what you started."

To drive home her point, she wrapped her arms around his neck and tilted her hips just enough to send lightning bolts of sensation through his rigid length. He sucked in a harsh breath, using every ounce of willpower he possessed not to start moving, and thrust himself to a glorious but premature end.

His nostrils flared as he took several measured breaths, counting to ten, then twenty. When he could finally speak without groaning or sweating too profusely, he said, "I'm all for carrying on, but as soon as we're done, I *will* want to talk about this."

She rolled her eyes. "Fine. I fully expect you to make my first time memorable, though."

A grin flashed across his face and the mood in the room instantly shifted to a less intense level. There must be traces of royal blood somewhere in Alandra's ancestry. She had the imperial air down pat.

"Oh, darling," he murmured, leaning in to cover her mouth with his, "you can rely on it."

He occupied her with kisses and featherlight touches on her breasts and abdomen. And at the same time, he began to move his hips, slowly and carefully.

By now, her body had adjusted to his size and invasion. Her muscles were relaxed, warm and silky smooth with arousal.

He used long, gentle strokes to start, not wanting to do anything that would hurt or startle her. He hadn't been with a virgin since he himself had been one, and he wasn't sure exactly how to act. How fast might be too fast. How much might be too much.

But Alandra seemed far from intimidated. Her arms and legs were in constant motion, shamelessly exploring his naked body. And she wiggled beneath him, making it difficult for him to hold on to his resolve.

He locked his jaw and concentrated on breathing. His body was alive with sensation, his nerve endings electrified with need and lust and desperation.

"Can't you move any faster?" she panted at last, her back arching and nails raking his damp flesh.

He raised his head to look down at her. Her face was flushed, her hair spread out in a gleaming mass on the pale satin sheets.

"Is that an order?" he retorted, torn between amusement and disbelief.

Her lips curved slightly. "A request. You're treating me like I'm made of glass," she told him, "and I most certainly am not. I may be inexperienced at this sort of thing, but I'm not fragile."

"I don't want to hurt you," he admitted.

She lifted up from the mattress long enough to give him a quick, hard kiss. "You won't. I can take whatever you have to give and then some."

There was only one way to respond. "My pleasure."

His tongue flicked out to tease a ripe pink nipple, and he was smugly satisfied to feel a shudder ripple through her long, lithe form. He kept at it, wetting both tips, suckling them into stiff, rigid peaks.

When he had her shivering in his arms, grasping at his hair and whispering his name, he began to scoot her back, sliding her naked, pliant body across the silky coverlet. Then he grasped her hips and rolled, bringing her over him while he lay flat on his back.

"They say a woman is responsible for her own pleasure. Show me what you want."

Alandra stared down at him, her heart fluttering as she went from being startled by the sudden change of position to feeling empowered by his sensual declaration. His low voice rumbled through her, bringing goose bumps out along her flesh, and he held her hips when she straddled him.

A dozen sultry images of being in the lead and having Nicolas at her mercy played through her mind, and she loved every one.

Spreading her fingers, she pressed her palms on his chest and leaned forward. Her hair fell around her shoulders, the ends tickling his skin. She saw his impressive pectoral muscles jerk, and felt him swell inside of her.

Biting back a grin, she brushed her lips across the line of his jaw. "This is nice," she murmured, kissing her way to his ear. "Having you beneath me, defenseless."

His fingers flexed where he gripped her. "I only hope I have the strength to withstand your torture."

"So do I."

Taking the soft lobe of his ear between her teeth, she tugged gently. At the same time, she rose up on her knees, just an inch, then slowly lowered herself back down. Nicolas groaned deep in his throat, and heat burst in her center.

"Do you know what I really want?" she asked, watching her breath flutter the strands of his brown hair.

"What?" The word came out harsh and strangled as he tried to hold back his base desires.

"I want you to touch me. Everywhere. I love the feel of your hands on my body."

Immediately, he began to explore. His palms drifted to her buttocks, where he gave a little squeeze before sweeping back up the length of her torso to her breasts. Again his thumbs wreaked havoc with her nipples, and with a moan of her own, she kissed him.

Sensations swamped her, raising her blood pressure and making her insides vibrate like the strings of a well-played violin. As good as she'd always thought sex might be, she'd never expected it could be *this* good. That a man—any man—could make her feel both hot and cold at the same time. Make her pant and purr, shiver and shake.

Instinct kicked in and she began to move, her body seeming to have a mind of its own. Her hips canted back and forth, and she rose and fell on his rigid length.

He filled her completely, pressing deep and rubbing with a glorious friction along her hidden folds. Pleasure wound inside her like a spring, from her lips all the way to the apex of her thighs, growing tighter and tighter as the two of them picked up speed.

Feeling as though she were about to explode, she sat up, gasping for air. Her eyes drifted shut and she dragged her nails across his chest.

Beneath her, Nicolas seemed possessed of the same frantic need to plunge and writhe and buck to completion. He met her thrust for thrust, pounding into her on every downward slide. And when that coil of delicious tension building up inside her finally sprang loose, he was right there with her, gripping her even harder and giving a guttural shout of completion.

Alandra's own body shook with climax, rocking her to her very soul before melting into a pile of boneless limbs and damp, exhausted flesh on top of him. His arms slipped around her waist, and where her head rested on his chest, she could hear his heart thudding beneath her ear.

Her last thought before slipping into sleep was that she was glad she'd waited all these years to be with a man. And that when she'd finally taken the plunge, she was glad that man had been Nicolas.

"Now tell me how it is that you got to the age of twenty-nine with your virginity intact," Nicolas demanded.

It was late, the sky darker than before. They were lying in bed, half-asleep after another bout of strenuous, passionate lovemaking.

He'd protested that twice in one night was too much for her, that she would be sore in the morning. But she was having none of it, and had proceeded to convince him otherwise.

Now that she knew the pleasures that awaited her, she had no intention of sleeping the night away. In fact, she was already anticipating the third time being especially charming.

At the moment, however, she was content to lie in his arms, blissfully sated and tucked between cool satin sheets.

"Don't you think my high moral fiber is reason enough?" she replied sleepily.

"It might be, if you weren't more beautiful than a supermodel, and hadn't recently been accused quite publicly of having an affair with a married man."

With a sigh, she pushed herself up on one arm, using her other hand to press the sheet to her breasts. If he wasn't going to let the topic go, she might as well tell him everything and get it over with.

"For the record, it wasn't an affair. Except perhaps in Blake's mind. Blake Winters," she clarified. "That was his name. I met him almost two years ago at a fund-raising event. He's charming and good-looking, and I admit I was attracted to him. He started calling, sending flowers and gifts.

We went out a few times, and he was nice enough, but I didn't think we hit it off quite as well as he apparently did. And I *didn't* know he was married and had a family," she stressed, finally finding the courage to meet Nicolas's gaze.

"Even after I decided not to see him anymore, he wouldn't leave me alone. He kept calling, kept sending presents. He attended my functions and did his best to get me alone. Just about the time his attention started to border on frightening, he stopped trying to contact me."

She shifted uncomfortably, readjusting the sheet around her torso as she went back to looking anywhere but into Nicolas's eyes. "I thought that was the end of it, and then suddenly photographs of the two of us showed up in the press. They were probably taken at the charity events, but they were just suggestive enough to get tongues wagging—especially when a so-called 'source' leaked the information that we *had* been intimately involved. I think it was Blake himself. I think he *wanted* people to believe we were having an affair, maybe even thought, in some sick way, that it would make me go back to him."

She shook her head and took a deep breath, shrugging off the bad memories and any lingering remnants of the shame she'd felt when the story—however incorrect—had broken.

The hair on her nape rose when Nicolas reached out to run the back of his hand over her bare arm. His knuckles rasped along her skin, drawing gooseflesh everywhere he touched.

"Poor Alandra, working so hard to take care of everyone else, but having no one stand up for you when you most needed it."

His words, as well as his tone, surprised her, and for a moment she let herself believe them. A second later, though, self-pity transformed into her usual streak of independence, and she gave an unladylike snort.

"I had plenty of people to defend me," she told him. "Unfortunately, my family is no match for all of Texas high society. In situations like that, the only thing you can do is lie low and try not to do anything even more newsworthy until it all blows over."

His hand moved from her arm to her back. The light stroking lulled her and made her want to curl up beside him once again.

"Is that what you're doing here, in Glendovia?" Nicolas asked softly. "Lying low?"

She snuggled down again, draping herself cozily along his hard length. Resting her head on the curve of his shoulder, she asked, "Is this low enough for you?"

He gave a chuckle, then shifted slightly and pulled her tighter against him, readjusting the cool sheets so that they were both covered from the waist down.

Silence surrounded them, heavy but comfortable. It gave her the chance to listen to Nicolas's breathing and the sound of his heart pumping rhythmically beneath her ear.

"That explains the scandal that surrounds you back in the States," he said at last, his fingers drawing random circles on her upper body. "It doesn't, however, tell me how you managed to remain untouched for so long."

Her mouth twisted wryly, even though she knew he couldn't see her expression. "I'm a good girl. What do you think?"

"I think you're a very good girl," he murmured, his words edged with innuendo. "But no one who looks at you would ever believe you were a virgin."

She cocked her head back to glower at him. "Why? Because I forgot to wear my sweater with the big red *V* on the front?"

"No," he responded calmly. "Because you're one of the most beautiful women I've ever met, and sexuality trickles from your every pore. No heterosexual man could be in the same room with you without wanting you, and I find it hard to believe that one hadn't convinced you to sleep with him before now."

Sighing, she relaxed and settled back against Nicolas. "I don't know how to explain it, except to say that no man has truly enticed me enough. I've dated a lot of men, yes. Wealthy, attractive men. And there were a few times I came close, a few I thought I might be falling in love with. But something always stopped me."

"Until now."

Beneath her ear, his heart seemed to jump against his rib cage and double its beat. Her eyelids, already half-closed, drifted all the way shut, his pulse acting like a lullaby.

"Until now," she agreed, her voice growing faint as sleep began to tug at her. "I guess you could say that your invitation came at a very beneficial time. For a number of reasons."

"One of those reasons being that it gave me a chance to finally get you exactly where I wanted you." With one sinewy arm around her waist, he dragged her up so he could see her face, jarring her into full wakefulness.

Alandra wanted to argue the point or chastise herself for falling so effortlessly into his trap. But right now, in the darkest part of the night, with him lying warm and solid beneath her, she couldn't find it in her to be angry.

Later, maybe, but not now.

Ten

Rays of warm sunlight slanted through the French doors, crossing the carpeted floor and part of the bed, and pulling Alandra slowly awake.

She stretched and yawned and reached out an arm, expecting to find Nicolas asleep beside her. When her hand met nothing but cool, bare sheets, she opened her eyes and blinked until her vision focused.

She was naked and alone in a tangle of pale, wrinkled bedclothes.

Sitting up, she glanced around the room, but didn't find him there.

A sliver of disappointment snaked through her belly. Maybe it had been too much to hope that she'd be able to wake up in his arms. It wouldn't do, after all, for him to be caught sleeping with the hired help.

With a sigh, she rolled out of bed and reached for her robe. Knotting the belt at her waist, she glanced at the clock, her heart pitching when she saw that it was well past 10:00 a.m.

Good Lord, how could she have slept so late?

Not looking forward to the greeting she would receive when she finally made her way downstairs, Alandra showered and brushed her teeth, then started to dress. She wore a simple white sheath with a silver-bangle belt, and white platform sandals. Nothing too provocative, but nothing too dowdy, either.

She wanted to appear cool and confident when she next ran into Nicolas.

Sleeping with Nicolas—a prince, her employer and the man who had propositioned her at their first meeting—wasn't the smartest move she'd ever made. She should have been stronger, more resilient.

Because there was no way she was about to become his mistress for the rest of her time in Glendovia.

Resolve firmly in place, she strolled along the palace corridors and down the wide, curved, marble staircase. There was no one around, not even a servant, making her feel even more awkward about sleeping in so late.

She made her way to the dining room, where she'd spent the majority of her time with the royal family thus far, but the room was empty, long ago cleared of any traces of breakfast. From there, she drifted back across the foyer and down the opposite hallway toward Nicolas's office. She wasn't in a particular hurry to run into him, but he was her primary employer and she was already late getting to work.

The door was closed and she rapped softly, half hoping he wouldn't be there. But he called for her to enter after the first knock.

She schooled her breathing and stepped inside, closing the door at her back. He was seated behind his desk, working, but raised his head to greet her.

Scorching familiarity flashed in his eyes. The look made her heart hitch in her chest.

"Good morning," he murmured, setting down his pen and rising to his feet. "I trust you slept well."

His tone was formal, more formal than she would have expected from the man who'd shared her bed only hours before, with no hint of teasing or double entendre. Yet his gaze consumed her, sliding over her like warm honey, and making her want to do nothing more than relax into it, surrendering her body and her will to him once again.

"Very well, thank you." If he could be this decorous, then so could she. "I'm sorry to be running late this morning. Just because the children's Christmas event was a success doesn't mean I should be allowed to dawdle on the other causes you brought me here to deal with."

She purposely avoided any mention of how they'd spent their time after the Santa gift giveaway, sticking to a professional mode. It was better that way and would help her remain on an even keel.

One side of his mouth lifted, as though he knew exactly what she was trying to do. "I don't think sleeping in a few hours can be considered shirking your duties. However, if you have ideas for other fund-raising events, I'd love to hear them."

He waved a hand at one of the chairs in front of his desk, motioning for her to sit down. As soon as she did, he returned to his seat.

"Actually, I do have another idea," she said, feeling some of the tension seep from her body. Talking business was much better than discussing last night. "Not for a fund-raiser per se, but for the development of an organization."

"Really?" His brows rose and he leaned back in his chair, propping his fingertips together as he listened intently.

"Yes. Back in the States, we have a nationwide organization that works to fulfill the wishes of terminally ill children. I've noticed that you don't have anything like that set up here in Glendovia, and I think it would be a wonderful project for the royal family to undertake. It would bring you some outstanding press, and also fill a very real need for kids who are sick in the hospital or even at home, with no hope of recovery. I thought we could call it Dream a Little Dream."

After considering her proposal for several long

seconds, he asked, "And what kind of dreams would we be fulfilling for these children?"

"Whatever they wanted. Their dearest wish, if it's at all feasible. At home, the organization arranges for children to meet their favorite celebrities, spend an entire day at an amusement park that's been rented out just for them and their friends, go for a hot-air-balloon ride or learn to fly a plane. Things that the kids have always wanted to do, but otherwise wouldn't get the chance to because of their condition."

Nicolas returned her grin. "I suppose that could be arranged."

"So it's something you'd consider?" She leaned forward eagerly. "There would be much more involved than simply planning a fund-raising event. We're talking about renting office space, hiring employees, enormous national and possibly international publicity, probably even a press conference or two. And the organization would need continued support long after I return to America."

She thought she saw a flicker of unease cross his face at the mention of her leaving, but it was gone in an instant.

"It's a noble endeavor," he said, shifting so that his elbows once again rested on the desktop. "A good cause, and something that would bolster Glendovia's reputation and its citizens' esteem. I'll have to discuss it with the rest of the family, of course, but I would certainly be in favor of getting the ball rolling."

"Excellent." She grinned broadly, pleased that he was in favor of a project she'd begun to feel very passionate about.

"You have only a little over a week left of your stay," he pointed out.

His mouth was a flat line and his words were curt, as though he found that fact distasteful. The ripple of unease low in her belly told her that she wasn't entirely comfortable with it, either.

When she'd first arrived and discovered exactly who Prince Nicolas Braedon was, she'd threatened to turn around and fly back to Texas, even if it meant breaking her employment contract with the royal family. But now that she'd been here for a while and had really begun to dig into the work, she was enjoying her visit. Enjoying the palace and the country and its people.

She missed her family and was eager to return

to Texas to be with them again, but she was no longer looking forward to leaving, as she had been only a couple of weeks before.

"Do you think that's enough time to establish this organization and get it to the point where it can be turned over to others and still run smoothly?" Nicolas asked.

"I do."

"Even with Christmas coming up?"

"I'll work through the holiday. I was planning to do that, anyway."

Without her family to share in the festivities, and with a multitude of servants who had already decorated the palace from top to bottom, she suspected Christmas this year would end up passing much like any other day.

She'd been prepared all along to spend that time alone in her room rather than intruding upon the royal family's celebrations. At least this way she would have a nice, meaty project to work on and keep herself occupied.

She thought she heard him mutter, "We'll see about that" beneath his breath. But then he pushed himself away from his desk and stood, and in a firmer voice said, "All right. I'll bring it up with the family and see how they feel about it, then get back to you with a decision."

Nodding, she rose to her feet as he crossed the office to hold the door for her. She took a couple of steps in his direction, then stopped.

"Is there anything else?" he asked, noticing her hesitation.

She curled her fingers into fists at her sides, then released them, fidgeting anxiously while she tried to decide whether or not to voice the concerns circling through her brain.

"Alandra," he murmured softly, and started in her direction.

Straightening her shoulders, she met his eyes, stopping him in his tracks. "About last night..." she began, steeling her nerves for a conversation that filled her with dread.

"Yes?" he asked without inflection of any kind.

Obviously, he was in no mood to make this easier on her.

"It can't happen again," she told him quickly and succinctly, as if pulling off a bandage before the pain or aftereffects sank in.

"Oh?" Again his voice lacked inflection, but this time he raised an eyebrow, the only hint that he had any interest in what she was saying.

"No. I realize it's exactly what you wanted, your whole reason for inviting me here to begin with, but it was a mistake and it's not going to happen again."

For a long minute, Nicolas studied Alandra, taking in her rigid stance and stern countenance. He wondered how annoyed she would be if he told her how attractive she looked when she tried to be authoritative.

Deciding not to risk her wrath over that, when he was about to commit a much worse offense to her sensibilities, he pushed the door shut with a quiet click and slowly closed the short distance between them.

"I'm afraid that's unacceptable to me," he replied, raising a hand to touch her hair, which hung straight and silky around her shoulders.

He watched her head tip just a bit away from his hand, as though trying to move away from his touch. And then the tendons of her throat tightened and released as she swallowed, her gaze not quite meeting his.

"It doesn't matter whether you agree or not," she said. "I'm simply telling you the way things are going to be. What happened last night isn't going to happen again."

She sounded resolute. So much so that he couldn't help smiling.

Not that he could hold her response against her. She hadn't known him long enough to realize that he was a man who got what he wanted. He had no intention of giving up so easily or letting her go purely because she claimed their lovemaking last night was a mistake.

He disagreed. Strongly.

Still grinning, he let his hand graze her soft cheek and tuck a strand of hair behind one ear. "I beg to differ. Last night was magnificent."

Her gaze flitted away and a pale pink blush started to creep across her face.

"You have less than two weeks left in Glendovia, and I fully intend to enjoy them. To enjoy you. I know that you'll need to spend your days working, especially if you undertake this new project you've proposed. But your evenings will be free, and I want you to spend them with me, in my bed."

"Absolutely not." She shook her head and took a step back, breaking away from his touch.

As much as he wanted to close the distance between them and grab her up, kissing the quarrel from her luscious, red-tinged lips, he remained where he was, allowing her to believe a few inches of space would keep her safe from him.

A wry smile lifted the corner of his mouth. "You think that I lured you here, created a position for you within my country, to sleep with you for only one night? Alandra," he breathed softly, almost teasingly, "even if you didn't know me well enough by now, you have to realize that no prince would go to such lengths for a single night of sex, no matter how spectacular that sex might be."

Determination straightened his spine and pushed his shoulders back. "I am a bit more dedicated than that," he added, slowly stepping forward. He was encouraged to note that her wide eyes remained locked with his, and she barely seemed to register his approach.

"And now that I've had you, I have no intention of letting you slip away. I wanted to make love to you, and I've done that, but I'm far from sated."

Even as his voice fell, becoming low and rich and seductive, his finger lifted to gently brush against her body. First the curve of her waist and the underside of her breast, then the tender flesh of her upper arm. He kept the contact brief and featherlight, just the tips of his fingers grazing the material of her dress and her bare skin.

And even though he was scarcely touching her, he still felt the shiver of awareness that rippled through her. It sent a jolt of white-hot sensation through his system, gathering and pooling in his groin. He went hard and heavy in an instant, nearly desperate enough to throw her to the floor and make love to her right then and there.

He wouldn't, of course, though it wasn't his royal blood keeping him from doing anything so crass. When it came to being alone in a room with Alandra Sanchez, his royal blood be damned.

No, it was Alandra herself who kept his more base instincts in check. She was already nervous and shy and regretful about what had passed between them last night, and jumping at her now would only cause her to crawl deeper into her shell, to move further away from him.

Instead, he knew he would have to go slowly again, returning to his original plan of smooth, flawless seduction.

Oh, he would have her in his bed again—tonight, if he had anything to say about it. But it would require a bit of persuasion to get her there.

Alandra's chest rose as she inhaled, and her bright, expressive brown eyes drifted closed for a moment, her head tipping down in defeat.

"Please don't do this," she breathed raggedly. "Don't make me do something that I'll hate myself for later."

Her eyes fluttered open and she raised her head to meet his gaze. Her expression was resolute, if somewhat sad.

"I don't want to be Prince Nicolas's secret mistress. A temporary entertainment to be enjoyed while I'm here, then sent away when you're finished with me, never to be thought of again."

Something about her words twisted his heart painfully, and for a second he reconsidered his single-minded determination to have her, regardless of the consequences.

He didn't want to hurt her, didn't want to bring that look of misery to her face.

He wanted to hold her, kiss her, savor her like a glass of expensive brandy.

Why should it be more complicated than that? They were both mature adults, able to make their own decisions and spend time with whomever they chose.

Leaning in slightly, he let his warm breath fan her cheeks as he hovered a scant inch from her lush, kissable lips.

"I don't want you to hate yourself," he murmured quietly. "I just want to be with you. And though I can't change who I am or the prudence my role in this family requires, I don't think it needs to have any impact on our time together. What we do when we're alone, away from the public eye, is no one's business but ours."

He threaded his fingers through her hair, holding her tight and tipping her head back so he could better reach her mouth. He brushed his lips across hers, tasting her, feeling her, absorbing her energy and spirit into himself.

"I only want to be with you," he said without

breaking contact. "And after last night, I believe you want the same thing. You'll have to work very hard to convince me that isn't true."

She didn't answer, didn't pull way. He wasn't even sure she was still breathing. Pressing his advantage, he kissed her again, deeper this time, until her spine bowed against his body and her nails dug into the material of his jacket.

When he finally raised his head, they were both breathing heavily. A shaft of satisfaction rolled through him at the cloudy, unfocused look in her eyes.

"Very hard," he whispered.

Eleven

It was beyond difficult to convince Nicolas that she didn't want him. So impossible, in fact, that she'd given up trying.

How could she claim she wanted nothing to do with him when one touch of his hands or mouth melted her insides like a pot of chocolate fondue?

He'd discussed the idea for the Dream a Little Dream Foundation with his family, even asking Alandra to draw up an official proposal he could take to them. He'd also done a bit of research on his own into its American counterpart, so he could show them what the end product of such an endeavor might be like.

Reaction so far had been positive, and she and Nicolas had been working together on a daily basis to plan things in more detail, crossing all the t's and dotting all the i's. Once the king and queen approved, as well as the board of Glendovian officials who oversaw this type of thing, she would be given the freedom to get the ball rolling on establishing the foundation.

Daylight hours were not her problem. She had plenty to do to keep her busy, and managed to make sure she wasn't alone with Nicolas any more than necessary.

The door of his office stayed open while they were working, and if for some reason it was closed, she found a way to get it open again. If they were alone and things began to feel too tense, too dangerous, she'd make an excuse to get someone else into the room with them.

It was nighttime that caused her the most anxiety. After dinner, when Nicolas would walk her back to her rooms…holding her hand, standing too close, leaning into her at the door.

He kissed her cheek or sometimes her lips. Stroked her hand or shoulder. And always, *always* his eyes blazed with the clear desire to sweep her up in his arms and cart her off to bed.

She prayed he'd never figure out how very often she wished he would do just that.

Obviously, she wasn't safe around him, and she didn't know how she was going to make it another ten days without either giving in or going crazy.

Ten more long, arduous days and she could fly home, fly away to safety.

For some reason, though, that knowledge didn't comfort her as much as she would have hoped. In fact, it almost saddened her.

But that was an emotion she refused to examine. Her entire existence had been turned upside down, and as soon as she arrived home, life would begin to right itself and return to normal.

She hoped.

For now, though, it was late, and she'd thankfully managed to survive another day, another dinner, another long, excruciating walk back to her suite.

She'd changed into a pair of comfortable black satin pajamas and was ready to climb into bed when a soft knock sounded on the sitting room door.

A petite young woman in the uniform of the palace's household staff stood on the other side.

"Miss," she said, bobbing a slight curtsy. "Prince Nicolas sends this message and requests an immediate response." She held out a square envelope.

It was Nicolas's official stationery, Alandra saw, with her name scrawled in his expansive script across the front, and a dab of wax sealant pressed to the back.

Whatever was inside, she suspected, was either very important or very private.

Running a finger under the flap of the envelope, she broke the seal and removed the folded sheet of paper.

Alandra—
Your presence is required at a very important meeting concerning Dream a Little Dream. We fly to the other side of the island tomorrow morning. Pack for at least one night. Be ready to leave at 7:00 a.m.
Nicolas

She wasn't sure exactly what response he was awaiting, since he didn't seem to be giving her much choice in the matter. He hadn't asked if she wanted to go or would be willing to go, or was even able to go…he'd simply told her to be ready.

Refolding the note, she stuffed it back in the envelope before returning her attention to the servant. "Tell the prince I'll be in the main foyer by seven o'clock. Thank you."

The woman nodded and hurried off, ostensibly to deliver the message. More like announce Alandra's compliance, she thought crossly as she shut the door and headed back to the bedroom.

Though she wasn't particularly happy about this new development, she dragged an overnight bag from one of the closets and began to pack.

By the time she'd finished, she was truly exhausted. Climbing into bed, she hoped for a good night's sleep.

She would need all the rest she could get if she was going to be alone with Nicolas—away from the palace. Overnight.

She met Nicolas outside the palace at exactly 7:00 a.m. The entire place, inside and out, was decorated to the nines in anticipation of the Christmas Eve party the royal family was hosting in only two days' time.

"Good morning," he said.

"Good morning."

"I'm glad you were able to accompany me to this meeting," he told her once they were inside the car and heading down the driveway.

"I didn't have much choice in the matter, did I?" she replied, avoiding his gaze by staring out the window.

"You always have a choice."

She turned her head, meeting his blue eyes. "Well, your note didn't seem to *ask* if I'd like to go with you."

"I was afraid that if I did ask, you would have said no," he confessed.

"Of course I wouldn't have said no. As long as this meeting actually does concern the Dream a Little Dream Foundation. Or did you just say that to get me alone and away from the palace for a few days?" she asked quietly.

A moment passed before he responded. "This trip *is* about the foundation, and though I could probably handle things well enough on my own, I think it's important that you're there. I think you'll be glad you came."

He paused again, letting the silence fill with tension as his sharp gaze bored into hers. "But I'm also quite happy to get you away from the palace and to myself. I think you'll be glad for that, too—eventually."

His voice lowered to a warm, honeyed tone, and it took all of Alandra's willpower not to suck in a deep breath of air to replace what had gotten stuck in her throat.

She should be angry. He was manipulating her again, moving her how and where he wanted her in an effort to change her mind about sleeping with him.

One thing could be said for Nicolas Braedon— he knew what he wanted and didn't take no for an answer.

She didn't want to admit it, not even to herself, but the truth was his single-minded determination to seduce her made her feel…special.

It wasn't her intention to play with him, to turn this…whatever it was between them…into a game, but she suddenly realized she was enjoying herself. She enjoyed knowing that he wanted her.

Instead of arguing or giving in too soon, she merely shrugged and said, "I guess we'll have to wait and see."

The flight to the other side of the island was a short one, and they went straight from the small private airstrip to the office where the meeting was scheduled.

Alandra was stunned to learn that they weren't simply meeting with a few people *about* establishing the new foundation, but were meeting with many people to actually get the organization up and running.

As the morning meetings progressed, she realized Nicolas had been right. She was glad she'd come along.

She was also thrilled with the amount of progress they were making in such a short time. Over a working lunch she met wonderfully enthusiastic people raring to get started. She had no doubt they would do an excellent job of running the organization, whether she was there or not.

She and the prince said goodbye to the future Dream a Little Dream staff at five, and Nicolas instructed his driver to take them to a hotel where the royal family kept a suite of rooms.

Alandra wasn't taken aback, and she wasn't upset. In fact, she belatedly realized she'd expected as much. After her little revelation in the car on the way to the airport that morning, she even found herself looking forward to what the evening might bring.

The royal suite was gorgeous. Nicer, even, than her rooms at the palace.

The walls, carpeting and drapes were all done in varying shades of blue, with touches of white and tan. A set of dark mahogany French doors opened onto a small lanai overlooking the city and the coastline beyond. One of the doors was open, allowing a cool breeze to ruffle the long, diaphanous curtains, bringing in the salty scent of the sea.

"Are you hungry?" Nicolas asked, stepping to a desk that held a thick, black binder of hotel amenities.

She nodded, moving slowly in his direction as she continued to take in her surroundings. She wondered if she should bother unpacking, or simply live out of her overnight bag.

"I'll have something brought up," he said, flipping through the room service menu and then calling down to order what sounded like a veritable buffet of appetizers and entrées. Before hanging up, he asked for a bottle of their best wine, and strawberries with fresh whipped cream for dessert.

"We have about thirty minutes before the food arrives." Loosening his tie and shrugging out of his suit jacket, he draped both over the back of a chair as he crossed the room. "Would you care to change into something a bit more comfortable before it gets here?"

His gaze raked her from head to toe, raising gooseflesh every inch of the way.

She knew when to admit defeat—and when to enjoy a very handsome man who was more than willing to pleasure and worship her, if only for a short while.

"Do you have any special requests?" she asked, slowly removing her watch, and then her earrings.

Next she raised a hand to the top button of her blouse, slipping it through its hole.

His eyes followed her actions intently, glittering with longing and sending sparks of awareness through her.

"Naked works for me," he murmured, his voice gravelly with desire.

She chuckled, feeling a thrill of empowerment swelling in her veins. "Not just yet, I don't think," she said, turning on her heel and heading for the bedroom. "I wouldn't want to shock the waiter when he arrives."

"If he sees you naked, I could have him killed."

She laughed again, facing him with her hands on the knobs of the double bedroom doors.

"Let's not turn this trip into a crime spree just yet. Not if we can help it," she told him as she swung the doors closed. "I'll see what I can come up with on my own."

She stayed in the bedroom until she'd heard the room service waiter deliver dinner and leave again.

Opening one door a crack, she saw Nicolas standing before the round table on one side of the sitting area. It had been set with an array of dishes and stemware.

Stepping the rest of the way into the room, she paused and waited for him to notice her. When he did, his hand froze on the silver serving lid he'd been about to raise, and his gaze zeroed in on her like a heat-seeking missile.

She'd changed into a long black nightgown with spaghetti straps and lace-lined slits running from ankle to midthigh on each side. Her feet were bare, her red-tipped toes peeking out from beneath the hem of the nightie, and she'd combed her hair out to fall in a straight, silky curtain around her shoulders. The look on Nicolas's face told her how completely he appreciated her efforts.

"It's not naked, but I hope you approve."

He swallowed hard. "Very much so. I didn't think it was possible, but that gown may just be better than full nudity."

An amused smile tugged at her lips. "I'm glad you said something. Now I know not to take it off, no matter how much you beg."

"Princes don't beg," he informed her, stalking slowly toward her.

"No?" she asked, her mouth going suddenly dry.

"No."

He was standing in front of her now, close enough to touch, but keeping his arms at his sides. Her heart was pounding in her chest and she had to fight the urge to wiggle nervously.

"What do princes do, then?" she asked, her voice husky with growing pleasure.

Reaching out, he stroked the back of his fingers across her cheek. "It would be better if I showed you."

"Won't dinner get cold?"

"Do you care?"

Twelve

Late that night, Alandra lay in bed, wrapped snugly in Nicolas's arms. She couldn't have been more physically comfortable and sated…but her emotions were in an uproar.

She had done the very thing she'd sworn not to—she'd become Nicolas's lover.

As disturbing as that was, as much as it made her question her own character, it wasn't what had her teetering on the edge.

She'd realized not an hour before—while

Nicolas was kissing her, stroking her and making her sigh—that she was falling in love with him.

She swallowed hard, blinking to keep the moisture collecting at the corners of her eyes from spilling over. Beneath her cheek, Nicolas's chest rose and fell with his easy breathing.

This was bad. So bad. An affair was one thing. But how was she supposed to leave for home with a smile on her face if her heart was left behind, broken and bleeding?

How was she supposed to pretend that what had passed between them was just a holiday fling, when it had become so much more than that to her?

Nicolas shifted slightly in his sleep, causing her breath to catch. When he didn't wake up, she relaxed, feeling a bit steadier.

Since she knew she was merely a temporary distraction for him, and that he didn't share her newfound sentiments in the least, she would simply have to deal with the situation as best she could. Hide her feelings. And then, when the time came, she would walk away.

Closing her eyes, she began to drift off, telling

herself to get used to the pain squeezing her heart. It was going to be with her for a long time to come.

They returned to the other side of the island the following morning, Christmas Eve, with many hours to spare before the family's annual holiday party. Nicolas had made certain Alandra knew she was to attend, though she wasn't entirely looking forward to it.

Stepping off the plane, they were accosted by a large group of reporters, all snapping pictures and screaming out questions. She had trouble making out the exact words, and Nicolas bustled her into the back of the waiting limousine before she could decipher them.

"What was that about?" she asked breathlessly as the car shifted into gear and headed toward the palace.

He shook his head. "The press probably caught wind of our travels and are trying to see if it's worthy of front page news."

The media attention still seemed odd to her, since the trip had been business-related and the palace likely would have already delivered a press release outlining the prince's plans. But she pushed aside her misgivings and relaxed in the comfortable, stuffed leather seat.

When they arrived at the palace, the queen was waiting for them in the main foyer. Her face was pinched, her mouth set in a flat, angry line. Though she didn't raise her voice, the disapproval in her tone was clear as glass.

"In the library," she snapped. "Now."

Nicolas and Alandra exchanged a questioning glance, then slowly followed in the queen's rapid-fire footsteps.

As soon as they stepped into the library and closed the door behind them, Eleanor spun back around, holding a newspaper in her shaking hands. *"What,"* she demanded through clenched teeth, "is the meaning of this?"

Alandra stood perfectly still, stunned by the queen's obvious displeasure, but unsure of the cause. As hard as she tried, she couldn't make out the headline of the article being waved between them.

Seemingly unfazed by his mother's mood, Nicolas reached for the paper. There, taking up nearly all of the top half of the front page was a close-up photo of Nicolas and Alandra. They were standing on the balcony of the hotel suite, caught in an unmistakable embrace.

The photo had to have been taken after they had made love, then gone out on the balcony for a breath of fresh air…only to end up kissing for long, stolen moments before drifting back inside to make love again.

Alandra's cheeks flamed at both the memory and the knowledge that someone had been out there, snapping pictures of a very private moment.

Above the photo, sending a wave of nausea through her stomach, was a bold, glaring headline that declared her Prince Nicolas's American Tart.

Nicolas muttered a dark curse beneath his breath and lowered the newspaper.

Still vibrating with anger, the queen said, "You and your little…*American* are on the front page of every newspaper in Glendovia. I told you, Nicolas. I *told* you not to get involved with her, that she would only bring shame and embarrassment to our family."

The sick sensation clawing at Alandra's insides grew worse. She'd come to Glendovia to get away from one scandal, only to find herself smack in the middle of another.

And this one was even worse, because now it was true. She hadn't had an affair with Blake Winters, as the American press had claimed, but she *had* been sleeping with Nicolas.

"Mother," Nicolas growled.

His jaw was clenched, and the single word was clearly a warning. One the queen chose to ignore.

"Princess Lisette arrived less than an hour ago—in tears. She's crushed, and her parents are furious. Do you have any idea how this indignity will affect your upcoming nuptials? If she backs out of the engagement, our family's ties with hers will be fractured. The political future of Glendovia could be in peril."

"I think you're overreacting," Nicolas remarked, but it was obvious from his expression that the entire situation had him concerned.

Alandra's brain had gotten stuck on two words that made her heart feel as though it were being squeezed in a vise.

She turned her head toward Nicolas. "You're engaged?" she asked.

"It's not what you think," he said shortly. "I can explain."

But she didn't want to hear explanations, excuses, lies or more of the persuasive and creative arguments he seemed only too talented at spinning.

It was her turn to shake her head as she backed away.

"I'm sorry," she murmured shakily, directing her apology to the queen, not Nicolas. She had nothing to apologize to him for.

"I'm sorry," she said again, "I didn't know he was betrothed. I certainly didn't come here with the intention of getting involved with Nicolas. I would never have knowingly brought any embarrassment or undue attention to your family. I hope you can believe that."

The queen's pinched expression did not change as she turned to look at her son. "I'll expect the two of you to keep your distance from now on. You will conduct yourselves with the utmost decorum and stay as far from each other as possible while we rectify this situation. Is that understood?"

Nicolas looked as though he wanted to argue, but Alandra was already nodding. She blinked to hold back tears of humiliation, even as she licked her dry, parched lips.

"You may go," Eleanor told her, clearly dismissing her. "And you," she said to Nicolas, "will speak with Lisette immediately, and do your best to repair whatever damage has been done. Is that understood?"

Alandra slipped out of the office, closing the doors behind her without waiting to hear Nicolas's reply, and hurried across the parquet floor for the stairs. All she wanted was to get away, get back to her rooms, where she could be alone. What a fool she'd been. Again.

Standing in the doorway of her suite, Alandra took one last look around to be sure she hadn't left anything behind. All had been erased.

Closing the door quietly behind her, she walked down the hall, pulling her wheeled carry-on behind her. Instead of heading for the front of the palace, where guests would be arriving for the Christmas Eve party, she slipped toward the back, where a car was waiting to take her to the airport.

Leaving now meant giving up the hefty bonus

Nicolas had promised for the charity of her choice, but she simply couldn't stay. She wanted to go home, where she would be surrounded by family. Where she could hopefully hide and start to heal.

At the moment, the pain in her heart didn't feel as though it would ever go away, but she was hopeful. Hopeful that the sooner she left Glendovia, the sooner she could put this entire incident behind her. That the farther she could get from Nicolas, the faster she would begin to forget that she'd let herself fall in love with him—and that he'd been lying to her the entire time.

"Thank you for all of your help," she said to the woman who had helped her arrange for the car and a flight back to the United States.

Alandra handed her a stack of thick files and paperwork, with a separate sheet of stationery clipped to the outside. Despite her eagerness to leave, she had taken the time this afternoon to make certain the foundation wouldn't be left in the lurch.

"Please see that Prince Nicolas gets this. It should be everything he needs to continue with the Dream a Little Dream project."

The woman nodded and offered a small curtsy. "Yes, miss. It was a pleasure to meet you."

"Thank you," Alandra said, swallowing back tears. In only a few short weeks she had grown unaccountably close to the palace staff and was sincerely going to miss them.

With her throat too clogged to speak another word, she walked to the waiting vehicle and climbed in the back. It was dark outside, and too dark to see much of anything through the tinted rear windows. But even so, as the car rolled slowly away from the palace, Alandra kept her gaze focused straight ahead, not wanting to catch even one final glimpse of the site where she'd experienced both an incredible amount of happiness and an incredible amount of heartache.

Nicolas kept his expression impassive throughout the night, giving no hint of his dark, foul mood. He was only too relieved when the Christmas party drew to an end and he was able to slip away from his family and their guests.

He muttered a curse through gritted teeth as he made his way down the long hallway to Alandra's rooms. This was *not* the way he'd hoped things would turn out between them, or how he'd intended her visit to Glendovia to draw to a close.

When he reached her suite, he knocked lightly, then opened the door and entered without waiting for her response.

The lights were on and he heard noises coming from the bedroom, but something seemed oddly out of place.

"Alandra?" he called, striding in that direction.

He pushed open the door, immediately taking in the stripped bed and the lack of Alandra's personal items, which had been scattered about the first night he'd spent with her. A second later, a maid appeared in the bathroom doorway and gave a little squeak of surprise.

"Your Highness," she said, bowing her head.

"Where is Miss Sanchez?" he asked, frowning in consternation.

"I'm sorry, sir, but she's gone. Left just before the party began."

"She's gone?" he repeated, feeling as though his feet had been swept out from under him.

"Yes, sir. I believe she left something for you, though, with Delores. Shall I get her for you?"

"Yes, thank you. Have her bring it to my office, if you would, please."

"Yes, Your Highness."

The maid rushed around him and out of the room. Nicolas trailed behind at a much slower pace, taking a back stairwell to the first floor and heading for his private office. Ten minutes later, Delores arrived. She had a stack of folders in her arms.

"Miss Sanchez left these for you, sir," she said, handing them across the desk to him.

He thanked her, waiting until the servant had gone before opening the note on top of the pile. Alandra's letter was oddly lacking in emotion, simply explaining that she couldn't stay any longer, regardless of the requirements of her contract, now that she knew he was engaged to be married and those pictures had become public. The files, he discovered, held pages upon pages about the Dream a Little Dream Foundation.

He should have expected that she wouldn't want to leave unless she was sure all of the project details were in his hands, and that the establishment of the organization would move forward as planned.

The problem was, he hadn't expected her to leave at all. Not without talking with him, letting him explain.

He should have told her about Lisette in the beginning. Should have let her know that it was an arrangement made by his parents and not necessarily his choice. That even though he was betrothed to the princess, they had never been physically involved.

Lisette and his mother would be delighted to learn of Alandra's departure. Without her presence in Glendovia, the scandal of their affair would die a quick death, and life as they knew it could move on, including plans for his upcoming wedding.

He only wished he felt the same. Instead, he found himself wanting to charge down the hall and be driven to the airport, follow Alandra all the way back to Texas.

If only she'd given him a chance to explain.

With a sigh of regret, he crumpled her note.

It was better this way, he told himself as he left his office and strolled slowly to his rooms on the second floor. Now that Alandra was gone, things could return to normal. He could get back to the matters at hand without being preoccupied with thoughts of making love to her just one more time.

Yes, it was better this way. Better for everyone.

Thirteen

The noise from the back of the room buzzed in Alandra's ears. She really didn't want to do this.

After arriving home from Glendovia in the middle of the night—Christmas night, no less—she'd done her best to get her life back on track. News of her affair with Nicolas had yet to trickle back to the States. But if anyone in her immediate circle had heard about the affair they'd wisely chosen to ignore the gossip.

Everyone except her sister. Elena had waited

until they'd gotten home from the airport to say anything, but she'd known instinctively that something had sent Alandra running back to Texas.

The minute they were alone, Alandra had broken down and told her sister everything, pouring her heart out about the situation and how she'd unwisely fallen in love with a man she could never have. And as always, her sister had understood. She'd listened and offered appropriate responses at appropriate times, but never acted as though she thought Alandra had been a fool to get involved with Nicolas in the first place.

Elena was also the one who'd encouraged her most strongly to throw herself back into her work, when Alandra had wanted nothing more than to curl up in a ball and hide under the covers for the next month or two.

Which was how she'd ended up backstage at the Gabriel's Crossing Country Club. Long before she'd left for Glendovia, she had not only helped finalize the evening's New Year's Eve bachelorette auction, but she'd somehow allowed herself to be roped into being one of the bachelorettes, as well, and now they were holding her to her promise.

The event was in full swing. Six other women had already pranced down the runway to a smattering of applause and generous, good-hearted bidding by the interested bachelors in the audience. Two more ladies were set to take their walks, and then she would be next.

She swallowed hard, taking deep breaths to keep from drowning in panic. This wasn't her idea of a good time. She far preferred to remain behind the scenes at these events. Being the center of attention—especially with all of the publicity that had surrounded her lately—made her knees shake and her teeth rattle.

One bachelorette down, one to go.

"Alandra," a woman who was helping out backstage called in a loud whisper. "Get ready, you're next."

Oh, God, oh, God, oh, God.

For a brief second, she wondered how far she would be able to run in four-inch heels. She probably wouldn't get far, but it was still worth a try.

Inhaling deeply and praying she wouldn't trip over the hem of her gown, she started slowly down the makeshift runway to the sound of scattered clapping and the voice of the master of ceremonies, who extolled her many feminine virtues and outlined the details of the date she'd agreed upon beforehand.

She felt like an animal at a zoo, on display for the whole world to gawk at and appraise. And as she neared the end of the runway, her stomach plunged when she realized that not a single bid had been called out yet.

Oh, Lord, please let the floor open up and swallow me whole, she thought.

At the end of the runway, she stopped and posed, more from embarrassment than any wish to act like a supermodel. Except for the MC asking if there were any bids, any bids at all, the room had fallen into utter silence. The scandals, it seemed, hadn't quite died down, after all.

Alandra blinked, feeling the stares of a hundred people boring into her like laser beams. She was just about to turn in disgrace and walk back to the curtain when a voice rang out from the rear of the room.

"Two hundred and fifty thousand dollars."

Her heart stopped, and she strained to see who had made such an outrageously extreme offer. The rest of the crowd did the same, twisting in their seats for a glimpse of the mystery bidder.

Elated, the MC quickly declared Alandra "sold!" to the gentleman at the rear of the room. At that announcement, the bidder started forward.

As the bachelor walked toward her, he moved into better light, and Alandra's heart stopped again, but for a much different reason this time.

Nicolas, in all his royal finery, stepped through the crowd. A couple of hulking, black-suited body-guards trailed behind, making his presence stand out all the more.

She opened her mouth to breathe his name, but no sound emerged.

At the end of the raised walkway, Nicolas stopped to gaze up at her. He stretched out a hand, his face showing nothing as he reached toward her.

"May I?" he asked in that rich, deep voice that sent shivers down her spine.

Without conscious thought, she put her hand in his and let him lift her bodily from the runway, then lead her back through the crowded room to the rear of the building. She let him take her away from her own event, away from the gawking stares and curious onlookers, to the limousine that waited just outside, on the paved country club driveway.

Nicolas handed her inside and climbed in behind her, allowing the driver to close the door. A second later, she heard the driver's door slam shut, but the partition was up, and she knew that for all intents and purposes, she and Nicolas were alone.

"What are you doing here?" she asked when she finally regained her senses and found her voice.

"I bought you," he replied easily, purposely ignoring the seriousness of her question.

The look in her eyes must have warned him he was skating on thin ice, because he sighed and shifted lightly on the leather seat.

"There have been some developments back in Glendovia since you left. Positive ones, in my estimation. For one, plans for the Dream a Little Dream Foundation are moving forward. We're estimating a March first start date for having everything up and running."

"I'm glad," she said softly. She was happy that things were moving smoothly with the plans she'd put into effect before leaving. But she doubted

Nicolas had flown all the way to America just to deliver an update.

"For another, I've reconsidered my original desire to have you as my mistress." His eyes met hers then, hard and unyielding. "It was shortsighted of me to believe that having you only temporarily would ever be enough."

Sliding across the seat, he wrapped his arms around her and tugged her against his chest. She went willingly.

"I've missed you, Alandra," he whispered against her hair. "I tried to forget you, tried to put you out of my mind and move on with what I knew I had to do."

His hands stroked her back, her neck, the side of her face. "But I couldn't go through with my engagement to Lisette when only one woman filled my heart. You're the one that I want, Alandra. Not as my lover or mistress, but as my wife."

Tipping her head back, she met his gaze, searching his startling blue eyes for the truthfulness in his words. And still she was afraid it was all a dream, that she would wake up to find herself alone, in her bed, with Nicolas nowhere around.

"I broke my engagement to Princess Lisette. It's caused a few hurt feelings and political problems between our two countries, but nothing that won't heal in time. And I've informed my family—my mother, especially—that I was coming to get you and wouldn't return unless you were at my side."

He slid his fingers through her hair, tugging loose the elaborate knot at the crown of her head and dislodging the tiny diamond clips holding it in place.

"Tell me you love me, Alandra, as much as I love you. Tell me you'll come to Glendovia with me, marry me and be my princess. My wife."

Her lashes fluttered as she struggled to absorb everything that Nicolas was saying. His determination and declaration of love, his willingness to put her before his responsibilities to the royal family and his country.

There were so many questions spinning through her brain, but when she opened her mouth, only one thing came out.

"I love you," she murmured, her own arms lifting to curl around his shoulders and hold him as tightly as he was holding her. "It wouldn't have hurt so much to leave if I didn't."

His mouth curved in a gentle smile. "I'm very glad to hear that. Does this mean you'll be my bride?"

A thrill of happiness squeezed her heart. She wanted nothing more than to say, "Yes, yes, yes!" and cover his face with kisses. But fear had her tugging away, watching his expression to be sure everything really was okay and that she could accept his proposal without making matters in both their lives so much worse.

"What about your mother?" she asked. "I don't need to tell you how much she dislikes me, and she was horribly upset about those photographs showing up in the papers. I can't imagine she'll be very pleased to hear you've asked me to marry you."

"Whatever problems my mother has with you are her own, and she'll have to learn to live with them. *My* feelings for you are what matter, and I can tell you quite unequivocally that I adore you." The corners of his mouth curved up in a grin, and he paused a brief moment to press a kiss to her lips. "And I'll have you know that the rest of my family is equally fond of you. They supported me one hundred percent when I told them of my plans to come here and try to win you back. My father included, and you can bet that he'll do his best to bring my mother around."

"You're sure about this?" Alandra asked softly. "I don't want to do anything that could hurt you or bring trouble to your family and country."

"I couldn't be more certain," he told her, and the conviction in his tone filled her with relief. "I would give up my title for you, and if you ask it, I will. You're all that I want, and I'll do whatever it takes to have you."

She couldn't decide whether to laugh or cry as pure delight poured through her clear to her soul. "Would you take me to a hotel—one without balconies, thank you very much—and make love to me?"

His eyes glittered dangerously, his hold around her waist tightening enough to have her gasping for breath.

"A prince's job is never done," he murmured a split second before his mouth touched hers.

* * * * *